The Thief's Tale

The Ottoman Cycle Book One

Revised edition

by S. J. A. Turney

For Alun.

I would like to thank everyone who has been instrumental in this book seeing the light of day in its final form, as well as all those people who have continually supported me during its creation: Robin, Alun, Barry, Charles, Nick, Alan, David, Miriam and of course Jenny and Tracey and my little imps Marcus and Callie who kept me entertained when I hit a wall now and then. Also, the fabulous members of the Historical Writers' Association, who are supportive and helpful.

Cover image by J Caleb Designs.
Cover design by Dave Slaney.
Revised Ed. editing courtesy of Canelo.
Many thanks to all concerned.

Roman Adventures (Children's Roman fiction with Dave Slaney)

Crocodile Legion (2016)
Pirate Legion (Summer 2017)

Short story compilations & contributions:

Tales of Ancient Rome vol. 1 - S.J.A. Turney (2011)
Tortured Hearts vol 1 - Various (2012)
Tortured Hearts vol 2 - Various (2012)
Temporal Tales - Various (2013)
A Year of Ravens - Various (2015)
A Song of War – Various (Oct 2016)

For more information visit http://www.sjaturney.co.uk/
or http://www.facebook.com/SJATurney
or follow Simon on Twitter @SJATurney

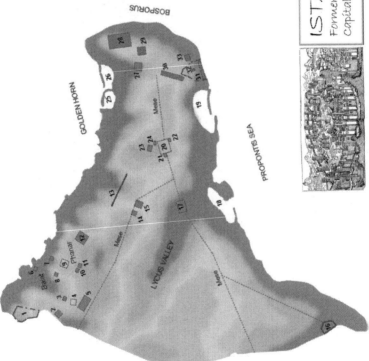

KEY TO LOCATIONS IN THE TEXT

1 Blachernae palace
2 Church of St Saviour in the Country
3 Petra Monastery
4 Spice Market
5 Aetios Garden cistern
6 House of Judah Ben Isaac
7 'Bloody' church of St Mary of the Mongols
8 Monastery church of the Pammakaristos
9 Fruit Market
10 Church of St John 'the Fore-runner'
11 Street of the Hercules Statue
12 Dry Garden cistern
13 Ancient aqueduct of Valens
14 Dulgerzade Mosque
15 Ruined church of St Polyeuktos
16 Yedikule fortress
17 Forum of the Ox
18 Harbour of Theodosius
19 Harbour of Julian
20 Forum of Theodosius
21 Byzantine Baths
22 Carpet warehouse
23 Janissary Barracks
24 Old Ottoman Palace
25 Neorion Harbour
26 Prosphorion Harbour
27 Basilica Cistern
28 Topkapi Palace
29 Aya Sofya mosque
30 Hippodrome
31 Bucoleon Palace (with ruined walls shown)
32 PPharos watchtower
33 Nea Ekklasia

ISTANBUL 1490
Formerly Constantinople,
capital of the Ottoman Empire

GOLDEN HORN

BOSPORUS

PROPONTIS SEA

LYCUS VALLEY

Phanar

Balat

Mese

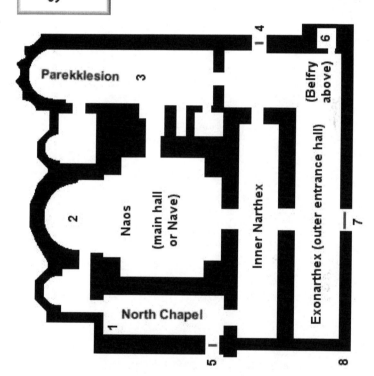

CHURCH OF
SAINT SAVIOUR
IN THE
COUNTRY

1 Altar and debris
2 Sleeping pallets
3 Hole in floor
4 South door
5 North door
6 Stairs to belfry
7 Main door
8 Water butt

To the street

Parekklesion 3

Naos

(main hall
or Nave)

2

North Chapel

1

5

Inner Narthex

Exonarthex (outer entrance hall)

(Belfry
above)

4

6

7

8

Prologos

* Plain of Yenisehir: Year of the Christian Lord Fourteen Hundred and Eighty One *

Bayezid i Veli, sultan of the Ottoman Empire for just a few short months, son of the greatest sultan the world had ever known, expert swordsman, poet, designer of gardens, patron of the arts and humble child of God and the prophet, scratched his neck and swatted away a biting insect.

'He still believes he can win, Nasuh.'

'Your brother is deluded, your majesty. Allah's hand is with us.'

The sultan raised an eyebrow, a smile playing around his lips as he glanced at the elderly agha.

'Allah's hand is notoriously flighty, my friend, but whether it is with us or not, at least the Janissary Corps are.'

The two men, sweltering in their robes, armour and voluminous turbans, watched the plain below the command post intently. The Janissaries – the elite corps of the sultan's army, formed of former Christian converts – were pushing back the left wing of the enemy's infantry with seeming ease.

'What will Cem think, I wonder, when he discovers that I have committed just a third of my Janissaries?'

1

The agha who commanded the Janissary corps stroked his long grey beard and smiled.

'I do believe that your ignoble and hateful brother will soil his trousers, majesty.'

The sultan turned to his most able officer and the agha was not sure whether the look of disapproval on his face was mock or genuine.

'Remember, Nasuh, that while he may have made unfortunate decisions, Cem is still a son of Mehmed the great and is beloved of God. I will see him fall here and, insha'Allah, I will see him dead for trying to take my throne, but I will mourn him and send him to paradise as befits such a prince.'

'Yes, majesty. My heartfelt apologies for my misspoke remark.'

'It is forgotten, Nasuh. Time to break them, I think. It is hot and dry and the battle wears into its third hour. Send in the rest of the Janissaries and the Six Divisions as planned. Cem's centre is in danger as he strengthens the flanks.'

The agha squinted down at the field of battle and frowned. 'It appears one of our orta on the left flank has broken formation and is attempting to destroy your brother's army on its own.'

Bayezid furrowed his brow as he followed the commander's pointing finger.

'The idiot. If he did not have a musket orta in support, they would be surrounded and butchered.'

The agha nodded. 'If he pushes any further, he'll fragment our left wing and we'll be flanked. Shall I recall the Six Divisions and commit them to the left, majesty?'

The sultan tapped his chin irritably. 'No. The cavalry must hit the centre or we will not break them. Send the Sipahi to the left and the other five divisions can attack as planned. That rogue orta must be recalled and put back in line.'

'Insha'Allah that will be enough to win the day, majesty.'

'As you say, Nasuh. Let us end this and let peace return to the Empire.'

Cem Sultan, son of Mehmet the conqueror and half-brother of the infernal Bayezid, sat astride a horse on the only slight rise available at this end of the field of battle.

'You chose the site badly, Hamid. Bayezid has the high ground.'

The agha of Cem's Timariot cavalry gave his master a sour look from behind where he could not be observed and prepared himself for a tirade.

'In fairness, my sultan,' – the lack of honorific would not go unnoticed either – 'we did not have the luxury of choosing the ground. Your brother,' he spat on the dusty ground, 'was too prepared for us.'

'Then you should have been more careful in planning, Hamid. You are careless.'

'The ground, my sultan, is not the issue. The Kapikulu are the issue – in particular the Janissaries. They are smashing our mercenaries like lions among deer. And we have not seen a sign yet of the Sipahi cavalry, which worries me.'

Cem turned his strangely ice-blue eyes on his commander and his face was a strange and unpleasant mix of disgust and anger.

'I have no care for the infidel scum that my brother cares to field against us. The Janissaries are a rabble of barbarian Greeks and Slavs who pay mere lip service to Allah. He brings Christians to battle, and even mercenaries drawn from the infidel east.'

Hamid nodded dutifully, though with mixed feelings. Deep in his gut he couldn't help but wish that their own force contained a few of those fanatic former Christians or eastern mercenaries.

'At least our army are all true followers of the faith,' Cem stated with the air of a man who believes himself on the moral high ground.

'Mamluks,' Hamid agreed unhappily, turning his gaze to the Egyptian expeditionary force that made up almost a quarter of their army. That he had been forced to defer numerous times in the campaign to a man that was born of a rebellious and murderous slave dynasty irked him beyond measure and he would secretly rather have fought alongside a cross-wearing Christian than this Mamluk detritus.

'Bring up the reserves. We have the wings strengthened. It is time to enfold Bayezid and squeeze him to death.'

Hamid bowed and left the command flag to give the orders to his officers, his relief at being away from the usurper sultan tempered somewhat by his personal suspicion that the enemy had not committed their best troops yet.

Deep in the press of men, Hamza Bin Murad, commander of the Sixty-Second Solak Cemaat Orta of Sultan Bayezid the Second's Janissaries, spat away the blood that coated his face. It was unseemly for an officer of his status to involve himself in the frontline fighting of his unit, not to mention dangerous, given the voracity of the enemy, and Hamza had been upbraided for this very thing several times in his career. In fact, it was one of the main factors preventing his rise to high office.

But the simple fact was that Hamza Bin Murad, unlike many of the self-seeking catamite orta commanders in Bayezid's army, was a true lover of battle. He never felt quite as good when he was not wearing the blood of the enemy like a veil. In a way it was a bad thing, though. While it made him a good warrior – and in his opinion a good officer – it put him at the very front of a battle that he was not truly comfortable being a part of. The very idea of his corps being involved in a bloody fight to the death with other Turkish brothers made him angry. The Mamluk scum yes, but the Turks less so.

He was a loyal Muslim, despite being born to Albanian peasant stock, and had served in the Janissaries since before the fall of Byzantium, but in his opinion it was not right for the sultan and his brother to bring civil war to the Empire. Especially when Cem had the prior claim. The vizier in Istanbul had named Cem as Mehmet's chosen successor, regardless of his being the younger brother.

And yet Hamza would fight until every last man on the field was dead if the sultan commanded it, for he was Janissary and it was his duty.

A series of cracks behind him announced another volley of fire from the arquebus handguns of the Sixty-First Orta and less than two yards in front of Hamza another Mamluk head exploded like a watermelon, spraying blood and brains across the struggling warriors on both sides.

May Allah strike the eyes from the head of Avranos the dog-molester, commander of the gunners behind them! The idiot always manoeuvred his unit so that he could fire over Hamza's head and more than once one of Hamza's own men had died in the volley fire. It was almost as though the lunatic was trying to kill him. Just let the bastard get in his way... Hamza's Janissary loyalties did not extend so far as to stop him putting a sword through the man's gut if he got the chance.

A Mamluk officer pushed aside the headless body as it slumped and was suddenly thrusting his round, studded shield at Hamza, a decorative axe pulled back over his head ready to come down in an unstoppable blow. Hamza could just see the fanatical gleam in the Egyptian warrior's pearly eyes through the eyeholes in the chainmail veil than hung from the ornate conical helm.

For a moment, the Janissary officer paused, finding a grudging

4

respect for this enemy who clearly shared the same love of killing as he himself. But he couldn't spare a man simply though a kinship of spirit. If he were to do that he could hardly justify fighting an Ottoman army at all.

As the axe started to descend towards him, he raised his own round shield, angling it carefully. Were the two to connect flat-on, the axe would cut a rent through the shield and dig deep into Hamza's arm, but at the right angle he could deflect the blow and send the axe falling uselessly towards the dirt. As his shield came up and he swept his own blade to impale the man through his exposed armpit, his kill was taken away from him as a curve-bladed pike with a wicked hook whistled past his ear and smashed straight into the Mamluk's face, sending broken links of mail, teeth, bone and blood out in a spray.

Hamza's fury at the loss of such a beautiful kill was compounded as he realised that the blade had also scythed through the ceremonial cotton tail of his armoured hat, leaving a tattered remnant of white cloth flapping at the side of his face while part of his ceremonial uniform, attached to the pike blade, was thrust deep into the Mamluk's brain.

Turning angrily, he saw the triumphant grin of the young soldier behind him and the blood rage came on, taking over his actions, leaving sense behind. Before he realised it he had thrust his curved blade into the young man's chest and ripped it back out, bringing chunks of rib and organ with it. For a moment he hesitated at the dishonour of killing his own, but quickly he resigned himself with a shrug. What were they doing on this godforsaken plain if not trying to kill other good Muslims? A death for a death. The boy had paid for stealing his kill.

Over the heads of the Mamluk infantry in front of him, Hamza could now see other Turks, pushing their way to the centre of the fight.

His thirst for blood leading him, Hamza elbowed his way past the shattered Mamluk before him and started pushing his way forward, shouting to urge his men on with him.

'Hamza Bin Murad!'

Surprised at the use of his name in the depths of battle, Hamza turned, allowing – with some irritation – his troops to swarm past him and into the enemy.

An officer of the Sipahi cavalry sat ahorse not three yards from him, coated from head to foot in gleaming mail and with a decorative helm from which hung a veil of chain. The man sat with a straight back, gleaming and pristine, untouched as yet by battle.

'Hamza Bin Murad, Corbasi of the Sixty-Second?'

'Yes!' spat Hamza, glaring at the man.

The Sipahi had the temerity to gesture at him with a sword and then swept it back to point at the hill behind them.

'You have been ordered to the command post. The agha is displeased with you. Leave the field at once.'

Hamza stared at the man and for the briefest of moments considered simply pulling him from his horse and gutting him; but that would be no solution. For all his insolence, the man was carrying out the orders of the agha, and possibly therefore of the sultan. Defiance would mean a painful, dishonourable and very public death.

'Very well.'

Sheathing his sword, regardless of the mess coating it, Hamza turned his back on the beloved thrill of killing and began to push his way back through the army towards the officers on the hill. He could anticipate what would happen: he would be chastised in front of the sultan for leading his men too far forward. He'd broken formation, but he could have won them the field had he been left to it.

'Allah protect us from commanders who lead like sheep.'

Whatever the horseman said in reply was drowned out by the fresh crack of volley fire from the guns of the Sixty-First.

Qaashiq straightened his rich blue overcoat and tucked his thumbs into the wide sash around his midriff next to an ornate short blade. Reaching up, he adjusted his turban and blinked away the dust and flies that seemed to swarm about him every four or five heartbeats. This benighted place was about the worst field he'd ever fought on.

With a gesture, he summoned his standard bearer.

'Sound the recall. Egypt is leaving the field.'

The standard bearer bowed and scurried off to perform his duties, and Qaashiq swiftly mounted his horse and rode along the rear of the lines of battle to where Cem Sultan, commander of the forces and claimant to the Ottoman throne, stood waving his arms and yelling at an officer. Calmly, he dismounted and walked his mount to the scene of the tirade.

After a few moments, Cem realised that his agha was no longer paying attention to the insults and was instead looking past him, and he turned in time to see Qaashiq come to a halt a few yards away.

'It is over, Prince Cem.'

'Sultan!' snapped the Ottoman angrily.

'No. The sultan stands on the hill over there. You are Prince Cem. Bayezid has produced two fresh corps of Janissaries and enough cavalry to grind your army into dust. The Mamluk forces here are unofficial and serving as mercenaries. We are leaving the field and returning to Egypt before this escalates into a war between our peoples.'

Cem pointed an accusing finger at the Mamluk nobleman.

'You promised me your all, Qaashiq! You gave me your word!'

The Mamluk shook his head calmly.

'I agreed to provide support as long as I deemed it reasonable to do so. This is no longer a viable cause. My force is not large enough to turn the tide in your war. Unless you can persuade the sultan in Cairo to back you, I must refuse further aid. I will not start a war with Bayezid without my sultan's permission.'

Cem stared in disbelief. His eyes strayed from the Mamluk before him to the serried ranks of his army, over which he had a reasonable view from this slight rise. It was clear to him now that the Mamluk contingent was leaving the field, performing a fighting withdrawal and reforming to the rear of the rise. Annoyingly, Bayezid's army was allowing them to retreat, while concentrating on Cem's own forces. Equally clear was the fact that the battle was over and that Cem had lost. His centre was in total disarray and his left flank was disintegrating.

'You will abandon me now, Qaashiq? What am I supposed to do?'

The Mamluk shrugged.

'That is your decision, Prince Cem. You can stay here and die in battle or under the executioner's blade, or you can flee the field and attempt to rebuild your army.'

'Will your sultan help me?' Cem asked, a hint of desperation in his tone.

'He may; he will ask a heavy price if he does. If he does not, however, he may just sell you to your brother. You may be safer asking the master of Rhodes for aid.'

'A Christian?' demanded Cem incredulously. 'One of those unwashed infidel knights?'

The Mamluk simply shrugged again and the Ottoman prince

turned in rising desperation to see his army finally break completely.

'Warn your train to expect a guest,' Cem snarled. 'Your sultan will help me even if I have to sell him half of Anatolia.'

Qaashiq smiled. 'Now you are thinking like a winner, Cem Sultan.'

* Istanbul: The Year of Our Lord Fourteen Hundred and Eighty Two *

The column of five hundred selectees of the Devsirme trudged along the dusty gravel road, the summer sun pounding mercilessly down on them and draining the last drops of moisture from every boy in the line. The enforced recruitment – some would say slavery, though not within earshot of the conquerors – of Christian children was an annual plague in the lives of the subjects of the Empire, but these past two seasons had seen a step up in the system. The wars between the two feuding brothers at the head of the Ottoman world had drained the armies of the Empire, and many strictures that protected the peasant farmers had been bypassed in order to restock the military.

'No family will have more than one child taken' had been stressed in the terms of the Devsirme, and yet the Orthodox Christian families in the lands around Hadrianople and Bizye had lost whole generations this past two years. The family of Parios the farmer had tried to hide one of their boys in the pig sty when the selection officers and their men had come, but the result had been all the worse: the boy had still been found and taken and Parios had lost his left arm below the elbow as punishment and would struggle on the farm in the future.

Parents had wailed and lamented, begging the officers for mercy, asking what would become of their farms with their children taken. Most of the soldiers and officials had been aloof and pushed aside the distraught parents, but the one who had come to the farm to take Skiouros and Lykaion had simply shrugged and suggested their parents start having children again.

Skiouros glanced across at Lykaion, and once more was impressed at how well his brother was taking the situation. Their mother had actually gone for one of the guards when they'd been pulled out from the yard, but their father had restrained her in his usual stoic, sensible way. Lykaion had apparently accepted his fate calmly, while Skiouros had kicked up enough of a fuss that he'd already been beaten twice before they were out of sight of the walls of Hadrianople.

The journey had been hell on earth. Four days of slogging along dusty roads in the endless heat, with only three ten-minute breaks from sunrise to sunset, each filled with a little bread and gruel and a few mouthfuls of water. Then they slept in the open within a ring of soldiers like the prisoners of some battle until the sun's first glow passed the horizon and the column of boys were heaved to their feet and goaded on once more.

And now, at last, the great city was before them and the trek almost over.

Again Skiouros glanced at Lykaion. The taller boy, older by two years and taller by a hand, had not spoken all day. It was as though every step that brought them closer to Constantinople drove the sparkle and the life from the curly-haired farm boy. Lykaion had always been taciturn and serious compared to his younger brother, but this was a noticeable change, and not one that Skiouros welcomed.

For the first two days of the journey, Skiouros had cried and despaired, fearing the bleak future of slavery and inevitable death that awaited them in the great city. Aisopos the trader had said that the boys taken in the Devsirme system were forced to renounce God the maker and worship their false Allah and his Arabic prophets, before they were sent either to be castrated and abused by the sultan or to die in his armies. Neither option sounded particularly good to Skiouros.

And then, during one disturbed wakeful night by a parched river bed, he'd had an epiphany and decided that the sultan was not the master of his fate. He would be his own master. The great city of Constantine was said to be full of wonder and promise even in these days of Turkish oppression. Skiouros had watched their guards and knew that he was fast enough and smart enough to evade them. When they were in Constantinople, he would run from the column and make the city his own.

The next morning, he had tried to discuss the possibility very quietly with Lykaion as they trudged, but had been forced to do so in whispers and fragmentary snippets whenever guard proximity allowed and the other boys weren't listening too intently.

At first, the older brother had been strangely uncommunicative but, as that third day wore on, he had finally turned to Skiouros and told him that he was being stupid. Their life may be forfeit, but that was the path upon which God had set them and to fight it was not

9

only to fight God, but to break the law and all rules of morality.

'Besides,' Lykaion had snapped with surprising force, 'what do you think will happen to Mother and Father if we disobey the sultan's men? Just walk and do as you're told.'

The rest of the day's attempts to convince Lykaion were even less successful, and by the fourth day, the older boy had fallen silent entirely.

Shouts in Turkish rang out suddenly at the head of the column, and the guards along the edges prodded and goaded their charges into a narrower column as they approached the walls. Lykaion felt the breath torn from his chest at the sight of the great defences of the city.

How had this place ever fallen to Mehmet the Conqueror? God himself could not smash these walls! By comparison, the walls of Hadrianople were a pile of bricks. Even the first barricade, a wide moat filled with brackish algae-covered water, presented an obstacle that Skiouros could hardly comprehend crossing were it not for the serviceable bridge either recently constructed or fully refurbished by the Ottoman lords. The column of boys, aged eight to eighteen, trooped unhappily across the moat without allowing their gaze to stray too much from directly ahead in case they incurred a jab or a slap from one of the guards. Skiouros, his curiosity too powerful to be contained by such a threat, carefully examined everything as they passed.

The moat was clearly deep enough to drown a man in armour or even a horse, and wide enough to discourage any thought of swimming, particularly given the phenomenal field of fire from the towers and walls beyond, where archers and crossbowmen would stand.

Beyond the moat lay a low wall, about the height of a man's shoulder, with a crenelated top behind which defenders could stand. As the column passed this low barricade, they approached the first of the true walls, showing the scars of repair but more than five times the height of a grown man and with projecting towers. There, they caught their first sight of the armed force that had ripped this great prize from the hands of the Romans and which kept the lands of the sultan safe from his enemies.

The men standing on the walls and watching the new recruits arriving were armed with bows and crossbows, spears and swords, sheathed in steel or mail, with gleaming helms. Men even stood with long muskets on their shoulder. Each man at that wall was better armed and armoured, and appeared stronger and more fearless than any of the Turkish soldiers who protected the low walls of Hadrianople.

As the column passed within the outer wall and Skiouros studied the great wooden gate that had opened for them, they moved out into the strange, deadly space between the two stretches of walls. Any attacker caught here was totally at the mercy of the men on the high inner wall – and what a wall it was. It was quite simply the most incredible construction that Skiouros had ever seen, had ever even imagined. More than half as tall again as the outer wall and with towers three times as wide, the inner wall was surely impregnable.

It was said that Mehmet had found a weak spot where his cannon had broken through in the end, but that even then it had taken more than a month. Skiouros could well imagine.

The great Gate of Charisius loomed powerful and unimaginably huge as they approached, the flanking towers bigger than any Skiouros had ever seen. The enormous arch welcomed them as the massive gates were swung ponderously inwards, and Skiouros and his companions saw for the first time the city that was going to be their home until they died.

If they submitted willingly to their new masters.

The interior of the city was less cluttered here than he'd expected. Hadrianople's buildings were tightly packed right up to the inner face of the walls, but then the city outside which the family farm lay was like a bug on a bison compared to this great ancient city of Emperors. They said you could walk for four miles from the walls before you reached the palace, so it was no surprise to find only sparse construction this far out.

Skiouros mentally adjusted his plans. There would be no chance to slip away here, with so few structures crowding toward them. He'd expected a warren like Hadrianople and not wide thoroughfares. Perhaps a little further in, when the city condensed a little...

On the column marched, the boys dragging their feet through the weariness of walking more than a hundred miles in the height of summer with insufficient rest or water, and with the reluctance of slaves approaching market. Their journey towards hell was almost over, but each selectee present knew what that meant.

Again, Skiouros glanced around to make sure the guards were paying him no attention and leaned closer to Lykaion.

'Nearly there, brother.'

A grunt was his only reply, and the larger boy kept his eyes forwards, his pace steady.

'I'm not going to let them make me die for the crescent, Lykaion.

11

And I'm not going to let them turn me into a woman for the sultan's pleasure.'

Lykaion's head turned slightly.

'You don't believe that shit, do you? Aisopos spun tales to entertain the children, and that's all that is. The sultan has wives. What use would he have for a castrated boy?'

Skiouros shuddered. 'I'd rather not find out. As soon as we're in a more built-up area and the opportunity arises, I'm leaving. God gave us the will to choose our destiny, Lykaion. Father Simonides used to say that, you remember?'

'I remember. But I gave my oath, as we all did, brother. I don't break my oath. I promised to obey and to serve and to do whatever they asked.'

'You promised with an oath on their unholy Qur'an. An oath on that is hardly binding to a God-fearing Christian like you, Lykaion.'

The larger boy glared at his brother. 'My oath is my oath, whatever it's given on, brother, as is yours. Our word is all we have, now!'

'I will not hold myself to a heathen oath I was forced to take. For the last time, Lykaion, come with me. Once we're safe we can decide what to do. We can either go back to the farm and try to do what we can, or we can forge a new life in the city. Either way we'll be our own men.'

'Be quiet and walk.'

Lykaion turned his face from Skiouros and concentrated on the road ahead. Skiouros opened his mouth to have the last word on the matter but a guard, having approached unseen, reached out and cuffed him heavily on the cheek hard enough to make him stagger, barking something at him in Turkish.

'And your mother's arse!' snapped Skiouros, ducking back hastily as the guard made to slap him again. The Turk moved on with a last warning glance.

'Well I'm going as soon as I can, whatever you decide to do.'

The pair strode on in silence along with the trudging column, the only sounds emanating from them the occasional shouts, orders and slaps of the guards, and the cries of pain or fear that resulted. Gradually as the first half-mile ground beneath their feet, the buildings began to close up and form heavier blocks, the streets narrowing and showing signs of having been planned in long-gone eras. The city was becoming truer to expectations.

'Constantinople is huge,' Skiouros announced, almost to himself.

'Istanbul,' said Lykaion quietly.

'What?'

'It's not been Constantinople since before we were born. It's Istanbul now.'

'Maybe to them.'

'To everyone, brother.'

Skiouros flashed an angry glance at his brother, but Lykaion was paying him no attention. To him, it was Constantinople and always would be. Their father and the other adults of the Adrianople district had refused to call their own city Edirne, so why would they adopt the Conquerors' name for the ancient capital?

Greeks, it was said, had long memories so that they could hold a grudge 'til doomsday.

'Will you help me if I go?'

Lykaion's gaze remained resolutely forward.

'I will have nothing to do with oathbreaking and your insane schemes.'

'Then I will have to wish you farewell now, Lykaion, for when the chance comes, I may not have time.'

At last the older boy turned his face to Skiouros, and the smaller brother suddenly found there was a lump in his throat as he saw a tear drop from Lykaion's cheek. The bigger boy rarely cried, and the look of almost heart-breaking loss Skiouros could discern in his brother's eye was almost unbearable.

'Don't do this.'

'I have to, Lykaion. I cannot serve them the way you seem to think you can.'

'What will you do? You're a farmer, Skiouros. You have no skills you can use here. You will be a vagabond; destitute. I don't want to make my way in the city and achieve something good only to find that one day I'm dragging the bodies of the diseased beggars from the street and it's my brother's eyes I'm looking into. Better to be a soldier for the Turks than a Christian corpse, eh?'

'I can't, Lykaion. It's not me.'

'Do you harbour that much hatred of the Turks and their crescent, Skiouros? I've never noticed you being so holy and pious before? You've never really embraced the cross, so why worry about the shape of your faith?'

Skiouros frowned. The brothers had long ago decided that God paid little heed to those with no power, and that consequently they felt

13

no pressure to return the missing attention, but they had been born, baptised and groomed in the eyes of the church. Like it or not it was ingrained in Skiouros, like a scar. Apparently not so in his brother.

'It's not that I hate the Turks with every ounce of my heart, Lykaion. You know that. God, I've never known a world without a Turkish ruler. They're just a people with a God like we are. But that's the problem: it's not our people, not our God. I'm a Greek, Lykaion, not a Turk, and no amount of forcing me to kneel in a mosque is going to change that.'

'Then it's just as well you're going,' the older brother said with a sad sigh. 'If you defy them things will just go badly for you.'

Skiouros opened his mouth to speak again, but that same guard was returning along the column and his eyes fell on Skiouros with a silent warning.

The column trudged on, the streets becoming more densely packed and built-up as they moved, to the point where they put Hadrianople to shame. The folk in the streets made way for the Devsirme column and gave them all a wide berth, but Skiouros noted with interest the prevalence of Ottoman inhabitants. It seemed somehow odd that only perhaps one in fifty people in the street was a non-Turk. Perhaps Lykaion was right in calling it Istanbul, for how could this now be the city of Constantine?

His chance, when it presented itself, was so sudden and unexpected that he almost missed it.

The same guard who seemed to have taken a personal dislike to him had been watching him almost continually since the walls, and Skiouros had begun to despair of the opportunity ever arising. Then, in a flash, it all happened. The guard turned to bring a ringing slap to one of the other boys, and at the same moment, a merchant with a handcart of melons appeared from a side street, bumped into a passer-by and his wares scattered and rolled from the cart across the street.

As the guard swung his arm, one of the rolling, bulky fruit bounced beneath his feet and his next step came down heavily on the curved skin, sending him bowling over with a yelp of surprise.

Skiouros was gone before the man touched the ground, past the surprised and panicky melon trader and into the narrow alley behind.

The guard's shouting and bellowing in the street was incomprehensible to him, but was almost certainly aimed at the fruit merchant anyway. By the time it was sorted out, the man had been beaten for his ineptitude, and the column had begun to move again,

14

Skiouros would be impossible to find. The guard would realise almost immediately, then, but it would be no use.

He was free.

Running like he'd never run before, grateful for the shade of the narrow alley despite the smell of warm dung that seemed to cling to the city, Skiouros ducked left and right, making sure to keep to the same rough direction and not to accidentally return to the main street. Heaving with painful, rasping breaths, he slowed for a time in an alley, and then stopped to take his bearings. A clothes line strung between two windows above him dipped at the centre to just above head height and it was then that Skiouros realised that he was dusty and travel-worn and wearing the shapeless smock of a country farm boy. If he was to survive here, he had best start looking as though he belonged.

Reaching up, he grasped a light grey linen shirt from the line and was then off again. Three alleys later he paused once more to discard his peasant smock and slip into the shirt.

'You throwin' that away?'

He looked up in surprise at the words and saw a woman standing by a door into a wooden house. By all that was holy, she appeared to be a non-Turk, and she was speaking his language! It was then he realised that the shirt he'd pulled on was also distinctly western in its cut and not the fine baggy wear of the Ottomans.

'Erm, yes?'

'Throw it here. It'll make cleaning rags if nothing else.'

As he stooped to pick up his discarded smock, he frowned.

'You're Greek?' he asked as he passed it over.

'And so are you. So?'

'But I've hardly seen any non-Turks here?'

The woman shook her head and rolled her eyes. 'You must be new. You're in Phanar – the Greek district.'

Skiouros smiled and turned a slow circle, taking in the tall, tightly-packed wooden buildings.

'The Greek district? I'm... I'm home.'

Again the woman rolled her eyes, and then she returned to her home, closing the door behind her. Skiouros stood for a long moment. This was it, then. This was where his new life would begin. He realised suddenly with regret that he'd not had the chance even to look at Lykaion when it had happened. He'd not expected to, really,

15

but he'd also not expected to feel such a wrench at the sudden absence of his brother.

Almost a mile away, Lykaion trudged along the street, his face a tapestry of cuts and bruises from the beating the guard had given him when he'd noticed the missing boy. The Turk had gone off to report to his commander after he'd run out of strength and had not been back since.

With a sigh, Lykaion wiped away the tear from his swollen, discoloured cheek. Skiouros had never even had the chance to look back and see his brother's final wave. It felt as though half his heart had been torn out and cast away.

'Go with God, little brother, and be well.'

Bourganeuf, France: Year of Our Lord Fourteen Hundred and Eighty Nine *

The two men-at-arms shared a look of relief as their sergeant left the room and closed the heavy oak door behind him.

'Well I for one will be pleased to get rid of the slimy bastard.' Pierre shivered. 'Every time he looks at me it gives me a cold spine.'

'I know what you mean.'

Abellard reached for the tower room's other door and swung it open, revealing the short passage that led to the suite of rooms which had belonged to the lady d'Aubusson only a few short years ago. The corridor itself was decorated in a style that disgusted the older soldier. A vivid-coloured carpet from heathen lands warmed the floor and the two guards took every opportunity to soil it with muddy boots. The wall hangings were silk from Egypt, and a gauzy curtain hung over the window like a woman's veil. It was all so damned unseemly for a good Christian castle.

And it was all because of the bloody Turk.

Pierre had only served here for five years, but Abellard remembered that winter seven years ago when Cem Sultan, apparently an exiled Ottoman prince, had arrived at the door under the escort of two dozen soldiers from the Order of the Hospitallers. The dark-skinned runt had apparently started a war between the Ottoman Empire and the Mamluks of Egypt but had ended up defeated and trapped and forced to seek the help of the Grand Master in Rhodes.

Master d'Aubusson had agreed to grant the heathen sanctuary for some reason known only to himself and to God, and within the year the exile had been sent back to France to keep him out of the reach of his Ottoman enemies.

'Why we aren't just sending the oily little runt back to his Turkish friends I don't know. It'd serve the heathen little bastard right. What do good Christian lords care if he gets offed by his brother?'

Pierre, always one with an opinion, and who claimed to have an understanding of higher matters despite the fact that he'd been brought up with pigs, shook his head.

'Too useful, that one. Started a war that's kept all them turbans kicking each other for a decade now.'

Abellard had to grudgingly concede the point. With all the trouble the exiled prince had kicked up between the eastern nations, the great crusader islands had had their first real breather in more than a century, and the Knights Hospitaller of Rhodes had been given time and space to reinforce and fortify a dozen or more fortresses along the Anatolian and Levantine coast. Moreover, it was said that some were calling for a new crusade and there would be no better time to attack the east than when it was already divided.

Saying that, Abellard had mixed feelings about a crusade. It would be a good thing to give those Turks and Arabs a sound thrashing, of course, but Abellard was no longer a young man and the thought of that long trek and a year or more labouring and fighting in the desert really didn't appeal the way it once had.

'Come on. Let's break the news to the little Turkish prick.'

The pair trudged heavily, and none too carefully, across the priceless Persian carpet, worn threadbare in places with their constant efforts, and approached the door to the suite. As Pierre knocked three times, respectfully stepping back, Abellard found a small tear in the wall hanging next to him and started to lengthen it quietly.

After a minute, the door opened and Cem Sultan peered suspiciously down at them. The look on his face made it abundantly clear that he thought as little of them as they did of him, and he peered down the length of his nose, nostrils flaring.

'What do you want?' he snapped in heavily accented French. It had taken him almost two years to learn enough to communicate with his hosts, but the men-at-arms had played dumb and dragged it out as long as possible just for the fun of it.

'Your unholy majesty is to gather his heathen shit together and get ready to travel.'

The Turk's nostrils flared wider and his eyes took on a hard, flinty look.

'Your master will hear of your insult.'

Abellard snorted up some mucus and paused long enough to make the Turk think he might spit, and then swallowed it back down. 'My master was the one who said it, Turk. Get ready.'

'Where am I to go now?' Cem demanded irritably. He was officially a free man and a guest of the Knights of Rhodes in the place, but every passing season made this enforced exile feel more like a prison sentence. Almost eight years and he still could not get used to how often the air got cold enough to ice over the water butts of the castle. It was not like home or Egypt, that was for sure.

Cem had been forced to seek the help of the Knights at Bodrum after the siege of Konya failed and he'd found his escape route back to his Mamluk allies cut off. The grand master Pierre d'Aubusson had granted him sanctuary, yet refused to return him to Egypt. He had been left with no choice but to agree when the knights suggested he be sent back to France 'for his own protection' and he'd wondered how long he might be confined in this freezing hell. The real question, though, was: where was he being sent now? Had a deal been struck to return him to Egypt, or were the knights about to betray his sanctuary?

'Well?' he snapped as the two soldiers looked at each other and grinned.

'There's a new escort waiting for you in the courtyard, prince Cem. Men from Rome.'

'Rome?' Cem's blood ran cold. What could the Pope want with him?

'Yes, Rome. You're going into Papal custody.'

The Turk's eyes narrowed. 'I am to become a prisoner?'

Pierre shook his head, smiling. 'You're just being transferred up from the holy Order of Saint John to their highest authority. Pope Innocent is looking forward to meeting you, I hear.'

Abellard frowned at his fellow guard. Had the young big head actually heard something, or was he just talking out of his arse again?

'Your Pope will not harm me?' There was a genuine note of uncertainty – fear, even?

'Far from it. It's said that your brother has paid the Holy Father a wagon-load of Gold to keep you safe and sound in Rome.'

'Where do you hear this horse shit, boy?' Abellard demanded, ignoring the look of sick horror on the exile's face.

'If you took your face out of the ale bucket for five minutes and started listening to things, old man, you'd hear it too.'

'Watch yourself, you little sod. I've got to look after this heathen animal, but there's no rule against giving you a good hiding.'

The pair descended into a slanging match, their attention totally removed from Cem, who stood in the doorway with a mixed sense of hope and panic. In a way, the transfer to Papal custody would take him another step away from tangible freedom. And yet it was said that Pope Innocent the Eighth was a reasonable man, for a godless Christian. He was supposedly an opponent of the crusading ideal, and the very fact that he had struck a deal with Bayezid suggested that he was open to other negotiation. If that was the case, and Cem could get a message to the Mamluks, he may be able to arrange a counter-offer to that of his brother.

It was faintly possible that this shift into even deeper Christian captivity might conceivably be a step towards his release.

Strange, the way Allah worked.

'Then if I am to meet your Pope, I had best move. I will come now and you can fetch my things afterwards.'

Stepping past the startled and angry faces of the two guards, he headed for the stairs to the courtyard.

Things were about to change. He could put his plan into motion as soon as he arrived in Rome, and Bayezid's days on this Earth would be numbered.

İstanbul

Capital of the Ottoman Empire (formerly Constantinople - the capital of the Byzantine Empire).

Year of Our Lord Fourteen Hundred and Ninety.

Autumn.

Çarsamba (Wednesday)

Now.

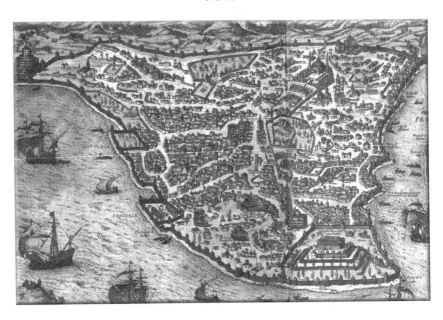

Chapter 1 – A dangerous choice of mark

* Çarsamba (Wednesday) morning *

S kiouros waved his arms angrily.
'Why do we end like this every time we talk? It's infuriating.'

'Because I am an adult with a position of responsibility and a path to paradise with the one true God, while you are a bottom-feeding, gutter-dwelling criminal infidel with no sense of justice or duty. Why you insist on trying to speak to me I truly have no idea and, insha'Allah, you will soon desist and I can stop dragging my weary backside across the city in my few precious free hours to spend them in this land of Christian hovels listening to your drivel.'

Lykaion fell silent, his hard, strangely-pale eyes boring into his brother's face and soul. Skiouros heaved a deep sigh, looking Lykaion up and down for the umpteenth time in the past uncomfortable five minutes. It was the first time the older of the two had come to the meeting dressed in his uniform, and it made Skiouros shudder to see it. Despite the lack of protective steel, Lykaion's green coat and Janissary hat were as impenetrable as any armour. His always-unruly dark wavy hair poked out from beneath the bronze decoration and long white tail of the hat, and his beard seemed thicker every time they met. At some eight inches taller and considerably broader in the shoulder than his brother, Lykaion was every inch the warrior, and would obviously have been so even without the uniform or the long, gently curved blade at his hip.

'Mother would drown in her own tears if she thought even for a moment that we could never speak civilly.' He ignored the sudden look of anger on Lykaion's face. 'Do you not recall Father's words: 'Remember that the world is iniquity and that, when it comes down to it, the only people you can rely on are kin'?'

'Father was a font of platitudes,' Lykaion snapped. 'Life has changed for us; for me, at least. It's a new world, brother, and I have made my place in it. You would do well to do the same, rather than clinging to old ways and a dead life.'

'This is not about religion, Lykaion, or even about culture. It's not about your precious Sultan. This is about family, plain and simple. Ships sail out of the Theodosian harbour every day, bound for a world where we could be free! Crete, brother! The Venetians are a power; we'd be happy there, without the taxes and restrictions.'

'Pah! When did you ever pay attention to taxes or restrictions, you little thief? And the Venetians are warmongering pirates, anyway. Why would I leave? I don't live in filth and thieve for a living. Freedom? I am free, brother, insofar as any man is free within the sight of God. Find yourself a trade and a woman, forget about me and live your life.'

Skiouros sagged. He was running out of strength to argue in the face of Lykaion's blind acceptance of his own enslavement. He scratched at the armpit of his threadbare grey doublet, appropriated from a washing pile in Galata last week. He might be shorter and narrower, and probably weaker, than Lykaion, but he was faster and, he was fairly sure, brighter. His hair would be the same as his brother's had he not continually trimmed it to an inch or so long – it would be asking for trouble to grow hair long enough for an enraged merchant to grasp.

One last try...

'I know they've persuaded you away from the cross to the crescent, and I'm no monk – I won't blather about turning your face from God, but how can you turn your back on Mother?'

He staggered as the back of his brother's hand connected sharply with his cheek in a ringing slap that left a painful red mark and a long scratch from the taller brother's ring.

'Don't you dare accuse me of that! I sent money back as soon as I started earning a wage and I kept doing so until Mother died in the summer.'

Skiouros blinked.

'Yes, I expect you didn't even know she'd passed on,' Lykaion snarled, 'since you never spoke to her. She died of the fever and the stinking flesh. I was given leave to return and see to her burial – which I performed in the Orthodox manner, I'll add. I even tried to find you to tell you, but how does one go about finding a homeless thief in a city of half a million people?'

'She's dead?'

'And with her every excuse you have left to bother me. Take this as my final word on the matter, little brother: we are kin by blood alone. Go back to your wasted life and sink ever further into depravity and leave me to my world, where I matter and I can make a difference.'

'Lykaion...'

'No, Skiouros. Just go, before I surrender to the urge to hit you again.'

The smaller of the pair took a couple of steps back and leaned against the brick wall of the so-called Bloody Church, his spirits sinking as he watched the green-coated soldier who had all but consumed his brother walk away, possibly for the last time. Perhaps twice a year, every year since they had come to the world's greatest city, Skiouros had arranged to meet with Lykaion. It had never gone well, but there had been a marked downturn in their relationship these past two years, since Lykaion had completed his training and made it to the most prestigious orta of the Janissary corps, charged with the personal safety of the Sultan.

It was not that Skiouros held a great enmity for the Sultan Bayezid the Second, or even his Ottoman world that had gradually suffused itself into even the lowest levels of life since the great city had fallen to them almost forty years ago. He would even say that he was more accepting than most of their Islamic ways, which had pushed the worship of the Greek church into one small corner of Constantinople. He had seen precious little evidence of any God in the past eight years of city life, and so it seemed as reasonable to 'salam' one's shoulders as to genuflect to the cross. Whoever it was watching over the family of Nikos the farmer didn't seem to be paying much attention.

Lykaion had gone.

Skiouros allowed his hearing to refocus once more. A man with a cart trundled past the entrance to the alley, selling bread and pastries. The general hubbub of the Greek enclave murmured in the background like a warm, familiar blanket which for once entirely failed to comfort him. After a minute or more of staring at the empty alley, he shook his head to clear it of the morbid and miserable. Grieving for his mother would have to wait. In a way, he was well prepared for it. He'd known she was weakening and had done ever since the Devsirme had taken her boys from her. In a way it was a relief, as she'd lived with backbreaking work and borderline starvation for almost a decade without husband or sons. At least their parents would be together again now.

As for Skiouros the thief?

If he wanted to pay another week's board at the hovel he called home, he would need more money. He'd spent his last few akce on a hearty breakfast this morning in preparation for the meeting. Reaching up, he became aware that a tiny trickle of blood was forming from the scratch on his cheek, which was deeper than he'd realised.

Time to earn some money.

Turning, he looked up at the small window in the brick and stone wall and past it to the small, circular tower, painted red and almost featureless, its dome invisible from this angle. He wondered for a moment whether to pray, but decided it would be hypocritical given his recent train of thought. With just a respectful nod at the cross that topped the dome and was just visible, he turned and left the small alley, entering the more major street and the bloodstream of the great city, life pulsing up the hill to the heart of Istanbul, as it was now known almost everywhere but the Greek enclave.

This district – Phanar – was the poorest in the city, lacking even the money of the Jews, and yet life went on here as though the Turks had never come. The maze of tiny streets and alleys, most of them vertiginous and affording a high-angled view of the Golden Horn, were home to almost the entire Christian population of the city, and the Turks were rarely to be found here. It was not unknown for an Ottoman wandering unaware into the Greek enclave to encounter a fast blade and a quick, quiet death, and to be stripped bare all within a minute. All the more reason why it had been surprising to see Lykaion in uniform, but then the Janissaries were powerful enough that a man would have to be both brave and foolish to attack one.

The stone-flagged and cobbled street led up towards the fruit market, which was one of the busiest areas of the enclave at any given time, and Skiouros made for the crowded square, pushing all thoughts of family and conquerors and Gods from his mind. Time to focus, now. Eight years of living off his wits and natural talents had taught him a few things, and the most important was concentration. Never be distracted, or the game could be over in an instant.

Strolling into the square, his gaze roved across the myriad of merchants and customers, delivery men with barrows of food brought from the countryside beyond the walls. Noting a stallholder duck behind his trestle to retrieve another basket of wares, Skiouros quickly swiped out an arm, fast as a snake, and pocketed a shiny red apple in his doublet. On he strode, his eyes selecting and discarding potential targets. Most were too poor to be worth the effort, and most of the stallholders were wary enough to make anything more than a swiped fruit too dangerous. Only busy and distracted customers were worth marking, and even then only those who seemed likely to have a bulging purse hidden away within the folds of their clothing.

His attention was so locked on the seething mass of people that he didn't notice the puddle of brackish water and escaped fruit juice until he stepped squarely in it. Silently, under his breath, he cursed as the stinking fluid seeped in through the hole in his right heel, making his foot feel cold and unpleasant and adding a sucking squelch to every step.

New boots.

If he could make enough to cover the week's board and a few meals and there was anything left over, he would either have to take these boots to a cobbler or give up on them altogether and fork out for a new pair. The early days of thieving in the city had taught him that he could purloin any amount of clothes and goods, but that boots should be bought and fitted; especially when one might require silence and stealth or be called upon to run at a moment's notice. These boots had cost more than half a year's rent, but had lasted for four winters now, and had been worth every akce he'd spent on them.

Shaking out his boot to remove the worst of the invasive liquid, he shuddered. While the autumn had not yet given over to winter with its snow and ice, there was an uncharacteristic chill in the air, and the cold foot did nothing to improve matters.

A mark.

That's what he needed: a mark. A good one. Preferably a merchant or a wealthy farmer come to sell his wares and returning with a fat purse and a lack of attention. Someone with money but no wits.

His gaze fell upon the man almost as if by providence. If ever there was a mark for a good thief, this man was it; he might as well be wearing a sign declaring his wealth. The man had a cloak around him, pulled tight against the biting breeze, but even the cloak was of rich, expensive wool, multihued with costly dyes and fringed with gilt tassels.

Without so much as twitching, Skiouros leaned against the wooden end-strut of a watermelon stall and crunched on his apple as though he hadn't a care in the world, his eyes taking in every aspect of the mark. He would have an escort. It was a pipe-dream to believe that such a mark would wander into a crowded market place without guards. It took only a moment for Skiouros to spot the two men standing respectfully nearby, a few yards away, yet intent on their master. It was something of a surprise to realise that the two men were Janissaries, their curved swords sheathed but hands resting on the hilts, ready for anything. Perhaps the mark was too much trouble after all. Messing with the Janissaries was always dangerous.

His doubts evaporated as he saw the richly-wrapped man reach through a purpose-made slit in his cloak and withdraw the purse from his belt – a purse that bulged fat and was clearly heavy. As Skiouros watched, the man counted out a few small, silver coins, but the young thief saw the distinct glint of gold in that sudden movement before the coins were pushed back into the purse and the container disappeared into the cloak.

His mind filled with conflicting thoughts. There were problems associated with such a mark. Quite apart from the guards, there was always a risk with someone so clearly wealthy that they were important and might bring unwanted attention and trouble if anything went wrong. And there was something else that seemed odd about the man. It took a moment for Skiouros to realise how uncomfortable he was with the fact that the cloaked man had handed over a good sized pile of cash to a scruffy oik at a stall, but had received just a small bag of lemons in return. There was something very odd happening.

As Skiouros shifted his legs to relieve a growing ache in one, his foot squelched and his intent hardened. The mark was dangerous, but he'd seen worse, and that purse would keep him for months.

The Janissaries were now moving off behind the merchant – if that was what he was – and their attention wandered here and there as they surveyed the crowd for potential problems. Their job, after all, was to keep the peace and prevent fires and troubles, as well as to supply a mailed fist to the Sultan's army.

To prevent fires.

Skiouros smiled to himself. Striding off to a nearby stall, he timed it carefully so that the owner was busy trying unsuccessfully to pile fruit on his trestle, lunging here and there to prevent them rolling off onto the street. As the merchant made a desperate and quite impressive catch of a pomegranate, Skiouros dipped and swiped one of the man's empty baskets from the stall's end. Moving at a tangent to the wealthy visitor and his two guards, he paused by a stall that was in the process of packing up for the day. Crouching, as the owner finished removing his wares to his cart and started to dissemble his table, Skiouros swept up the dry leaves and packing, avoiding the litter that was stained with the wet juice of fallen fruit. He put the fibrous offcuts and leaves into the basket, nice and dry as tinder, waiting until he had it almost packed before standing again and moving off.

The merchant and his Janissary guards were moving through the market with surprising slowness and, despite the delay as he'd gathered his tinder, Skiouros found that he had to adjust his pace to keep his intercept course true. As he walked, his nimble feet dodging him this way and that among the thriving crowd and affording him a regular if intermittent view of the mark, Skiouros reached to his belt with his free hand and withdrew his flint and steel. Hooking the basket over his arm, he made sure his course was still correct and then dropped his eyes to the fire-starting tools, which he took in both hands. A few strikes was all it took to start small sparks dropping into the dry leaves and fibres in the basket.

By the time the flint and steel were back in his belt pouch, a thin tendril of smoke was drifting up from the basket. Blinking in the tiny column of smoke, Skiouros returned his view to where the mark should be and was rewarded with a picture of the merchant bent over a stall not far away, the two guards off to one side yet close and alert, their eyes straying constantly across the crowd.

Taking a deep breath to steady himself, Skiouros found a stack of dry wooden crates at the end of another stall and, with barely a falter in his pace, dropped the basket among them. Even as he moved away, unnoticed in the mass of people, the thin tendril of smoke became a billowing torrent as the flames took.

By the time he was halfway to the merchant, sauntering slowly and casually, and occasionally pausing to examine a stall's fruit, the owner of the pile of crates was shouting his alarm and stamping at the growing conflagration. A murmur of alarm began to grow among the crowd and in a beautiful moment of almost perfectly planned response, Skiouros saw the two Janissary guards' heads flip round to the source of the shouts. It was unlikely that either man spoke Greek, but they would be familiar with a few choice words and phrases, and 'fire' would be high on the list.

The two men shared a quick look and then glanced only momentarily at their master before turning and running through the crowd, pushing the innocent citizens out of the way in a less than polite manner. Skiouros almost broke into a smile. With a wealthy man under their protection, the Janissaries would pay little attention to most incidents: petty thievery, assault or suchlike. But fire? Fire was a different matter. More than nine tenths of the city consisted of highly flammable wooden housing and each year saw a disastrous and costly conflagration hit some neighbourhood or other. Even with this being the Greek enclave, the Janissaries could hardly afford to risk a small market fire turning into something that wiped out a square mile of buildings and which might spread to a more important region.

Keeping his face locked in an expression of mild surprise, Skiouros hurled a half-hearted curse at the two men as they elbowed past him to the stall that was now producing a thick column of smoke. The merchant did not even appear to have noticed that they'd gone.

Standing with his back to Skiouros, the cloaked man was examining a table of bananas – a hideously expensive fruit imported from the old Persian east – and paying no heed at all to the growing chaos of the market behind him.

Carefully, as nonchalantly as a human being could manage and as inconspicuous as a rat beneath the stalls, Skiouros ducked between two trestles and appeared a few yards from the merchant, just in time for the man to turn, his attention finally drawn by a particularly piercing shout. Even in that split second, as Skiouros turned and picked up a crate of fruit, placing it on the stall-holder's cart to blend into the background, the young thief was suddenly struck by how outlandish the mark was.

An Ottoman stood out in the Greek enclave, for sure, and the two Janissary guards were no exception. Their master, however, was clearly not cloaked against the chill, but against drawing too much attention. The man's face was a dark chestnut colour, round and full with a thin, oiled moustache that protruded at the ends. He would stand out as much in the Ottoman neighbourhoods as he did here.

Skiouros rubbed his hands together to remove the muck from the crate of fruit and lowered his face to his 'work', peering up at a difficult angle to keep the man in sight. The dark-skinned foreigner seemed to take in the fact that there had been some incident that was apparently coming quickly under control, and turned back to the banana stall.

Without further delay, knowing that his window of opportunity was short, Skiouros took six quick steps across the intervening space, nipping between the crowd members who drifted hither and thither, and walked with an air of hassled irritation past the foreigner. Mouthing a curse in Greek he stumbled and his fingers whipped into the large slit in the man's cloak.

Once more he was grateful for his secret weapon, purchased from an Arab some years ago. The small razor sharp blade, only an inch and a half long, was guided by the two rings in its hilt that settled over his two smallest fingers, and in less than a heartbeat, the keen edge found the purse-string and severed it, the reassuringly heavy weight dropping into the remaining three fingers. His hand was back out of the slit and reaching into his own doublet in another thump of his heart, before he had even righted himself and moved on.

Success.

'Hirsiz!'

Skiouros' heart skipped a beat and then made up for it by beginning to pound dangerously fast. The Turkish word for 'thief' was well known to him, and the only people in this market that would use it were the two Janissaries.

Forcing himself to continue at a steady pace, on the very small chance that he was not the target of the shout, Skiouros turned his head with an expression of mild interest. The two Janissary guards were pushing their way through the throng, pointing at him, one of them waving an already-drawn blade.

Thanking God in a blind, almost automatic fashion that they were armed only with swords and not the guns now being wielded by some of their number, Skiouros turned his eyes from them to the merchant. The rich man had recognised the shout and his hand had immediately reached into his cloak. As the foreigner gave another shout in a distinctly Arabic tone, pointing at Skiouros, the Janissaries had switched to stilted Greek.

'Thief! Stop the thief!'

In another heartbeat, Skiouros was running, all thought of new boots and platters of food gone from his mind as he simply ran directly away from the foreigner and his guards.

His eyes lit upon the narrow street that led from here, up yet another slope towards the former Pammakaristos monastery. If he could get into that street, he could easily lose himself in the warren of narrow alleyways that he knew so well. No Turk would stand a chance of catching him there.

A big man thrust out an arm from his stall, grasping for Skiouros as he ran, and the nimble thief ducked and slid under the grip, his boot heels skidding across the flags before he came up running again. His heart fell as he saw three heavy-set middle-aged stallholders and customers move to block his exit up the street.

Now the foreigner had been lost to sight somewhere in the crowd, but the two Janissaries were on him like the Sultan's greyhounds on a palace rabbit. As Skiouros changed direction, angling away from the outraged locals who blocked his path, he glanced over his shoulder to see the two Turks gaining on him with surprising speed, barging citizens out of the way as though they were mere sheep – which, to most of the Ottomans, the Greek Christians might as well be.

Swallowing and forcing himself to continue with deep breaths that calmed his system and facilitated an easy speed, Skiouros ducked beneath a stall and made his decision. Ahead, two carts, piled almost head high with fruit boxes, stood close together, waiting to be taken away from the market. Angling towards them, but slightly off to one side, Skiouros made for the main street leading from the square, which led past the great sunken wreck of the 'Dry Garden' cistern and the great mosque of the Conqueror, and off towards the heart of the Sultan's great demesne. It was the obvious direction to take. The sheer numbers of people in the street would make pursuit troublesome. Even though it was a wide avenue, Skiouros would have a chance.

And that was what they would naturally assume.

As he pushed past a stack of boxes, raising a cry of anger from the stallholder, Skiouros ducked sharp right and disappeared between the two high carts of crates. Pausing long enough for a pursuer to assume he would have moved on, he edged out from behind the cart at the far side and strolled nonchalantly, holding a laden box, towards the edge of the square.

The shouts became more frantic but more distant as the two Janissaries, fooled by his sudden disappearance, searched ahead where he should have been, pushing towards the main street. Skiouros, all but invisible to them now, staggered across the less busy side of the square under the weight of his box and made for the nearest door.

Like most of Constantinople, and certainly the Phanar district, the buildings that ringed the square were heavy, two-storey constructions of dry timber, precarious staircases leading up inside a courtyard around which dozens of families made their home. The houses were so tightly packed together that the shoulder-wide alleys between them were almost pitch black and stank of dung and refuse, but no one entered them anyway, barring the stray dogs that roamed the streets or beggars with no place to stay.

As he passed from the bright, cold light of the square into the dim entranceway of the wooden housing he shivered, but sagged with relief. Continuing at the same steady pace in case of casual observers, he dropped the box of fruit in the hall and stepped into the narrow courtyard.

He was safe, for now. It would take a few minutes for the foreigner and his Janissaries to realise they had been deceived and turn their attention back from the main street to the other exits from the square. It was possible, however unlikely, that they might manage to summon other Janissaries or officials to their aid, aside from the bulk of the law-abiding populace of the market. The upshot was that his apparent security was a fleeting state. In five minutes, or ten, a stallholder would answer a question and remember someone of Skiouros' description coming in here. And then he would be trapped somewhere even more confining.

Fortunately there were few folk in the whole of Phanar, or the city as a whole, who could navigate this neighbourhood like Skiouros. With only a moment's pause for decision making, he crossed the courtyard, climbed a stair at the far side and entered the dusty wooden corridor. Four residences led off the long passage, their doors standing resolutely shut. To the inexperienced eye it was clearly a dead end.

And so it would appear to angry pursuit.

But Skiouros was a little more aware than the average citizen or Janissary. Glancing along the corridor, he settled on the last door to his right and made for it. The other three doors stood closed but clear, indicating regular access and therefore the possibility that they were currently occupied. The fourth, however, had a pile of old, unpleasant blankets bundled up near the door, smelling of faeces, suggesting that one of the city's many vagrants was using this corridor to shelter from the chilly autumn weather. It was a very common sight at night, but only happened outside the doors of those houses that stood unoccupied and had no owner to shoo the homeless on. In some cases the vagrants even moved into the houses, but the penalty for such an act was extremely harsh if they were discovered, and so few dared to try it.

Stepping carefully so as not to disturb the various offending and offensive articles, Skiouros reached the door and pushed. As expected it opened slowly and stiffly, following some weeks or even months of disuse; few doors in Phanar had locks, barring the wealthier owners, and at least one member of the family would always be at home to keep their possessions secure.

Inside, the house was dim and smelled musty and disused. A number of unseen creatures scuttled away from this sudden intruder, and Skiouros paused for a long moment to let his eyes adjust before closing the door behind him, carefully enough to leave little or no sign of his passing.

Almost enough, but only a fool would consider himself safe yet.

With another steadying breath, the nimble thief stepped across the dimly lit room towards the far side, where two shuttered windows blocked out most of the light. His choice had been a good one; many of these buildings around the square would back onto another similar structure with just a dark stinking alley to separate them. Not so this one, as the bright white light forcing its way through the cracks around the shutters confirmed.

Stepping up to a window, he leaned to the side, so as not to be seen clearly, and unlatched the shutters, pulling them inwards. Again, he paused to allow his eyes to adjust. Behind the house, as he'd anticipated from his excellent sense of position and geography, the ruins of an old Roman bath house stood among choking foliage, rotting slowly into oblivion. One day, some enterprising person would rebuild or demolish it and the open space with its derelict ruin would be no more, but for now...

Skiouros smiled to himself and checked quickly to be certain there were no observers, before slipping lightly out of the window, his feet finding minimal purchase on the wooden boards of the outer wall above the four foot drop to the undergrowth. Carefully and slowly, he pulled the shutters closed again, using agile fingers at the last moment to lift the latch-hook and rest it on the staple of the other shutter. With a dextrous motion, he jerked the shutters closed, the latch falling into place on the far side and hiding signs of his passage to all but the most observant of men.

Dropping lightly to the ground, he stepped through the undergrowth, avoiding the brambles and descending the slight slope towards the shattered ruin of the bathhouse. Disused for several centuries, the complex was little more now than a shell, with a few passageways open to the air and dangerous, uneven floors, scattered with tesserae from broken mosaics.

Pushing aside a springy branch, he scurried into the open doorway and navigated the ruin with the skill and surety of a man who had used this structure as a hideaway more than once. Along the corridors he moved, slipping through a huge break in a wall into a room next door, where half the floor had gone to reveal dozens of piles of bricks set in regular ordered rows, as well as the green, mossy half-cellar they filled. The figure of some heathen deity stared accusingly at him from a ruined wall, his features surprisingly distinct given the condition of the ageing painting.

In the corner, a wooden chair lay on its side, with two old wooden crates nearby. Righting the chair, Skiouros glanced around over the low, ruinous walls for any sign of pursuit and sank into the chair with a sigh of relief. He was free.

Free?

In Ottoman 'Istanbul' there was precious little true freedom for a Greek Christian, however liberated they were officially. Oh, the conqueror Mehmet had apparently been remarkably tolerant of his new subjects, and even Skiouros' father had been surprisingly complimentary about the man. Moreover, this Bayezid the Second was already being referred to as 'The Just', but how free could a man be when most of his own city was a foreign nation, and his religion only tolerated so long as it did not intrude into his masters' lives?

For a man like Skiouros, however, freedom was no illusion. His choice of profession, dangerous and illegal though it might be, allowed him a freedom that few others in the city could experience.

With a sense of achievement and satisfaction, the thief leaned back and withdrew the heavy leather purse from his doublet. Weighing it in his hand, he couldn't even begin to estimate the haul he'd just taken. Certainly it felt like a goodly amount.

Savouring the moment, he examined the purse and came to the conclusion that the leather article itself was probably worth more than some of his days' takings. The whole thing was decorated with intricate stitching, singeing and staining depicting an Arabic desert scene surrounded by delicate patterns. The catch was of polished brass.

Smelling the rich, oiled leather and noting a hint of spice about the odour, Skiouros finally relented and undid the catch. The cold sunlight filtering down through the weeds and branches that formed a natural roof over this corner of the room glinted on a variety of metals: copper, silver and even gold.

Skiouros dragged the crate over and turned it so that the upward-facing side was the most solid and flat. Then being careful to contain the distribution with his free hand, he tipped the purse's contents out onto his makeshift table.

The first thing that caught his attention was the disproportionate amount of high currency to low. There was enough gold in there to buy a house – or more. The second was the nature of the currency. He had seen enough Turkish coins in his eight years of filching them to identify them, often right down to the mint that had issued them, this despite not having a grasp of the written word in any language. These coins were clearly not Turkish but Arabic of some sort. Who was this strange man? A foreign merchant seemed the obvious answer, but what would a rich Arab merchant be doing in the poor Greek quarter? It was a puzzle that he was beginning to dislike even the look of.

With a sigh of mixed relief, satisfaction and faint worry, he scratched his head. He would take a stroll to the Jewish quarter. There was a dealer in antiquities there called Judah ben Isaac, who would be able to identify the currency and could read a dozen different scripts. Judah would tell him what these coins were and might even be able to change them for less distinctive Turkish currency at the same time. Yes, he would head there in an hour or so, as soon as he was fully convinced there was no chance of his pursuers picking up his trail again.

With a grim nod of satisfaction he decided to put the haul away. No point in tempting fate; best to keep them stowed safely for now.

Reaching down, Skiouros picked up the largest of the gold coins, admiring it as it glinted in the sunlight, turning it over a couple of times to admire the workmanship, biting lightly on the edge to test the quality of the metal. It was not just gold, it was good gold. With a grin of true satisfaction, he lifted the purse again to slot the coin in and realised that it was not quite empty. A small piece of paper had caught against the lip and remained within.

Intrigued, Skiouros removed the scrap and examined it. Once more, the writing on it was completely indecipherable, but it had been penned in a fluid and graceful script. Turning the paper over, he discovered nothing on the reverse. Just two short lines of text. Another job for Judah, then.

Slowly, allowing plenty of time to pass and examining each in turn for design, presumed worth and metal content, Skiouros replaced the coins in the purse and then added the piece of paper. After perhaps half an hour, his impatience to learn more about his haul overcame the desire to stay hidden for longer and he stood, stretched, and pocketed the purse.

Feeling relaxed and a little excited by this intriguing development, he strode out of the room with its shattered floor, past another chamber with a rubble-filled half-moon basin in the corner and then a broken hall with niches along one wall, and out into the world once more.

He emerged, a shiver running through him as the enforced period of prolonged inactivity had cooled his muscles. Rubbing his hands together for warmth, he pushed his way through the hanging whip-like branches of an invading tree and appeared in the open ground on the deep, untamed grass.

So immersed in his mental whirlwind was he that he almost fell over the woman sitting on the ground, and had to perform a strange jig to keep his feet and balance.

Idiot! It was inattentiveness like that which killed his kind.

His hand went to his waist, where a knife hung on his belt, as he spun to examine this woman who had no legitimate excuse for loitering and lurking in such a rarely-visited place.

Relief filled him as he recognised the figure for what she was: a Romani – one of those nomadic magicians from the east who were now to be found all over the former lands of Byzantium.

'I nearly trampled you, old woman,' he said.

The old woman looked up, holding her arms out to her sides, and Skiouros realised now what she had been doing, hunched over the grass. On a patch of dry dirt, the wizened, lined and leathery old woman had the corpse of a crow laid out flat and was busily removing the bones with infinite care, one by one. Involuntarily, he shuddered.

'Amri tuti!' she snapped, making an unfamiliar but clearly unpleasant gesture at him with her outstretched arms.

'I'm sorry, but I have no idea what that means,' he replied calmly.

35

'Are you...' he shuffled uneasily. 'Are you a witch?'

'If you say,' she replied noncommittally, narrowing her eyes at him.

'I...' He had no idea what to say, and surrendered to the obvious. 'I have to go.'

'Flee to shelter,' the old woman said, bending back to her work.

'Sorry?'

'A storm comes. Big storm. You find shelter.'

Frowning, Skiouros looked up at the chilly clear blue sky and shook his head.

'No sign of a storm, old witch. I think you're picking over the wrong bird.'

The woman paused in her gruesome task once again and looked up at him. There was something about the glint in her eye that sent a chill through him – a chill which had nothing to do with the weather, and which made him feel like a five-year-old afraid of the monsters in every shadow of the farmhouse.

'A storm comes and it brings death and pain. Find shelter now and stay there.'

Narrowing her eyes, she gestured with worrying accuracy at the very place beneath his tunic where he had secreted the purse.

'And forget about that. No good comes of it.'

'You only say that because you haven't got it. Go back to dismembering birds, old woman. God reigns in the city of Constantine; not your weird ways.'

The woman gave him a gap-toothed smile that contained all the humour of a burial chamber and which sent yet another chill through him.

'Go.'

Without needing any further urging, Skiouros turned his back on the old witch and her grisly pastime and strode through the undergrowth to the alley that would lead him towards the empty shell of the Pammakaristos church. All the way out of the bath-house's surrounding vegetation, he could feel what he was sure was her gaze boring into his back, filling him with uncertainty and superstition.

The Romani were strange ones, with powers that no-one could explain. The Orthodox priests called them children of the devil, and the imams of the Ottoman mosques had no better words to say about them, but there was definitely something about them that felt not-of-this-world. Skiouros was still feeling eerily chilled and uncomfortable even when he moved into the current of people that was the lifeblood of the city.

Feeling at least relieved that there was precious little chance of being pulled up for his adventure in the marketplace, while still under a cloud somehow caused by the Romani witch, Skiouros strode down the hill that led from the Greek district of Phanar to the Jewish area of Balat.

Despite the well-known, unmarked delineation of the nations, the architecture and atmosphere hardly changed at all as Skiouros passed from the Greek to the Jewish enclave. Only the personal appearance and habits of those people wandering about the streets labelled this a Jewish area. Over the past eight years in the city, Skiouros had spent a great deal of time in Balat and had come to know a number of its residents on what he considered friendly terms. For a man in his profession it was a godsend to have such a collection of shrewd traders, monetary experts and merchants nearby, many of whom were happy to deal with a man suspected of being on the wrong side of the law. After all, it was Ottoman law these days and the Jews had fared much the same under their rule as the Christians.

Fifteen minutes' walk brought him to the house of Judah ben Isaac, a man who dealt in treasures, fine sculptures, coins and other similar goods, supplying the houses of those wealthy Ottomans who exhibited a taste for the artistic, and slowly becoming the richest non-Muslim in the whole city. Ben Isaac maintained a modest house, but with his unseemly wealth and the patronage and support of some of the most influential Turks in the city, he was a man with a great deal of understated power. It was said that he ran other businesses on the shadier side of the legal system, but that was something that Skiouros was happy to avoid. Organised crime just meant more people to take a cut of your pickings. One thing that stood out, though, about Ben Isaac's residence was its construction. It rose like an island of stone among so many timber structures.

At the door, David met him as usual. A hulking man who seemed incongruous with his ringlets and skullcap, given his enormous muscles and reputation for causing damage, David had long since become a friend, or at least a friendly acquaintance.

'Skiouros.'

'Shalom, David. Is Master ben Isaac available? I have a few questions to put to him, and possibly a healthy commission.'

The brute nodded, the shiny black ringlets bobbing beside his lantern jaw, and gestured inside. 'Usual place.'

Skiouros bowed slightly in respect as he passed the big enforcer and stepped into the house. An 'office' of sorts sat off to the right of the entrance corridor, the desk and chairs arranged in just such a way as to make the visitor feel humble and to emphasise the power of the building's owner. The first dozen times Skiouros had been here, he'd been met in the office. These days he was allowed to greet the house's master in the casual atmosphere of the second room.

Mounting three stairs, the thief turned into the next doorway and smiled.

'Master Judah. Shalom, my friend.'

The elderly Jew, his ringlets silvery white and his shoulders slightly hunched, looked up from whatever he was doing and focused on the visitor, an expression of noncommittal recognition passing across his face. He returned to examining the lists on his desk.

'Shalom, my Greek filos. How can I be of assistance?' His words were pleasant and to the point, but his attention remained riveted on the paper lists.

'I need some help, Master Judah.'

'Of course you do. Those with no need of help do not seek me out. Elucidate, my boy.'

'I have some coins with which I'm not familiar. If you will tell me about them and how to get them changed, I will let you keep five of them of your choice.'

'Five coins is a pittance for my work, young man.'

'Not these coins, I suspect.'

For the first time, Judah ben Isaac's attention shifted from the paperwork to his visitor and he looked up with an interested gleam shining out from beneath his bushy grey eyebrows.

'Intrigue me.'

Without saying more, Skiouros withdrew his new purse from his doublet and unfastened it with a flourish. As the Jew frowned, he tipped the contents onto the table, where they scattered on the felt cover. He almost grinned at the sudden change of expression on the old man's face and the hint of hunger in his eyes.

'Interesting, then?'

'Six coins,' the old man said with an air of finality. Skiouros chewed his lip for a moment, but nodded. It was worth the extra coin to keep the good faith of a man like Judah ben Isaac, and six coins out of this pouch would still leave a small fortune.

'Six; agreed.'

The ageing Jew pored over the offering, turning over the coins and examining them with great interest.

'You don't know what these are?'

'No.'

Judah ben Isaac shook his head as he leaned back. 'These are Mamluk coins, from Egypt. They are of little use to you.'

Skiouros felt a cold shiver run through him. The Empire had been in a constant state of hot-and-cold war with the Mamluk Sultanate for nine years now, ever since the usurper Cem had allied with them in his failed attempt to take the throne. His mind furnished him with an image of the man in the wealthy cloak with the dark skinned face and narrow moustache, apparently engaged in some nefarious activity in the fruit market. The Mamluks?

'Can they be exchanged?'

'I would be interested to know how you came by them, I have to say,' Ben Isaac frowned, 'but not interested enough to pry. Some things are best left unlearned, I find.'

'But can you change them?' Skiouros repeated urgently.

'I can change them, yes, but not through a local source. Given the war, these are less than useless in the Empire. No Ottoman will handle a Mamluk coin at the moment, and their very presence here raises some dangerous and uncomfortable questions. I will have to change them with a western dealer. I can exchange them for Venetian ducats, but the relationship between Venice and the Mamluks is cold at best, so I do not anticipate a good rate. And then, of course, I will have to change the ducats for good Ottoman sultani and akce. I would hazard a guess at this haul being worth perhaps fifty ducats – after my deduction of six gold coins, of course.'

Skiouros' mind raced. He'd handled ducats a few times. Fifty sounded like an enormous sum.

'And then,' Ben Isaac went on, 'when I change the ducats to local coinage, we'll be looking at perhaps two thousand akce – forty sultani. I cannot guarantee this, of course, but that is my estimate.'

The young man swayed a little on his feet. He'd managed to lift a few sultani here and there in his time, but had never in his life held more than two at a time. Forty? Just one would buy his new boots with coin to spare. He looked up into the calculating eyes of Judah ben Isaac, who tapped his chin.

'Bear in mind, my Greek friend, that there is no guarantee that the deal will go through. It is very likely, but such a large sum in a coinage belonging to an enemy state will make many a trader nervous. Are you comfortable leaving the money with me?'

Skiouros fought down the urge to say no. Ben Isaac was not a man to insult and when involved in a business deal, he was known to be trustworthy; in all fairness, the money was probably more secure in this house than anywhere Skiouros could keep it.

'Of course, Master ben Isaac. But I am... a little light at the moment?'

The elderly Jew laughed and leaned forward once more, his fingers tracing motions around the gold coins on the table.

'Up my commission to seven coins, and I will give you fifty akce to take now.'

It was a poor deal, and both men knew it. Despite the dangers of refusing this man, Skiouros cleared his throat. 'A hundred. Two sultani if you prefer. My boots leak.'

There was a silent, dangerous pause, then Judah ben Isaac threw his arms wide in defeat.

'Alright, my boy. You win. Haggling with a Greek, they say, is like trying to ride a two-legged donkey: it takes too long and you'll wish you hadn't tried. Two sultani it is. Buy yourself new boots. And get yourself a bath; you smell like a midden.'

Skiouros grinned and watched the old man reach into a drawer in the back of his desk, removing a small brass tin, unlocking it with a key from within his voluminous robes, and producing two shining gold coins, each bearing the likeness of Mehmet the Conqueror. He slapped them down on the far side of the desk and Skiouros swept them gratefully into his grip. Taking a deep breath, he reached down to the empty purse, still in his other hand, and removed the piece of paper he'd kept inside with a carefully-placed fingertip.

'One last thing, Master Judah. Could you tell me what this says?'

The house's owner reached out and took the paper gently, holding it up and peering myopically at it.

'Are you sure you want to know?'

'Yes,' he replied, placing the purse on the table as he secreted away the two coins in his own pouch.

The old man narrowed his eyes and swept out a hand to take in the spread of coins. 'Bear in mind the trouble you're skirting with all this. I ask again, are you sure you want to know?'

Skiouros frowned at the old man's manner. What was he suggesting?

'Yes, I want to know.'

'Very well. This note was written in true Arabic, but not by a native speaker. I suspect it was penned by a Christian, as I believe the line was written incorrectly from left to right. It is an address and a date. The date is today, and the address is Zagan Pasha Caddesi – the house with the yellow marble columns.'

'I don't know the street.'

'I suspect you do, though in your Greek quarter it is still known mostly by its old name: The Street of the Hercules statue. Out by the Church of Saint John?'

'Thank you, Master Judah, I know the one. I will leave you to your work now, and call again in a few days to finalise the transaction.'

The old man nodded and held out the paper. 'Take this with you. I want nothing to do with whatever it means.'

Skiouros took the paper and stuffed it into his doublet, bowed, and left the room almost vibrating with excitement. In his hand was as much money as he'd ever owned at one time, and he could anticipate perhaps twenty times that amount in a few days. He had enough to buy new boots, pay his rent and eat well all week, with plenty of change to spare. He knew for certain that Ben Isaac had seriously short-changed him and that his haul was likely worth at least twice as much, but there was simply no alternative channel for such a take and it was better to be certain of a small fortune than to jeopardise a large one.

He barely noticed the hulking David as he left and made his way back up the slope towards the Phanar district; indeed, it only occurred to him as he passed the edge of the Jewish residences that he had dropped the ornate leather purse on the table in the house and neglected to retrieve it before he left.

Ben Isaac had been singularly reticent in revealing the contents of the note, and the fact preyed on Skiouros' mind as he climbed towards the street where his rented rooms were to be found. Admittedly, anything that might link him to a Mamluk spy in these days of strife was a serious danger to life and limb, but still the old man's reaction had seemed a little over the top.

Walking steadily towards the house, he remembered that his

primary goal should be a cobbler and turned around, he headed for the road which would lead him to the Mese, the great central street that split the city and formed part of the edge of the Greek enclave. There would be many boot sellers on the Mese, some with expensive Italian footwear as well as the soft, yielding Turkish garb.

And then, when he'd returned and paid his board, he would go to the Dionysus taverna on the corner near the 'Dry Garden', have a solid meal and a few flasks of good, strong, imported Bulgarian ale while he pondered what to do about this mysterious piece of paper and the address named upon it.

Chapter 2 – The house of the yellow marble columns

* Çarsamba (Wednesday) evening *

Skiouros tapped the gold coin on the surface of the table, eyeing his used dinner plate with slightly blurred contentment. The lamb had been succulent and well sauced, and the olives and spiced bread fresh and piquant. He'd often watched wealthier occupants of the taverna eating the owner's best fare and wondered what it tasted like, given the wondrous aromas. Now he knew. It would be hard to go back to eating the ordinary rubbish that he accepted: offcuts and leftovers, reheated meat and stale bread that cost a fraction of the price of the taverna's better food. But return to his old ways he would have to. He had made a small fortune from this haul, but there was no guarantee that the near future would be as good to him, and to squander such a reward on a few good meals was tempting providence.

No. Perhaps once a week he might treat himself to a quality dish. Plus, of course, he had his new boots. Glancing down beneath the table, he took in the fine fawn leather of Florentine origin, the pointed toe and the folded top. They were exquisite, though they would take some breaking in and would pinch for a few days.

On his return journey, he had seen a tailor on the Mese with a slashed black doublet of Italian manufacture that he would dearly love, but which would have to wait until the rest of his payment showed up, as would a fresh linen shirt and new braes and hose. But the boots were a good start.

Reaching across the table, he grasped the ale and almost missed, his fingers scrabbling at the bottleneck and righting it just before it rolled over. Three empty flasks lay nearby, testament to his celebratory evening.

There had been gambling and games of chance in the taverna's main room, and he'd been sorely tempted to try his hand, or even to lighten a purse or two the easy way, but had forced himself to sit in virtual solitude at a shadowed table in the corner. He had drunk too much for that kind of escapade and he knew it. The temptation was evidence enough: one should never shit on one's own doorstep, as they said, and to consider it was all the proof he needed that he ought to stop drinking.

But he could never afford to waste ale, even with spare coin in his purse, and it would be a criminal act in itself to abandon such a good brew. Grinning to himself at his logic, he tipped the last of the ale down his throat, splashing some of it down his chin and onto his doublet. Ah well. In a few days he would have a fine, new doublet.

Common sense still floated on the lake of ale in his head, and he knew that the longer he stayed intoxicated and in such a place, the more chance there was of something going wrong, or of him trying something stupid.

Sliding his chair back from the table, he stood slowly and swayed for a moment. Fresh air and a walk. That was what he needed.

Slowly and very deliberately, he moved the chair safely out of the way and turned towards the door. Oil lamps lit the tavern's interior in much the same fashion as they had since the days of the pagan emperors, but the doorway was illuminated by two flaming torches just without, one to each side, and the heady smell of the burning pitch was starting to infiltrate the main room, having been burning for over an hour now since sundown.

Carefully, so as not to cause undue attention, he moved towards the door, concentrating as though walking a rope like the acrobats at festivals. One foot in front of the other, time and again until he was outside. It was half a good thief's task to build a shell of complete ordinariness to the point of becoming almost invisible. Drawing attention to oneself was tantamount to surrendering to the authorities.

His head fizzing gently with intoxication, he strolled out of the door without the slightest wobble and into the chilly nighttime air of the city. The cold hit his brain like a block of marble, sending the ale pulsing round his body and infusing every inch of him. He was suddenly dangerously unbalanced, but knew that it would begin to wear off soon. Fresh air brought it all to an immediate head, making the effects worse temporarily, but speeding the recovery no end. Better this way than the long drawn-out lie-down in the warm.

Just in case, he moved diagonally across the road and leaned against the wooden wall of the house opposite, pausing long enough to gain a semblance of sobriety. A rainwater barrel stood at the building's end and he reached in and scooped up a few chilly mouthfuls with his hands.

Which way to go?

Perhaps he could visit Lykaion and try and patch things up?

Stupid! He knew damn well that there was no chance of that, particularly in this state. Besides, it would be more or less suicidal to wander up to the Janissary barracks. Normally he passed a message inside with one of the numerous new recruits or slaves who attended the everyday chores of the complex. That would not be possible at night.

Stupid even to think about it.

He could just go for a walk – stroll around Phanar and Balat, or even into the Ottoman area. While there were distinctive living regions for the non-Turkish residents of the city, there was no physical boundary and Greek subjects could quite legally move through the rest of the city, providing they were not visibly armed and paid due deference and respect to any Turk they encountered.

He considered the possibility.

Every week or two he would spend a day and an evening wandering the city, getting to know its byways and streets, its great civic buildings and open spaces. It was good to be acquainted with the place in detail, and over the eight years he had been doing so he liked to think there were few places within the city walls that he didn't have a reasonable geographical grasp of.

The only downside of such an outing was the inherent danger of being a foreigner in the Ottoman regions. While Sultan Bayezid the Second might be 'just', most of his citizens were 'just' capable of tolerating the Greeks as long as they kept to their own quarter. It was not even uncommon to hear of a Greek merchant making a delivery to an Ottoman household to have been beheaded for 'acting in an offensive manner' to a Turk. Such acts sometimes included walking and breathing.

Still, the non-Turkish population should thank providence that such a man as Bayezid did rule the city. It was said of his brother that he had boiled men in oil for delivering his food cold. And in the interests of a fair view, Skiouros' own grandfather had told tales of the Byzantine Emperors that had horrified him as a child: beheadings, blindings, roastings, impalings and so much more, and that to their own kind!

Still, Ottoman Istanbul was too dangerous; out of the question for tonight.

Leaning against the wooden house, he fumbled in his pocket and withdrew the scrap of paper, lifting it to the vague glow of the burning torches opposite as though that would somehow give him the ability to interpret the strange, snake-like scribbles upon it.

The Street of the Hercules Statue.

He knew it well – well enough, even, to picture the house in the address. Somewhere around halfway along the street stood a house that was somewhat unusual in the area, its lower courses formed of old Byzantine or Roman brick with timber above. Two huge columns of golden-coloured marble stood flanking the door, supporting a wooden porch. It was an interesting building, though nothing more than a house, for sure. Too poor and wooden to be the residence of the wealthy, albeit a single house rather than a shared residence like those that covered much of the city.

Well, he could at least take a look at the place.

With the confidence of the slightly inebriated he straightened and strode off down the street. His sense of direction unimpaired by his condition, he strode through the streets of the Phanar district, paying no heed to the numerous folk still abroad despite the cold. Turning corners here and there, he soon found himself at the small church of Saint John the Forerunner, from which led the street named on the paper.

The church, tiny even for one of the multitude crammed into the ancient city, was the shape of a small apsed cross no more than fifty or sixty feet across and with a circular tower, all formed of the traditional decorative brick and stone that was to be seen in public buildings all over Constantinople. At the side of the church by the small apsidal end stood the statue for which the street was named.

No one knew where the 'Hercules' had come from originally, and there was little about it to definitively confirm such an appellation, but some enterprising early Christian had chipped away whatever the statue had originally held and replaced it with a large wooden crucifix, which it still held after all this time. The statue appeared to be glaring at him, or possibly at the street to which he had come. A shudder ran up his spine.

If he were a man given to superstition or fear of the divine, he would turn and flee right now. After all, a Jew, a witch and now an ancient God had all apparently tried to urge him away from the place.

'Stick it in your back passage, Hercules!' he snapped quietly at the statue and shrugged his shoulders against the chill, turning away and striding down the street. He was starting to feel a tension at his temples and the rising pressure in the centre of his skull that suggested his hangover was going to be visiting him early – a consequence of the fresh air and exercise combined with his imbibing.

This street was deserted as he made his way down it. Despite lying in the heart of the Greek region, the thoroughfare itself and all the others that surrounded it were entirely residential, and little activity would be found outdoors of a cold autumn evening.

Wooden housing fronted onto the street as it did in the entire district and most of the city, though many of those to be found here were individual houses rather than the conglomerate structures housing a dozen families that covered the lower slopes leading down towards Balat and the river.

Slowly, a sense of wariness beginning to build within him, Skiouros moved down the street, strikingly aware of just how alone he was. After only a few moments he could see the marble pillars on the house near the centre, glowing in reflected moonlight among the dark and seasoned timbers.

Was he being stupid? Reckless?

Certainly the ale was informing his decisions tonight. Sober, he would have waited until morning. He knew himself well enough not to even pretend that he would have left the place alone and ignored the note entirely, but he would certainly have waited until a more sensible time presented itself. But the same natural inquisitiveness that meant he would never be able to pass off the note and its address as unimportant had been magnified by alcohol and now refused to let his mind leave the subject he'd fixated upon.

With a wariness that belied his inebriation, he slowed as he approached the house and came to a halt opposite the door with its grand columns, leaning against a wooden wall and watching the house that was the subject of the paper scrap.

Despite the slight idiosyncrasies in its architecture, the house was in no way out of the ordinary. Four windows were visible from the front, as well as an opening below the roof, and the houses lining the street were so tightly packed here that there was not even room for a man to squeeze between them; in many cases houses that had settled and sagged were even leaning against their neighbours for support. Only one window had any sign of life: a flickering golden glow in an upstairs room barely showing behind heavy curtains that were drawn most of the way across.

Skiouros watched the building for some time, wondering, now that he'd actually come here, what he was supposed to do about it? To knock, or even to enter, was strange and probably stupid. Doubtless the occupant was expecting someone today and that person would either already have visited or would bear no resemblance to him. Either way, he would find himself speechless, uncomfortable and in trouble when the door opened.

But the door was open…

His eyes began to pick out details as the realisation started to bring him forcibly back to sobriety. The thumping in his head receded as his brain began to function at a higher level once again. Sometimes inebriation could be killed off simply by surprise.

The door was ajar, rather than wide open; hardly inviting visitors. Sometimes, in the heat of a hot Propontian summer, when the flies made the evening air unbearable and the smell of warm dung filled the streets, the people of the city would leave their doors cracked at night to cool their houses, but the weather was hardly stifling at this time of year, and a draft would be chilling the room within.

An accident, then?

Something was tremendously wrong with the situation and alarms were triggering all through Skiouros's body. 'Run,' his subconscious urged him.

He took a step towards the house, feeling the hairs rise on the back of his neck. His expert gaze took in more points that alarmed him as he took three further steps into the middle of the street.

The door was creaking and moving slightly with the chill wind, but in a specific and odd fashion. The wind blew down the street, hitting the outer face of the door and trying to slam it shut, but something small must be caught in it, as the portal bounced slightly with each gust and returned to its slightly-open state.

Within, a thin, low glow of golden light at ground level suggested a light source stood on the floor just out of sight around the corner from the door. The chances of that being a purposeful decision were tiny. A fallen light; a jammed, half-open door. Not good signs.

'Run!'

Skiouros clamped down on his subconscious urge to flee the scene and took a few steps further towards the creaking door. The owner of the house was far from poor. Three yards from the entrance, he could see the felt lining on the inside of the door – additional draft-proofing – and the expensive Anatolian rug that led from the entrance into the room.

So... a person living in the Greek enclave in a modest but private house, but with notably costly furnishings; someone to whom the interior of their residence was more important than the exterior. If the owner had been more conservative with their furnishings, they could have perhaps afforded one of the few brick or stone buildings that were warmer and more stable and fire-proof than the wooden ones.

Anonymity was the goal, perhaps? He had walked past this house countless times in his eight years of city life and only really noticed it in terms of architecture – the lower courses of brick and the twin columns. It had never occurred to him that it might be anything more than a simple residence the same as all the others.

There was plainly no point in trying to fight his curiosity any more.

With a deep breath and a quick glance up and down the street to check for observers, he stepped up to the door and grasped the edge, slowly pulling it open and wincing at the creak and the tiny squeal that issued from it.

A quick glance in, and he ducked to the side, not allowing long enough for any occupant to get a good look at his face or to aim a weapon, but long enough for a brief appraisal of the situation.

Empty.

The main room behind the creaking door was unoccupied and silent. A crude-oil-burning lamp, its tall glass chimney decorated with engraved tulip buds and Ottoman patterns, lay on the floor at an angle against a cushion, miraculously positioned just right to keep the oil reservoir contained and the lamp burning. A lucky escape for the neighbourhood, for sure.

But other than the lamp, there did not appear at first glance to be any sign of a disturbance or a struggle. A door led through into the rear of the house, while a narrow staircase led up to the next floor.

The décor was quite startlingly expensive, and coloured silver, white and blue.

Skiouros leaned back against the wall beside the door, his heart pounding noisily in his own ears and the slight thump of his all-but forgotten headache blending in with it. Despite the ale, he'd never felt more sober. Amazing what a little nervous action could do. He'd still need to watch his step, though. His alertness and senses might be back in condition, but there would still be a sluggishness and unpredictability to any delicate activity.

Since no further sound or sign of movement issued from the room, Skiouros stepped back to the open doorway and peered inside, taking in more detail this time. A second door, almost out of sight behind the staircase, led to another area of the ground floor. A plush blue couch rested against the far wall of the room, cushions adorning it. There were three rugs in total on the floor and a small area in the corner was strewn with floor cushions, the oil lamp among them. Cupboards and desks dotted the periphery.

His eyes were straying towards the wall decorations when something registered in his brain and his gaze snapped back to the lamp, his vision focusing this time on the hair-thin wire that looped around the glass chimney of the lamp and ran across the floor at a height of four inches, barely visible except when it caught and reflected the lamp-light.

Frowning, Skiouros followed the wire's line to the front door, where it ran through a staple and across the opening at ankle height. The hastily inserted tack to which the far end of the cord had been attached was the object preventing the door from slamming closed.

A trap? A foolish one, if so. Anyone entering would almost certainly trip it and set light instantly to the soft furnishings. The house would be an inferno in half a minute and, while no unprepared visitors would have the time to prevent the conflagration, they certainly would have time to get away from it. So what point was the trap?

All caution thrown to the wind now, restraint submerged beneath Skiouros' driving need to know more, the thief raised his leg and with infinite care stepped over the wire and into the room, bringing his other leg over after and then stepping away from the line.

For a moment he tried to decide whether it would be prudent to leave the trap in position rather than removing all doubt that someone had been here, but the fear of a fire raging through the streets and blocks of the city won out and he crossed to the oil lamp, straightening it carefully and removing the loop of wire from the neck before lifting it and placing it on one of the decorative inlaid sideboards. With the tension taken from it, the wire sagged back to the ground and the trap was disarmed.

Again, Skiouros looked around. The décor was truly fine and rather at odds with the exterior, the interior being largely Ottoman in nature while the house presented an Orthodox image in the Greek district. Something about it, though he couldn't quite put his finger on what, suggested that the owner of the house was a woman. The room in which he stood was clearly furnished and decorated for entertaining guests – Ottoman guests by the look of it.

Method to everything. Never change floor until you're certain that the ground is clear, else you could find yourself trapped and your exit blocked. A quick glance at the staircase and a pause to listen confirmed his initial impression that there was no activity up there.

Crossing to the furthest door, he listened intently. Other than the distant clatter of something outside in the wind, nothing could be heard. Inching open the door, he peered inside, allowing time for his eyes to adjust to the dim interior. Nothing. A kitchen and pantry with a storeroom, all devoid of movement or sound. Noting the firmly closed door leading out of the rear of the building, he returned to the other exit from the front room.

A cloak room, filled with small boxes and crates; a fine lady's robe hanging on the wall displayed some of the finest Ottoman-style work to be had in the city. Next to it, another lady's cloak hung, dowdy and plain in the Greek style.

A woman of two cultures, then? Or a woman with a habit of masquerading as what she was not? Despite the growing sense of danger, Skiouros' blood pounded excitedly with each new discovery, fuelling his curiosity.

The ground floor was clearly empty. What of the upstairs? That was, after all, where a light had shown through the window. Just because he could discern no activity from here didn't mean there was none.

Crossing to the stairs, Skiouros peered closely at them, taking in the first nine before the staircase turned for its final ascent. A dim golden glow emanated from the corner, indicating a light source somewhere near the top. While reasonably maintained, the boards showed signs of wear, and he picked out the third and fifth boards as ones particularly likely to bow beneath his boot and groan loudly. With a last indrawn breath, he placed his left foot at the very edge of the step, next to the wall, and moved up, putting his weight on it slowly. The step gave what seemed like an alarmingly loud creak, though he knew from experience that his heightened senses and imagination were amplifying what was in truth only a tiny noise.

Another step.

Another creak.

A pause.

There was still no sign of activity from above, and Skiouros carefully skipped the third step and planted his foot on the fourth, hauling himself quietly up with a gentle groan of tortured wood.

Still no sound.

Skip again to step six, and he could see the landing where the stairs turned. A thick, warm rug lay there, probably purposefully made for the task, given the perfect fit.

With stealth and speed, he padded up the remaining steps to the corner and paused for another listen before peering round it.

He could see part of the upper floor now. Strangely, it appeared from this angle that the entire top floor was given over to one room. The golden glow came from somewhere out of sight to the left, hidden behind a wall until he emerged at the top. He did, however, have a reasonable view ahead, and in the far corner of the room stood a bronze bathtub, surrounded by a wall of white and blue tiles. The owner had combined her private bathing area with the sleeping room. Functional, if a little unorthodox.

Still no sound issued from the room, so Skiouros crept up the last few stairs, the room opening up to him first allowing him to take in the floor ahead, and then out to his left as the wall came to an end, giving him a full view of the sizeable upper room.

The first thing that drew his attention as he moved in was the bath and its surroundings, directly ahead. The bronze bathtub with its lion-paw feet stood upon white and blue tiles of the same style as the wall, though the tiles were covered with a wet, swirling pattern of red, where the blood and water from the tub had overflowed and pooled beneath.

He'd not had time to fully register his alarm or react to the sight when his eyes strayed to the left and he took in the second grizzly scene.

Most of the room was taken up by an exceedingly large bed. The walls around it were hung with golden drapes here and there, but not enough to hide the murals that showed every carnal act Skiouros could imagine, and a number he had trouble imagining.

Upon the bed, though, was the true immediate focus of his attentions. A naked man lay sprawled upon the white and gold silk sheets, awkwardly splayed upon a lake of his own blood that had saturated the entire bed and even run to the floor at one side.

Again, Skiouros' instincts told him to run, and again he fought them. There was no inherent danger here now, with the occupant – occupants? – of the room in this condition. And as for the perpetrator of this nightmare? Well, he'd clearly been and gone, leaving the lamp...

A connection clicked in his mind as he realised that the lamp and cord were not a trap but a cover-up. The first person to enter the house after the killer had left would cause a fire that would likely demolish a sizeable section of the Greek enclave, and would certainly have removed all evidence of this butchery. Moreover, it would happen at some random point long enough after the killer made his escape that he would be far away and safe from both flame and discovery when it happened. Indeed, the lamp would have had enough oil to burn for much of the night, the wire and angle were so carefully set as to guarantee a fire unless the visitor was almost preternaturally aware – like a thief. How the killer could know someone would happen by in the next few hours was...

The answer struck him as his eyes took in the murals again: this lady was distinctly no 'lady'. Her clientele were probably carefully timed and would certainly be most numerous during the evening. She would probably have at least two more visitors tonight.

A sudden invigorating sense of urgency thrilled through him as he realised that he might be discovered here by her next client at any time.

He would have to be quick.

Hurrying over to the bed, he put his hand to his nose and mouth. Lykaion might be a soldier, bloodied on the field of combat against both Turk and Mamluk, but Skiouros was a thief, not a killer, and had no taste for blood. The tinny odour stuck in his nose and throat, cloying and thick and threatening to make him retch. A quick glance at the body close up forced him to avert his gaze for a moment until he could master his gullet. Trying not to breathe too deeply, he turned back again.

The man was a Turk, and a well-groomed one, with a neat beard and moustaches. His body would have been a healthy golden colour were it not currently almost white. The killer had cut the man's throat with one stroke from ear to ear and there was no other sign of struggle or incidental wounding. A quick and efficient kill. The man had died without even trying to make it off the bed.

Staggering back from the body, Skiouros turned and shuffled over to the bronze bathtub, already knowing what to expect.

He was mistaken. Hideously mistaken.

Where the Turk on the bed had been killed with a clean quick stroke, the woman in the bathtub, bobbing around in the dark red water, had been dealt with in the most horrible fashion.

Skiouros almost fell, one hand shooting out to grasp the side of the bath, making it wobble and almost upending it as he vomited copiously into the bloody slick at his feet. In the water, the dismembered body parts sloshed around with the sudden activity, shins knocking into shoulders, the head bouncing off a foot and coming to rest almost comically with a hand across its mouth as if mocking him.

Again, Skiouros staggered, this time away from the bath, still trailing a string of vomit, his face blanching. His foot caught on something and he almost fell. Looking down, he saw a long red robe with an extremely expensive cut and the look of a high-ranking Ottoman's wear. Nearby lay a golden shirt of silk and dark red trousers piled onto very expensive shoes. Whoever he was, the victim on the bed was important.

Quickly, Skiouros hurried over to the bed again, trying to hold down what remained of his fine dinner, and scanned the body for anything of use. His gaze fell upon the signet ring on the man's hand and he reached down for it, flinching at the cold shudder that ran through him at the touch of the dead man's cold, grey hand and the sticky blood that pulled and sucked at his palm as it was lifted from the bed. The ring came off with just a little work at twisting, and Skiouros spared it just long enough a glance to make sure it was an identifiable signet before closing his hand around it, stuffing it inside his doublet and into the pouch at his belt.

Feeling the next wave of nausea rising to break on his palate, he turned and fled towards the stairs, skidding to a halt at the last moment as a thought struck him.

Until he worked out whether he was entirely in the clear and what else should be done, it would be better if no one else came across this horrifying scene. That meant discouraging any further clients.

Taking a deep breath at the stairs and steeling himself, he hurried back across the room, pulled all the curtains tightly across the windows and extinguished the lamp. These things done and satisfied that, at least from the street, it would appear that the house was empty or the occupant asleep, he rushed to the stairs once again, this time pounding down them with no thought for silence. Entering the lower room, he crossed to the door and pulled it tightly shut. Unlike most houses in the city, this door was equipped with a lock in which the key still sat, and Skiouros thanked the Lord in his heaven for a small mercy. Turning the key, he effectively sealed the house. With a quick glance out into the street to be sure he was not being observed, he pulled closed the heavy curtains and then paused. Memorising the floor plan and crossing to the cupboard, he closed his eyes and counted to ten to attune his sight to the darkness and then blew on the lamp, extinguishing the flame.

When he opened his eyes once more, he was in a pit of darkness, the only visible light being the faint cracks of moonlight slipping between the curtains. The darkness smelled of burned oil and the tangy blood still raking his nostrils.

Slowly, his eyes began to pick out details in the room, and he crossed it lightly, without touching anything, to the rear door, which he opened slowly and carefully.

The kitchen area was still dark and empty, pristine and tidy. Closing the interior door behind him, Skiouros crossed to the other door that led out to the back of the house. No expensive key lock here; this door was fastened with a small locking bar that could be drawn back or pushed home. Cursing the fact that he would have to leave the rear entrance unlocked, he slid back the bar and opened the door.

The cold air hit him like a welcome wave, cleansing him a little of the stink of blood and death and of burned oil. He shivered, and not entirely with the cold, as he stepped out of the building and into the narrow alley behind. As with all such passages in the city, this one stank of ordure and threatened to ruin his new boots – not that such mundanities were a high priority for Skiouros tonight. Turning, he pushed the door to and hoped it would stay that way in this sheltered position, before hopping around the worst of the mess and scurrying out towards the alley's end.

As the moonlight grew, heralding open space ahead, Skiouros paused and took a deep breath. Even the smell of the shit and the animal carcasses out here in the alley was bliss after the prostitute's house. Approaching the corner, he slowed and looked carefully but very quickly this way and that. There was no sign of life in the main thoroughfare and he had, thankfully, emerged on the far side, at the opposite end from the Church of Saint John, and into a cross-street.

The sound of a couple of happy drunks bellowing in Greek issued from the next junction and, before they made an appearance, Skiouros stepped out into the open, quickly looking himself up and down in the moonlight.

He probably appeared deathly pale after his vomiting session, but that was no real issue. His boots had been in blood, but then they had also been in offal, shit and dusty gravel, so there was little chance of that being evident. The only real indicator that anything untoward had happened was the smear of tacky, drying crimson on his hands where he had gripped the bath side and then twisted the ring off the man's bloody finger.

Easily solved.

Still trying to calm his racing heart and return his breathing to normal, his spine tingling with both fear and horror, Skiouros stuffed his hands into the pocket-slits at the sides of his doublet to hide the mess and strolled on down the street.

The drunken revellers turned the corner, there being evidently three of them, rather than the two he'd heard, and staggered past him with barely a glance.

Without paying any further heed to them, Skiouros hurried on to the corner, turned left, right and left again and closed his eyes in relief as he came to the ancient fountain that still provided good drinking water. A grinning face with beard, curly hair and bulging cheeks, carved from a single solid piece of stone, spat a constant stream of crystal water, brought from the hills north of the city, into a wide stone trough. The overflow ran away into a gutter that trickled off down the sloping street towards the Golden Horn.

Wasting no time, Skiouros removed his hands from his doublet and gave them a thorough scrub in the icy water, removing every trace of blood from between his fingers and beneath his nails. That task complete, he flicked the excess water from his hands and reached into his belt, unhooking his pouch. He noted with irritation the blood smear his hands had left on the soft calfskin, and then opened it, tipping the coins and the signet ring into his other hand.

For a long moment, he stared at the ring with an almost accusatory expression, as though the ornate item had intentionally ruined his day. The very presence of the ring weighed heavier than the gold itself and briefly he considered disposing of it and forgetting all about it. Something deep inside, however, clamped down on his thoughts and he shook his head and straightened.

Carefully, he placed the coins and ring on the flat stone next to the face and gave the pouch a thorough scrub inside and out until only the faintest hint of discolouration remained. Then, hanging it from an iron nail that protruded to one side of the fountain, he proceeded to clean off the ring and each coin before depositing them back in the bag.

As the last silver akce dropped inside, Skiouros heaved a sigh of relief, returned the pouch to his belt beneath the doublet, and set about quickly rinsing the transferred blood traces from the stonework.

Within a minute all was done and he looked the same as usual, but for the paleness of his sickened face. Again he was grateful for the cold evening weather that was keeping most people off the streets in the more residential areas. Had a passer-by happened across him cleaning the blood from his money, he would have been forced to air a convincing story, and he felt ill equipped to try such a thing right now.

Shaking the remaining droplets from his hands and then wiping them on his braes, Skiouros strode off around two more corners with a sense of purpose, only slowing as he laid eyes on his chosen destination: the Olympos Taverna. While he had no urge and no intention of getting drunk, he certainly needed to fortify himself right now and, after all, he'd just ejected every last drop of alcohol from his body.

A drink. And a think.

Walking inside the busy, warm brick structure, Skiouros strode up to the bar, purchased a flask of costly, imported Italian wine, and found himself a space at a table in a shady corner.

The world began to slow and refocus for him as he took a sip of the wine and sagged in the chair. Time to take stock of what had happened.

Clearly the murders in the whore's house had been very deliberate. Their connection with the man – probably a Mamluk – in the market was a little hazy, though. The man had apparently not written the note himself – despite being in Arabic, Judah had believed it written by a Christian and therefore the Mamluk had clearly received the address from someone else. Presumably he had only recently done so, or he would not be carrying the evidence in his purse – thus it had probably come from one of the stallholders in the market. Assuming the dark-skinned man had something to do with all this, he would have to have ordered the killing between receiving the address and it being stolen by an unfortunate Greek thief.

No; that wasn't true. The Mamluk would be able to read and could easily have committed an address that short to memory. The murders had been less than an hour old when Skiouros had arrived at the house, so there had been plenty of time for the Mamluk to pass on the details during the time Skiouros had been visiting Jews, shopping for boots and eating a hearty meal. It was faintly possible that the Mamluk himself had done the deed, but Skiouros rather doubted that. The man was slightly overweight and well dressed, with immaculate features. He was no blood-stained killer, but more the sort of man that would hire one.

That made sense then. It also explained why a Mamluk would be in the Greek region. If he was looking for the best time and place to kill a certain Ottoman noble, where better than in bed with a woman of the night? And this Ottoman clearly had a penchant for the western girls – and so must a number of others, given the clear success of her endeavour. Until tonight, of course.

Why kill the Ottoman, who must surely be the principle target, in such a professional manner, and yet savagely butcher the woman, though? He tried to hope that the prostitute had been dead before the dismembering began, but he knew in his heart that was unlikely. Had the killer a hatred of women? Of whores? Of Greeks or Christians? Likely one of those.

So... Some Mamluk plot to murder an Ottoman noble, which had clearly succeeded. What had occurred now seemed fairly clear. What to do about it was something else.

The killer – and therefore likely his master the Mamluk – had gone to great pains to arrange covering up the mess in such a way that it would be distant enough from them to avoid likely incrimination. And if they wanted it covered up, then it was likely important that word of the murders reached the authorities.

Could it be in any way tied to Skiouros if that happened?

He could see no real way. The Mamluk or the two Janissaries might conceivably recognise him, but it seemed very unlikely. He had been one fast moving Greek youth in a sea of Greek faces. As soon as he changed his clothes – a new doublet must be high on his agenda to purloin before the night grew much older – he would be indistinguishable from any other Greek as far as they were concerned.

There was the possibility the Mamluk might investigate his stolen purse and try to track down any sudden influx of foreign coinage in the city but that would be dangerous for the foreigner, and no one in the Jewish, Greek or Armenian enclaves, or even the small Venetian post in Galata, would sell out Judah ben Isaac.

No. There was no realistic way any of this could be traced back to him.

That left one huge hanging question: why should he care?

The question struck him with such surprise that he blinked and paused before taking a heavy slug of wine, pondering his answer to the mental dialogue with his baser nature.

The answer was very simple, really, and came in two parts.

Firstly: Skiouros was a thief, and by choice, but he did not believe that made him a bad man. Others would disagree, of course, and yes he stole for a living, but he had never had cause to be violent, other than punching a man once in a drunken brawl. In fact, he would say with certainty that he actively despised such violence. And the viciousness that had been perpetrated in the house on the Street of the Hercules Statue was of the most appalling nature that it should not go unpunished.

Secondly: although he espoused the view that his people were little more than servants or pets to the conquering Ottomans, he was often more vociferous than his beliefs truly warranted. The Ottomans were surprisingly tolerant in these strange days, and the situation could quite clearly be so much worse. If the dreaded Mamluks of Egypt should gain power here, life under Bayezid the Second would seem like a lost heaven.

It was important that this incident not be discovered by accident by an Ottoman and blamed erroneously on the Greek community, and the authorities would have to know so they could track down the killer. If all was well, they would be able to piece it together and put things right…

…but without locating the Mamluk's missing monies, of course.

59

That must not be part of it, or both he and Ben Isaac would be endangered.

Another swig of wine helped seal the deal on that decision.

So the next question was: how to go about bringing this to light? It would have to be soon. The next morning at the very latest. The longer the room was left as it was, the more chance there was that a client with a missed appointment would take it upon themselves to gain entrance to the house, or that the smell would start to become noticeable enough that it would draw attention from outside.

An anonymous note to the authorities might be easiest, of course, but that presupposed he could find someone to write it for him, and there was simply no one in the city he trusted enough for that barring Master ben Isaac, and he was loath to endanger the powerful Jewish businessman any further.

The fact that there was only one feasible solution had not escaped him and, as he quickly brushed aside all other options, he took another large pull of wine to cushion the distasteful thought.

He was going to have to meet with Lykaion again.

As a member of the Janissaries, his brother would have easy access to men in high authority who could do something about this. Moreover, despite everything Lykaion had said to him in their numerous hurtful exchanges, he felt certain that if he revealed a little more information than strictly necessary, Lykaion would gloss over it and protect him.

It was settled in his mind. By dawn he would be waiting outside the Janissary barracks to catch the first non-soldier to come outside. He would deliver a message to Lykaion, the two would meet, and this could be resolved.

And then he could retrieve his small fortune from Ben Isaac and live happily for a few months.

MILES PRÆTORIANUS.
five Janizarus.

Chapter 3 – The lie will out

* Persembe (Thursday) morning *

Skiouros crouched in the shadows cast by the carpet-merchant's warehouse that stood at the southern edge of the square, trying not to be too conspicuous. This great square, once a forum constructed by the emperor Theodosius, was a testament to the city's great history through the reigns of so many rulers – as indeed was the warehouse itself. Shattered columns rose from a variety of long-gone structures, some patterned with teardrop shapes, lending a sadness to the ruins. Little remained of the once famous arch or the column of the emperor – now a sad, quarried stub at the square's centre, but a great dry cistern perhaps four centuries old stood near the western edge of the open ground, one end torn away and displaying a veritable forest of columns.

The carpet warehouse occupied the shell of an ancient structure to shoulder height, finished to a second floor by one of the Byzantine rulers and now patched with wood by a struggling merchant. Three empires that had made the city their heart all represented in one ramshackle structure packed with mercantile goods.

It was a fascinating place, and a sad one, which Skiouros had visited many times over the past few years, but it was not the square itself or the ruins therein that captivated his interest this morning, as the chill wind tore along the streets and alleys and whirled around the square, sweeping up dead leaves and twirling them in eddies. The sky was inky purple in the pre-dawn light, and the barracks of the Janissaries stood at the far side, visible as yet only as a series of regular lamps which made it stand out in the gloom. Beside it, the former home of the sultan stood silent and cold, still owned by Beyazid even though he now resided at the new Topkapi palace, left empty until a suitable use could be found.

The small thief hunched down into his corner, wrapping his arms tight around himself to maintain what little warmth there was. This routine was so familiar to Skiouros after years of visiting his brother's barrack that he could have done this in his sleep, and probably would have done if there had been even the slightest possibility of slumber in the aftermath of last night's horrors.

First the tense, expectant silence.

Across the city many thousands of Ottoman citizens paused, waiting, cloaks in hand and shoes already on.

Then a voice rang out. The muezzin in the wooden minaret that rose from the great Aya Sofya a mile or so away began his Fajr call, summoning the faithful to the dawn prayer. Despite his Christian upbringing, Skiouros had been born into a world where the call to prayer was a matter of daily life, even in Hadrianople, and he had to admit in the core of his soul that it remained a beautiful and evocative sound, even if it was part of the Ottoman's heretical religion.

As usual, within moments the call echoed from the other scattered minarets, and the people of Ottoman Istanbul began to stir from their residences, shuffling into the streets, yawning and scratching. As though the Fajr call were some sort of trigger, the city seemed to suddenly burst into life. Even the animals seemed to have been poised, birds suddenly cawing and chirping out their morning conversations, stray dogs and cats emerging from alleyways, scratching themselves and hunting for a free meal.

And as usual the servants and slaves and the new recruits of the Janissary corps used the call as a morning alarm, hurrying to be about their assigned tasks before they were ordered. It was bad form for even the lower occupants of the Janissary barracks to have to be ordered to do something when they were expected to already be at it.

Skiouros had once queried his brother over how these lessers managed to somehow skip the morning prayer when they were officially required to attend as any other good Muslim. Lykaion had been extremely coy and evasive, mumbling about peculiarities in the worship rites of the Janissaries, but had refused to be drawn further, grasping the 'nazar boncugu' – the stone bead on his neck thong which protected the wearer from the evil eye. Unconcerned with oddities within Janissary worship, Skiouros had shrugged it away. Certainly less focus on the rigidity of religious observance would make the organisation and daily running of the barracks considerably smoother.

Skiouros watched the boys and adolescents rushing out of the three staff exits of the building, some with pails for collecting water or milk, some with a purse of coins to purchase necessities, others with chitties to deliver or collect goods from smiths, tailors or other manufacturers. The doors were well guarded by men in full uniform with guns, and Skiouros had discovered in the early days just how defensive and unfriendly they could be, fleeing the scene with the barrel of a gun trained on him.

As usual, Skiouros waited a few minutes for one of the half-dozen water bearers. They were the first to return during the pre-dawn ritual, having only to move down a side street to one of the great monumental fountains in order to collect their burden. They would use three different local fountains and make a game of it: who would be first to complete their daily task. Skiouros waited as two boys ran past towards the fountain and prepared himself.

Each water bearer would make a dozen journeys, and the tired yet constantly alert thief watched as a young man with distinctly Slavic features came barrelling back along the alley next to the carpet warehouse, cold clear water sloshing over the lip of his heavy wooden bucket. Ignoring the inquisitive look of the other boy who was rushing up behind with his own bucket, Skiouros stepped out in front of the Slavic servant and held up a hand. Alarmed, the boy skidded to a halt, spilling water. He babbled something in Turkish – a language of which Skiouros had a reasonable grasp – but so fast and thickly accented that it was barely intelligible, regardless. Skiouros held out his other hand, in the palm of which were two silver akce coins. The boy's eyes widened greedily.

'For the delivery of a message,' Skiouros said slowly and carefully in Turkish. The boy nodded, his eyes never leaving the coins, and licked his lips.

'The message is for the Janissary known as Hussein Bin Nikos.'

Lykaion's official Turkish name, given to him on his arrival at the Janissaries, always left something of a sour taste in his mouth. 'He serves with the Fourteenth Cemaat Orta.'

The boy nodded, though his eyes left the coins now and registered discomfort with something. Something about Lykaion's unit? Whatever it was clearly was not enough, however, to overcome the boy's desire for silver, and he nodded again.

'Tell Bin Nikos that his brother must see him urgently by the church. It is vitally important that he come. Can you do that?'

The boy nodded, dropped the heavy bucket to the floor and reached for the coins. As his hand grasped greedily, Skiouros' fingers snapped shut on the coins. Shaking his head, he kept one contained in his palm and held the other between thumb and forefinger.

'Only if the message arrives. You get one coin now and one from my brother when he returns from our meeting.'

The boy looked taken aback and slightly uncertain, but quickly overcame his objections and snatched the coin.

'Hussein Bin Nikos of the Fourteenth.'

'The Fourteenth Cemaat,' clarified Skiouros patiently. 'Now go before you're late with your water.'

The boy collected his bucket once more and scurried off with it towards the barracks, struggling under the weight.

Pausing only to make sure the boy made it back through the small guarded doorway and into the building unmolested, Skiouros hurried away from the square and marched the one and a half miles back to the Phanar district and the relative security of his own people.

As he walked in a roughly north-westerly direction, wishing he'd had even an hour's sleep, the sun began to rise behind him, casting the shadows of Byzantine domes and tall wooden houses along the street, separated by lines and cracks of golden light. The call to prayer ended quickly and the city fell curiously silent as its occupants filled the numerous mosques crammed into the city.

Word was that more of the ancient grand Byzantine churches of the city were earmarked for transformation into places of heathen worship, since they were left empty and unused, but at this time, very few had had their crosses replaced with crescents. Both Mehmet and Bayezid had had the sense as rulers to make the transition of the city from Christian to Muslim slowly and carefully, so as not to provoke trouble with their conquered populace.

By the time Skiouros moved through the main market in Phanar, purchasing a loaf of hard, unleavened bread and some goat's cheese en route, his feet were aching from the new, stiff boots, but the world was beginning to come to life.

The young man shook his head wearily. With the children laughing in the streets and hawkers calling their wares, the general hubbub of civilisation thronging the ways of the city, it was almost impossible now to picture what Skiouros had stumbled across the night before and the horror seemed somehow muted and unreal.

The Bloody Church of Saint Mary stood glowing fiery red and somehow hostile in the early sun as he found his usual spot by the brick wall and sank gratefully down on an old shattered Roman lintel that formed a good seat, rubbing his eyes and then removing his left boot to massage his sore foot. Almost immediately, his toes chilled in the cold wind and he found he was rubbing more vigorously to both massage the soreness and bring life back into the frozen flesh.

Time passed slowly and quietly as he repeated the process with his other foot and then launched into his bread and cheese like a man possessed, his teeth tearing hungrily at the loaf and his nimble, slender fingers dipping it into the soft white cheese. Despite his considerable distance from any Ottoman neighbourhood, the faint odour of spice and meat from the Turks' morning meals made him hunger for something warm and somehow enhanced the chill as it worked its way into his bones.

A quick glance at the sky showed nothing but icy blue, promising only colder weather to come. While he had no love of rain, at least clouds would warm the world a little in their grim blanket.

By the time Lykaion put in an appearance, at least an hour later, Skiouros was seriously considering leaving to purchase more food – hot food from an Ottoman stall trader. In truth, while he'd never even considered the possibility that his older brother might not turn up, over the past quarter of an hour he had started to worry and wonder what he would do next if their latest argument had soured things for good.

'This had better be important, little thief,' Lykaion said, his voice as icy as the alley's breeze, hands on the hips of his green uniform jacket, curved sword swinging beneath.

Skiouros rubbed his knees and, standing, leaned back against the wall in a casual manner.

'Good to see you too, my brother.'

'Just get to the point. You said it was urgent. I'm theoretically on my way to the port to oversee the arrival of new artillery from Bursa, and I can only delay for a few minutes.' He narrowed his eyes. 'And you owe me an akce to pay that little Slavic runt.'

'It is important, Lykaion. I need your help.'

'Of course you do. What is it this time? Some offended merchant offering money for your head? You've fallen foul of that Jewish criminal and his thugs? What?'

'Worse than either of those, but it's not my fault.'

'I doubt that.'

Skiouros sighed and lowered his voice. 'I won't go into too much detail, but suffice it to say: last night I stumbled on the site of a murder.'

Lykaion rolled his eyes. 'Have you any idea how many people are killed in this city every day? The number will surprise you, I'm sure.'

'The Janissaries are supposed to police the streets.'

The older brother straightened the sleeves of his uniform jacket, emphasising the 'double sabre' symbol of his unit. 'I am of the Fourteenth Cemaat Orta, which serves as the Palace guard. I do not sweep the streets of the Greek slums looking for murder victims. That is a job for the Boluk Ortas – like the camel-humping Fifth!' He spat on the ground at the mention of the provost unit – never the most popular.

'It's not that simple, Lykaion. You know I can't just go and see the provost's orta. I'm a Christian and a Greek; they'd laugh me out of the building before beating me blue. But I'm fairly sure the authorities will want to know about this.'

The taller brother shook his head in exasperation and held up his hand to signal an end to the conversation. 'I'm a Janissary guard with a job to do. Whatever trouble you and your Greek friends have got yourselves into you can sort it out without me. I'm away to the port and if you even consider bothering me again over such paltry matters I won't stop at a quick slap next time; you understand me?'

Skiouros stared at his brother with nervous eyes.

'It's not that simple,' he repeated.

'Go away.' Lykaion turned his back and walked away towards the alley's entrance.

'They're not Greek!' blurted the younger brother urgently.

Lykaion paused, his head turning slightly.

'What?'

66

'What I mean to say is that one of them isn't Greek – the victims. He's a Turk!'

'What trouble are you in?' demanded Lykaion, turning back to him.

'I told you: it wasn't me. I only found them by accident. She's Greek – a whore. He's an Ottoman.'

'A whore? Then it really isn't something to bother my orta with. Some merchant led by his dick gets himself knifed? Not my problem.'

'I think he's a nobleman.'

Again, the older brother had turned to leave, and again he turned back.

'He's a what?'

'He's certainly rich. And I think powerful too.'

In a blur of motion, Lykaion was back across the alley and face to face with his brother, so close Skiouros could smell the spicy kofte of the morning break-fast on his breath.

'What do you know of nobles and money? The most money you've ever had was some poor merchant's daily takings!'

Scrambling in the pocket slit of his doublet, Skiouros brought a small object up in his clenched fist and opened the palm flat to reveal the signet ring. It took a moment for the older brother, staring intently into those wide eyes, to realise that an object was being displayed for him. Taking a step back, he looked down at his brother's hand.

'Where did you get that?'

'From the dead Turk.'

Lykaion's head snapped up to meet his brother's gaze again.

'You stole it from a corpse?' he demanded angrily.

'Not stole. I just needed something to identify him with. See? It's an expensive signet. He must be a noble.'

Lykaion glared at him for a moment longer until his gaze dropped once more to the ring. Swiping it from his brother's hand, he lifted it and turned it in the dawn light to examine it more carefully. Squinting, he peered at the design on the flattened surface, a tense silence falling. The cold golden sunlight flashed and danced off the intricate script.

'If I could read Turkish...' Skiouros began.

'If you could read at all!' Lykaion snapped. 'Now shut up and let me look.'

'But you…'

'Shhh!'

Skiouros watched his brother uncertainly for a long moment.

'Subhan'Allah!' Lykaion exclaimed breathlessly. 'What have you done?' Tightly gripping the ring in his right hand, his left lunged up, grasping his brother by the doublet's neckline, pushing him roughly against the wall.

'Nothing! I swear, Lykaion.'

The older brother's eyes bored deep into Skiouros' and finally, against all expectations sensing no duplicity, he released his grip and stepped back.

'You found this on a body in the house of a Greek whore?'

'Yes brother. He was clearly a client. He was… naked when I found him.'

'By the grace of the prophet, this is not good, little brother.'

'I didn't know you could read,' Skiouros noted, apropos of nothing.

'Unimportant. What is important is this ring and the man who wore it. This is going to cause widespread ripples. I don't even know how I'll go about reporting it.'

'Why? Who is he?'

'Specifically, I don't know. But the ring says enough on its own: he's a vizier – one of the sultan's close advisors.'

Skiouros felt his blood run cold, images racing through his mind in quick succession: a naked bloodied corpse; a dismembered woman; an old Jew wanting nothing to do with the matter; a Romani witch telling him no good would come of it; the accusing glare of an ancient God; and back to the blood… so much blood.

'Perhaps I was wrong, Lykaion. I shouldn't have brought it to you; shouldn't even have taken the ring. Maybe we should leave it well alone if he's that important? I could put the ring back?'

Lykaion snorted and turned away, stamping a few steps along the alley before turning back and displaying the ring in his hand.

'How can I leave it alone now that you've told me? You should have kept it to yourself. Now I have to look into it, whatever that might bring.' He snarled as he moved closer again. 'And if I have to look into this, be assured that you will be helping me and that any involvement you haven't told me about will soon come to light. Is there anything you want to tell me?'

Skiouros stared at his brother, fighting for control over his nerves and struggling with the urge to tell of his deeper connection. How could he do that, though?

'No. Nothing.'

Lykaion narrowed his eyes disbelievingly. 'Then let the truth come out later and on your shoulders be its weight. Where did you find the ring?'

'A house in Phanar. Not too far from here. Five or ten minutes' walk, perhaps.'

'Take me there. I want to see it.'

'Are you sure? It's not pretty. Cost me a night's sleep.'

'Just take me there.'

Skiouros paused for a moment and then left the alley, scurrying out into the main street, already thronged with people going about their ordinary lives. On any other day, the younger brother would scorn such folk for their unadventurous, dull existences. Today he found himself envying them. Lykaion thumped along the street behind him in his over-the-knee boots.

'What we must look like!' thought Skiouros. He, scruffy and unkempt with his newly 'acquired' and slightly stained burgundy-coloured doublet, being followed closely by a Janissary guard in full uniform with his ceremonial tailed-hat proudly erect and a warlike blade slung on his hip. It would appear almost like a prisoner escort.

Quickly they moved through the streets of Phanar to the church of Saint John where, trying not to meet the gaze of the disapproving God with his incongruous crucifix, Skiouros came to a halt.

'What?' asked his brother irritably.

'Best we go through the back door. When I left, I locked the front to keep the scene closed off.'

'I can't wait for you to decide to tell me what you were doing in a whore's chambers in the first place,' Lykaion grumbled sarcastically. 'Take us to the back door, then.'

Peering cautiously down the street, Skiouros continued on past the turning and around the church until he saw the narrow opening of the alley that ran down the back of the wooden housing. Even in the cold morning air and out of the sun, the stink of offal and faeces issued strongly from the opening. Lykaion shook his head.

'No way you're getting me in there in my good boots. You go open up the door. I'll wait at the front. Which house?'

'Is that a good idea?' Skiouros countered. 'A Janissary at the door will certainly rouse comment.'

Lykaion shrugged. 'Let them talk. I'll be reporting this as soon as I work out how best to go about it. Now, which house?'

Skiouros cleared his throat. 'The one with the yellow columns.'

Waving his brother off, the older of the two strode back out to the main street. As Skiouros disappeared into the shit-steeped alley in his ragged clothes and stolen doublet, Lykaion shook his head at the madness of it all. Taking his time and moving with the slow, deliberate pace of a man of authority, he made his way towards the front of the house Skiouros had named.

Whatever his younger brother had caught himself up in now, it was clearly a step up from his usual mischief, but despite the venom with which he'd spoken, Lykaion was fairly certain at heart of his brother's relative innocence. Clearly some dubious activity had led Skiouros to a whore's house, but the young man was a thief – not a killer. Try as he might, Lykaion just could not picture his brother up to his elbows in blood, murdering a man with cold purpose. It simply wasn't him.

Once more, and for the umpteenth time since they had set off from the red-painted church where they met for their latest argument, Lykaion found himself quailing on the inside at the idea of informing his superiors about this. It would have to be done, and it would have to be dealt with by the Janissaries – initially, at least, before the sultan was made aware. An ordinary soldier like Lykaion could hardly march up to the office of the agha and ask to see him, so everything would have to go through channels; the chain of command.

And that meant Hamza Bin Murad.

Lykaion's superior officer – the 'corbasi' of his orta – was not a patient or understanding man. Despite being the most senior of the commanders beneath the agha himself, it was commonly said that Bin Murad would never be chosen for high command due to his temper and his bloodthirsty tendencies. Lykaion had fallen foul of his commander half a dozen times in his past two years of full service, and had the lash marks from one particular occasion to remember it by.

No. It was not going to be a pleasant task appraising the corbasi Bin Murad of this incident. For a moment, Lykaion even considered dropping his brother into the whirlpool of the man's inevitable anger. Anything that might help deflect it.

Lykaion came to a halt outside the house with the yellow columns. Was it his imagination playing tricks on his senses, or could he truly smell the tang of blood emanating from the building?

The house looked ordinary but the longer Lykaion spent standing in the cold street and looking at it, the more he was starting to get the feeling that the building actively loomed. He was just considering turning and leaving when there was a quiet click and the front door of the house swung slowly open.

Skiouros appeared in the dark rectangle, his face a picture of uneasiness. As Lykaion stepped towards the entrance, he realised what it was that had drawn that look to his brother's normally optimistic and eager features. The smell was already appalling before he'd even crossed the threshold. Despite the chilly weather, the enclosed house had filled with the stink of blood, offal, and the other unspeakable products of a violent death. Reaching down, Lykaion undid the decorative brass buttons on his green wool jacket, hauling up the shirt beneath until he could just cover his nose and mouth with it.

Slightly better prepared, he stepped into the house.

'It appears undisturbed.'

'There were signs,' Skiouros admitted. 'The killer had left a nice little trigger that was intended to burn down the house and all its evidence. I unset the trap and blew out the lamp.'

Lykaion nodded his approval. 'Lead on.'

Skiouros crossed the room, ignoring the two downstairs doors, one of which stood open allowing a cleansing draft to blow through, and began to climb the stairs slowly and carefully. Lykaion followed on, noting the steady increase in the potency of the smell. By the time they turned the corner and emerged at the top it was almost too much to bear, the air cloying and sickly-thick; nearly unbreathable.

Emerging into the room, the young Janissary soldier glanced around with an eye that might appear calm to an outsider. He certainly had no wish to show any sort of weakness in front of his brother. But the smell...

He gagged a little, and covered up the reaction by moving swiftly across to the bed, pulling the shirt up a little more, for all the use it was. It was like trying to keep out the sea with a cotton kerchief.

'I've seen him before,' he announced, trying to keep the sickly swallowing noise out of his voice. 'When I've done duty at Topkapi, he's been in and out. One of the viziers, and a fairly prominent one, judging by his regular visits to the sultan.' He bent over, his constant gulping to halt the gag reflex barely concealed beneath his wrenched-up shirt collar, and examined the body.

'This was done very neatly with one blow; and from behind.'

Standing, he mimed the kill, more for his own clarification than for the sake of his brother who was standing nearby looking extremely unhappy.

'A hand went around his front like this, just to keep his arms out of the way. The other held the knife – left hand with the knife – and cut from ear to ear with one slice. Very deep. Cut almost to the bone. The vizier would have been dead in moments, and no chance to scream with his windpipe cut. It was very professional and the attacker was fast, silent and very strong. Not the job of a random killer, and not even the job of a soldier; we're trained for speed and efficiency, not subtlety. Kill and move on. A soldier doesn't make such careful blows. The culprit here is a man who's trained to do just this. Silent and instant.'

Skiouros was suddenly next to him.

'But if he got the man from behind and by surprise, the woman could have screamed. Probably did. Why do away with him silently yet risk the woman screaming?'

'The sort of noises that probably come out of this place, no one would pay attention to her scream. A man's death scream, though, is different; that would draw unwanted attention.'

He stepped back. 'Yes, he killed the vizier first. Even took the time to lower him down to the bed on his back and didn't let him fall. Probably didn't want to risk incriminating blood spray on his clothes. He might well have remained completely clean throughout the attack, since he went in from behind.' He glanced to the other end of the room. 'As long as only his hands got bloody he could clean them in the bathwater.'

'I don't think they'd get much cleaner,' Skiouros noted sourly. 'Come on.'

Striding across the room, the younger brother stopped just within sight of the bathtub's grizzly contents and pointed.

'Tell me that's neat and professional, then.'

Lykaion almost lost control of his gullet as he closed on the tub and its meaty soup.

'No. No assassination, that.'

Skiouros nodded his agreement.

'But I have seen its like before,' Lykaion added.

'What?'

The older brother sighed. 'Fighting the Mamluks across the channel in Anatolia. Some of their more fanatical men used to take their time when they came across isolated Christians. 'Course we had Christians in our army last year – mercenaries, you know? Venetian crossbowmen and suchlike. And when the fighting reached the worst point, the Mamluks were even poisoning wells in our villages to stop us resting there. We'd find our Venetian allies – ones that had been taken captive by the Egyptian bastards – stripped naked and cut to pieces, floating in the soured wells.'

'You're saying this is the work of a Mamluk?' Skiouros asked quietly, his blood running cold as his memory dutifully furnished him with an image of the rich foreign merchant who had started this sequence of unpleasant events.

'More than likely.'

Once more, Lykaion turned on his brother, a gleam in his eye that was somewhere between anger and desperation.

'Again, little brother, and for all our sakes, I'll ask whether there's anything you want to tell me?'

Skiouros trembled under the fierce gaze and almost broke.

'There is more, Lykaion, but I wish I didn't know it, and so will you if you get any deeper. I think we need to hand this over to the authorities and then move on.'

The taller brother continued to glare for a moment, and finally nodded wearily.

'You might be right. This is going to cause enough problems. Perhaps you should have let the building burn. Too late now, though.'

Turning, he strode towards the stairs.

'What are we going to do now, then?' Skiouros called quietly, hurrying after him.

'I'm going to return to barracks and report this. I'll tell them that a local vagrant drew my attention to the place – it's more or less the truth.'

A joke it may have been, but Skiouros could hear no humour in the voice.

'And me?'

'You?' Lykaion barked, coming to such a sudden halt on the stairs that Skiouros almost walked into him. 'You will lie low. Disappear entirely if you can. I won't mention you, so you should be free unless they turn anything up that drags you into it, depending on whatever it is you haven't told me. If I need you, I'll scratch my Greek name into the church wall, alright? Other than that, your part in this is done.'

Skiouros nodded, somewhat too meekly for Lykaion's liking, suggesting that the younger man thought otherwise. Giving him a hard glare for good measure, the older of the two turned and marched purposely down the stairs. At the bottom he paused and examined the front door, spotting the key in the lock.

'Come on. Out the back again.'

Skiouros shook his head. 'What's the point, now the front's open?'

'Because the fewer people who can testify to you even being here, the better. Now go out the back.'

As Skiouros moved through the kitchen and stepped out of the back door into the alley, Lykaion followed him, pausing at the threshold.

'Can we meet again soon?' Skiouros asked hesitantly.

'Not if we can possibly avoid it. Now that I'm a full serving Janissary it's very difficult for me to find time to slip away, and I risk punishment detail every time. I don't know about you, but to me that doesn't seem worth it for an argument with a bloody-minded thief.'

Skiouros sighed. Better to leave it there than to prove Lykaion right.

'Go. Watch the church wall, just in case.'

Before the smaller brother could reply, Lykaion shut the door and slid the bolt across, sealing out both the cold world and his troublesome sibling. Turning back, he crossed the kitchen and then the front room, removing the key before leaving, then using it to seal up the house.

On the doorstep he paused for some time, breathing in fresh air in desperate gulps. Feeling like a child who has damaged a parent's precious possession and now faces the inevitable and uncomfortable confession, he made his way slowly across the city towards the barracks and his martinet officer.

'Show me the ring,' Commander Hamza Bin Murad snapped in his usual fashion, holding out his hand flat and snapping his fingers irritably.

Lykaion, having only just finished working through his story, winced at the anger in the voice – more of it even than usual. Fumbling in the pouch at his belt, he withdrew the ring and dutifully placed it in his superior's palm.

Bin Murad rocked back in his seat, his hand coming up so that he could examine the ring closer in the dim light of his office. His ageing grey moustaches twitched, and his hard, well-worn eyes widened as he turned the ring over and examined the seal.

'You have no idea whose it is?'

'Barring that it's a vizier's ring, master. I vaguely recognised the face from his visits to the Topkapi while I've been on duty. Foul to think that a man of such position has been consorting with a Christian whore, master.'

'If that's what's happened,' Bin Murad replied, suspiciously.

'Sir?'

'This is the ring of Muharrem Bin Yusuf, the vizier of his majesty's treasury. As you surmised: a very important man. And 'til now a man of taste; above reproach. It seems unlikely that he had willingly placed himself in such a position. I've never heard of him consorting with the unclean infidel; he has a wife who is both noble and comely, after all.'

'It appeared very much voluntary to me, master.'

'Quiet!' snapped Bin Murad. 'Your information is important to me; your opinions are not.'

Lykaion bowed curtly – as low as custom demanded, yet almost shallow enough to convey an insult.

A silence fell over the room, and Lykaion was suddenly less pleased at their solitude. When he'd first entered and begun to relate his tale, he'd been grateful they'd been alone, given the likelihood of a tongue-lashing. Now, as the situation had moved beyond that and into the vague region of indirect accusations, he was wishing there was some kind of witness in the room with them. It was not unknown for Bin Murad to lash out and seriously injure a man merely to assuage his own temper.

'None of this adds up very convincingly, soldier.'

'Sir?'

'A beggar in the street accosts you on the way to the harbour to look at a potential incident halfway across the city? Ridiculous!'

'I expect I was the nearest Janissary the man could find, master. We are rarely to be found near the Greek and Jewish areas – even the policing forces of the provost.'

'And with good reason!' Bin Murad spat with apparent distaste. 'The scum should be kicked out of the city or enslaved, converted and utilised. It is an offence in the eyes of Allah to have this holy city infested with such infidels.'

Lykaion had his mouth almost open to rebut with a gentle

reminder that both Sultan Bayezid and his father had been proactive in attracting and settling the foreign populations, albeit in their own regions, and that Bayezid was actively encouraging Jewish immigration. Gainsaying the commander of the Fourteenth Cemaat Orta, though, was a fast track to reassignment in a shitty duty. And/or pain...

'Well whatever we turn up,' the commander resumed, 'you're going to have to answer some searching and difficult questions.'

'I understand, master.'

'I will bring this matter to the attention of agha himself. Until he is fully briefed and decides how to proceed, you are confined to barracks. You will not leave your room, except to perform your ablutions and to eat in the mess hall. Is that understood?'

A sinking feeling driving all the enthusiasm from him, Lykaion saluted.

'I do, sir.'

'Then go.'

Without another word, and rather grateful to be leaving the office, the young soldier turned and strode from the room. A last glance before he left the doorway and rounded the corner revealed Hamza Bin Murad rising from his chair with the most astoundingly unpleasant smile on his face that Lykaion had ever seen. He shuddered as he turned the corner to the outer vestibule which, although decorated in expensive marble and gold, felt to Lykaion like the corridor that leads to the execution ground. The offices of three lesser orta officers stood along the outer wall along this corridor: the standard bearer, the barrack chief, and the 'Asci Usta', second only to the commander.

Even before Lykaion had fully rounded the corner and disappeared from sight, Bin Murad's voice roared out from his office, calling for the Asci Usta. The second in command, a long-standing veteran and the nearest thing the commander had to a friend, came barrelling out of his office, jamming his ceremonial hat on his balding pate, and ran for the office, almost colliding with Lykaion on the way but paying him no more attention than a brief irritated glance. When Bin Murad called, you ran; simple as that.

Lykaion strode to the end of the corridor and opened the heavy, decorative door that separated the senior officers' area from the general rooms of the soldiers. Allowing the portal to slam shut, he ignored the half dozen men in the wide passageway beyond, two of whom were polishing unit insignia, one carrying an armful of partially-finished gun stocks, and the others chatting amiably. Taking a deep breath and grateful that he'd been granted time to think some more about his story, he slumped back against the wall.

It had been stupid, and he knew it.

He'd been considerably more rattled by what his brother showed him than he'd allowed Skiouros to know. The entire journey back across the city, he'd tried hard to concentrate on formulating a convincing story, but images of dismembered women – all of whom bore a disturbing mental resemblance to his mother – kept encroaching on his thoughts and wrecking his concentration. Moreover, even the fish market he passed had failed to remove the stench of death from his nostrils. He should have continued with his duty for the day down at the port, and then spent the night contemplating his course of action first – would have done, if he'd been thinking straight.

But no.

He'd hurried straight into Bin Murad's office and started pouring out the story. May Allah, the Prophet and the Prophet Isa damn Skiouros for doing this to him. He'd been halfway through the story, watching the suspicion and anger building in his commander, before he'd even noticed all the gaping holes and obvious falsities in it. Now he would have to spend the next night in his room thinking up every possible answer and excuse for every conceivable question in preparation for a grilling by the higher authorities.

It suddenly occurred to him that there was the very real possibility that this could go very badly for him, and his mind filled with images of the cells at the Blachernae palace where suspected traitors and spies were dealt with.

He shuddered as he realised that all he was doing by protecting his brother was putting his own hide in danger. It would soon come out when they questioned him that Skiouros had been instrumental in all of this and that Lykaion had merely been a messenger – perhaps an interpreter. But by then he would be bleeding and singed in the cells.

Damn Skiouros!

Why should Lykaion suffer questioning and torture to save the little thief?

Standing, his hand reached for the door handle before he paused again.

Would revealing that his brother had some part in this really make any difference? Could he truly put Skiouros in the firing line in order to protect himself? He'd always been actively disapproving of the idiot's life choices, and treated him with anger and even contempt, but much of that was born of a desperate need to try and turn Skiouros around and make him grow up. He'd never contemplated harming him beyond a reproachful slap.

Biting his lip, Lykaion fumed in his quandary. Perhaps there was a way he could do something other than assigning or accepting culpability? He could reveal that he had been on the way to see Skiouros at the time. That would explain why he was in the Greek enclave. From there, he could easily claim the rest of the story as truth. It would be considerably more plausible, for sure; that would explain the geographical anomaly in the tale. There was the very faintest possibility that someone would remember a deserter from the Devsirme intake all those years ago, but the chances were very small. More than half a decade of war had been fought since then, and the record keepers of that time would be long moved on or dead now.

Revealing his fraternal connections and visits would mean punishment for breaking regulations, but he could stand a beating or cessation of pay, or a cut in rations. That way neither he nor Skiouros would have to face real danger.

It was the only clear answer.

Setting a grim look and a firm jaw, Lykaion pulled open the door to return to Bin Murad's office and take a little punishment to prevent a greater one...

And his world fell apart beneath his feet.

'You'll find Bin Nikos in his barrack room,' the commander was saying. Lykaion froze in the doorway. Something about the tone of his voice was not right – not angry, but malicious.

'Are you sure, master?'

'You would question me, Asul?'

'Of course not, master. It just seems so incredible.'

'Have him taken away immediately. We cannot risk this killer roaming the barracks freely. Make sure you use a strong escort who are not considered close to him. I will inform the agha and we will then investigate the house.'

'By your command, sir.'

Around the corner, the cracked-open door in his hand, Lykaion's blood ran cold. Surely there was no reason? No evidence? This couldn't possibly be happening.

'And Asul?'

'Yes, master?'

'Before you do so, have the barrack entrances sealed and the other orta commanders informed. Let's not risk this murderous dog evading you.'

Lykaion had to resist the urge to let go of the handle and run. If the door slammed, it would alert Asul and Bin Murad to his eavesdropping. Slowly, he inched the door silently shut and stood still, shock and disbelief flooding him. What should he do?

What could he do?

There was no evidence tying him to the crime, but then there was no evidence to the contrary either. And, damn Skiouros to an eternity of pain, any in-depth questioning would reveal that he was absent from the barracks for a time that could be seen to fit the killing, despite the fact that he was actually arguing with his brother at the time. He was trapped, and the vicious, blood-hungry dog that was Hamza Bin Murad would tear him to pieces in short order.

He had to run! So many years building up a reputable position in one of the most important orta in the Empire, faithfully following Islam and the specific doctrines of the Janissaries, of serving the sultans and protecting Ottoman interests – and it all came down to this. Two choices: run like a criminal and shatter any doubt of his guilt in the eyes of his peers, or stay and take what was almost certainly a death sentence and probable torture due to his inability to prove his innocence.

Allah help me!

Something deep in his soul beseeched another God he'd almost forgotten.

He had to run, but first he would have to get to his room and collect all his effects.

No. No time for that. His frowned-upon Christian amulet that lay hidden in his goods – the only reminder of his family and his former life – would only incriminate him further, but if he should return to the room and retrieve all things of import, he would risk being too late and becoming trapped in the barracks.

Feeling his body shaking with uncontrollable fear and fury, he turned and moved with a very deliberate and casual slowness along the vestibule, praying over and over that his shaking was not openly visible and that the sweat he could feel pouring from his brow and soaking his shirt would not attract undue attention.

The three chatting soldiers leaning against the wall opposite looked across at him as he walked and Lykaion felt the chill of fear as he saw suspicion and accusation in their faces. The shaking reached his knees and he had to force himself to walk on, almost breaking into a panicked run. One of the guards smiled in faint recognition and nodded at him, forcing him to realise just how much his nerves were influencing his senses.

Maintaining a forcibly steady gait, he turned into the corridor that led to the kitchens. The word would be going out now to the guards at the various doors, but the main front entrance and the stable and artillery gates would be the first places to be locked down. Other, smaller doors would follow, but the scullery entrance that the slop-slaves and water-bearers used would be one of the last to receive the order.

Trying to appear purposeful – no one ever questioned a man with a purposeful look and a steady stride – he entered the kitchens, where a number of veterans were busy preparing the food for the noon meal, the servants and slaves rushing about their assigned tasks. The kitchens, pantries and stores for the Janissary barracks were cavernous and sprawling, and it was easy for a single soldier to blend in and become lost within them.

As an afterthought, he moved alongside a lengthy wooden table and swept up a stack of flatbreads on a tray of Persian walnut. Bearing them aloft as though performing a chore, he strode through the kitchens, virtually invisible through his mundanity.

Turning into a passage, he strode past the butter and cheese storage pantries and the racks of yogurt maturing in its goat-skin bags. Ahead, at the far end of a long corridor of storeroom entrances, he could see the door that was his ultimate goal.

Servants and slaves scurried in and out of the doors bearing trays, bags and bowls, and Lykaion found that he had to weave in and out of them, holding aloft his tray.

One of the servants paused in his work and touched his forehead in respectful recognition, a happy grin plastered across his face. It took a moment for Lykaion to realise it was the Slavic water bearer who'd delivered him a message and to whom he'd given a silver akce that Skiouros still owed him for.

Nodding absently at the boy – it was important right now to appear entirely ordinary and unobtrusive – he strode towards the door. Before the last approach, he dipped into an unoccupied side room, placing his tray of loaves on one of the few shelf spaces available. With a deep breath, he reached into his purse and withdrew Bin Murad's stamped order from this morning, sending him to the port to oversee the arrival of new cannon. Hopefully it would still seem appropriately valid; it was still only mid-morning, after all.

Returning to the corridor, adjusting his coat and collar, he approached the two guards of the Third Cemaat Orta, whose area of responsibility was the kitchens, reaching out with the orders, his other hand on his belt within easy reach of the sword hilt, in case things suddenly turned bad.

The two men bent forward to look over the orders and one nodded and stood back. The other paused and frowned and Lykaion's heart skipped a beat before the man straightened and grinned, handing the slip back.

'You're late leaving. That ship'll have docked hours ago. Wouldn't want to be you when your commander finds out.'

Lykaion forced a grin and hoped it didn't look panicked and false.

'It's my commander that caused the delay!'

'Isn't it always the way? Good luck out in the cold.' The guard heaved open the door and Lykaion strode through into the fresh air, tension still holding him stiff and rigid until the door clicked shut behind him. Suddenly all the pent-up fear and anger flooded out of him and he almost collapsed, the jelly-like shaking in his legs nearly unmanning him.

He was not safe yet, though. The orders would even now be racing around the barracks: lock the doors; bar the gates; find the murderer Hussein Bin Nikos.

His blood pounding in his ears, legs shaking uncontrollably, Lykaion strode slowly and purposefully across the square until he passed the old Byzantine bath house at the corner of the Mese street and turned the corner, the barracks disappearing from sight behind him.

There was only one clear destination in his mind: the 'Bloody' church of Saint Mary of the Mongols, where he would scratch his name and wait for Skiouros.

His life in tatters, Lykaion ran.

Chapter 4 – Acts of Gods and men

* Persembe (Thursday) afternoon *

Skiouros clambered blearily from his bed, kicking aside the cheap, itchy wool blankets and dropping his feet to the uneven wooden floor and its threadbare ancient rug. Sunlight streamed through the inadequate curtains with their moth-eaten holes and dappled the mouldy wall. He'd managed four hours of sleep, interrupted only briefly by the second call to prayer of the city's muezzin, and the afternoon would now be wearing on.

It had been clear as he had left Lykaion that he would achieve nothing else that day without at least a little rest, and he'd been asleep almost before he touched the thin mattress. In a way it was a shame, since he'd intended on hovering near the house of the yellow columns to try and observe events, but exhaustion had scuppered that plan and he'd retired to his room instead.

Very likely the whore's house was now neat and clear, the Janissaries having performed every check they could and made their important discoveries. The woman's body would have been delivered to the church of Saint John the Forerunner – where the priest would have fainted at the sight – while the vizier would have been cleaned up and borne to the palace. And Lykaion would be fuming over having become involved in the matter in the first place and calling down the wrath of his heretical

Allah on him.

The image of his brother popped into his mind and he decided that it would have been inopportune anyway to have tried even subtly to observe the Janissaries at the house without checking first that he was safe.

And that meant a visit to the Bloody Church.

Flapping his arms in a birdlike fashion to try and diffuse the odour of sleep-sweat, he threw on his doublet, leaving it unfastened, and pulled on his new boots, shivering at the cold even in his small room. This particular building had been subdivided by its greedy landlord into single rooms, each of which was rented out for a small fee that suited the purse of the more impoverished citizen, yet which netted him a tidy sum when combined. With eight rooms on each of three floors it was a healthy investment, and a number of men in the city had become quite well off catering for men like Skiouros.

Pulling aside the curtain, he made his habitual check of the street for angry merchants, short-changed Jewish moneylenders, cheated thugs, irritable zealots and inflexible Ottoman Janissaries, all of which were a constant possibility and threat. The narrow alley that ran around the back of his building was empty apart from a stray dog eating something unpleasant among the murk. A glance up to the balcony of the room above – a balcony cost an extra two akce a week, which was hardly worth it for the rickety death traps – told him that his upstairs neighbour was busy with his washing as a shirt and braes, washed in the fountain at the street's end, dangled, dripping, from the rail.

Skiouros pulled away irritably as a heavy fat droplet of water burst on his forehead.

Back inside he crossed the room, pulled open the door sharply as though expecting a lurking menace outside and, finding nothing, closed it behind him and sauntered down the stairs. On the rare occasions he had anything worth protecting, he would set small traps at his door, but generally only a spare shirt and his ruined boots sat in the room, so he sometimes even left the door open invitingly. Better they didn't damage the hinges getting in to find out their time was wasted.

Jogging lightly down the wooden stairs, he played a game that had become second nature over the years.

Left; right; right; skip a step; left; left; right; centre; left; skip to left; skip to right; right; left; drop the last two steps to the ground floor.

The ancient wooden staircase included five steps that were weak enough to give way under a heavy step and everyone in the building knew which ones to avoid. They could seriously hamper the day of any visitor, should the building contain anyone who was worth visiting – which it didn't. With only a few safe patches large enough for a footstep, even the well repaired steps were noisy and relatively poor.

With a sense of light relief, Skiouros stepped out into the street at the front of the building, hurriedly fastening the doublet against the chill wind that blew up the slope from the Golden Horn. Today could be the best in many years. Despite the unpleasantness of last night and this morning, he had actually felt closer to his brother during the morning argument than he had for half a decade, and this afternoon he would visit Judah and see if there was any news on the money. He'd been told 'a few days', but with that kind of money involved, Skiouros suspected the old Jew would have the money pushed through in short order.

With a spring in his step, he bounced down the street and ducked into the side passage that led to the Bloody Church of Saint Mary. The afternoon light shone on the barest wall of the church, leaving the badly-upkept brick façade where the brothers habitually met in a sliver of shade. Rubbing his eyes and aware that sleep would still be of great use, Skiouros crossed to the wall. The majority of its length consisted of the traditional Byzantine decorative brick where the plaster bearing the red paint had come away, leaving the bare core.

The chances of Lykaion having further need of him were small for certain, but there was always that niggling possibility, and better to spend a few minutes in the cold searching the church walls than give Lykaion any more ammunition to use against him in future.

His gaze rose as high as he could have reached on the red paint and began to stray back and forth in a zig-zag pattern down the wall, searching for the scratched legend 'Λύκαιον' – a warning that his brother needed to see him. As his gaze reached the bottom of the wall and he felt a sag of relief, having found only crude graffiti and meaningless scrapes, he suddenly became aware of a noise behind him.

Turning, expecting to see one of the many stray dogs making a gagging choking sound, he almost laughed out loud as he realised that the peculiar noise was his brother trying subtly to attract his attention.

Lykaion stood in the lee of one of the local houses, almost shrouded in shadow opposite where Skiouros peered at the wall. His smile faltered and then fell into one of worry as he noted the expression of desperate fear on his brother's face and the nervous twitch of his hands as he gripped the wooden wall and pushed himself back out of sight.

'What?'

Lykaion made a hissing noise and used his hands to mime a need for silence. As Skiouros frowned, his brother beckoned. Shrugging, the smaller brother crossed the open space and ducked into the narrow stretch of shade with Lykaion.

'What is it?' he hissed.

'Trouble!' Lykaion snapped, his voice little more than a whisper. 'Big, big trouble.'

Skiouros' hand went automatically to his belt knife.

'What sort of trouble.'

'I'm wanted by the Janissaries!'

This time, Skiouros couldn't help but let out a small chuckle.

'I'm serious!' Lykaion snarled, his voice rising unintentionally.

'For what?'

'What do you think? For the murder of the vizier!'

'But that's ridiculous. Why would they think that?'

Lykaion sagged against the wall. 'I don't know whether they're just being stupid and mistaken – maybe they need someone to pin it on very quickly before the sultan finds out; sometimes the truth is not as important as having someone to punish in the Ottoman court. Maybe my shaky story didn't help? It was hardly convincing, I have to admit. I don't know. I have the horrible suspicion that Bin Murad is pinning this on me out of spite. The man is a spiteful old snake.'

'Who's Bin Murad?'

'My commander. He's put out a call for my arrest. By now every Janissary in the city will be aware of it and on the lookout. And given the nature of the killing and the victim, they'll be none too careful in arresting me. It won't go too badly for them if they deliver me as a corpse instead of a prisoner.'

Skiouros shook his head in bewilderment. 'This is all insane. There's no evidence against you, a Greek court would laugh it aside.'

'There's no such thing as a Greek court, brother, and the Janissaries will deal with it any way they see fit. And with the death of a senior government official, it'll be something vicious. I don't know what to do.'

'Well we'll have to try and come up with something that

exonerates you.'

Lykaion barked a laugh. 'Unlikely, since we've nothing to go on. All things are as Allah wills them. I must have offended God. Probably by consorting with thieves and whores.'

Skiouros bit his lip and stepped back into the sunlight.

'I may have something that could help, but the first thing to do is to get you changed. Look at you: you might as well be running around shouting that you're a Janissary.'

'I took my hat off and turned my jacket inside out,' the older brother retorted somewhat defensively.

'It's still green and very official looking – doesn't look like a peasant jacket; just like an inside-out Janissary jacket. And you're wearing your red leather boots, your blue trousers and even your sword. You need to change completely.'

'Tell me about this "something that could help'', Lykaion said with a suspicious frown. 'I knew you were keeping something from me.'

'I'll tell you, but we need to make you blend in first. Come with me.'

Lykaion began to object, but his brother had hold of his cuff and was already dragging him out into the sunlight. Spluttering his panic, the older of the pair found himself unceremoniously hauled out and hurried along the narrow road by the church. They turned several swift corners in a row until Lykaion had no idea where they were.

'Where are we going?'

'Local tailor. Need to get you changed.'

'I haven't much money on me.'

'You've enough for this tailor,' Skiouros announced with a grin as they turned a corner into another narrow street, cross-crossed with lines of people's washing.

'No. I won't steal clothes,' Lykaion said flatly.

'But I will.' Leaving the older brother with his arms crossed, resolutely shaking his head, Skiouros jogged off along the street, his eyes checking the doors and windows in advance of his run as they sized up potential items.

Hurrying along past the few open doors or occupied windows, the thief's arm shot out three times, snatching items off lines as he ran – items carefully selected in advance. Lykaion watched in a mix of amazement and disapproval as his younger brother reached the far end of the narrow street, having acquired a full suit of clothes without attracting even a shout of consternation, and disappeared around a corner.

He stood nervously for some time, wondering where his brother had gone and starting to worry about standing here near so many now-missing garments, until a tap on his shoulder nearly caused him to lose bladder control. Skiouros stood grinning behind him, gesturing back the way they had come.

The pair hurried through a few more streets and into the shade of a tiny alley mouth, where Lykaion came to a breathless halt and looked his brother and their haul up and down.

'No. Not stolen clothes.'

'It's that or you risk both our lives. How long do you think it's going to be before your brothers in arms start to search the Greek enclave, given your history? Get that kit off.'

The older brother stared helplessly for a long moment, shaking his head, but there was no clear alternative and in the end he began to divest himself of the jacket and the cotton garments beneath it.

'Leave the shirt,' Skiouros noted, pointing. 'No one will notice the shirt. You'll need to keep the boots for now too, but here's a brown doublet and braes and a scratty short cloak you can throw over the top. When we get to my room, you can try on my old boots. They might be a bit tight for you, but we'll have to make do for now. Boots are a "must buy", sadly.'

With considerable distaste, Lykaion removed his outer clothes and shrugged into the stolen garb. Despite his disapproval of the clothes' origin, he had to marvel at Skiouros' eye for detail. Each item was a perfect fit, clean and yet nondescript. The resulting look made his official red leather boots stand out all the more. With a sigh, he began to belt his sword back on.

'Not the sword.'

'What?'

'The sword's costly and Ottoman. Too obvious. You'll have to throw it away.'

'No.'

'It's too much of a giveaway. Drop it and your Janissary clothes into that dung pit at the end of the alley.'

'No. I'll throw my jacket and trousers, but the sword I'll carry under my cloak. I can hide it in your room. I'm being hunted by the Janissaries, and I won't simply throw away my only defence.'

'Keep your knife on your belt too, then. That's fine in this quarter and you might even get away with it in the rest of the city.'

As Lykaion hid the curved sword in the voluminous folds of his ragged cloak, Skiouros peered out of the alley entranceway and nodded in satisfaction.

'Come on.'

As nervous as he'd ever been, Lykaion followed his brother back into the main street and up the hill, turning corners until they arrived at the wooden building that Skiouros had called home for almost four years now.

With warnings and guidance from Skiouros, the pair climbed the stairs, avoiding the dangerous planks, and pushed open the door only when the younger man had checked to make sure the room was unoccupied, peering through the crack between the hinges.

'Come in.'

As Lykaion entered the small space and looked around with barely-concealed distaste, Skiouros collapsed onto the bed and fished around underneath, pulling out a pair of ragged, leaky boots covered in stains. The older of the brothers stared at them in disgust before taking them gingerly and examining them.

'Horrible,' he remarked.

'Just put them on.'

Lykaion joined him, sitting on the edge of the bed as he removed his expensive red boots and pushed his feet with some difficulty into the ruined brown ones.

'Tell me the whole story,' he said quietly as he struggled with the footwear. Skiouros flashed a nervous glance at him for a moment and then sagged back onto the bed, lacing his fingers together behind his head. After a long, cleansing breath, he began to relate the story of the previous day, from the moment Lykaion had left angrily right to the fountain where he'd cleaned off all the blood. Throughout the tale, the older brother nodded as though Skiouros was simply confirming his worst suspicions. Finally, when he'd finished, Skiouros squeezed his eyes shut and rubbed his short hair.

'We could go and see Judah ben Isaac, though I'm not sure how well he'll take being queried and I'm not sure I want him knowing what he's almost involved in.'

He'd expected Lykaion to argue, but the older brother simply nodded knowingly. 'Ben Isaac is a vicious piece of work when he's crossed. If we get on the wrong side of him, the Janissaries will look like the easy option. I think you need to forget about him. Forget all about your stolen hoard and have nothing else to do with the man and his pet thugs.'

'It's a lot of money,' Skiouros objected defensively.

'I'm sure it'll be very useful for you when you're floating face down in the Propontis for putting the old bastard in danger. Anyway, he's peripheral to this whole thing. He's only involved because you dragged him into it, and the coins will tell you nothing beyond when and where they were minted.'

'So what...'

'The Mamluk.'

Skiouros scratched his chin. 'But he could be anywhere.'

'Not so. There are precious few places in the city a Mamluk can go without causing comment or being attacked. And you say you think he was accompanied by Janissaries?'

'Definitely.'

'There are maybe half a dozen places an enemy of the Empire could hide in the city. But with a Janissary guard he's here officially. And that narrows it down to two or three. He could be one of the few Mamluks that are actually serving the sultan, which would put him at Topkapi, the Yedikule fortress or the Blachernae Palace. He could be one of the merchants with trade authority, who are still permitted to ferry goods between here and Egypt, in which case he'll be restricted and should be spending most of his time at the ports on the Golden Horn. Or he's one of the officials – an ambassador or other noble – in which case he'll be in the Bucoleon palace on the Propontis shore.'

'None of which you're likely to get into, even if you kept your uniform on.'

Lykaion nodded. 'But I might not need to actually get inside if only I knew where to look. Five places to watch and only one of me. Is there anything else you can tell me? There must be more.'

'I've told you everything I can remember, short of the colour of his underwear.'

'Clothes...' mused Lykaion, tapping his lip with a finger that he then eyed suspiciously, wondering whether it might be deadly poisonous after touching Skiouros' old boots. A frown crept across his face.

'Clothes. The Janissaries' clothes. Can you describe any peculiarities of them? We might be able to narrow it down by his guards.'

Skiouros nodded, gazing into space as he cast his mind back to the image of the two guards throwing themselves over the trestle tables in the market in an effort to get to him. They all looked very much the same. They were almost identical to the uniform Lykaion had been wearing earlier. Only the cavalry or the axemen or musket orta or suchlike were distinguishable. Except for...

'I can do better than that,' he grinned. Lykaion raised a questioning eyebrow.

'They both had the same insignia as you. Does that help?'

'The Fourteenth?' Pieces of a frightening puzzle were starting to click together in Lykaion's mind as he thought it through. 'So if this Mamluk is connected to the killing – which seems undeniable – and his guards serve Hamza Bin Murad, then it's no longer surprising that the commander might immediately pin the blame on me. Something very serious and important is going on here, little brother.'

'Does it help narrow down where to look?'

Lykaion nodded. 'The Fourteenth are Palace Guard. We serve at Topkapi and the Bucoleon. The Blachernae Palace and its dungeons are in the hands of the Provost Corbasi and his men.'

'Down to two, then?' queried Skiouros.

'Describe your Mamluk again.'

Dredging his considerable recall, Skiouros once more detailed everything he could think of about the Mamluk. When he finished, Lykaion nodded again.

'And that's definite. All absolutely correct?'

'Yes.'

'Then I go to the Bucoleon palace.'

'You've seen him?'

'Quite the opposite. I am assigned to the Topkapi, and I've seen the four Mamluks who work there dozens of times over the past months. Three of them have full beards – two grey and one deep black. The other is always clean-shaven – I believe him to be a eunuch. If your Mamluk in the market sported a thin, oiled moustache, then he is not at the Topkapi.'

Skiouros pursed his lips as he tried to picture the Bucoleon palace. It would be as impossible to get inside as the sultan's own Topkapi palace, but considerably easier to watch.

The old imperial walls that had turned three grand structures into a single massive palace complex, with its own lighthouse, chapels, churches and ancillary buildings, now stood unguarded and with the doors removed, even demolished in places. The main structure of the

90

former complex was the only part now inhabited and was itself commonly referred to as the Bucoleon. This building – a grand edifice on its own – stood directly on the sea-shore, with two sides opening out onto land within the city and two onto the waters of the Propontis. There was an impressive water entrance, but that would not be opened in these days; particularly not if the building were serving as the quarters of dignitaries and ambassadors for an enemy nation.

That left only two sides, and there was no entrance on the western wall. The only remaining façade, which opened north into the heart of the city, had one grand entrance, and one smaller servants' door. It would be easy enough to keep watch over them.

It was feasible. And yet still an inferior choice to the alternative that had been forming in another corner of his mind as he talked.

'There's another option,' he said quietly.

Lykaion, his mind still riveted on the Bucoleon and his next move, looked up in confusion. 'Hmm?'

'I said: there's another option.'

'What?'

'Leave the city.'

Lykaion shook his head decisively. 'No. I am Janissary.'

'No you're not. Look, brother: even if you can find this Mamluk, what will you do with him? How are you going to prove his involvement and clear your own name, especially if half your own comrades think you're guilty? You're heading down a path to self-destruction.'

'I cannot flee and leave my name in ruins.'

'It's not your name. Hussein is some construct of the Janissaries. You are Lykaion, son of Nikos of Hadrianople. I don't care whether you bow to God or Allah or some piss-faced pagan, but you are my brother. I'd rather we were both free and gone from here than dead in an Ottoman ditch.'

'No. You might be able to run…'

'Lykaion, you've been trying to persuade me to stop my thieving ways for years. How about I make you a deal: we'll go down to the port of Theodosius and get on a ship bound for Crete. We can hide out here until she sails and when I get to Judah ben Isaac, he'll give me enough money to pay for the journey and start us on something new when we get there?'

'No.'

'Come on, Lykaion. It's the only sensible thing to do.'

'I won't run and leave the guilty to revel in their success. If this is Bin Murad's doing I'll see him dead for it.'

'I hear that Crete is quite welcoming of defecting Turks…'

'No, Skiouros, and that's an end to it. You can flee, but I must track down this Mamluk.'

The pair lapsed into silence, and finally Skiouros let out a burst of air and rubbed his temple, his brow furrowed.

'You look like a man planning a battle,' Lykaion commented, looking sidelong at him.

'After a fashion, I am. We go to keep watch on the northern face of the Bucoleon then?'

Again, Lykaion shook his head. 'I will not drag you into my darkness, brother. You may be a thieving sinner in the eyes of the prophet, but you're a lucky one and a born survivor. Stay away from me.'

'I am more than a mere thief, Lykaion. I'm your brother. Whatever else happens, I'm not about to let you face trouble alone.' He gave a light laugh. 'Besides, you have the street sense of a sick donkey. You wouldn't last two minutes in the backstreets without me.'

'It will be difficult, and dangerous, and there is very little chance I will succeed.'

'I know. Believe me I know. And that's why I'm coming along. Once you've seen this Mamluk and found out what he's about, you'll realise there's nothing else you can do, and I think – I hope – you'll see the error of your ways. Then we can go to the port and arrange passage.'

'Unlikely.'

'We'll see. But you'll get nowhere without me watching your back, that's for certain. So to the Bucoleon it is… via somewhere for me.'

Lykaion narrowed his eyes suspiciously and then sighed and nodded. 'Come on, then.'

With a brisk pace the pair descended the stairs once more and, as Skiouros reached for the door handle to throw it open to the street, Lykaion's hand fell on his and held it firm.

'Listen,' he hissed.

The two fell silent, the only noise in the building a tuneless hummed ditty issuing from one of the rooms on the top floor. As Skiouros listened, frowning and trying to work out what his brother had heard, a regular pulse began to draw his attention. A drum. A drum being rhythmically pounded in the street, not far away.

'Janissaries?' he asked quietly. Lykaion nodded and moved Skiouros' hand aside, inching the door open little more than a crack and angling his head to peer through. A small party of four guards were making their way down the street and shouting, a pounding drum warning the Greek second-class citizens to stay out of their way.

'Stupid,' Skiouros whispered.

'What?'

'If they're looking for you, I mean. Stupid to advertise their presence with a drum.'

'They're not looking for me. They're distributing my name and description to the public and the details of a reward. That's how they do it, particularly in the foreign enclaves. They know they have no chance of finding me themselves, but they also know that someone here will turn me in for the money.'

Sure enough, as Skiouros listened he could hear the names 'Lykaion, son of Nikos' and 'Hussein Bin Nikos' being shouted. He was impressed that the guard were offering a gold sultani for his brother's capture or information leading to the same. It was a sad fact that there was no one he could think of who would stay silent for even a couple of silver akce, let alone gold.

'We'd best not be seen in the street, even if you're now less obvious.'

Lykaion took a deep breath. 'Will they find your room from Father's name?'

'There must be the children of a hundred Nikoses living in Phanar. No. They need more than that. Come on.'

Swiftly, Skiouros led his brother back along the narrow wooden corridor, past the staircase and to a small door that led out into the stinking alley behind the building. Wrinkling his nose at the acrid assault on the senses, Lykaion followed the thief out into the alley and moved along it hurriedly, trying not to tread in anything too unpleasant, and failing repeatedly.

Despite having spent almost the same number of years in the city as his brother – barring brief actions against the Mamluks in Anatolia – and having sporadically met with him at the Bloody Church, Lykaion's geography of the city was largely confined to the areas to which his duty took him; largely the higher class areas with open boulevards.

As Skiouros expertly navigated the alleys and streets, nipping into apparent dead ends, only to bring them by some tortuous route out onto another street, the older brother quickly became quite hopelessly turned around until, almost half an hour later, they emerged from a narrow alley's mouth and into an open space.

The Mese streamed with life in both directions and it took Lykaion a moment to orientate himself, with three landmarks standing out. Ignoring the Roman aqueduct that ran between the Third and Fourth hills and which still brought water to the population, he focused on the Dulgerzade mosque across the road. Two Turkish nobles stood by the street entrance, chatting absently as carts and pedestrians flowed past them. Instinctively, given his situation, the fugitive Janissary pulled back into the shadows of the passageway. Skiouros came to a sudden halt and turned to him.

'What are you doing? We need to keep moving.'

'We're in too much danger. Everyone here's Ottoman. We'll stand out too much – attract attention. We should have waited 'til dark.'

Skiouros shook his head and reached out to take his brother's cloak by the shoulder. 'There's dozens of Greek merchants and beggars in the streets. So long as we move quietly and quickly, as if we're on our way somewhere, we'll be ignored. If you start panicking and lurking, that's when you'll draw attention. Now come on; we're going to church.'

Lykaion fought his grip and pointed at the building opposite where the two Turks' attention was now straying around the street. 'I can't go in there. Are you mad?'

'I wasn't talking about the mosque. There.'

Lykaion followed his brother's pointing finger and his eyes fell on the third landmark. The sprawling ruins of a once-great church stood next to the Mese a hundred yards away. He'd walked past the crumbling structure any number of times when reporting to the city walls, but had never given it a moment's thought. Even for a church it had seemed unworthy of his attention, the missing windows staring out of a cracked and crumbling façade in a manner that reminded him disturbingly of a skull.

'What?' he demanded incredulously.

'I told you I wanted to stop somewhere on the way. And at least you can guarantee none of your Janissary friends will be in there.'

Lykaion was too confused to fight his brother's grip any more and staggered out into the street, turning to follow him as casually as possible when he realised how his sudden jerky appearance must look.

'I think that in fairness I'd rather risk a visit to the Dulgerzade Camii,' he hissed.

'Stick to Greek. If you start speaking Turkish you really will attract attention.'

As they neared the ruins, a chilling gale blowing up the valley between the Third and Fourth hills and through the gaping arches of the ancient aqueduct bridge, Lykaion viewed the tall, jagged and roofless brick face of the church's north wall with something of a mix of nervousness and distrust. The building seemed faintly threatening, despite the fact that he'd spent much of his youth in smaller churches of the same style praying to the Christian God. The mounting sense of panic almost turned him back and, as they approached the worn and damaged steps, Skiouros grasped his shoulder once more to drag him onwards.

Lykaion felt a cold shudder as he passed across the threshold – entirely a product of his own imagination, he was sure. The ruined church was missing almost all of its roof, and the great dome that had formed the centre was visible now only as curved ribs reaching up to the cold blue sky. The interior was almost entirely demolished or removed, fragments of once fine marble at the bottom of the walls showing how the floor had been taken away to decorate some other structure. Many of the pillars had gone, making Lykaion worry for the structural soundness of the remaining walls.

Whatever had caused the destruction of this church, it had clearly happened long ago and it was no victim of Mehmet's conquest. That knowledge somehow put his quailing heart a little more at ease and he began to take something of an interest.

'Why are we here?' he asked his brother quietly as they passed through the first hollow space and under a wide arch into the main hall.

Skiouros glanced sidelong at him and smiled strangely.

'This, dear brother, was the church of Saint Polyeuktos. Took me some asking around and research to find out much about it. See the altar over there?'

Lykaion peered through the undergrowth beginning to take command of the church's central floor, past a shattered colonnade screen and to a heavy marble altar that bore the marks of both time and deliberate ruination.

'Yes?'

'That's where the head of the saint used to be kept.'

'Until you stole it?' The older brother gave a nervous half-laugh.

'That's not particularly funny, Lykaion.' He took a deep breath and scratched his short hair fiercely. 'Actually, it seems that no one knows what happened to the head. Regardless, this is the one church in the city that I can come to where no priest is going to demand a confession of me or badger me for a donation.'

'You're not that pious, brother. You never were. Why are you bothered with a church at all?'

'No, I'm no zealot, but Saint Polyeuktos has become something of a personal mascot for me. His church saved me from your friends the first year I was here. I was trapped in plain sight by that very altar and half a dozen Janissaries walked straight past me. It's the only time in my life I've ever believed in miracles.'

Lykaion frowned as they neared the altar.

'So you've come here to pray? Don't expect me to join in, brother.'

Skiouros gave him that strange smile again.

'Hardly. But the thing is that Polyeuktos is also the patron of promises and deals, and I feel I need to tie you to one.'

Coming to a halt, the younger brother slapped the flat of his palm down on the chipped and damaged marble of the once fine altar. Lykaion could just make out worn Greek script around the edge, but with no hope of reading it.

'Put your hand on the altar.'

'I left your church behind long ago, Skiouros.'

'I'm sure God doesn't care – or Allah. Put your hand down.'

Obediently, and not entirely sure why he was agreeing to this, Lykaion slapped his palm onto the cold marble. A plethora of nesting rooks suddenly exploded into life in the arched ruins just below the dome, bursting up into the air in a chorus of croaks and flapping. Panicked, Lykaion withdrew his hand.

'Nature,' Skiouros smiled. 'Nothing more.'

Still nervously eyeing the departing black birds, Lykaion placed his hand back on the chilly hard surface.

'I'm going to make a vow to you,' his brother stated in a quiet, forceful manner, 'but in return I want one back.'

'That depends on the vow.'

Skiouros patted the marble fondly. 'I vow in the sight of God and

Saint Polyeuktos to help you try to achieve retribution or justice in every way I can, as long as it is possible.'

He locked Lykaion in a piercing gaze.

'In return, I want you to swear that the moment it becomes obvious to you that our task is impossible, you'll come with me on one of the Venetian traders and head for Crete?'

'Skiouros...'

'I lost something of my brother to the Janissaries almost a decade ago. I won't lose the rest to bloody-minded pig-headedness. You'll only leave with me when you agree that there's nothing more we can do. Surely you can avow me that?'

Lykaion looked down at his hand, doubt over giving his word on the subject vying with nerves at doing so in a church of the Christian God. It seemed, curiously, to feel both wrong and right at the same time.

'I swear it.'

'On the head of Saint Polyeuktos?' prompted Skiouros.

'Don't push it. I swear; leave it at that.'

Skiouros swept his hand from the altar. 'Thank you. Right now you can only see the need to revenge yourself and clear your own name, but I can see the impossibility of it. I can wait for you to join me in that realisation and leave the city, so long as you don't get yourself killed in the meantime.'

Lykaion pursed his lips and sighed.

'I think you're wrong, but we'll see.'

As the older brother pulled his own hand away, Skiouros smiled. 'Then in that case, let's go and have a look at the Bucoleon palace; see if we can't spot a Mamluk murderer.'

The journey on from the sprawling ruins of the church became at the same time easier and more dangerous. The main road that they followed south towards the great Theodosian harbour was thronged with people of all colours and classes, as was always the case in main thoroughfares radiating from a port, and the pair found they could easily lose themselves in the flow of varied life.

In the Forum of the Ox, the situation was much the same, there being hardly room to walk between the press of people, lending the pair perfect anonymity. From there, two small side streets full only of the lowest strata of society took the brothers to the long, winding road that followed the line of the Propontine sea walls, another route that

97

thrived with busy multicultural workers and low characters. Here, Lykaion noted, they were more likely to be set upon by thugs than by the authorities, and he observed that his brother seemed to be of the same opinion, judging by the fact that they had both placed their hands on the pommel of their knives as they walked.

Despite the tension and potential trouble, though, their worries proved unfounded, and after another forty minutes of walking they emerged into a wide street and were confronted with the vast, monumental arc of the hippodrome's southern curve.

Lykaion peered at the towering, breath-taking and graceful curve of the long-abandoned structure, sadly now missing much of its white marble and displaying only heavy walls of brick. He'd seen it many times before, but it remained to him one of the city's most astounding images, despite its frowned-upon pagan nature that made imams spit venom. Legend had it that the city had almost been destroyed by fire in a riot that started in that very stadium. If the ordinary Turkish settlers who now filled its homes thought that the Mamluks were assassinating viziers within the city – particularly with the aid of an Ottoman officer – there might very well be another city-threatening riot. Now there was food for thought.

Turning his eyes from the hippodrome's magnificent curve, he focussed instead on the expanse of the Bucoleon ahead. One of the old Emperors had walled this section of the city off with thick, high defences, creating a small, fortified, self-contained palace, but the Ottoman rulers had their own palaces and fortresses, constructed of delicate arches and arcades, domes and turrets, all in the city's high places. They had abandoned old Imperial residences like the Blachernae and the Bucoleon, utilising them instead as barracks, diplomatic quarters, prisons and more. Little over half the great Bucoleon wall now remained, and the buildings that constituted the palace complex were once more public and open.

Moving on away from the hippodrome arches, the pair made for one of the demolished sections of the wall, through which a broad avenue now ran and there, sitting at the end of the road, stood the huge, white marble bulk of the Bucoleon palace. With its delicate arched windows and decorative stonework, it remained the most stunning of all the secular works to remain from the old city, supplanted in beauty only by the new Ottoman palaces and minarets. If one were to be a foreign ambassador from an enemy nation, there could surely be no more fabulous place to be imprisoned.

The thought turned Lykaion sour once more as he reminded himself that if he was not mistaken, that Mamluk was anything but a prisoner.

'Have you given any thought as to where we'll wait?' Skiouros asked quietly as they slowed, nearing the building. A wide space had been left open before the palace's north façade: a broad boulevard with an extra area of gardens and fountains to the north that prevented any other building from intruding upon the former Imperial residence. The statues of Gods and emperors that had filled the garden had all long gone, but the bases that had held them remained in irregular patterns throughout the park and along the side of the wide street.

Lykaion nodded as he eyed the front of the palace carefully. There were no guards outside either the major or minor entrance to the north. Presumably any sentries assigned by the Janissaries would be in guardrooms inside the building; after all, their official duty was to keep foreigners inside the building rather than intruders out.

'There's two places that should have a good view of the doors. I've done a couple of stints of duty in the Bucoleon, and I think they should be safe enough from view. The Ilyas Chapel is the closest with the most direct view of the door, but it's ruined, unstable and dangerous. Even the staircase is partially gone, so I don't fancy trying that. The pharos tower will give the best view, but it's further away, at the far end of the gardens.'

Skiouros scratched his chin thoughtfully. 'The pharos is the obvious answer. Question is: can we get in? It's still in use, yes?' He'd passed it several times on his infrequent tours of this end of the city, but had never lingered to investigate, being so close to a place where Janissaries patrolled.

'In a way,' Lykaion replied. 'There's rarely anyone in it and if they are, they'll be up at the top, where the important workings are. If we can get to the first walkway a third of the way up, we can stay there and watch with relative comfort. The downside is that the door will be locked. We'll have to break it down and risk the possibility that someone will come along and discover it.'

'We could always use a grapple and climb the wall on the north side where it can't be seen from the palace – I know where to lay my hands on the tools back at the harbour.'

'No. No grapples or climbing.'

Skiouros raised an inquisitive eyebrow.

'I'm not good with high places these days. I'll be alright once we're on the walkway behind a parapet, but I can't climb it in the open.' He shuddered at the very thought.

'Then we'll have to go in my way.'

Lykaion opened his mouth to comment, but the smaller of the brothers was already moving down the street past the ruined walls, where he stepped off the main thoroughfare into the gardens, all-but disappearing among the shrubs and trees, the statue bases and the fountains that played their constant tinkling tune.

As they moved across the small park, Lykaion scurrying along behind his brother, they peered at the legends on the statue bases: VALENS – ANASTASIOS – ANASTASIOS II – LEO IV – NIKOPHOROS PHOCAS. Between these squat blocks that had once borne rulers of the world, others had suffered greater wear and were all but indecipherable.

Moments later Lykaion reached the wall of the pharos and leaned on it, drawing in deep lungfuls of air. Like his brother, he had only walked through the gardens, not run, but the nervous tension had led to him holding his breath as they moved, his eyes flitting this way and that.

The walls of the great watchtower that represented the terminus of a warning system that covered much of near Asia disappeared upwards a hundred feet and more up into the chilly blue afternoon. Built on three distinct levels, the tower's lowest was a heavy square base with slightly tapering walls of creamy stone, flush-fitting and perfect. Looking up the line of the wall, Lykaion could see the parapet that marked where the first level ended in a fortified walkway before the second level, circular and vertical, began.

Turning his attention back to his surroundings and starting to worry that perhaps they were taking too long looking suspicious in the open, he leaned round the corner where his brother had disappeared a moment earlier.

Skiouros was nowhere to be seen.

In a momentary panic, Lykaion's wide eyes searched this way and that, noting with small gratitude that the windows of the palace seemed to be empty and unoccupied. At least they didn't appear to be being observed, but where had the little thief gone now?

'Come on up.'

Lykaion craned his neck sharply at the sudden hissed words, only to see his brother's grinning face peering down from the battlements before he disappeared again from sight. Hurrying around the corner, Lykaion strode on to the heavy door with its complex lock that kept the city's warning system secure from tampering only to find the portal standing wide open with no sign of damage.

Shaking his head irritably at the unfortunate necessity of relying on his brother's sinful skills, Lykaion threw up a quick apology to Allah and begged Mohammed and Isa to forgive the manner of their entrance. Whether it was right or wrong, he was grateful for Skiouros' ability and, as he shut the door behind him and climbed the staircase to the first parapet, he prepared himself for the long wait.

Chapter 5 – A new use for an old church

* Persembe (Thursday) evening *

Skiouros started sharp awake, his hand going reflexively to the knife at his belt before his refocusing eyes picked out the form of Lykaion against the porphyry sky. The last copper-coloured bands of sunlight streaked the air above the horizon, just visible over the roof of the Bucoleon palace. Lykaion's eyes gleamed with alertness, while Skiouros' were still blurry and gritty from the two short stints of sleep he had managed and which, between them, had entirely failed to equal a good full night's worth.

'Shhh!'

Skiouros frowned at his brother. He wasn't aware he'd made any sound.

The pair had waited on the first-level parapet of the pharos tower for only an hour before the younger brother had succumbed to his weariness, pulling his tattered cloak around him, and snuggled down as best he could on the hard stone, falling almost instantly into a deep, dreamless sleep. Lykaion had crouched in a position where he could see down across the small strip of gardens and the wide road to the palace's two entrances without being uncomfortably close to the parapet and the drop beyond, and didn't appear to have moved since then.

'How long have I been asleep?' Skiouros mouthed with almost no sound, blinking away the salty grit.

Lykaion showed two fingers and then folded one and used the other to point over the parapet. Skiouros slowly unfolded his tired legs and shuffled as quietly and carefully as he could to his knees, peering over the edge.

It took him a moment to pick out the figures to which his brother was drawing his attention.

Three people were moving with a slow and confident pace along the street from the palace's main entrance and were passing the pharos now, just the short stretch of park land separating tower from road. While one was cloaked and could have been almost anyone, the other two were quite clearly Janissary guards.

Skiouros leaned close to his brother and cupped his hands to Lykaion's ear.

'He's definitely the one? I can't see his face.'

'He's a Mamluk with Janissary guards,' the older brother whispered back. 'Don't think the sultan will allow too many enemy ambassadors into his city at once, so I think we can safely take the chance he's the one, or at least in league with him. He's heading towards the southeast, though; not into the city. Why? There's nothing that way but old Byzantine ruins and poor Turk housing. If he was going anywhere important, he'd have gone up past the hippodrome.'

Skiouros took his hands away from Lykaion's ear, aware that the three men were now far enough away that a low whisper would be lost in the winds that blew colder and wilder this close to the headland.

'If he's involved in murders and the like, he's probably up to something he needs to keep quiet. He can't do that in crowded Ottoman spaces under the nose of the sultan, can he? Come on.'

With a nod, Lykaion struggled to his feet, his knees aching from the hard floor. The pair hurried inside, with a quick check to make sure that no one had entered unseen, though the chances were small with Lykaion on watch above the door. Finding the interior empty, the brothers scurried down the stairs and to the front door.

Gesturing Lykaion aside, Skiouros inched the door open just a crack and peered through. The three men had disappeared from sight along the street, past a section of the old imperial palace wall that had not been demolished. Motioning to Lykaion, he stepped out into the evening chill and pulled the cloak tighter round him before hurrying across the gardens and to the street. His brother loped along behind him with the speed and grace of the wolf for which he was named.

Opposite them stood the second of the great residences that had been part of the Imperial palace. Much of the roof had fallen in through decades of disuse, and the inky sky was visible through the high, decorative windows. Despite the best efforts of the Janissaries in the adjacent palace, Skiouros knew the building to be the haunt of numerous homeless beggars. Momentarily, he prayed the three men had not entered that building. The one time he'd done so, he had quickly realised just how unsafe and precarious the structure was. Some day soon dozens of beggars would be buried in the rubble that the palace was destined to become.

His prayers were answered as they reached the corner where the garden ended and the main street ran off to the southeast, and he peered along it, spotting the ambassadorial party some four hundred yards ahead, past the walls. There was no one around on the streets here, and following the three men would be extremely difficult. If the Janissaries were even remotely alert the brothers would stand no chance.

The pair paused, frustrated for a moment, becoming aware with irritation that they had not thought through their plan beyond waiting for the Mamluk to put in an appearance. Was it even safe to follow him? As the brothers looked around for options, the thief found himself looking up at the purple sky and the silhouette of the rooflines.

Skiouros smiled and gestured up to the roof of the wooden building next to which they stood, using his fingers to make a walking mime and shrugging the question. Lykaion shook his head vehemently. Again, the younger man thought hard. The street was long and open and if they followed the three men straight, it would only take one glance over a shoulder for the guards to spot them. Coming to a decision, he pointed first to himself and then to the roof. Then he pointed at his brother and gestured towards the parallel street that ran behind the houses.

Lykaion nodded and ran off along the side of the wooden structure. Taking a deep breath, Skiouros grasped one of the planks of wood that jutted slightly from the house's façade and, hoping the noises he was about to make would not draw attention from the occupants, used it to haul himself up to the tiny balcony of the next floor.

He had used the rooftops of the city several times in the past few years, though mostly in the Phanar district, and only when he had to, given the inherent dangers in the unsafe wooden constructions. The roofs often provided an avenue of escape when all other routes appeared blocked, for many of the passages and alleyways could be jumped by a man with a healthy understanding of his own abilities and control of his fears. In addition, the poor quality of the timber structures meant plenty of hand- and foot-holds, and a man did not have to be an expert to achieve the roofline.

A few seconds was all it took the thief to drag himself onto the more-or-less flat roof with its gentle camber to keep the house clear of rain and snow. Without pause, knowing that time was of as much essence as was subtlety, Skiouros sprang to his feet and began to run along the row of houses.

The roofs were of varying heights but with all the buildings in the area consisting of only two storeys the difference was only a few feet each time and the thief bounded and loped along each roof with a delicate jump up or down as required. The gaps between houses were rarely more than two or three feet and several had actually settled into leaning against one another, closing the gap at the top, so there was little danger or effort really required – he had seen the poor boys of the city making games of it.

As he sprinted along the row, Skiouros dipped first to one side and then, jumping the dark, stinking alley between the housing rows, to the other, making sure the three were still visible in the street, and gesturing to Lykaion in the parallel road, who looked up and nodded, picking up the pace a little.

Sure-footed and swift, the thief skipped from roof to roof, catching up with their quarry while moving with relative silence in the whistling wind.

As they reached the ruined walls of the palace complex, which presented no barrier at roof level, Skiouros took another glance down into the street and noted the three men approaching the Nea Ekklasia – a large, ancient Byzantine structure close to the ruined wall, but on the outside, beyond the former palace grounds.

The building was a church, or had been – a big one too – and was being reused by the Turks for some government or military purpose. He had passed it a number of times over the years, and had noted on every occasion the Janissary guards at the main door, with the other entrances all bricked up. Why in the name of God would the Mamluk be going there?

Pausing, his interest piqued, Skiouros watched with narrowed eyes as the Janissaries on guard at the door nodded to their counterparts and then calmly opened the door and stood aside for the Mamluk to pass within. The ambassador's escort, however, remained outside with the door guards, where they stood blowing on their cold knuckles and chatting casually in the manner of unobserved soldiers everywhere.

With a frustrated sigh, Skiouros realised that there was no feasible way to follow the man within. The doors and windows around the church's ground floor were well sealed, as he'd tested on other occasions and, with guards on the front, there was little or no chance of gaining access. Crossing the house and jumping the narrow alley, he moved to the parallel street and had to hiss to attract the attention of Lykaion, who was already moving ahead.

The older brother stopped and looked up to see Skiouros clambering down the building's side, using the protruding edges of boards and the balconies to grip and pivot.

'What's happened? You haven't lost them?'

'Hardly. They went into the Nea Ekklasia.'

A hint of worry pervaded Lykaion's taut expression.

'What's the matter?' Skiouros asked, his brow furrowing.

'That's our main powder store for the city – the Nea Ekklasia here and the Anemas Tower on the walls, anyway. What in the name of Allah would he want in there? And why would the guards let him in? There were guards, yes?'

'Yes. What sort of powd...' began Skiouros, pausing as his eyes widened. 'You mean gunpowder?'

'Gunpowder, yes. We have to get in there, little brother.'

'I'm not all that sure I want to. That stuff makes me nervous. Anyway, the place is sealed tighter than a nun's undergarments.'

Lykaion gave him a disapproving look and tapped his lip.

'Can you not break in? Like you did at the pharos?'

'Not this place. The lesser doors were bricked up. I've looked before. There is an entrance from the old portico garden, but that's solid as the Clashing Rocks and barred from the inside.'

'I won't ask why you've looked. I know the windows were sealed up with timber, too; I've been inside a couple of times on duty. I can't imagine what the Mamluk is after, but I need to know. Find us a way in, Skiouros.'

The thief breathed a heavy sigh and scratched his head.

'Do you get birds in there?'

'What?'

'Birds. Flapping things with feathers?'

Lykaion frowned in irritation. 'All too often. They shit on everything when they get trapped inside, and we find the odd dead one.

'Well if they can get in that means at least one of the windows is accessible.'

The older brother shook his head. 'All the windows are sealed over with wood.'

'Logic tells us otherwise – pigeons are resilient, but I've never seen one pass through a solid plank of wood yet. If all the windows you've seen are boarded up, though, then we're probably looking at the domes. I can't imagine your friends bothered boarding up the windows up there.'

Lykaion's eyes widened. 'Not a chance!'

'You want in? Then you're going to have to climb. I'll help you, though.'

'I can't.' The renegade Janissary had suddenly gone very pale and Skiouros noted a nervous shake to the man.

'Then we have to walk away and forget the whole thing. Remember your vow at the altar of Saint Polyeuktos? Just give the word and we can make our way to the harbour and book a passage to Crete. I know I will be a lot happier.'

A look of helpless desperation fell on the older brother's face and he walked forward, Skiouros padding along behind. A hundred yards further on, they reached the end of the street and Lykaion peered cautiously around the corner. The once great church of the Nea Ekklasia stood in its own open ground as though the Ottoman structures were too nervous to encroach upon its ancient space. Four Janissaries huddled at the door, deep in conversation and apparently paying no attention to the world around them.

Lykaion's eyes slid upwards from the guards, past the great, monumental doors, up to the sloping tile roof that covered the narthex – the front porch – and past that to the main wall of the church with its arched windows displaying only blank timber. As his mind furnished him with a height estimate of perhaps sixty feet, he shivered. Above that, the next sloping tile roof marked the top of the church itself, above which rose five domes – four smaller protrusions surrounding a larger central one. Skiouros was right. Even from here he could see the difference in colour as the moonlight shone on the glass in the dome windows.

There was a way in.

Lykaion felt the distinct urge to retch.

To give in to his fears, though, was essentially to abandon all hope of unravelling this nightmare. It would mean admitting defeat to Skiouros and taking his offer of flight to the assumed safety of a foreign land.

No. He would not flee.

'How do we go about it?'

Skiouros, at his shoulder, raised his brow in surprise, but concentrated on his answer, his eyes roving across the building's facade.

'We go round the back of the church, away from the guards. First we get up onto the lowest roof. That should be easy enough – there's a huge porticoed garden attached to the back.'

'Can we not just get into that garden?'

Skiouros shook his head. 'You can, and I've done it, but remember what I said? The only door into the church from there is very solid and locked and barred from the inside. I've looked at it before.'

Lykaion nodded unhappily as his brother resumed his plan.

'From the first roof, there's a side aisle with a second roof maybe fifteen feet further up. The whole building's good Byzantine brickwork with lots of good hand- and foot-holds, so we get onto that side roof and then to the central cross of the church. The only tricky parts will be each time we get to a roof section, which'll create an overhang. I'll go first so I can pull you up. Then, when we're on the roof, we can just walk the slopes to the dome and... well from there we'll have to see what we can do. I've never been inside.'

Lykaion swallowed nervously.

'I think that might be a problem. Most of the interior is just one big open space and the big dome's above that. The smaller ones I don't know about.'

'Come on. Let's find out.'

Lykaion nodded nervously as Skiouros took a quick look at the guards by the door and then stepped confidently out into the open, affecting a slight limp as he moved from the street end around the side of the Nea Ekklasia as if simply passing by. Lykaion swallowed noisily, paused for a count of fifty, and then followed, trying no such deception. Two limping men close together would start to look idiotic, like some sort of disabled parade. Quickly, he caught up with Skiouros, only catching the guards out of the corner of his eye – to look across at them directly might draw too much attention. The four men glanced at him but

108

paid no further heed, returning to their private conversation.

The far side of the church presented a potential climb that sent a cold shiver through Lykaion, but he did not have much time to study it as Skiouros was already moving to the wall. Despite the open space, the darkness of the evening and the cold in the streets which was keeping most people indoors, there was always the possibility of a stray passer-by happening upon them moving furtively around the former church or scaling its walls. Indeed, it would only take a lucky local peering out of his window at the right time and in the right direction and they could be undone.

A sudden need for urgency filling him, Lykaion followed his brother across the open space and to the rear of the church, where the main building and its square rear portico met in a convenient shadowy corner. Indeed, as the fugitive Janissary closed on the corner, he could barely see Skiouros in the darkness, and it took him a moment to pick out the climbing figure nearing the top of the twelve-foot wall, his hand hooked over the roof edge, where three courses of decorative brick extended outwards at increasing lengths, topped by rows of tile so ancient they had probably seen pagan days. His heart pounding with sudden fear, Lykaion watched his brother with a mix of terror and awe as the young thief grasped the tiles and somehow vaulted over the edge, coming to rest face down on the slightly sloping roof.

Skiouros waved him on.

Feeling an imaginary cold lead weighing down his boots, trying to prevent him approaching the wall, and the icy grip of unmastered fear all over his flesh, he stepped into the shade and took a firm grip of the brickwork. The long-gone and forgotten architects of this marvellous building had built designs into the walls through the masterful use of differing brick styles, and the result was bands of decorative work that ran around the walls between and above windows and doors, strange concave fake window arches, false columns of brick and mortar and so much more. It was quite fascinating, and created a healthy selection of holds for climbing, so long as the climber had strong fingers...

...and no fear of falling.

Lykaion's feet were only four feet from the ground when he first made the mistake of looking down. Quickly, he pulled his eyes back to the brickwork as icy fingers probed his spine and he felt every muscle and tendon in his body tighten. His fingers whitened on the brick as though he might crush it.

'No. Nononononono.'

His fingers slipped from one of the bricks as he made the conscious decision to drop back the four feet to the floor, but suddenly a vice-like grip wrapped itself around his wrist and he felt himself being pulled upwards. Panic ran through him as he scrabbled for the brick to try and back down.

'For the love of God, climb!' hissed Skiouros, his eyes wide with effort and the tendons in his wrist standing out like cords as he struggled with his brother's weight.

'I can't.'

'Then the Mamluk wins.'

Lykaion ground his teeth in irritation. Before he even realised what he was doing, his fingers had curled around the protruding tile of the roofline. Taking a deep, terrified breath, he pulled himself over the lip with his brother's help and came to rest on the gentle sloping tiles of the first roof, his heart hammering in his chest. Opening his eyes, he looked back and wished he hadn't. The ground was only the height of two men away, but the roof edge jutting out and cutting off the direct view down somehow amplified it and made it look distant and terrifying.

'One down, two to go,' Skiouros breathed.

Lykaion's blood ran cold as he looked up at his brother and saw the rest of the ascent behind him. The next stage was theoretically very similar to the first, but with the added horror of already being a dozen feet up; beyond that lay a climb of at least twice that height, and then the undulating roof and its domes.

His bladder suddenly threatened to empty itself.

'I can't do it.'

Skiouros pursed his lips. 'I know it's an old cliché, but don't look down. Concentrate on where you've got to get to and it'll help take you there. If it makes you feel any better, I'm much the same with tight spaces.'

'It doesn't.'

The older brother watched in abject horror as the thief sprang to his feet on the sloping tiles and started to stride up the slope towards the side aisle wall. The wind up here suddenly felt very powerful and Lykaion could feel it rippling through his cloak and wished fervently he had had nothing to do with all this from the start. Not trusting his feet on the roof, he stayed almost flat to the tiles as he started the ascent to the next stage on his belly.

By the time his fingers closed on the lowest courses of brick, Skiouros was already at the next roof, leaning over in what looked to Lykaion like a suicidally dangerous manner, arm dangling ready to help him up. The older of the pair steadied himself with a deep breath and pushed himself to his feet, his hands whitening as he gripped the decorative brickwork hold. His knees had suddenly become fluid and useless and, as the first gust of wind hit him, he almost passed out with sheer panic, pulling himself close in to the wall and flattening himself to it.

'Come on,' hissed Skiouros. 'We might be missing something.'

His mind locked onto an image of a Mamluk ambassador standing over the bloodied corpse of a Christian whore and an Ottoman noble and the picture filled him with such frustrated anger that he actually snarled as he reached up to grasp the next brick jutting out and hauled himself upwards. A minute later he was being pulled over the edging tiles and onto the aisle roof. Skiouros was grinning.

'What's so pissing funny?'

'You,' Skiouros laughed. 'You don't know what you sound like.'

'This is not amusing.'

'It is when you climb a wall saying "fuck, fuck, fuck" over and over, like one of your Dervishes in full swing. Nearly pissed myself.'

'Glad I can help. Now move up.'

The anger was continuing to build in Lykaion. His blood was boiling with the combination of the image of the murderous Egyptian among the innocent citizens of the city, his commander's apparent involvement – despite the vows of the Janissaries, his own impotence in the whole situation, and now his brother's jibes.

And yet the anger was helping.

While Skiouros skittered up the tiles to tall walls with rows of windows and arches, Lykaion followed up on his belly, feeling the wind ripping at him, trying to throw him off to his death. Half a minute was all it took, and yet it felt like half a lifetime until he finally wrapped his fingers round the brickwork. Once more, Skiouros was already climbing and far ahead of him.

Just a single look up froze the older brother to the spot.

At twice the height of the previous two climbs, this wall seemed to rise into the heavens like a construction of Allah himself. The small part of his mind that was still processing logical thought and was not

111

given over to blind panic or driving anger told him that this section would actually be easier, for all its height. While the previous two ascents had been short, they had been on flat, featureless walls with only the brickwork itself to aid them. This section had columned window edges, brick arches, protruding sections of wall similar to shortened buttresses and so much more. In his childhood days, Lykaion would have seen this climb as a fun challenge.

The knowledge that he was mid-way up, and that it would be at least equally terrifying to shuffle to the roof edge and contemplate climbing back down, drove him to the first few holds. He was perhaps halfway through the main ascent when the anger was no longer enough to conquer the panic and he stopped dead, fingers gripping the stone, feet frozen and knees shaking dangerously.

'Come on.'

'No.'

Skiouros peered over the roof edge and extended his arm. Their fingertips would still be an arm-length apart, even if he stretched.

'No.'

'You have to, brother. We're nearly up, and you can't just stay there.'

A sudden gust of wind whipped Lykaion's cloak about him and one hand came free. As his bladder gave an involuntary squeeze and leaked a little, the white-icy blindness of panic gripped him and he flailed and grasped for the brick again, almost crying out in terror.

Somehow, in the desperate thrashing of his arm, he found purchase again and pulled himself flat to the surface.

'Can't!'

But when he looked up, Skiouros was not there. Lykaion hadn't realised just how much positive effect his brother's company had been having on his fear until that comforting presence was gone. He felt sick. Perhaps he'd been sick; certainly his mouth tasted funny. His head began to spin with the sensation of falling and he shuddered uncontrollably.

'Get up here now, Lykaion!'

The terrified climber's head snapped upwards again to see the welcome face of Skiouros peering over the edge.

'The Mamluk's in there,' he went on, 'waiting for someone. Stay there and we'll miss it.'

'Can't.'

'Yes you can. Trust in God, or in Allah if you like, or even in me, but do it.'

Slowly, Lykaion released the brick with one hand and desperately reached up and grasped the next one, his heart pounding. He would do it; had to do it, or give up and die here. His fingers were rapidly numbing with the cold and when it got too much for all his digits, he would plummet almost thirty feet to a roof, bounce down it, fall another dozen or more feet and then repeat the process to the paving stones of Mill Street – odd that. Here in the heart of the Ottoman city, a few streets retained their old names.

He was aware at a deeper level that his mind was wandering to avoid facing the current dilemma, until suddenly he felt fingers close on his wrist again and haul him up. Pulling himself, shaking, over the lip, he collapsed flat onto the roof – or as flat as he could on the sloping curved lines of tile.

'Shit, shit, shit, shit, shit!'

'Come on. We're taking too long.'

Lykaion glared at his brother, but Skiouros was already vaulting away up the roof towards one of the smaller domes, where a window stood wide open. The panic still present and hovering on the periphery of his senses, Lykaion followed his brother up the slope of tiles, taking considerably more care and time, and reached the dome with great relief, his fingers folding tight on the window sill.

Skiouros had already disappeared inside, and Lykaion pulled himself up to the window and peered inside without thought, his brain suddenly reeling and swirling as he looked down some fifteen feet to a stone floor. Gripping the window edge tight and shivering uncontrollably, he pulled back from the drop, though not too far as the roof sloped away behind him and down to a horrible descent.

It took him a moment to realise that Skiouros was hanging from the inside of the window frame by his fingertips and, as Lykaion leaned in to question his brother, he saw the thief let go and drop to the floor, where he landed lightly as smooth and professionally as an athlete. A moment later Skiouros was standing and beckoning him. Lykaion swallowed nervously and clambered onto the window, his heart pounding so rapidly it felt like almost one constant hum, the beats melting together. Slowly, and feeling the panic mount again, he swivelled, lowering his feet and then legs over the drop inside, gradually shuffling and inching down until the sill grazed his armpits. Then another drop to his fingertips, and he felt the panic recede. He was only about eight feet from the floor.

The drop was not subtle.

Unlike his brother, who had landed with catlike grace, Lykaion hit the floor with the slap of leather boots on stone. He looked guiltily around as he rose slowly to see Skiouros wincing. The pair stood very still for a long moment, breathing as lightly and quietly as they could until suddenly the silence was rudely broken by the crashing open of a door somewhere below – the front one; all the others were blocked.

Skiouros beckoned to his brother and the pair made for a staircase that led down the inside of one of the outer walls. Moving as quietly as they could, the brothers' footsteps were partially masked by the heavy rhythmic thump of another pair of boots marching through the church below.

A voice suddenly sprang up, barking out authoritatively in Arabic, and a second speaker replied, a note of anger or irritation in its tone.

Lykaion reached the bottom of the stairs and turned to find his brother creeping forward between huge wooden kegs. The very thought of what those containers held was chilling to the blood. The Janissary guards were not allowed even an oil lamp in this building, and it was quite obvious why. As the renegade moved between the aisles, following his brother as quietly as he could, he lost count of how many rows of barrels he could see. They packed most of the former church's ground floor and were stacked two high.

The thief came to a sudden halt and gestured to Lykaion as the deeper of the two voices switched to Turkish.

'Did you hear something?' it said.

There was the tense pause of two people listening intently, and when a pigeon suddenly burst from the low arch of the side aisle in an explosion of flapping and feathers, the second man burst out laughing.

Lykaion's heart pounded all the more with the sudden shock.

'You, friend Qaashiq, are entirely too nervous. Pigeons! This place is alive with the vermin. Look at the shit all over the floor. Don't fall prey to unnecessary panic; this is one of the most secure buildings in the city. It's why I suggested it.'

Creeping forward to Skiouros' position, Lykaion peered between the kegs and the centre of the building opened up before him. Despite having only a narrow peephole, the angle served well to display much of the open space at the centre. In a small arena formed by a circle of powder kegs, passages radiating off between them, two men stood four yards apart. The Mamluk appeared tense and stood with his arms folded, while the new arrival leaned on a stray keg in a relaxed fashion.

Lykaion pointed to the Mamluk and shrugged questioningly at his brother. Skiouros nodded and returned the gesture, pointing at the visitor. Lykaion took another look, just to make sure, and nodded back. Yes; it was Hamza Bin Murad, Corbasi of the Fourteenth Orta. If the fugitive soldier had still harboured any doubts about the culpability of his commanding officer, he felt them melt away at this damning scene.

'I am uncomfortable speaking in your tongue,' the Mamluk spat with a perfect Ottoman inflection.

'You are in my city, at the whim of my Janissaries, so you will speak my tongue. Do not mistake my willingness to take a part in this affair for any kind of respect or pleasure at your presence. You are my enemy, no matter what happens.'

'Perhaps we chose you wrongly, commander?'

Bin Murad's lip curled into an unpleasant sneer.

'No. You chose correctly. No other officer would even countenance your plots.'

The Mamluk shifted uncomfortably.

'But you are different? To be willing to defy your own and sell out your nation.'

Hamza spat on the floor, his hand going to his sword pommel. 'Be very careful how you speak to me, Mamluk. I could live with myself if this all ended here with your brains smeared across the floor.'

'There is no need for such antagonism, commander. You asked for me to come; I'm here. These meetings are dangerous, so I suggest you say your piece and we depart.'

There was an angry pause and then Bin Murad nodded, his hand slipping down from the sword to hang by his side.

'The treasury vizier has turned up with an unfortunate second mouth just beneath his chin. Caught me off-guard, since I wasn't expecting it yet, and forced me to do a little improvising. Your killers are getting ahead of themselves.'

'You never specified a timescale – just a deadline.'

'It was implied, you fool. The longer this is drawn out, the more danger there is. One day. All in one day, I meant.'

The Mamluk took an angry step forward. 'Do not presume to lecture me, Bin Murad. This is not your game, nor mine. We do as we are bidden and will receive our rewards in due course, following which, insha'Allah, we will never have to set eyes on one another again. Now, was there anything else? This meeting is too stupid and dangerous to call for putting forward a simple complaint of no real substance.'

This time, Bin Murad took the step forward and pointed angrily at the ambassador.

'You use fools. Your hashishin or whatever you want to call them these days are clearly overzealous in their devotion to Allah.'

The Mamluk unfolded his arms and clapped his hands condescendingly. 'Some might argue that there is no such thing as too overzealous in the eyes of God, commander.'

'Your killer performed his task on the vizier perfectly, but took time to cut a Christian bitch to pieces in his fervour. While I approve of removing the vile heathens from the world at every opportunity, this particular death was idiotically unnecessary. Such a murder could point unhelpful fingers; it certainly made it too difficult for me to pin it on the Christian, which I would have preferred. I have managed to deflect suspicion so far, but if your other two assassins are no more careful, this is going to become too big and pubic for me to contain. Curb your murderers, Qaashiq. Just tell them to do the job they're paid for and stop dabbling with personal killings.'

The Mamluk nodded slowly as if conceding the point.

Skiouros and Lykaion shared a look as the young thief mouthed the words 'other two' silently. Suddenly it felt very exposed and dangerous in here.

'So if you are dragging the timescale out,' Bin Murad said irritably, 'when will the agha die?'

Lykaion felt his blood chill at the question. Just as the viziers were the men who ran the civil side of the Empire, so the aghas were the men who commanded the military at the very highest levels, and the only agha to whom Bin Murad could possibly be referring here and now was Ahmed Ali bin Nasuh, the commander of the Janissaries. He was the only agha who spent any real time in the city.

'Leave the details to me' the Mamluk said quietly. 'Suffice it to say he will be dining in paradise the day after tomorrow. Other than that, the less you know, the better.'

Bin Murad nodded at the truth of that.

'Just remember your side of the bargain when the army is yours,' the Mamluk said, a note of threat in his quiet voice. 'A deal has two sides. We are not doing this purely for your benefit.'

Bin Murad gesticulated angrily.

'I know what I am to do, Mamluk, and I am not doing this purely for my benefit, either. You would do well to stop treating me as a traitor. I love my Empire and I love my Corps. If it were not for what you can give me, I would have your head on a pike over the Edirne Gate by morning. Bayezid must die, but I take no pleasure in it. Just you make sure your Cem 'Sultan' remembers those who made this possible.'

Lykaion almost staggered back into the kegs, the colour draining from his face as the full impact of what the two men had revealed hit him. Even Skiouros looked shocked. The sultan? Who would even consider moving against the most powerful man in the world? Surely not Cem? The failed usurper was said to be imprisoned by the Pope of Rome and the sultan paid him good money to keep it that way.

'I know you, Bin Murad,' the Mamluk sneered. 'There is nothing that gives you more pleasure than killing. Your reputation after the battle of Yenisehir carried even to Mamluk ears.'

'The sultan is an affront to all good Turks!' Bin Murad spat. 'He dilutes our city and our Empire with heathen Christians – ones that don't even have to convert to stay here – and twisted Armenians and...' he paused to spit on the floor again, 'even Jews. The money-lending filth are starting to take over.'

The Mamluk's nostrils flared, but he folded his arms once more and nodded sagely.

'My own sultan allows these Coptics and Jews in our cities, but they have their place, even if they peddle their heathen ways. Anyway, I am not here to argue religion and race with you. I very much advise against any further meetings until the deeds are all done.'

'We will meet any time I deem it necessary,' Bin Murad snarled. 'And we are safe here with my men surrounding us. But there is one more thing, before you go.'

The Mamluk narrowed his eyes suspiciously. 'A problem?'

'Hardly. One of my Janissaries knows of the murder and is on the run in the city: Hussein Bin Nikos. We will catch him soon enough, though. I have a bounty on his head that would make his own mother turn him in, and he is accused of the very deaths that he reported.'

'Careless, commander. You should have had him executed.'

Bin Murad bridled. 'Just leave it to me. I only mention it at all out of courtesy.'

'Perhaps I can help,' the Mamluk replied, scratching his chin. 'One of my Fida'i is done with his mission. I shall set him onto your fleeing pup. Let him take his knowledge to the grave.'

For a minute Bin Murad stared at the Mamluk as though dumbstruck, but finally he nodded his assent and pointed to the door through which he'd entered.

'Go back to the Bucoleon and stay out of sight.'

The Mamluk – Qaashiq – bowed curtly and turned, striding away from the room. The brothers, wide-eyed and pale, looked at each other in disbelief and turned back to the narrow viewing gap just in time to see commander Bin Murad's temper snap and the officer lay into a keg of powder with his bare fists, pounding on the wood and raising a faint cloud of black dust as he worked out his fury on the container.

Skiouros tugged at his brother's sleeve and pointed to the side aisle. Lykaion nodded, and the pair padded as quietly as they could towards the church's outer wall, any noise they made being masked easily by the raging of the Janissary commander.

Quickly, they moved into the aisle and then along the line of arches and frescos until they were sufficiently distant from the centre to breathe easily.

'What now?' Lykaion asked in a whisper.

'You tell me? This is too big for us.'

'I didn't mean that. I meant getting out of the church. We can't use the front door, but I can't climb that again.'

Skiouros smiled wearily.

'Thought of that.' Leading his brother to the end of the aisle, he rounded a couple of corners and gestured to a small, heavy wooden door, held fast with a lock and with a beam across it.

'You lift the bar and I'll deal with the lock; then we'll be in the garden out back.'

Lykaion sagged with relief and reached up, lifting the heavy beam and crossing to the wall, where he carefully and quietly stood it on its end against the plastered surface. By the time he'd turned back, Skiouros already had the lock dealt with and was replacing some dubious tool in his belt pouch. As the thief gently inched the door open an icy blast hit them, whipping up a cloud of black dust from the floor that alarmed Lykaion enough to make him barrel out of the doorway, propelling his brother before him.

The huge porticoed courtyard garden that had belonged to the church had gone to wrack and ruin, the water system broken and weeds running riot throughout. Despite the neglect, however, the place was still structurally sound, and the columned portico kept its roof intact, surrounding the forgotten flower beds, fountains and lawns. While it did nothing to keep the chill wind away, it kept them nicely shaded and covered.

'What now?' Skiouros asked in a nervous voice. 'Don't suppose you feel like that trip to the harbour yet?'

'We do nothing until we've had time to think and to work this out' Lykaion replied, leaning against a column. 'We go back to your rooms, unless you think your landlord or neighbours are likely to try to claim that bounty?'

'None of them know who you are or even that you're there, and I've not used father's name in many years.' He gave an aggravating smile. 'Besides, we Greeks stick together. No one would sell a countryman out.'

'I think you overestimate the pride of our people, Skiouros. But let's go anyway. I feel the distinct need for a rest somewhere warm. Now get us out of this cloister.'

Chapter 6 – Observations and their consequences

* Cuma (Friday) evening *

Skiouros glared at his brother, his gaze packed with indignant impotence. Lykaion ignored him and kept his own eyes locked on the door of the Bucoleon palace as though he could bring forth their quarry by will alone.

The brothers had exchanged few words that morning and through the afternoon, and the longer the uncomfortable silence grew, the more difficult it became to break it.

After the revelations at the Nea Ekklasia church the previous evening, the pair had returned to Skiouros' room, where they had begun a frank discussion as to the options available; a discussion that had rapidly become a bloody-minded argument as the brothers refused to compromise and repeatedly gainsaid one another.

The subject of the argument had not been the options open to them, per se; half an hour of thought and discussion had easily narrowed down their available options. There was no one in authority they could go to with the problem, no way they would be able to gain access to the agha or the sultan to warn them of the danger they were in, and no feasible way to try and prevent the coming murders since they had no idea where the three assassins could be found. Add to these stumbling blocks the fact that the Janissaries were actively hunting Lykaion and had now been joined in the task by one of the assassins, and doing anything at all was becoming a life-threatening option. The only clear possibility was to maintain their watch on the Mamluk and hope that it would lead them to something useful. It was, simply, the only path available if they wanted to investigate the matter any further.

And there was the crux of the matter and the cause of the row.

Skiouros simply could not comprehend how his brother held any further interest in the matter. He had returned to arguing for the course of flight, offering to pay for and secure the passage himself to any safe haven Lykaion cared to name – even a Muslim one. Anything to get him away from this mess.

The fugitive Janissary, however, refused to move from his position. To flee was not only dishonourable, cowardly and low, but was also permitting agents of an enemy nation and an exiled traitor free reign to continue their campaign of usurpation against the sultan.

It was hard to argue with Lykaion's logic, certainly. That Sultan Bayezid the Second – The Just – deserved the murder planned for him was not something even a devout Christian could claim, and certainly not Skiouros, who had no real enmity towards the ruler, despite the gulf in cultures. And the agha of the Janissaries – a man Lykaion claimed to be of the highest honour and valour – whatever he was like, had to be a preferable man to have in charge of that elite unit than this traitorous Hamza Bin Murad. Even if it came down to simple nationality, Skiouros had to admit that the Greek population of the Empire would experience a new age of terror and pain if the Mamluks were to gain any influence in its running. Lykaion was correct in everything he said, with one glaring exception: it did not have to be their problem.

Their mother and father had gone, the farm no doubt swept up by one of the local Ottoman landowners, and so the only kin the pair had in the city was one another. Neither of them had any career or property to save, now that Lykaion's military life was effectively over. When it came right down to it, Skiouros couldn't actually name anyone other than his brother in the city who he counted as a friend. There was nothing, as far as he was concerned, to keep them in the city. They could watch the implosion of the Ottoman world from a safe beach in the west.

The honour angle was hammered again for a while, and Skiouros had to admit that it felt uncomfortable leaving things to fall on their countrymen, but his counter-attack was, once again, their impotent inability to do anything about it.

Which was why, in Lykaion's opinion, they had to return to

watching the Mamluk and not seek to flee.

And so the argument returned to its root and began the cycle again.

By the time the pair slept, they were hoarse from arguing and as angry as at any meeting they'd had over the past half decade. It was only as they lay down in the blankets, Skiouros on the bed and Lykaion on the floor, that it struck Skiouros just how loud they might have been in the throes of fury and consequently the danger in which they had placed themselves.

Then this morning, when the argument had lulled and there was that precious opportunity to lay it to rest and reconcile, a fresh disagreement had arisen over Lykaion's intention to take his sword out into the city. Skiouros had flatly refused to countenance the idea, arguing the certainty that the sword would be impossible to hide effectively about his person and therefore the very high likelihood of the pair ending up in the clutches of Lykaion's former comrades. The younger man had threatened not to lead his brother through the city's backstreets to the Bucoleon, but Lykaion had pointed out that he now knew the way. The matter had only been settled when Skiouros stated vociferously that he would not open the pharos tower's door for them if Lykaion insisted on such an idiotically dangerous path.

Not long after dawn, and still seething and flatly refusing to speak on the matter, the two had made their way once more to the pharos tower by the ambassador's palace and settled in on the first level's parapet to watch for the architect of this whole nightmare.

The morning wore on in silent and angry monotony.

This session of observation had seen a change in the assigned Janissaries, though still of men from the same orta on rotation, and therefore presumably as culpable in the matter as those being replaced. Around noon a figure had emerged with the appropriate Janissary escort and, though he was not the Mamluk, Skiouros had watched him with interest and curiosity. Dressed in a heavy sheepskin coat and felt hat, huge, furry boots and leather belts with hanging pouches, the man sported an untidy beard and wild hair. The high, angular cheek bones and slight incline to the eyes suggested he might belong to one of the Nomadic tribes from Asia and, having heard the members of the Golden Horde referred to as yellow-skinned, he decided that the fellow in the warm, functional clothes must be the Tatar ambassador. Other than the change of guard and the interesting easterner, however, the day had been one of excruciating dullness, marred even further by the overhanging air of discontent.

In the early afternoon, Skiouros had disappeared up into the city near the great hippodrome, where a man selling koftes and salted breads took the opportunity to seriously overcharge his non-Turkish customer. Upon his return, Lykaion had taken some of the bread and meat and eaten without a word.

And now, as the light began to fade once more and the sun slid into the Propontis, making its waters glow red and casting a bronze shimmer across the horizon, Skiouros had spent so long being silent and glowering that he actually coughed and wheezed with a crackly voice as he tried to talk. He moved sharply back from the parapet and reached for Lykaion, who was leaning back against the wall, giving his tired eyes a break.

'What?' snapped his brother, quietly.

'Something's happening,' hissed Skiouros, pointing to the palace, out of sight over the low stone battlements.

Lykaion was suddenly moving and the pair leaned into the parapet and gazed down on the door of the palace.

The peasant Skiouros had seen approach the doorway, and who had prompted him to disturb Lykaion, was standing patiently waiting, shifting from foot to foot as though nervous about being where he was. The young boy was perhaps nine or ten years of age, dressed in the dirty, colourless rags of the innumerable beggars of the city. One of his arms was gnarled, twisted up in front of him, and it swayed involuntarily as he moved.

'It's just a beggar,' hissed Lykaion.

'It's a beggar visiting the main door of the palace for foreign ambassadors! That's not normal, surely?'

'True,' conceded the older brother, peering down. 'He must be something to do with the Mamluk.'

As the pair watched, their arguments forgotten in the face of this development, the door of the palace swung inwards and a Janissary guard appeared. Lykaion knew from experience how the guard felt about the peasant beggars of the city, regardless of their race or creed, and the suspicious nature of the arrival was only heightened when the beggar handed something to the Janissary and received a coin in return. The beggar said something quietly to which the guard nodded and, retreating inside, closed the door. Outside and once more alone, the boy secreted the coin about his person and then started back along the street towards the hippodrome and then right uphill to the bulk of the old city.

'Come on…'

Skiouros frowned. 'What?'

'We might as well follow him. Whoever he is he knows something.'

Skiouros shook his head. 'He just delivered a message. That was a scrap of paper and there's no way that boy could read and write.'

'But he can still talk,' Lykaion replied ominously.

'We can't follow him.'

'We have to.'

Skiouros grabbed Lykaion's hand and held it up to the dying rays of the sun.

'Look at that.'

'What?'

'Your hand; your skin. You're as pale as me. You might have served with the Janissaries for years, but you're still a Greek to look at. How far do you think you'll get sneaking through the streets after a beggar while there's a price on your head all over the city?'

Lykaion bridled. 'Then you lead. You keep getting me between Phanar and here safely enough!'

'That's different, brother. There you're in the Greek enclave, port areas and the industrial streets down near the water. People just don't notice strangers there, as many of them are killers and thugs. That beggar's headed into the heart of the Ottoman city. You won't last five minutes.'

'Well there's nothing else happening. Are we going to sit here for days in the hope the Mamluk shit makes an appearance?'

Skiouros' eyes flashed angrily.

'Not if I can help it. I'm still for taking ship before I end up riding a pointed stake in the Blachernae dungeons. Death by Ottoman torture is not high on my list of priorities.'

'I am not leaving.'

'Then if you're set on this course, we're going to have to find some way to blend in better than we do. I know a few tricks. It's heading towards freezing now the sun's gone down, so let's go home and then tomorrow we can disguise ourselves a little and come back. That way we can try a pursuit if we get the opportunity. But not now.'

Lykaion glared at him for a long moment and then nodded. 'Phanar again, then.'

'Come on.'

By the time the two brothers had reached the familiar street in the Greek enclave, the sun had disappeared entirely and the streets were lit only by the silvery shimmer of the moon in its icy, crystal sky. The wind blowing up the thoroughfares from the Golden Horn was bone-chilling, and the pair were grateful to reach the security of the wooden tenement.

Entering the room, the brothers threw off their cloaks, despite the cold that breached even the house's walls and shutters. Skiouros added to his list of requirements the theft – or more likely the purchase, given his brother's disapproving presence – of more blankets for the room, and possibly even a cushion or two. Perhaps tomorrow he could add a trip to Balat and the house of Judah ben Isaac to his plans? Apart from retrieving the money for such purchases, it would also be nice to have in pocket the funds to cover a passage to Crete, should Lykaion suddenly see the light.

Gritting his teeth at the whole mess, Skiouros lay on his bed, watching his brother wrapped in blankets on the floor, and wishing that just for one moment he would stop being so bloody-minded and arrogantly superior. He was still pondering how like their father his older brother was when he fell into an exhausted and deep sleep.

It wasn't the creak that woke Skiouros. Some strange God-sent inner sense snapped his eyes open just in time to hear the first deep groan of the board. Hardly daring to breathe, he lay still and silent, listening intently for confirmation. It came a moment later with the slightly flatter tone of the second step giving under a light foot, probably in a soft leather boot.

By the time the third step gave the barely-audible squeak that indicated an unaware climber had placed his foot centrally on the board, Skiouros was sliding soundlessly out of bed and reaching for his doublet that hung on a wall peg near his head. Stepping lightly across the room, he crouched and grasped Lykaion's shoulder.

His brother's eyes shot open in a panicky manner, his mouth opening to cry out in alarm just as Skiouros' hand closed around it, the index finger of his other hand coming up to his lips in a 'shushing' motion.

Lykaion, his expression betraying his confusion, sat up and stared as Skiouros mimed someone climbing stairs with slowness and great care, his hand raised as if brandishing a knife. Pointing at the door behind which the stairs descended, he handed Lykaion's doublet to him and began to pull on his boots.

Still listening for the tell-tale squeaks, creaks and groans, Skiouros stepped past the bed and carefully, quietly, pushed open the window shutters. A hiss from somewhere on the stairs bore the very distinctive sounds of a blade being drawn. Now, Lykaion was with him, sheathed sword in his hand, fastening it to his belt with altogether too much noise for his brother's liking.

Gesturing out of the window, Skiouros motioned his intention swiftly and silently. Lykaion's eyes widened as he shook his head. Time was, however, running out, and Skiouros simply replied with a nod, climbing up, crouching on the window sill. In half a heartbeat, he turned back to the room and, a crazed smile on his face, leaned back over the drop. In a fluid move, with the grace of an acrobat, the thief let go of the window frame and grasped for the jutting balcony of the room above.

His fingers finding easy purchase, he moved on without a pause, launching his feet from the sill and using the momentum of his swing, directed by the pressure of his hands, to sweep his legs up and hook a foot around the balcony's rail.

There was an ominous creak from the ancient, feeble structure, but it held and, in a heartbeat, Skiouros was gone from sight, one floor up.

Lykaion, his heart pounding with terror, stepped forward to the window and made the mistake of looking down.

As he clung to the window sill, he heard the shuffling of feet outside the door of the room. The intruder had reached their residence and was still maintaining his own silence, though he could not know how alert and prepared his prey was.

The decision was a tough one. While his rational mind told him that even if he fell from the window, a one-storey drop would be likely to at most break his leg, his fears told him that the window was a one-way trip to screaming agony. Yet whoever this person was who was about to reach for the door, he felt confident enough in his abilities to come alone, and clearly had death in mind, from the sound of the blade being unsheathed. Lykaion was an able soldier, but a far cry from a master swordsman. And what if the man also had a gun? If he was Janissary it was more than possible.

His mind was made up as he saw Skiouros appear in the window once more, his lower half anchored on the upstairs balcony, his torso hanging upside down in empty space as his hands beckoned for Lykaion. Damn it! Clearly the thief had done this before.

There was the faintest sound that the renegade soldier felt sure was the noise of a gloved hand on the door handle.

Bracing himself and mouthing 'Allahu Akbar' in silent prayer, the older brother lifted his foot to the window sill and, without a pause – he knew for certain that any pause would see him falter and abandon the decision – used the bent knee to launch himself out into the open air.

A thousand images raced through his mind in a split second: Hadrianople and the family farm; Mother reaching out as her boys were taken from her; Father telling him the old Greek tales of heroes; Skiouros pounding away from the Devsirme column into the unknown streets; a Mamluk killer standing with his own commander.

He was barely aware of the hands of his brother as they caught his wrists, mid-flight, and the pair swung for a second.

'Climb!' hissed Skiouros, but Lykaion needed no such encouragement. He was already reaching up and grasping his brother's shoulder in a desperate attempt to clamber up from the empty space.

As Lykaion climbed, Skiouros peered at the window. It would have been easier to drop to the alley, of course. It would only have been an eight-foot fall once they were out and hanging. But there were problems with that. There was always the possibility that the intruder was not alone, and any sort of flight into the alley might well run them straight into even deeper trouble. Moreover, he knew from sad experience that if he dropped to the alley and ran, any intruder who got to the window would see him before he reached a corner.

Better then to appear entirely absent. He had practised swinging up onto the balcony a dozen times and knew he could easily manage it as a flight route before being spotted. He'd never tried it with a passenger, though, and certainly not one who hated heights. But it was still the best way. Skiouros was a thief, not a killer, and a thief learned quickly to run and to evade, if he wanted to be a thief for very long. Never stick around for trouble if there's a way out. Why could Lykaion not learn that simple lesson? They could have been lounging on a merchant galley far across the Propontis by now, out of the reach of the city's authorities.

In the same moment, he felt relief from pressure as his brother reached the safety of the balcony and let go of him, heard Lykaion's almost explosive release of tension above, and saw the figure move into the room.

It was just the blink of an eye.

The intruder was cloaked, lithe and short. Little could be made out in the shadows but for the clear murderous intent, a short, straight blade of the Caucasus type glinting in his grip. The briefest flash of filigree-fine thread in the other hand told Skiouros all he needed to know, and he hauled himself up to the balcony and out of sight half a heartbeat before the figure turned to regard the open window.

Motioning Lykaion to absolute silence, Skiouros crouched down low, trying not to cause the wood to groan, and put an eye to a crack between planks through which he could just make out the open square of darkness in the wall below.

He felt a chill run through him as the intruder's knife suddenly appeared through the window with a swift, neat slashing motion that would have wounded any flesh outside within a foot of the frame. Then, assured of the fact that no one waited by the sill for him, the man's head appeared, hooded in his dark cloak, through the window. The hood moved this way and that, scanning the street and then the walls of the building.

Finally, the head turned, the hood falling away with gravity's pull, and the face looked up at the balcony above. Skiouros shut his eye on the improbable chance that the intruder might see the white gleaming through the crack.

But he'd not been so quick to squeeze his eyelids shut that he'd not got a quick look at the man who had clearly come here to kill them. That he was an assassin had been clear as Skiouros had hung from the balcony and seen the steel-wire garrotte in the man's hand. More details had fallen into place as the man's face turned towards him and the hood fell away, revealing the walnut skin, darkened eyes and sharp nose of an Arabian or Egyptian Mamluk.

The brothers remained absolutely motionless, barely daring to breathe, and Skiouros could hear the faint rustle of the clothing and cloak as the assassin made another pass of the alley and walls before retreating in through the window.

As the thief's eye snapped open once more, still at the crack, he briefly saw the cloak billowing as it disappeared inside.

The man was alone. The brothers could have used the alley, after all, but the decision he'd made had still been the sensible one. Leaning across to Lykaion, he cupped his hand to his brother's ear. The lightest of whispers would be lost in the cold wind blowing along the alley, after all.

'Mamluk assassin,' he hissed.

Lykaion nodded with no sign of surprise, and then cupped his own hand and leaned in to Skiouros. 'He won't stop until I'm dead.'

Skiouros felt his spirits sink as he realised his brother was right. He'd blindly assumed that the man would now depart and look elsewhere, but that was short-sighted at best. 'He'll come after me now, too.'

Lykaion frowned, so Skiouros leaned in again. 'If he's come here, he knows about me, and must assume I know what you do. We're both marked now.'

'Then we've got to kill him now.'

Skiouros leaned back, shaking his head with wide eyes and mouthing the word 'assassin'. Lykaion leaned forward and spoke almost silently.

'Maybe he only knows about you. Better to get rid of him now before he starts rounding up friends.'

'You can't fight an assassin!'

'I don't intend to,' hissed Lykaion and, leaning back, he mimed knifing the man in the back, a hand over his mouth. Skiouros leaned in again, his face bleak.

'How?'

The former Janissary paused. He hadn't thought that far ahead yet. He could go into this balcony's room and down the stairs to get to the intruder, but the owner was probably in there. There would be a noisy fuss and the game would be up very quickly. As for over the balcony... well, Lykaion didn't even want to think about that. He'd only managed to get up here through the split second decision that he couldn't stay and fight and the fact that it had been so fast he had not had the time to panic properly.

'Exactly,' Skiouros whispered, seeing the look on his brother's face.

There was a moment's pause, and then they both heard the room's door being closed again. The assassin was leaving.

Skiouros closed his eyes and heaved a sigh of relief but when he opened them, they widened in astonishment.

Lykaion was holding out a knife, hilt first, a look of challenge in his eyes.

'What?' the thief mouthed at him, and the older brother's eyes slipped to the balcony's edge and the drop to the street. Though already wide, Skiouros' eyes bulged as he grasped what his brother was suggesting.

'No. I can't.'

'You have to. This will be the only opportunity we'll ever have to take him by surprise, and neither of us will be able to kill him in a straight fight.'

'No.'

'If you don't he'll only find us again, and next time we might not see him coming. You fancy a knife in the neck in the dark?'

Skiouros shuddered; not at the thought of a knife blow, but his imagination was furnishing him with a fairly good idea of how it felt to have that loop of steel wire drop around his neck and pulled tight. Try as he could to fight it, Lykaion was right. If they could end it now, they had to do just that.

And it would have to be him.

Reaching out with a grim expression, Skiouros wrapped his fingers around the knife's hilt and took it from his brother, examining the gleaming blade with distaste. It was reasons like this that he'd run away from the Janissary intake in the first place.

Momentarily he considered a quick prayer for luck, but reasoned that God probably frowned on people about to commit murder and, instead, gripped Lykaion's shoulder briefly and then moved to the rail and climbed lightly over. Jamming the knife between his teeth, he lowered himself until he was hanging from the balcony by his fingertips and then let go.

There was just the faintest 'slap' as the thief's feet hit the alley, sending up a dried cloud of desiccated shit and other muck. Rising from the bent-kneed landing, Skiouros looked up to give his brother the 'all fine' signal, but Lykaion was nowhere to be seen. Of course, the drop would encourage the older brother to stay away from the rail.

Without allowing himself time to start panicking, Skiouros scurried over to the back door of the building. There was always the chance that the assassin would leave by the front entrance onto the main street and he would not have to do what they'd decided, but he knew in his heart that the kind of man who carried a garrotte, and whose mere skin tone would mark him as an enemy of the Ottoman people, would have used narrow alleys to get here and would use the back door for access.

With a deep breath, he peered into the doorway, noting with a thrill of fear the sound of a man carefully descending the creaky staircase. Seconds were all that he had. Gripping the knife as though it had a life of its own and were struggling to escape his grasp, Skiouros stepped to the side of the door and flattened himself against the wall. Briefly, he looked up at the balcony just above and a few yards along the wall, but there was still no sign of Lykaion.

A heartbeat later he heard the last stair creak.

Thump – his heart pounded in the silence.

No sound from the corridor.

Thump.

The faint sound of footsteps padding along the corridor.

Thump.

Louder steps.

Thump.

The swirl of a cloak's edge in the doorway. Skiouros flattened himself back against the wall so hard he wondered if he might splinter the wood. If only it could swallow him whole. Holding his breath, he tensed, the fingers of his free hand flexing momentarily while the knuckles of his right whitened on the knife's grip. He braced his left foot ready to lunge.

The assassin stepped from the building, but at an oblique angle, off towards the far side of the doorway. Even as Skiouros was lunging forward, one hand raised to hook round a head that was now out of reach, a blade moving to penetrate a back that wasn't there, he realised he'd underestimated the killer.

The assassin, clearly prepared for such an attack, had neatly sidestepped the possibility and his own blade, still unsheathed, swept through the space Skiouros had expected him to occupy and sliced a neat line along the thief's upper arm; not deep, but enough to make him cry out and withdraw sharply.

Darting back to his original position, Skiouros raised his knife defensively, as though it would do him an ounce of good.

The hood fell away once more to reveal the Mamluk's clean-shaven head, his gleaming white eyes and teeth showing up sharply in contrast to his skin in the shadowy alley. The blade in the man's hand no longer glinted, as it blurred and whirled in the expert grip of a highly trained and talented killer.

The knife was suddenly in the man's other hand, so fast that Skiouros couldn't have predicted it and, as the thief watched the killer's blade-hand carefully, the second blow came from the wrong place.

The knife point struck his eye-socket and by some miracle slid on the bone and scraped along his cheek, taking a nick out of his ear instead of sinking through the eye and deep into the brain as the man had clearly intended. With a cry of agony, Skiouros leapt back, flailing helplessly with his own knife. Through the fiery pain he tried to concentrate, though suddenly his left eye was blinded with a rush of blood and he had to blink it several times and then keep it squeezed shut.

The Mamluk laughed and said something in Arabic – a language incomprehensible to the Greek thief. He had a reasonable grip of Turkish, and some words transferred between the two, but not enough to help.

The assassin changed footing and the blade moved between hands again twice in quick succession.

Then he lunged.

Skiouros tried to counter with his pitiful defensive blade, only to find that the blow had been a feint faster than he'd believed possible. One blink of his clear eye and the man's left hand had been driving for his face with the gleaming blade – the next, that hand was empty as it came forward. Skiouros had only a fraction of a second to register the blade, now in the other hand, streaking towards his breast. He was going to die with that carefully chosen blow.

God in Heaven...

The Mamluk, his feinting free hand and the deadly knife suddenly vanished from sight as one hundred and sixty pounds of fugitive Janissary landed on him from a two-storey drop.

Skiouros stared as his brother's feet smashed the assassin aside, sending him sideways with a gasp to land in a heap in the ordure of the alley, his knife skittering away and disappearing into the shadows.

Lykaion, his face white as death with fear, rose slowly from his landing, his knee buckling slightly.

'Never... again!' he declared, shaking. Skiouros grinned.

In the alleyway, winded and wounded, the Mamluk killer rolled over, groaning, trying to get to his knee. Skiouros' darting eyes gave Lykaion the nudge he needed and, gritting his teeth, he drew his sword and took three steps across the alleyway to the fallen assassin. His curved blade had killed three Mamluks in battle over the past two years and he had no qualms about adding a fourth to his list.

The assassin was on one knee now and reaching into the folds of his cloak with a little difficulty, given how the garment had twisted as he fell. Not allowing him time to produce some horrible weapon, Lykaion stepped one more pace and drove his sword down at the Mamluk.

As the point hit the man just above the collarbone and began to drive inwards, the assassin screamed 'Murderer!' in Turkish.

The sword slid home into the man's chest, slicing through a lung before exiting near his spine below a shoulder blade, the curved point turning up towards the wall opposite.

'Murderer!' the man repeated, this time in Greek, but as a breathless rasp and with no real power.

Somewhere out on the main street there was a cry of alarm. Lykaion withdrew his blade, watching with dispassion as it came free from the man's neck with a sucking sound and a spray of blood that spattered his braes.

Skiouros was suddenly by his side, one hand going up to wipe away the blood at his eye and ear. The initial pain was dying away now, leaving a dull throb, but the blood still flowed free. 'Come on!'

Another voice called out on the street. The agonised cry of the Mamluk had attracted attention; probably just late-night drunks returning to their homes, but even that was too much of a danger to hang around for.

'We have to go!' Skiouros added as Lykaion stared down at the Mamluk.

'Half a minute,' the Janissary replied in an emotionless voice. As Skiouros watched, itching to move, his elder brother took a step back and bent his knee, bringing his curved blade out to one side. The Mamluk, still struggling to breathe, bloody froth bubbling from his lips, looked up with an unrepentant expression – one that stayed on his face even as it bounced along the street and came to rest in the gutter.

Lykaion watched the headless body fall to the alley floor and then grasped the dead man's cloak, using it to wipe the crimson mess from his blade.

'We should search him,' Lykaion said quietly.

Skiouros, however, was listening to the sounds out in the street and noted the addition of several new voices to the noise now, including one in Turkish.

'We have to go now!'

Lykaion glared at the corpse and finally straightened and nodded, turning as he sheathed his sword.

'Where, though?'

'Follow me,' Skiouros said, turning and jogging along the street in the opposite direction to the growing sound of approaching people. Lykaion gave a wistful look at the corpse he'd not had time to search and then ran off after his brother.

At the end of the street they turned and made their way along a tiny passage, not much more than shoulder wide, between houses, before bursting out into another alley. Skiouros paused.

'Put that away,' he gestured at the sword. Lykaion blinked and then nodded, realising just how much attention he could attract running with a drawn sword if he was seen. Sheathing it, he unfastened the buckle from his belt and gripped it, holding it tight to his side so that it was less visible and did not swing as he ran.

'I wish we'd had time to search him. What if he had something about his person that condemns us?'

Skiouros shook his head. 'He's a professional. He wouldn't carry anything that dangerous with him. I doubt anything will lead back to us. He's a Mamluk – an enemy of the Empire – with an assassin's weapons, dead in an alley – in the Greek quarter, no less. If anything, the Greeks hate the Mamluks more than your Ottomans. He'll be stripped bare of anything interesting or valuable and will turn up on the doorstep of the nearest guard post in the morning.'

'That might be good,' Lykaion smiled unpleasantly. 'Would be a nice message to Bin Murad and his friends.'

'I certainly doubt it will be an end to it, though. We can't go back to my room.' It was said with a deep sense of regret – not because he'd become emotionally attached to the place, but because he knew it inside and out; knew how to defend and protect himself there and all the quick exits. And because he was still paid up rent-wise for weeks.

'So where do we go?' Lykaion asked quietly. His years of service in the army, either in battle against the Mamluk or policing the streets of Ottoman Istanbul, had failed to prepare him for the possibility of being on the run in the old city where the Turkish influence was small. He felt utterly lost.

'I have an idea. You might not like it, but we're running low on options so you'll just have to trust me.'

Glancing suspiciously at him, Lykaion gestured onwards.

They ran.

Not once in the next ten minutes did they pass a place that Lykaion recognised and it surprised him just how little he knew of the area. There was, of course, a bright side to that. If he, as a Greek-born Janissary, knew so little of the city, then very few of his comrades would know any more. Essentially, they were relatively safe from the Turkish authorities here.

The same could not be said about Greeks hungry for rewards.

Or Mamluk assassins, of whom Lykaion had to remind himself there were still at least two in the city.

Suddenly, they rounded a corner and the thief leading them came to a halt. Ahead, where the street opened out into a wide area of grass, stood a sprawling Byzantine church.

'You have to be joking,' Lykaion said sourly, a cold shiver running through him.

'Find me a better hiding place and I'll think on it,' Skiouros said quietly. Lykaion glanced around as they took a few steps forward to the edge of the grass. Old Greek tombstones jutted here and there, but many were lost. Much of the grass was deep and untended, while in one area off towards the left the grass and tombs had been cleared entirely. A blocked-in arcade fronted the building, though the central arch contained a solid door, and the others presented a high arced window at the top, where the blocking had stopped to allow light to penetrate within. Some of the closed arches had heavy beams resting against them.

'What's happening here?'

'Your noble sultan is planning to convert the place into a mosque. Work started last year and they've done bits, but all the workers were pulled off the project this spring and sent to some other work. The place has stood empty half a year. Welcome to the former Church of Saint Saviour – the "country church".'

As Lykaion eyed the building with discomfort, his brother padded across the open ground towards the building. Following him, Lykaion glanced around. The church was surrounded by the grassy cemetery but beyond that the jumbles of timber housing formed an almost continual circular perimeter with very few windows or gaps.

Seemingly the occupants had no wish to look out upon the graves of their ancestors. The only thing that gave him an idea of their location was the looming bulk of the city's great walls jutting up behind the buildings.

Despite his inherent discomfort with the idea of taking shelter in a house of the Christian God, he had to admit that it was as good a hiding place as they could hope for.

He quickly caught up with his brother at the central door arch as Skiouros was finishing some arcane manoeuvre that ended with a click and the portal swinging open. The thief put away his tools and smiled at Lykaion.

'I realise that you don't like this but bear in mind that our deal still stands, and you'd be a lot more comfortable on a Venetian merchant ship.'

Lykaion shook his head and nipped past his brother into the darkness of the church's interior. Skiouros shrugged and followed him, closing the door behind them and allowing a moment for his eyes to adjust to the darkness. He had been in here a number of times over the years. The church had stopped serving as an active place of Christian worship following the city's fall to Mehmet, and the interior had begun to decay with the surprising speed that such buildings do with only a decade of neglect. Indeed, the Ottoman workers and architect had done nothing on their plan for 'Islamicising' the building beyond repairing some of the worst damage and removing broken or dangerous stonework. It had become a useful place to pass the time when angry eyes were searching the enclave for a young thief.

Strolling into the outer narthex – the church's entryway – he trod lightly on the hexagonal tiles and passed through the archway and into the inner narthex, a highly decorative passage with streaked marble walls and a ceiling of mosaics. Barely glancing left and right, he stepped on through the doorway opposite and into the main church.

Despite his care and time in allowing his sight to adjust, he still almost fell over a bag of mortar mix next to a barrow left carelessly beside the door by a departing worker. Walking on past them and cursing with words rarely heard in a church, he entered the naos and moved into the very centre beneath the dome. Looking up, he saw the beautiful mosaic picked out strangely by the moonlight shining in through the small, high windows around the circumference. Glancing around and through the door, he spotted Lykaion in the side chapel, his neck craned, looking up at the astoundingly complex and ancient mosaic ceilings.

Smiling at the fascination that seemed to hold the attention of a man who was nervous over even entering a Christian church, Skiouros strolled across the naos and through the connecting doorway.

'Beautiful, aren't they?'

Lykaion nodded absently, his face upturned. 'They are astounding. Don't have them in the camii – the mosques. They're forbidden. This will all be plastered over when it changes. I love Allah and his prophets, but there are aspects of my worship I would change if I could.' He frowned. 'The prophet looks sad. I fear he looks at me, actually, with sadness.'

'The prophet?' Skiouros fell in alongside his brother.

'Isa. Christos as you call him. He seems to disapprove of me.'

'Perhaps he wants you to go board a ship for Crete?' Skiouros replied with a weary smile. 'Watch out!'

Lykaion looked sharply at Skiouros as the younger brother leapt forward and grabbed him, hauling him aside and preventing him from striding straight into the deep hole in front of him. Had Lykaion continued to walk forward with his gaze locked on the ceiling, he would most certainly have fallen in.

'You see?' he said as he teetered on the edge, peering into the darkness. 'Isa Christos disapproves of me.'

'It's the crypt. They're replacing some of the flags and repairing the church's sub-structures. Just be careful. There may be other holes. Now settle in. I'm going outside to wash my head and clear off this blood. I think the cuts are drying up.'

Lykaion stared down into the black, trying to decide whether the pit might just be the entrance to hell. Or whether, given the past two days, it could instead be a convenient exit from it?

Chapter 7 – A house divided

* Cumartesi (Saturday) morning *

Skiouros awoke with that strange lurch of a person who feels they should be doing something and have been caught napping off guard. His eyes rolled around and his surroundings reasserted themselves in his consciousness. The church; they were in the church. Nothing untoward had happened; it was just morning. His cheek and ear throbbed with yesterday's dulled pain.

His roving eye scanned the building in the watery, cold morning light that shone in through the high windows and the glazed triple aperture in the east wall. The church's extensive decoration which flooded the senses was all the more startling and eye-catching in the light, and it took a moment for Skiouros to notice Lykaion's cloak lying rumpled beside the straw mattress on the floor across the room, where he'd slept. The sudden sense of alarm that he felt disappeared almost instantly as he heard his brother's footsteps off in the parekklesion chapel, the sound of Skiouros' old worn boots familiar even with someone else's feet in them.

Slowly, shivering in the church's chilling air, he unwrapped the cloak from around himself and then, standing, fastened it about his neck once more. Quietly, he padded over to the door that led to the extraordinarily decorated side chapel, a pleasant and awe-inspiring assault on the senses. Every wall and every inch of ceiling was cluttered with painting or mosaic, the floors tiled in fascinating marble shapes.

Lykaion stood close to the hole down which he'd almost fallen the

138

previous night, his cloak and the cold apparently forgotten, his neck craned as he studied the images, chin cradled in one hand.

'Good morning.'

Lykaion turned at the voice and nodded at his brother before returning his gaze to the ceiling.

'It is, of course, an affront to God to have images like these. Just as the Bible condemns idolatry, so does the Qur'an. But I have to admit to sadness at the thought that these will all disappear under white plaster soon.'

'Paintings can be repainted,' Skiouros replied with a shrug.

'Some things can never be replaced, brother. Something similar can be put in its position, but it will never quite be the same.'

He unfolded his arms and uncradled his chin, pointing at the frescoes.

'See there? That is the most appalling image to a true believer. The prophet Isa – Christos – resurrecting, as though he were God himself. That is why the faiths will never be at ease. And yet, I feel no discomfort looking at it.'

He turned, a strange look on his face. 'Do you realise how odd that is? I've avoided setting foot inside a church for so many years, not because it's forbidden or because I hate them, but because I was a little nervous about how it would feel.'

'It's only a building.'

Lykaion's nose wrinkled a little. 'To you, perhaps. You were never a pious boy, if I remember rightly. I was Father Simonides' little disciple, while you were always in search of the next thrill. It seems somehow ironic that you who are still an open worshipper of the Christian God devote so little of your soul to him while I who am a true son of Allah was once a devoted child of the Church and can see more grace and power in these images than you.'

He turned and gestured to the various frescos with a sweep of his arm. 'I wonder if the other Janissary converts feel like this? It is not a subject openly discussed in the guard. I find that, despite knowing in my heart that Allah is the only God and Mohammed his prophet, I feel comfortable with the idea of Christos rising as the offspring of Allah. After all, we in the Janissaries follow the Bektasi – a Holy Trinity of sorts; if I can feel comfortable with that, why not with a "son" of God?'

Skiouros frowned. It was strange to hear his brother in such frank and reasoned discussion after so many years of heated argument between them, but the simple fact was that the subject was counter-productive... or was it?

'There is still time for us to leave the city, you know? To turn our back on all this trouble and seek out some peace, like both Holy books urge.'

'No. Sometimes there are things that have to be done, even if there is no chance of success or possibility of reward. I think you misunderstand my thoughts, brother.'

'You've come to some sort of understanding, I see. It would certainly make it easier for you if we went to Crete.'

'It is the very reason we cannot do so. I and the good men in the Janissaries are sons of Allah, but we were all once sons of the Church. I suspect it gives us a unique perspective. And yet, Sultan Bayezid seems to have a level of acceptance that I had not understood until now. He is – more so even than I am – a son of the prophet and of God until death, and yet he advocates peaceful coexistence with the Christians and the Jews; even the thrice-cursed Armenian ones. He can see beyond the trappings of their religion to the fact that they are men, and he treats them as such.'

'He taxes them heavily.'

'Mere mortal commerce. Imagine what would happen if that throne were occupied by a Mamluk zealot? Or a man such as Hamza Bin Murad? Someone has to try to stand in the way for the sake of all that is good and reasonable in the world.'

Skiouros sighed. 'I was uncomfortable enough with the honour thing. Let's not turn this into a crusade as well.'

Lykaion smiled oddly. 'Interesting choice of words from a Christian. But that is the long and the short of it, brother. The sultan will paint over these images and inscribe the teachings of the Qur'an over the top, but some churches are still yours, and he does not attempt to rework men's beliefs the way he reworks a church – beyond the necessity for the Janissary intake. If he is removed and his enemies take the throne, we may see every Christian and Jew in the city placed on the hook, or the cross, or the stake. Imagine Phanar and Balat full of pointed pales, each bearing a stinking, screaming, writhing body. Could you in all truth flee to your wonderland of Crete and leave that to happen? I, for one, would suffer with a dreadful conscience for the rest of my life.'

'I believe I could live with it, since the alternative is very possibly ending up on one of those spikes myself.'

'But I could not. And if you were a "good" Christian, neither could you.' He sighed. 'Anyway, we took vows over the altar of your patron vow-taker in that ruined church. I promised only to leave when I saw no alternative, and I still see an alternative. You promised to stay and help me. Well once you've done what you said you would do this morning, I will free you from that vow.'

'Lykaion...'

'No. I must stay and face whatever comes my way and try to stop this, but if you do not feel the same call to the task, you should leave. I want you to leave; to know that at least my brother is safe somewhere, and hopefully away from the path of crime.'

'I'm not going and leaving you here. You and I are the only ones left.' Skiouros grinned. 'Besides, you'd not last a day on these streets without me.'

Lykaion scratched his chin. 'Perhaps you're right. Perhaps not. But I will welcome the aid for now. You will go soon enough, though.'

'Not yet. For now, stay here and keep out of sight. I must go to the market and grab a few things quickly. I'll be back in ten minutes.'

The older brother nodded and waved Skiouros away calmly, going back to his study of the figures on the walls and ceilings.

With a last glance at his quiet, serious sibling, the thief rubbed his hands together for warmth and strode off towards the church door. Carefully, he peered through the grille near the handle to make sure the front was unobserved and, seeing no one, opened the door and scurried outside, closing it behind him.

The sun was still low enough that its presence behind the houses was only indicated by a lighter patch in the sky, and a white frost had formed on the grass around the church. Skiouros did up the collar of his doublet and pulled his cloak tight around his shoulders before hurrying out into the street beyond the encircling wall of wooden housing, his breath creating a white cloud that drifted away on the chill breeze.

It occurred to him briefly that there was the faintest possibility that he too was now being sought after the events of last night, but the chances were small. There was no obvious tie between the Mamluk's body and Skiouros' room and, while the information could easily have been leaked from the Mamluk assassin and his master to Bin

Murad, that was obviously not the case, or it would have been an orta of guards that had come for them in the night, and not a single killer. Clearly at this point the assassins were still working independently of the Janissaries, thank the Lord.

Satisfied at his logic, Skiouros moved into the streets and made his way to the spice market that filled the open space between the Petra monastery and the Aetios gardens. Already, the market was thriving, with new arrivals still filling their stalls and early shoppers moving about haggling and arguing over the quality of the goods on offer.

A cold chill that had nothing to do with the weather ran through Skiouros as he moved among the stalls. A mere three days ago he had strolled into another market in the district after a meeting with his brother, and the events of that morning had snowballed into somewhat cataclysmic proportions.

Trying not to think too much on the matter, he perused the stalls until he spotted a Syrian merchant balancing the last of his wares on his trestle. Such foreign traders were uncommon in much of the Greek enclave, but were not an uncommon sight in the spice markets, since such goods naturally came north and west through Syria, Persia and Arabia. The better of the traders would spend five days of their week in the city selling in the great Spice Market in the Ottoman centre, and would then spend two days touring the outer enclaves to rid themselves of the lower-quality or excess goods before returning to their caravans and heading south once more.

'You see something you like?' the merchant oozed at him, his Greek language surprisingly good, but with a thick Syrian accent.

'This is the last of your cinnamon. You have no more? None fresher?'

'Fresh? Pah! It is sealed in containers for the journey and only open this one week.'

'And we shall not mention the half a year it languished in there first?' Skiouros asked with a grin, the familiar cut and thrust of the haggle taking over.

'For you I offer cheap, yes? Ten akce for a bundle.'

Skiouros pulled a face. 'Ten? Are you insane? The sandstorms of your desert have worn away your brain, my friend. Even many times fresher I would only offer you five.'

'Then you waste my time with your babble, Greek. Move along and bother someone else.'

'I will give you two for a bundle, but I will take all seven bundles.'

The merchant feigned a horrified expression, his shrewd eyes making a calculation even as he blustered. 'My poor wife who waits for me in Dimashq would never stop screaming at me. For two akce a bundle, one of my children starves for a month! Could even a Christian stoop to starving a little girl just to save a measly coin?'

Skiouros pursed his lips. 'I've never met your children, but if they are as untrustworthy as their father, they will undoubtedly steal whatever else they need to survive. Sixteen akce for the lot, then?'

'Thirty for all seven bundles. Then my child will eat and honour the name of the Christ prophet in thanks.'

'I don't give a swollen fig about the Christ prophet's name in Syria. Twenty.'

'Twenty-six.'

'Twenty-three.'

'Done.'

The two men clasped hands in agreement and the merchant, grinning like a man who had pulled off a great trick, bagged up the cinnamon bundles.

'Is there anything else you seek, my Greek friend?'

'Yes, but I doubt you'll have it. I look for khave?'

The merchant nodded sadly. 'I wish I had such a thing. It is a rare commodity here and those who bring it from Arabia go home bedecked with gold. Half a dozen traders I have spoken to came with it but mostly it is sold to the Kiva Han – the coffee house near the great mosque. You might find some here, but only on the expensive stalls and even then it will be the floor sweepings that the Kiva Han would not take.'

Skiouros smiled. 'Floor sweepings sounds just right for me. Thank you my friend. May your return journey be smooth and calm.'

The merchant gave him a sour look. 'Not from what I hear. Across the straits the lands are wracked with terrible storms. I might just have to spend much of my profit wintering in this northern hole.'

Skiouros frowned as he suddenly pictured the Romani witch and her warning outside the ruined baths three days ago. A shiver ran through him.

'Perhaps the prophet will be kind and send the storms elsewhere so that I may take my earnings home,' the man added with upcast eyes.

'Well it's important to worship the profit, eh?' Skiouros smiled, though with little humour.

The Syrian laughed and passed over the bag of cinnamon. 'Good day. May Allah and his prophet smile upon your endeavours this day.'

'I would like that. Goodbye.'

Trying not to think too hard on the storms across the Hellespont, Skiouros moved on through the stalls until he spotted an Arabian merchant with what looked suspiciously like a khave sack beneath his table, a measuring scoop jutting from the top. That it stood open, unprotected from the elements, confirmed its low quality.

Quickly, Skiouros approached the merchant and began the process of haggling once more, though his attention was quickly divided. A chance mention of the word 'Janissary' at the next stall drew his ear. Rattling through the sales routine automatically, failing to achieve the best deal with the merchant and not really paying attention, Skiouros concentrated on the two men chatting at the other stall.

'How?' asked one.

'Poison, they say,' said the other in hushed tones.

'Fucking Janissaries deserve it. Someone should poison the whole bunch.' Skiouros felt his heart start to beat faster as he listened to the two Greeks.

'I don't disagree; they'd gut you as soon as look at you, but you're missing the point, Andros. We're not talking about some piss-filled little convert carrying a cooking pot. This is the damned agha we're talking about!'

Skiouros felt his blood run cold and finally stopped paying any attention at all to his transaction. The merchant had finished anyway and was tipping two measures of the brown powder into a bag for him. The Janissary agha! Poisoned?

'It means they'll be all over the city trying to pin it on someone, and it's always a Greek. We'll have a hundred Janissaries on every street by tonight, beating people to death just for fun.'

'Don't panic,' the stall owner interrupted, leaning forward and lowering his voice conspiratorially. A Slav with a stall of garlic and precious paprika, the man was likely no lover of his Ottoman overlords. 'They say it was an inside job; one of his own men.'

The two shoppers leaned back in surprise.

'It's true,' the trader hissed. 'I heard it from three different sources. They're hunting some rogue soldier for it.'

'Holy mother! That must be the one they were stamping around shouting about yesterday.'

Skiouros turned back to the khave merchant at his own stall, carefully measuring his breath. To panic and run would be to draw unwanted attention. He wracked his brains trying to remember what price he'd agreed on and dropped the coins into the merchant's outstretched, expectant hand. The man frowned and then passed two coins back suspiciously. Skiouros shrugged an embarrassed apology and took the bag of khave, turning away and striding back through the market, ignoring the interested look on the trader's face.

As soon as he rounded the corner into the street, he took to his heels and ran, making his way down two back alleys before coming out onto another main street down which he could just see the glowering shape of the Church of Saint Saviour. As he reached the grassy area around it, he slowed and took a deep breath, wondering how best to approach the coming conversation. Directly was probably the best way. Lykaion was made of stern enough stuff to learn his peril had just doubled without buckling under the weight.

Opening the door, he slipped inside and, bags in one hand, scanned the various junk left by the workmen. Spotting some splintered rotten beams which had been removed from the structure and a wooden crate now lying empty, he moved on into the church's centre, hearing the reassuring tap of Lykaion's boots in the north chapel. Dropping the bags to the floor, he crossed to the straw pallets that he and Lykaion had used – nasty, uncomfortable things that had accommodated the workers while they repaired the place. Very quickly, he removed a few handfuls of straw and started to pile them in the centre of the room.

'Brother?' he called as he strode back to the workmen's junk piles.

Lykaion strode calmly into the room as his brother was busy taking an iron crow to the crate, shattering the cheap, thin wood.

'That was quick.'

'It's getting a little dangerous out there,' Skiouros replied as he gathered an armful of broken wood. 'Can you bring those two pieces of rotten beam?'

Frowning, Lykaion did as he was bade and carried them across to the small fire that his brother had been constructing in the centre of the room.

'Are you serious? You'll fill the place with smoke!'

'I only want to heat up a pan of water. Then we can put it out. Five minutes. I've got news, too.'

The ominous tone of his voice made Lykaion pause, and the older brother dropped the two pieces of timber for Skiouros.

'Go on.'

'The second assassin's already struck.'

Lykaion's face fell. 'When?'

'Not sure, but the news is in the streets this morning. The agha was poisoned and – sorry about this, brother – they're attaching the blame to you.'

The former Janissary simply shrugged. 'They can hardly make things worse for me now. One murder, two, what difference? If they catch me, they'll impale me for either, let alone both. Or we manage to stop them getting their third target and then the sultan can discover the guilty parties and proclaim my innocence himself. Either way, it makes no difference, though I am sad for the agha. Ahmed Ali bin Nasuh was a good man.'

Crouching, he watched Skiouros strike steel and flint, sending sparks into the mattress straw until the small fire smoked and burst into life. For the next minute or so, the thief fed the fire with small pieces of wood, and then disappeared into the exonarthex and returned with a small brass pot.

'Where in the name of the prophet did you find that?'

'The workmen had it in a pile near the door. I don't know what they used it for, but the inside's black. Probably not something you'd want to prepare food in now.'

'Then what are we doing with it?'

'I told you: boiling water.'

Leaving Lykaion tending a fire that was sending a coiling column of smoke up to the beautiful dome, Skiouros took the pot out into the narthex, pausing and tutting at the empty font. Checking for watchers and then ducking out through the door, he made for the small water butt he'd spotted at the church's corner and dipped the pot into it, grateful that the weather was not quite cold enough to have iced the barrel over. A minute later he was back at the fire with the pot of water, forming a frame from two sacks of mortar lime, the iron crow and a long metal piton. Carefully, he balanced the pot on the frame above the fire.

'Keep the fire fed until the pot boils.'

Lykaion began to add small pieces of wood to the pile beneath the little cauldron while his brother found two shallow bowls that had been

146

used for mixing plaster, as the remaining crusty mess confirmed. The brothers sat in silence, each with his own thoughts, as the bubbles began to appear in the water. Finally, Skiouros wrapped his cloak around his hands and lifted the boiling pot from the fire, tipping half the water into each bowl. Placing the empty pot back on the frame, he unwrapped his bundles and tipped several dozen cinnamon sticks into it.

'What are you doing?'

'Disguising you.'

'With cinnamon?'

'Yes. And khave.'

Lykaion shook his head at the clear idiocy of this and watched as Skiouros tipped his small bag of khave into one of the mixing bowls, where it combined with the water to form a very liquid sludge. The older brother watched with distaste as Skiouros stirred it, making it more liquid as he worked.

'Time to strip down.'

'You jest.'

'Just to the waist,' the younger brother replied, removing his own doublet and shirt and shivering at the cold. 'I need to make sure our hair is black enough to pass for a Turk and seriously darken our arms to the shoulder and face right down to below the collar bones. It has to be done right. Too many disguises are undone by cutting corners. Every bit of flesh that might possibly be seen should be uniformly dark.'

'And we do that with khave?'

'No,' Skiouros said, stirring the cinnamon and watching the oil forming in the bottom of the pan. 'We do that with cinnamon. The khave is for the hair. Yours needs to be about two or three shades darker and mine needs to be a lot more.'

As Lykaion stared at him, Skiouros returned to the brown sludgy mix and dipped his fingers in the warm mess, pulling them out coated with gloop. Reaching across, he made for Lykaion's hair. The older brother pulled back, but the thief leaned forwards and grasped the curly locks in his messy hands. For the next minute or two, he worked at Lykaion's hair, carefully pulling the strands through his fingers, coating every inch with khave mixture and noting with satisfaction the darkening as he went. Finally, after only a short stint, he leaned back, satisfied with his efforts, then dipped his hands once more and began to work furiously at his own, shorter hair, massaging the mess into it, hissing with pain each time he touched his damaged ear.

Once his own hair had achieved the same almost black-brown as Lykaion's, he stood.

'Right. Drain the oil from the pot into the other bowl and then you can tip the used cinnamon on the fire. Try mixing it in, then, and I'll be back in a moment.'

'You're going out like that?' Lykaion asked, gesturing to his half-naked brother and the dark brown gloop covering his hands.

'Only to wash my hands.' Grasping the bowl of coffee paste he left the room and, striding to the door and checking for observers again, hurried out through the freezing air to the water butt. Bracing himself, he dipped both the bowl and his hands in, rubbing them all until the chilly water cleaned off the muck. When he was happy with the result, he dipped the bowl in, collecting more water, and then scurried inside the church.

Back at the centre, beneath the dome, he nodded his approval of Lykaion's mixing efforts as he tipped most of the cold water onto the fire, sending a thick choking cloud of black smoke up to the dome. The cinnamon oil had combined with the hot water to create a rich, mahogany-coloured stain. Crouching, Skiouros added the last of the cold water to the mix, cooling it to a comfortable temperature.

'Stand straight with your arms out like this,' he instructed Lykaion, who did so with a nose wrinkled in distaste.

'I'm going to smell like a khave house.'

'Not after a few hours. The smell will dissipate by lunchtime, and by evening it'll only be noticeable up really close. Now don't flex anything unless you have to. I want to get this even.'

Dipping a rag into the mix, he stood and began applying it to his brother's face.

The two young men who crouched behind the first-level parapet of the pharos tower that morning would not have drawn undue attention had they been purchasing fruit in the great bazaar of Baghdad, their skin swarthy and dark, their hair almost black. Acquiring native Ottoman dress was not difficult and had taken Skiouros only a minute, his ability to judge the fit of clothing still impressive in his brother's eyes. Now, the only thing that spoke to the casual observer of their Attic ancestry was the pale colour of their eyes, and such a viewer would have to find themselves in very close proximity to see them well enough. The brothers were effectively invisible, dressed as poor Turks.

The morning had passed mostly in silence, though not due to the aftermath of an argument this time, but rather through a sense of tense expectation and the need for something to happen.

Lykaion had run over in his head everything that had happened and everything they had discovered time and again, hoping that something useful would occur to him that he had somehow missed before, yet to no avail. The more he thought about the problem, the more it became apparent that the Mamluk ambassador was the only possible lead they had. Of the three assassins, one was dead and the location of the other two entirely unknown. Of their targets, two were now dead and the third so totally out of their reach they had more chance of a personal audience with the moon. The authorities were out of the question, given the complicity of the Janissaries and the absence of any of the other military aghas, who were serving in Anatolia in the war.

Lykaion had briefly contemplated seeing if Skiouros was in touch with any of the city's more dubious organisations that might be able to provide aid, but not only did activity with such criminal groups come with a price that was usually too steep to pay, it also went against everything that he stood for.

And so he sat, and watched, and fervently wished for something to happen.

Skiouros had spent the morning in equally fruitless mental debate, trying to discern any possible way he could persuade Lykaion to abandon this dangerous path and come with him to safety. The problem was that, despite his vehemence in all their arguments, and several ideas that might nudge his brother in the right direction, something Lykaion had said to him had taken root in his soul and refused to budge, infecting his decisions with its oppressive presence:

A conscience.

The thief had worked hard for many years now to eradicate that nagging voice and the many doubts that had assailed him from his early days in the city. A thief who fell prey to his conscience was useless or doomed, or both. He'd never been the most reverential of Christians, and had been cast as a sinner every day of his young life, but he had always been careful to keep his crimes to a misdemeanour level – a social irritant that warranted punishment perhaps, but was

149

never wicked enough to put his life in danger. It was this fine line that he'd walked which kept that nagging conscience quiet, and he had become an expert in keeping it boxed up and silent.

But he knew for certain that Lykaion was right. If they fled the city without doing whatever they could to prevent the coming disaster, he would never be able to silence that voice again and, if it came back in full flow, it might well drown him in the torrents of his past crimes.

Without realising how much damage his argument had done, Lykaion had effectively removed flight as a possibility for either of them.

And so the brothers watched, tense and silent, each face a walnut-skinned mask of self-torture as they tried to solve their unsolvable problems. Morning wore on into afternoon, and the possibility that the early autumn sunset would fall upon a fruitless day was starting to sour the brothers' moods.

Their introspection had become so involving that they did not notice the door of the Bucoleon palace open until the Janissary guard emerged and walked purposefully off towards that dangerously unstable former Imperial residence close by. The brothers shared an unspoken question: should they follow? To do so was dangerous and also left them unable to keep watch on the palace door. The question was rendered obsolete a moment later as the Janissary came to a halt in plain sight outside the main door of the crumbling palace shell and waited.

The two observers watched with nervous excitement as, a moment later, a homeless Turkish street boy came running from the door and approached the guard. The big soldier leaned down to the boy and exchanged words, handing over a silver coin. With a smile, the urchin turned and ran towards the pharos. The brothers disappeared below the parapet, pushing themselves back against the stone, a momentary panic that the boy was coming for them quickly dissipating as the unlikeliness of that became clear. The boy pounded along the street past the tower, heading directly up the hill through small, little-used alleys and roads, up towards the heart of the Ottoman city. By the time the Janissary returned to the palace and closed the door, the urchin was lost to sight and the watchers fumed quietly in the realisation that there was no way they could catch up in time to follow him.

Instead, they returned to watching the palace and were rewarded only a few minutes later when the door opened again and the Mamluk ambassador stepped outside, the two Janissary guards at his shoulder, and walked off towards the headland.

Lykaion and Skiouros shared a look and a thought: the Nea Ekklasia. Despite the fact that it was still a cold, light afternoon with a few locals abroad in the streets, and that the brothers could now easily pass for Turks, it would still be unnecessarily dangerous to follow the Mamluk too closely.

Skiouros shrugged. Guessing the man's destination was a gamble, but lessened the danger of the pursuit. Lykaion thought for a moment and then nodded his agreement. With no further pause the pair pulled their unfamiliar Ottoman short jackets tighter against the wind and descended the staircase, scurrying out into the chilly afternoon and ducking to the side, making for the street that ran parallel to the one walked by the Mamluk.

Without need for secrecy, the two pounded along the street, praying to their respective Gods that they had judged the man's destination correctly. If they went to the church only to find he had turned away en route and gone somewhere unknown, they would have effectively had two leads dangled before them this afternoon and missed both.

At the far end of the street, the pair paused, pressed against the wooden house wall, and peered across the open space before the former church. There was no sign of the Mamluk and his escort, which either meant they were far enough ahead to have beaten them to the church, or that the church had not been their destination after all.

'Do we wait?' Skiouros whispered.

'No. We have to try. I just hope that door's still free.'

Skiouros nodded. The thought of making that climb with his terrified brother once more was unappealing. Taking a deep breath, the pair ran out into the open space, fervently hoping that the Mamluk wouldn't appear at that moment, emerging from the parallel street. There was no sign of him as they ran past the frontage of the church and to the side wall, where they came to a stop, leaning on their knees and heaving deep breaths. It was as Lykaion looked up that he saw their quarry appear before the church from the other street, and he pulled himself up tight against the wall, pushing Skiouros back with an arm.

Indicating the three men's arrival with his fingers, he waited until Skiouros nodded and then the pair ran off along the side of the church to the rear. Here, they sought out the ruined door to the colonnaded peristyle garden and clambered past it into the abandoned, overgrown interior.

A quick jog along the portico and they reached the back door of the church, which they had used to escape the last time they had been here. Tentatively, Skiouros reached out to it, drawing something from his jacket. When they'd left previously, he had pushed the door closed until the latch clicked, visible as a sliver of horizontal metal in the crack. Now, he pushed a filament-thin blade into the gap and pushed upwards. The latch moved with a faint rattle and the door immediately creaked open by an inch.

Grinning, Skiouros put his blade away once more and then fully opened the door and stepped inside. Clearly none of the guards who had been here in the past two days had been thorough enough in their work to notice that the blocking beam had been removed, and had left it unlocked.

Lykaion followed his brother inside and quietly shut and latched the door behind him, sending up thanks to Allah and the prophets that he had not had to contemplate that blood-chilling ascent of the north wall once again.

Moving at a slow pace and lifting their feet carefully with each step to keep the sound down to a bare minimum, the brothers moved around the church's periphery until they found the place from which they had observed the last life-changing meeting that had taken place here.

The smell of the black powder was acrid and filled the air, and both brothers had had to stifle sneezes by the time they had reached their viewing position. Clearly some of the kegs had been moved recently and the resulting cloud had continued to swirl in the stagnant air of the building ever since.

Falling into a crouch and watching, the pair spotted the Mamluk, alone, pacing back and forth in an angry manner. Seeing the man angry made both brothers feel a little more comfortable, as though they had somehow leeched some of the man's happiness into themselves.

'I thought these meetings were supposed to be dangerous,' barked an unseen voice, quickly followed by the slamming shut of a door and the steady approach of booted footsteps.

Hamza Bin Murad!

'They are!' snapped the Mamluk in response, as the newly-arrived commander joined him.

'And in broad daylight.' The Janissary officer shook his head. 'I knew you were trouble and dangerous, but I had not figured you for an idiot.'

'Watch your tongue, Bin Murad. I am already incensed!'

'Am I supposed to care? Just play your part and stay out of sight. Stop calling meetings like this; I have a job to do, you know?'

'One of my Fida'i has disappeared. I receive regular reports from them and the one I sent after your rogue soldier has gone!'

'Risks of the profession, Qaashiq, I'm afraid. I won't even ask for a description to match him up to the body that was left dumped in an alley of the Greek enclave late last night. I doubt there are too many armed Mamluks around the city.'

'Your information suggested that the target was a common soldier and not even a veteran. He should have been no match for one of my Fida'i. You have misled me.'

'I cannot help the bumbling of your foolish men.' Bin Murad rolled his shoulders. 'I'm just grateful they seem to have been more effective against their primary targets. I very much suspect, though, that your man never even met the runaway. A Mamluk in the Greek quarter is somewhat noticeable and your people are very, very unpopular – more so with the Greeks even than with the Turks. Risky business even crossing a street there unless you're one of their own.'

'I do not believe one of my highly-trained professionals fell foul of street thugs!' Qaashiq snapped. 'Something here is not what it appears.'

Bin Murad pointed at the Mamluk. 'I personally do not care about your men's state of health or their ability, so long as they do their jobs. Two targets are down and you have two men left. Concentrate on Bayezid now and stop pestering me.'

'No. The assigned Fida'i will stay on the sultan, but the other will take over the hunt for your renegade. We can not afford to leave loose threads dangling where someone might pull on them. Just tell me anything else I need to know about the target. What is unusual about this Janissary?'

'Nothing, Qaashiq. I've told you all about him. He only finished training two years ago. He's been in a few engagements across the water, but he's just an ordinary soldier. I don't care how you deal with him, so long as the primary target remains your main concern. Tomorrow is the deadline and I want Bayezid's head.'

The Mamluk nodded and folded his arms. 'Tomorrow is the day of

Ashura and the city will turn out to mourn, but the sultan will not reach the Aya Sofya alive.'

'Make sure that he does not. Then this feeble nation can be remoulded into a strong Empire of Islam and the stinking infidels can be dealt with.'

The Mamluk watched Bin Murad with dispassionate revulsion. Religious fanatics were dangerous men to work with. They tended toward irrational acts and unpredictable moves. Qaashiq could hardly wait for Bayezid to lie bleeding out his life and the Janissaries to be marshalled under a new command so that he could finally get rid of this lunatic. There would be no room in the new Mamluk-influenced Empire for such men. He already had his eye on the replacement agha, and it most certainly wasn't the bloodthirsty Hamza Bin Murad.

'I am leaving now,' the officer said flatly, 'and I do not expect to be called away to meet you again for such paltry, pointless matters.'

Bin Murad turned and strode away, stomping towards the front door of the church and leaving the Mamluk alone. Skiouros and Lykaion shared a look and nodded, creeping away from the viewing point and towards the rear door, where Skiouros opened it quickly for them to step through before shutting it tight with a quiet click.

'Tomorrow!'

'Their window of opportunity is going to be ridiculously small,' Lykaion mused as they strode through the garden, their breath pluming faintly in the cold air. 'The sultan will be safe from harm until he leaves the Topkapi Palace's main gate, and he'll be too difficult to touch once he's inside the Aya Sofya. So there's perhaps five minutes in which he's vulnerable. It can't be more than six or seven hundred yards between the two doors. He'll be travelling quite slowly so the crowd can adore him, but even then it won't take long.'

'We can talk about it later. For now, I think we should get away from here and back to Saint Saviour's so we can discuss it in private.'

'Agreed.'

The two crossed the garden and slipped out through the broken door into the open street, first making sure that no one was observing them. Slowly and without speaking, they passed around the outer wall of the church towards the main façade, each silently contemplating the very real possibility that the Empire would have a new ruler and a new direction by the time the sun set tomorrow.

Lykaion let out a sharp breath as they reached the church front, and pulled his brother back against the wall, out of the open. Skiouros leaned out slightly trying to see what had spooked Lykaion, and then ducked back sharply.

The Mamluk – Qaashiq – was standing in front of the church with his two Janissaries. Pausing, the brothers took a breath and reached a silent accord before creeping to the corner and peering around it. One of the Janissaries was striding across the street.

Skiouros focussed on the building he was approaching and saw with interest two young beggar boys hunched together in the doorway, trying to shelter from the cold. The guard exchanged quick words with the boys and then all three returned to the Mamluk.

Skiouros and Lykaion watched intently as the ambassador leaned close to the urchins and issued instructions, accompanied by silver coins. Satisfied that they could repeat back his instructions, the Egyptian waved the boys off and then strode back in the direction of the Bucoleon with his guards.

'The Mamluk or the beggars?' Lykaion asked quietly.

'The beggars,' Skiouros replied. 'Their boss is going nowhere this evening. But one boy, or both?'

'Both,' Lykaion said with a deep breath. 'Just in case; this may be the only chance we get. We follow at a distance and don't get too involved. Just find out where they're going and see if we can work out why. Then we meet back at the church, yes?'

Skiouros nodded. 'Then pick your target and I'll see you soon.'

Lykaion watched the beggars. The first had strolled off north, up the hill towards the Ottoman centre, while the other was heading back towards the pharos along the parallel road they had themselves taken.

'I'll go uphill. I know the headland area and the First Hill well. Good luck.'

Skiouros nodded and, with a final clasp of his brother's shoulder, turned and strode off after the beggar, towards the tower and the bulk of the city beyond.

Chapter 8 – The hunt begins

* Cumartesi (Saturday) evening *

The sun touched the level waters of the Propontis, sending rippling sheets of gold out towards the city. Few ships moved in the harbour but the streets were as cluttered and busy as always as Skiouros ducked into the doorway of one of the new hamami – the Ottoman baths which so closely resembled the ancient Roman ones – that were springing up all over the city like mushrooms in a damp meadow.

The young urchin seemed to be entirely unaware of the fact that his every step was being shadowed but Skiouros took no chances, employing every device and trick he knew to make himself barely visible.

Whatever the boy's errand, it appeared not to be a matter of urgency, and the lad strolled through the city streets at a tardy pace which irritated the thief who followed. The sunlight was slipping from the world and a shroud of dark falling upon the streets of the ancient city as the boy turned into a street in the valley that ran between the Fourth and Seventh hills, from the walls down to the Theodosian harbour.

Skiouros crossed to a house at the far side of the street and two doors down, which stood dark and closed, and there he made a quiet and subtle show of searching for a key. It was not unknown for houses in this area to have quality locks, as merchants and businessmen lived there. Pretending to find a key, despite the fact that the urchin had not even glanced at him, he drew his picklocks and clicked open the door easily. A good ruse was one where you kept up every detail no matter how closely you were being observed.

Entering the house, he turned and closed the door, quickly pausing for any giveaway sound – though he was positive the building was empty – and ducked down to the window shutter, peering through the crack.

The door of the house diagonally opposite opened suddenly and Skiouros had only a moment to discern dark, Arabic features which flashed this way and that around the street before the boy was unceremoniously yanked inside and the door closed.

For almost two minutes, Skiouros crouched irritably at the window, wishing he could both see and hear the exchange across the street, and was just contemplating either giving up and leaving or trying to find a better vantage point when the door opened again and the urchin reappeared, a gleaming coin in his hand. The door slammed shut behind him and the boy turned and left the way he had come.

Skiouros bit his lip. It would be a simple matter to follow the boy back, but was it worth the time and effort – not to mention the danger? There seemed little doubt that the boy would return either to his home in the damp wreckage of the former palace, or would head to the Bucoleon and deliver another message to the Mamluk, which Skiouros would not be able to observe from close enough to make any difference.

But he did now have one lead.

He had the room of one of the other two assassins.

At this point it would probably be best to meet Lykaion and pool their findings before deciding what to do about the killer living in the Lycus valley.

His mind made up, Skiouros hurried back through the house and slipped out of the back door, leaving it unbolted, dropping into the dung-filled alleyway and trotting along it to the next opening, where he re-emerged into the main streets and turned towards Phanar and home.

The Church of Saint Saviour cast a somehow threatening shadow this evening as Skiouros passed between the last houses and entered the grassy area of the former graveyard. The moon cast a silvery light on the far side of the building, throwing the structure into a stark silhouette from this angle, unrelieved by lights or apertures.

For some reason a chill ran through the thief – a chill that was entirely unrelated to the weather. The strange atmosphere was enhanced by the threatening sky. Where for many weeks now the sky had presented a clear blue infinity, the wind appeared to have changed with the falling of the darkness, and tatters and shreds of cloud were now scudding past the white orb at an astounding speed. Approaching the abandoned church, Skiouros tried very hard not to think about Romani witches and their predictions or traders who spoke of devastating storms to the south.

The south, from which this fresh wind came, dragging a torn shroud across the sky.

Opening the door, the young man slipped inside, into the gloomy interior of the exonarthex and then the inner narthex. The moonlight, shining in through high, narrow windows in the small cupola above, did little but pick out some of the upper decoration in ghostly white, and barely touched the lower reaches of the corridor. The faint shapes of painted saints were somehow threatening as they were picked out by the dim glow.

Trying to shake off this gloomy, uncomfortable feeling, Skiouros crossed through the inner narthex and into the main hall of the church, where he settled down on his pallet to wait for his brother, his shabby cloak pulled about him for warmth.

Some strange otherworldly sense alerted the young thief that something was wrong. For almost an hour he had sat in the naos of the church, picking through every detail he could remember of the assassin he had seen, and now he suddenly stood, the hair rising on the back of his neck in response to some primeval warning.

He had already crossed the church hall and moved into the darker narthex when the knock came at the door. The wind had only increased over the last hour and could be heard howling around the church and battering shutters in the nearby houses, the sound of it hissing through the trees audible even inside. And yet that knock had cut through the noise like the leaden doors of a tomb closing.

In response to some deep-rooted caution, he suddenly changed direction and, instead of crossing into the exonarthex and the outer door, he took a circuitous route that brought him around the church's edge, through the parekklesion and towards the door at an oblique angle.

Pausing, he deliberated over his next move. Whoever it was outside, it was not going to be his brother; Lykaion would not have knocked. A faint flicker of orange that just showed beneath the door suggested that whoever it was had torches burning outside. The Janissaries? Surely they would not have knocked.

Why would anybody knock?

The answer, quite obviously, was 'to get him to open the door'. Which meant that the very last thing he should contemplate right now was opening that door.

Briefly, he considered running to the corner and climbing the staircase of the belfry where he would be able to observe much of the exterior grounds, but he decided that such a move could also potentially trap him like a rat. Instead, he approached the enclosed arch in the outer wall next to the main church door, now home to a plain and unadorned tomb. With a brief, silent apology to whatever priest or bishop it contained he clambered onto it, gritting his teeth at the scraping noises he couldn't avoid making.

Where the arch of the former external arcade had been sealed with a solid block, it had only been closed up to the curve, the very top forming a window that was now covered with an iron grille and glazed against the weather.

Breathing lightly, his nerves pinging, Skiouros raised himself up on the tomb and managed to pull himself high enough to peer through the window at the scene outside.

The young thief bit into his lip, blood welling into his mouth. As his breath stopped entirely and he almost toppled from the tomb, his fingers gripped the edge of the window, whitening.

It was Lykaion.

At least, partially.

Even with the darkened skin and hair, courtesy of the morning's efforts, Skiouros would recognise his brother's face anywhere.

The head sat on the rough ground some twenty feet from the church door, a flaming torch planted either side of it illuminating it in ghastly detail. Even at this distance, Skiouros could make out details he'd rather not.

The eyes were gone, as were the ears, the mouth rent and covered in blood, suggesting strongly that the tongue had been removed also. The base of the neck where it met the ground was jagged and messy, with crimson fleshy tendrils hanging loose. There was nothing neat or surgical about this decapitation.

Skiouros closed his eyes as he felt the next shudder almost pull him back off the tomb.

Momentarily, he cast up a prayer to the Lord – and to Allah, just in case – that Lykaion had died quickly and that this defilement had occurred after the soul had gone. Not that he believed it, but he had to hope.

His world collapsed.

Standing on the tomb, shaking, his gaze locked on the illuminated head, Skiouros was suddenly bereft of everything. For so many years he had lived with his brother's absence in the knowledge that despite all the arguments and ill-feeling, at least he was still there and still strong. They might not talk cordially, but they had never failed to acknowledge their link. The regular meetings had failed to reconcile them, but there had always been hope. Even through all that time, Skiouros had never allowed himself to contemplate the possibility of a life without Lykaion.

He tried to focus; to concentrate on the important – the here and now.

But his eyes just would not tear themselves away from the desecrated head of his brother, and that gruesome sight filled his mind and senses and left no room for rational thought.

The glazed half-moon window suddenly exploded in shards of jagged greenish glass as an arrow nicked Skiouros' ear before clattering off the wall and disappearing off into the exonarthex. Instinctively, the young thief's eyes closed in an instant, probably saving his sight as fragments of glass scored his face.

Unable to maintain his precarious stance, Skiouros fell back from the tomb, landing with a heavy thud on the marble floor of the passage.

In an instant, Skiouros was alert once more, scrambling to his feet. The shattering glass had forced him to shut his eyes and that had finally detached him from Lykaion, freeing some part of his mind to deal with the immediate problem.

There was no way to confirm how many people there were out there but Skiouros would have been willing to wager that the attacker numbered only one. Were it the authorities, there would have been none of this grisly showmanship, but a brutal assault on the church – possibly with gunfire – and capture. So that left only the assassins. Lykaion had apparently been careless or unlucky and the man he'd been observing had caught him.

That meant that there was only one man out there. But it also meant that he was a trained killer.

Could he flee? Certainly one man would have difficulty keeping watch on the entire exterior of the church. But he had a bow, and that seriously diminished any chance Skiouros had of reaching the safety of nearby housing. He would have to be fast as lightning to cross the wasteland graveyard before the assassin could get off a bowshot, unless the assassin were to be distracted somehow.

Fleeing would probably do no good anyway. If these assassins were good enough to track down Skiouros' room purely through his brother's associations, and then this place, there was little chance of him finding any level of safety.

No; unless the opportunity of escape suddenly presented itself, he had to deal with this killer – but how?

He was no soldier or assassin. He had a little skill with his knife, but had never taken a life and had never intended to. How could such a man deal with the trained killers of the Mamluks?

Briefly, his mind's eye reminded him of Lykaion's sword, wrapped in a shabby sack, lying next to the straw mattress. It would be easy enough to get, but would it do him any good? He'd never used a sword in his life. The theory was obvious, of course: you held the rounded bit and used the pointy and sharp bit to damage the enemy. But to think he might be able to best the assassin was sheer idiocy.

Quickly he discarded the sword as a possibility. He would be better unencumbered. The only advantages he had were the ones he'd always had: wits and speed.

What to do, then?

Perhaps he could buy himself enough time with a trick; enough time to get away from the place without being within arrow shot?

Again, the belfry presented itself as an option, and he glanced across to the doorway of the spiral stairs before discarding it once more. Being trapped in a tower was asking for trouble.

A soft click from the main door brought home the urgency of the situation, and he was up on his feet and running in an instant, heading towards the tower stairs purely because that happened to be the way he was looking as he stood.

Behind him, the door creaked open. Even as the figure moved inside, the cloaked head swinging this way and that, trying to ascertain the location of his quarry and any source of danger, Skiouros had disappeared around the corner, his back to the wall, trying to control his breathing.

A distraction was what he needed, but what?

He could hear the swish of the assassin's cloak as he turned on the

161

spot, his eyes picking out every detail of the exonarthex in the gloom. Taking a deep breath, Skiouros reached into his pouch and drew out a single coin, trying to muffle the sounds as best he could inside his doublet. With a short, fervent prayer, he tossed the coin across the open space and into the stairwell to the belfry.

He might be no fighter, but years of living by his agility had lent Skiouros excellent throwing skills. The small, silver akce disappeared into the darkness of the stairwell and hit the wall high up, tinkling as it bounced back down and coming to rest on the lowest step.

Without waiting to see if his ruse had worked, Skiouros turned and tip-toed through the door into the inner narthex. It was a gamble. If the assassin ignored the somewhat obvious coin-toss and walked straight forward, they would be face-to-face any moment.

Three heartbeats with no sign of the killer, and finally Skiouros heard the gentle sounds of the man's light footsteps as he moved towards the tower.

With a small sense of relief, Skiouros moved along the inner corridor to where its doorway opened up to the exonarthex and the main church door. If the assassin actually climbed the stairs, he could get away, could even take Lykaion's remains with him.

Taking a steadying breath, he leaned round the corner and then pulled his head back sharply. The assassin was at the tower stairs but had not begun the ascent, his head moving back and forth like some sort of predator, scenting out his prey. Skiouros noted with grim acceptance that the man had shut and barred the church door behind him as he entered. It would not take much effort for Skiouros to move the bar, but it would slow him down and the sound would be obvious.

His eyes dropped to the floor and took in the glittering points of dozens of caltrops scattered across the inside of the door.

Quite clearly no escape that way, then.

He knew from earlier explorations that there were two other exits from the church, but the one in the south wall had been sealed up thoroughly when the building had been deconsecrated, and the northern one was blocked by piles of workmen's rubble outside. It was one thing to know that your hideout only had one approachable entrance, but when you were trapped in it and that one entrance became only one exit, the benefits were considerably less beneficial.

With a sinking feeling, he realised that the chances of running had all but evaporated. No matter how much time he could buy now it would not be enough to get him away from the killer.

A quick glance around the corner confirmed the worst. The assassin had not fallen for the trick, and had turned, peering down the corridors of the parekklesion and the exonarthex. Skiouros managed to duck back just as the man's gaze swept past him.

What to do? Skiouros' desperation was becoming palpable now. He was truly trapped.

Carefully and as quietly as he could manage, Skiouros backed away from the door and prepared to creep along the corridor and into the north chapel, in the opposite direction to the assassin and as far from him as it was possible to get within the building.

What happened next came as a blur that felt like slow motion.

Even as he stepped back from the door into the centre of the inner narthex, so the assassin also stepped from the outer corner to the inner narthex doorway.

Skiouros caught a glimpse of the movement out of the corner of his eye and threw himself forward and into the church's main naos even as a thrown knife, only two inches in length, ripped through the shoulder of his doublet, becoming fast within it.

It had not been an elegant dive, and Skiouros had to recover himself quickly in the church's cavernous centre before running once more, horribly aware of the pounding feet out in the corridor behind him.

What had been a silent stalking of hunter and prey had now become a chase.

Grateful for his solid knowledge of the church's plan, Skiouros crossed the naos and ducked through the small door into the north chapel, almost falling over a workman's barrow as he did so. Weaving past the barrow, he ran into the main long, decorative chapel, pausing only to confirm that the assassin was following him and that he hadn't doubled back to wait for him ahead.

A moment later, he turned the corner into the inner narthex once more.

How long could he realistically keep this up? He was fast and nimble, and he knew the layout well, but the assassin would be just as fast, and every step he took in this pursuit increased his knowledge of the place.

Realising his options were running out, Skiouros pounded down the inner narthex and through the door into the parekklesion.

As he rounded the corner two small blades clattered off the stonework next to him, chipping the centuries-old images of saints.

The plan formed even as he looked down the parekklesion, trying to figure his next move. His feet were already running, but he slowed his pace. It wouldn't work if he was always a corridor ahead.

There was an inherent danger, of course.

Clearly, the assassin had discarded his bow as he came inside – shouldered it most likely. A bow was no weapon for fighting in a building. That left only his short throwing knives or any number of horrible hand weapons he might carry. He had to trust to luck that he would not fall to a thrown blade before the plan could pay off.

The assassin was almost at the corner now, and Skiouros had barely moved.

They were close enough. Close enough for the killer to keep his attention on Skiouros and not his surroundings.

Picking up the pace again, Skiouros ran down the parekklesion, the assassin only a few steps behind him – almost close enough to smell the spicy scent of the man and to hear his measured breaths with each stride.

Much to the thief's relief, the assassin drew a curved blade from his belt. A strange relief it was, but at least that horrible razor-sharp blade in hand meant no more thrown knives.

Without even looking down, sure of his surroundings, Skiouros turned his run into a short, gazelle-like leap, landing and continuing to pound on into the dead-end of the curved parekklesion chapel where he put out his hands to stop himself at the beautifully-painted apsidal wall.

His success was announced by a panicked squawk.

Turning at the wall and heaving in a deep breath, Skiouros looked back along the passage. There was no sign of the assassin.

Two or three times in the past days, Skiouros had debated over whether to cover over the deep hole that had almost claimed Lykaion on that first evening. Clearly the saints were with him that he'd never got round to it.

Gingerly, he approached the hole that he'd leapt over mid-run and which his pursuer had fallen foul of. The man probably had more throwing knives.

The assassin lay on the floor of the vault below, his leg and an arm twisted at an impossible angle, groaning with pain.

Skiouros stepped back.

As his breathing and pulse began to settle back down to their normal pace, a cold and angry scowl reached his face, contorting his usually genial features. Paying no further heed to the man's groaning, he stepped off to the side, where a small pile of debris remained, testament to the workmen's labours. Selecting an appropriately hefty piece of cracked marble cornice, he bent and lifted it with some difficulty.

Straining and grunting with the effort he staggered back to the pit where, carefully peering into the darkness to identify the shape of the crippled assassin, he held the stone out as far as he could before his arms gave out, and then let go.

The heavy marble block fell the ten or more feet into the crypt, smashing onto the fallen assassin's ribs and splintering them to tiny fragments, flattening organs and crushing him to death quicker than Skiouros would really have liked.

The assassin let out an agonised wail that echoed around the corridors and rooms of the church – a wail that turned, as it descended, into a rattle and hiss and then finally, silence.

Skiouros peered down, swaying slightly and having to step back from the edge in case he joined the assassin in his cold tomb.

As he turned away, back to the parekklesion, emotions flooded him and he suddenly felt overcome. His knees seemed to lose the ability to hold him up, and he collapsed to the floor. After a minute or so he realised that the agonised wailing that was filling the church like the singing of the most heart-breaking, disharmonious liturgical hymn was, in fact, himself.

For countless eons he sat on the floor of the parekklesion, screaming out his grief at being the last of the family of Nikos the farmer. He shook and sobbed, wracked with pain, his hands continually curling and uncurling as if trying to hold onto something that was as tangible as smoke.

Skiouros couldn't have said how long he stayed there, but by the time he stood, slowly, on shaking legs, the moonlight that had filtered into the church and given it its only illumination had gone, leaving the place dark, and the sound of light rain battered the roof above, like a distant sizzle.

Resolutely ignoring the hole in the floor with its crushed occupant, Skiouros walked slowly and unsteadily back towards the entrance of the church. A quick side-trip into the naos and he collected one of the rough, twig brooms the workmen had left, which he used to sweep the numerous barbed caltrops away from the door.

Slowly, with weary, weakened muscles, he hauled the blocking bar from the exit and dropped it aside, pulling open the door.

The rain must have started some time ago, completely unnoticed by Skiouros, for it had extinguished both torches, and Lykaion's head was now visible only as a faint circular shadow on the floor.

Ignoring the cold downpour, Skiouros stepped outside and strode across the intervening space, bending and picking up his brother's head by the hair.

Somehow the realisation that his brother's body would almost certainly never show up was actually worse than lifting his severed head. Lykaion, even in death, would never be whole again.

And nor would Skiouros.

Turning, he strode back into the church, the head swinging by his side.

A dim recollection struck him – a memory of something he'd seen when he'd scouted out the interior that first night and, with a sour and unpleasant sense of purpose, he turned and strode into the north chapel. At the far end of the place a pile of debris from the workmen's exertions was piled up beside the altar. The front of the holy table had been stove in – to get at the holy relics within, presumably – but among the pile of refuse beside it sat the thing that Skiouros remembered.

Crouching, he retrieved the wood and leather container. Some time in the past it had rested in that very reliquary, probably containing the skull of a saint, given its size. The gold edging had been ripped from the container, but the box itself remained intact and usable... and the right size for a head.

Carefully, Skiouros placed the box on the holy table and opened it. There was, as expected, nothing inside, and it smelled faintly musty with great age.

With a fresh tear from eyes that had almost been drained of moisture, Skiouros lowered his brother's head into the box and closed it. Crouching, he slid it into the reliquary space in the centre of the altar once more.

'I'm sorry, brother, if this is wrong, but it's the best I can do. Whether your God or mine actually exist, both of them should appreciate having the remnants of a good man interred here temporarily.'

He straightened, his sense of purpose filling him.

It would be temporary.

As soon as it was light, he would make his way down to the Theodosian harbour and book that damn passage to Crete. Then he would go and see Judah ben Isaac, collect his money, and then this casket, and make his way down to set sail.

Whatever he'd vowed with his brother back in the ruined church of Saint Polyeuktos a few days ago, it was now rendered null and void. Lykaion was dead, and nothing remained to keep him in the city.

Still cold to the bone with grief, Skiouros returned to his straw pallet and lay upon it, pulling his cloak about him for its scant warmth, and failed to sleep.

Chapter 9 – An Anatolian Tempest

* Pazar (Sunday) morning *

Skiouros rolled onto his back. The night had not been kind. The cold had lifted a little as the sky grew overcast, but not enough to take the chill out of the air, and the winds had become wicked, battering the deserted church and tearing the branches off trees in the locale, ripping tiles from roofs and destroying anything not thoroughly shut tight.

The rain had come and gone numerous times, though with the power of the wind behind it, it was more often than not horizontal and driving. The intermittent hiss and clatter of it on the church had been interrupted violently at one point when it had actually managed to break a fragile window in the north chapel.

Such conditions would not normally have perturbed the thief, who had spent much of his recent life in a rickety, cheap wooden room with cracks and holes in the walls and inadequate shutters, but the fresh memory of Lykaion's brutal demise the previous evening and the ensuing grief, still ever-present, had simply removed any possibility of calm or relief.

Sometime in the early hours, before the window had broken, still restless and unable to find the elusive peace of slumber, Skiouros had wandered into the north chapel and pulled out the reliquary box from the altar, sitting cross-legged before it in silence, unable to bring himself to open it. Ridiculously, it seemed that the strange and eerie one-sided conversation that followed had been the longest and calmest one the brothers had shared since reaching Constantinople all those years ago.

One-sided in a way, at least.

Whether it was the power of this once important and holy place influencing his thoughts, or just the fresh grief playing tricks on his mind, he almost could hear Lykaion's voice taking his part in proceedings, barely audible above the storm outside; an echo of thoughts in his head. No matter how much he looked around, there was no physical sign of the unfortunate brother, though.

'Why could you not leave with me?' Skiouros had pleaded with the plain wooden box, its surface marred only by the scars of forced entry and the removal of the decorative metalwork. In a way, the box, with its lack of frippery, stripped down to its honest essentials, was a suitable analogy for Lykaion's physical presence.

'Because it would not have been the right thing to do, I know...' he replied to the ghostly, imagined voice. 'I know that, and so does God. And because you chose the right path, are you rewarded, brother?'

He paused, listening to the voice that could be the wind forming words.

'Some reward,' he spat in the end. 'And whose God, anyway? Yours or mine?'

He looked up at the altar and the carved cross in the lip, wondering whether the workers would simply sling out the holy table or whether it would be reused for the greater glory of Allah.

'"Does it matter?" is the question, I suppose. Those who quibble over the details and kill on the urging word of an overzealous priest are missing the real word of God – people like your friend Bin Murad who can't tolerate differences and fall prey to the sheer love of death that tarnishes their souls. We do what we must so that men like Bayezid the Just can change the world, one step at a time, and so that men like Hamza Bin Murad fail to do so.'

He shook his head to some unheard reply as the wind howled its fury around the church.

'No. It's what you would do, Lykaion, but I must go – away from here, I mean. I can't finish this without you – I don't even want to. It was your quest, this, not mine.'

He cocked his head to one side, listening to the vehemence of his dead brother's reply in the howling of the storm.

'"I will do what I must"? Lykaion, what I must do is leave this place and take you too. Beyond that? Even God doesn't know. Time and fate will tell.'

Skiouros lowered his eyes, perturbed at the strangeness and the frankness of the ethereal conversation. 'Have I offended you with all this?' he asked quietly, gesturing at the altar. 'This box, I mean? This altar? This church? No. I suppose not. You always did see things in better perspective than me. I assume you're with whatever God wants you, and I'll be content when I'm sitting in a taverna in Crete. I'm taking you with me when I go.'

'I cannot leave and nor, I suspect, can you.'

The words were so suddenly clear that Skiouros spun around sharply, expecting to see his brother standing behind him, but there was nothing there. Perhaps the words had been his own, unintentionally voiced aloud.

'I think you underestimated the strength of my survival instinct, Lykaion. I should have gone days ago, and I should have taken you with me. There is nothing here for me now. The man who killed you is dead, so vengeance is served. I am gone with the afternoon tide at the latest.'

And yet now, with the advent of dawn, as Skiouros clambered upright from his makeshift bed and pulled his doublet tight, lacing it up and pulling on his fine boots, he began to wonder about that vehement decision of flight. He was determined to go, but something about those words of Lykaion's ghost – if that's what it had been – had settled into him.

I cannot leave and nor, I suspect, can you.

The phrase formed a couplet with an earlier memory of his brother's advice: 'I, for one, would suffer with a dreadful conscience for the rest of my life.'

So it came down to whether Skiouros had the mastery over his conscience that he hoped. He would go; had already decided that, with no possibility of changing course. But would he live easily with having made the decision? As Lykaion's unseen spectre had said, only time would tell – not fate, though. Fate could go hang.

Biting down on his lip, he threw the cloak about his neck and fastened it, turning to face the door of the north chapel.

'I'll be back for you before I leave, Lykaion. Be sure of that.'

With a last sad smile, he took a breath and turned to the main door and the potential of a new world. Time to see what that fate had in store for him. Down to the harbour to book a passage; Crete if possible, but he would accept Cyprus, Venice, Genoa or even Athens if that was the only voyage available. What mattered most was to leave Constantinople as soon as possible. Then, with the voyage organised, he would hie himself to Ben Isaac to collect his money. Finally, back here to pick up Lykaion's remains, and then the journey could begin.

Crossing through both the inner and outer narthex, Skiouros approached the door with trepidation, the memories of the last time he had opened it all too clear. Outside, the rain had let up again, but the winds were howling and clattering through the timbers of the city, threatening a new downpour. A storm had hit the city, but he had seen much worse in his time – some storms that had almost ruined the farmers of Hadrianople. This was more of a gale with bad squalls. Gritting his teeth, Skiouros pulled the door open and surveyed the scene.

The ground was soaked, much of the grassy area waterlogged, and rivulets of mud ran through the rest. Two blackened stumps of torches sat on the ground to either side of a faint stain that had been almost entirely erased by the rain.

Nothing to keep him here.

Taking a deep breath, he shut the door behind him and strode across the ground outside, subconsciously taking a gently arcing path that avoided the torches and the stain they guarded, bringing him by a circuitous route to the road.

Skiouros prided himself on his alertness and care. They were the traits that had seen him survive his chosen path in the streets of one of the world's greatest cities these past eight years. And so it almost threw him when, as he passed from the former church cemetery into the narrower street beyond, a cough rang out from the side of the street only a few feet away. He'd seen no one...

His head shot round to the featureless wooden wall of the nearest house and his eyes dropped to ground level, to where a sack of something best unexamined stood, surrounded by debris.

The black garbed figure of an old woman with ragged black hair and a leathery, weather-beaten face crouched leeward of the sack, nominally out of the wind.

The Romani witch.

Skiouros' blood ran cold.

'You!'

The old woman raised an eyebrow as she regarded him the way a surgeon looks over the corpse he's about to dissect. As her head moved there was a hollow clatter and Skiouros noted with some distaste the bones of a bird woven into the gnarled tresses of her hair.

His mind leapt back a few days to a scene of the old woman boning a crow and he shuddered.

'Are you mocking me?' he snapped, referring to her repeated presence at the worst moments of his life.

The old woman frowned and shrugged, reaching down to a small bowl between her feet that contained some form of dried plant life. Producing a piece of flint and a chunk of red-gold rock, she proceeded to smash the two together over the bowl until sparks fell and caught in the fibrous material, causing a tendril of blue smoke to rise. Throwing him a strange look, the old woman bent over the bowl and breathed in the smoke heavily.

'I said: are you mocking me?' he repeated. 'I pick a purse that causes all hell to break loose and you're there with your cryptic yapping. Then my brother dies and I'm forced to kill someone – something that I hope never to have to do again – and here you are again.'

The old witch remained silent, breathing in the blue smoke until she gave a rasping cough and sat up, her eyes fixing him with a disturbing scrutiny that felt as though she had just seen through his eyes and into his soul.

'No one is to blame for your predicament but yourself, farmer-thief. You were warned away from this path, but you took it anyway, and now that the path has you, it will not let you wander off it.'

'How did you know about the storm? It's just a bit of wind and rain, I know, but how did you see it coming in clear blue skies?' He narrowed his eyes. 'You talked to the spice merchants, didn't you?'

'I know the signs,' she replied quietly. 'This storm will damage the city, and it will damage you. And you will damage the city, too. But do not try to fight your path now. Follow it to your final destination.'

'My final destination is far from here.'

'Yes. But not today.'

Skiouros pursed his lips, his jaw set firm, as the wind whipped his cloak about him and threatened to extinguish the woman's strange burning bowl, despite her meagre shelter.

'Do not presume to tell my future, witch. Neither God nor Allah has any say over where I go, so I'm not about to follow the advice of an old woman with bones in her hair!'

'God and Allah!' the witch cackled. 'God and Allah!'

Skiouros shook his head and straightened.

'I go now to book passage away from this place, from you and the

Janissaries and all that the city has thrown at me.'

'You go to disappointment, young fool. Quo vadis, eh? Tu Petros, sa-phal Theodoros. Bater, eh?'

'I told you before: I don't understand your tongue, even when you mix it with Greek names.'

His nostrils flaring angrily, Skiouros turned away from the old woman with her smoke and bones and scurried on down the street, away from the walls and into the Lycus valley at the end of which lay the harbour of Theodosius, the greatest of all the city's ports.

Turning the corner at the top of the hill to face down the valley, almost directly south, Skiouros' breath caught in his throat. The view here was one of the best in the city, as the valley of the now-subterranean Lycus river ran down between two of the city's most prominent hills to the Propontis sea and the great harbour. It was a view that Skiouros had seen a hundred times in his years in the city.

But he'd never seen it like this.

The battering, howling winds were rushing up the valley towards him, stirring leaves and debris into eddies in the side alleys and house frontages, and grit and dust scoured his face and eyes. Scudding clouds above promised more imminent rain squalls, but the horizon...

Where the steely grey sky above, marred with torn clouds, dipped down towards the horizon, they met a wall of dark purple, so deep it was almost black, obscuring the land not far beyond the Asian shore a few miles south.

It was a storm, but it was more than a storm. It looked like the judgement of God given form. Even for a pragmatic man like Skiouros, the very sight of that approaching nightmare brought a lump to the throat. The witch had been right, after all...

His step lent a new urgency, Skiouros hurried down the street, quickly sidestepping passers-by and ignoring all but the great harbour ahead and the promise of blessed escape that it offered.

Something else was nagging at him as he ran, but he had neither the time nor the attention to devote to it.

By the time he reached the Forum of the Ox, where the slope began to level out towards the shore, he was almost jogging, his eyes repeatedly straying up to the dark band of the approaching storm. He realised he knew nothing about tides other than that ships tended to sail on them. Did they have to? Or could they sail between tides? If they did have to sail on them, when precisely were they, and had the morning one been?

Across the great forum with its somewhat dilapidated arcade and the frontage of the once important Eleutherius palace he hurried, down through the last few streets which were largely clear of the usual bustle of people – not surprising, really, given the conditions. Exiting the city proper through the Gate of the Jews, he hurried towards the warehouses that marked the landward edge of the harbour complex.

Finally, with pounding heart and tingling nerves, Skiouros ran into the port and along the main quay, a relatively modern structure that had moved the focus of the port further out to sea to account for the silt build-up around the mouth of the Lycus. A dozen or more jetties jutted out into the water around two sides of the harbour, the third given over mostly to slipways for the construction of ships. Warehouses and offices stood inland, on the silted up area, arranged with the ordered and bureaucratic method visible in all remnants of the former Byzantine Empire.

Ships of a number of styles and nationalities sat in the water at the jetties, but the something that had been nagging at him suddenly penetrated into his consciousness and he realised what it was: the harbour was quiet.

There were the tell-tale sounds of shipwrights at work, and men were hauling goods in and out of ships and warehouses, of course, as was normal and to be expected. There were the small groups of soldiers at the end of each jetty with their guardhouses; not Janissaries here, but a lower-grade private force under the aegis of the Vizier of Trade. They watched the visiting vessels as always, checking crewmen in and out to make sure the city was safe from harm or foreign infiltration.

But apart from the mercantile, security and construction facets, there was something missing from the port: sailing.

Despite the two dozen merchantmen of different nations, not a single ship was out on the water of the harbour, each remaining tied up safely to a jetty. The Propontis beyond the harbour walls was empty even of the small fishing craft that perpetually dotted its surface.

Most tellingly, the great wooden harbour gates were shut.

Skiouros felt his pulse quicken. Surely this was too much for a mere storm, even one as bad as the lurking nightmare on the horizon? Turning, he ran towards the merchants' hall next to the harbourmaster's office.

The huge structure, formed of old Byzantine brick and stone, was a two-storey building that housed temporary offices which could be rented by the captains of ships or the city's merchants to do business in, and some of those offices had now been taken by traders in perpetuity.

The door of the building stood open and unguarded, as all were welcome within, especially if they had available goods or a few spare akce to spend.

Hurrying over the threshold, noting the warm dry interior and the wet footprints in the entrance, Skiouros stepped inside. In his years in the city, he'd been past the merchant's hall numerous times, but had never had cause to enter it. Such a place contained a lot of money and therefore everyone who transacted within it had their wits about them. It was a brave thief indeed who tried for pickings here, as the three spiked heads near the harbourmaster's office attested.

The ground floor was mostly given over to a social area with seating and tables – a 'meyhane' or wine house, its trade forbidden by religious law but tolerated by the wise Sultan Beyazid as a necessary evil in a cosmopolitan city such as this – another unwelcome reminder of what was coming. Here, traders and their crews and teamsters were able to shelter from the weather and pass information and laugh, sing and drink. Around the edge sat the offices, with two staircases leading up to a balcony that ran around the periphery to another floor of offices, these upper ones more private and exclusive and therefore more costly.

The social centre was not Skiouros' current concern, and he doubted the top floor would be of much use, so he strode around the edge of the ground floor, examining the boards that advertised each trader's business.

Without a command of the written word, much of it was gibberish of course, but a lot of information could be gleaned, regardless. Of necessity the offices were also advertised with images, given the low rate of literacy among the sailors and teamsters.

Those he was interested in, for instance, would have an image of a ship, to denote that they were a trader preparing for an outbound journey. They could be further narrowed down by locating a national flag. He was not, for example, interested in any office displaying the Crescent and Stars of the Ottoman Empire. It would be dangerous to try such a route at the moment. He sought the Lion of Saint Mark for Venetian merchants, the Red Cross and Gryphons of Genoa, or the White Cross on Blue of Venetian Crete – the so-called Kingdom of Candia. All might well present an opportunity for transport at a reasonable rate.

Almost a third of the way around the circumference, he found his first port of call, a Genoese ship captain, but changed his mind and hurried on as he realised that the man was in the throes of a deep argument with a man in the uniform of a Janissary. There was almost no chance that the man was here in any manner connected to Skiouros or his brother, but this was not a time to take chances.

Moving on, he found a second office in the far corner of the building that seemed more likely: a small room bearing the arms of Candia. At the side of the small office, an ebony-skinned boy from Africa was loading bales of something atop one another in an attempt to make more space, while the merchant himself sat at the rear of the room behind a table, with a set of charts spread out before him and some arcane brass device. Tutting to himself, he gripped the stem of a wooden beaker and drank a draught of something before returning to the chart and frowning at it as though it had offended him in some way.

Skiouros peered in at the man, sizing up the possibilities before entering.

The merchant captain was dressed in a purple doublet that had seen considerable wear and salt-spray damage. His boots, jutting out from beneath the table, had clearly been purchased for comfort and wear rather than style. His hair was a sandy corn colour and his face pale in comparison to those around him, adorned by a slightly ragged beard.

Skiouros nodded to himself. The man called no one master – that much was clear – but was also struggling to maintain a healthy income, as was clear by the fact he apparently did not own a second suit for land-work as many wealthier captains did, and he wore his sea apparel even here.

With a preparatory swallow and clearing of his throat, Skiouros stepped into the office.

'Good captain. Could I beg a moment of your time?' It was only as he fell silent that he realised he'd become so accustomed these past days to the automatic use of the Turkish tongue that he – a Greek – had automatically addressed a Venetian in it.

The sandy head lifted, and beleaguered, tired eyes fixed on him. For a moment Skiouros wondered whether the man had any Turkish, so he switched to Greek and repeated his opening comment.

'Yes?' the captain replied in good Greek with a southern, presumably Cretan, accent.

'I am seeking passage to Crete.'

The captain looked his visitor up and down, sceptically.

'I don't have room for thieves, vagabonds and stowaways, and I have no space for extra crewmen working their passage. Paying travellers only, I'm afraid.'

Skiouros sighed and gestured to his clothes with both hands.

'Do not let this garb form your opinion for you, Captain. I have more than moderate funds in the city; funds which I will be withdrawing this morning as soon as I am finished here. I can pay my way – on the clear assumption that your fee is not over-exorbitant, of course.'

Again, the captain regarded him with shrewd eyes, calculating his worth.

'I take only akce and good Venetian ducats. The cost will be ten ducats for standard passage with hammock. Fifteen for a bed. Twenty-five if you require a cabin – I have precious few.'

Skiouros pursed his lips and folded his arms.

'I'll agree to the fifteen for a good bed, if you'll throw in the storage space for a sea chest. I note you have not mentioned luggage rates yet.'

The captain grinned. 'Can't pull the wool over a Turk's eyes, eh? Alright. Fifteen with a bed and luggage.'

Skiouros wondered for a moment whether to explain that he was no Turk, but the fact that he was made up as one would raise even more questions and likely deny him passage, so he bit down on the words and nodded. The cinnamon stain would still colour his flesh for a week and by that time he could be in Crete before he apparently changed ethnicity again.

'When do you sail? I presume we've missed the morning tide.'

'You don't know much about the sea, do you, lad.'

When Skiouros looked at him blankly, the captain leaned back in his chair.

'You seen that storm out there? That, my lad, is what we in the trade call a "bastard of a storm". No sailor in his right mind would take a ship out in the face of that. I was due to sail on the morrow, but now, it seems we'll be trapped in port for a few days first.' His eyes narrowed suspiciously. 'Unless you're in a hurry?'

Skiouros sagged.

'Not in the way you mean, captain, but I would rather leave before the storm.'

The sailor laughed and leaned forward onto the table again.

'Not a chance, lad, I'm afraid. No ships will cross the Propontis now for days. Nothing will enter or leave port until the vizier fellow in charge of the harbours gives the all-clear.'

'I will have to decline then and find someone prepared to leave now.'

'Are you not listening, lad?' the captain sighed. 'No one will be leaving. Even if anyone here was insane enough to want to try, there's an Imperial edict against it. As long as that vizier says so, the harbours stay closed and we're all stuck here. Why do you think there are so many seamen out in the tavern area getting drunk?'

Skiouros pinched the bridge of his nose. The world seemed to be conspiring against him today. Or was it Lykaion's ghost trying to keep him to his task?

'You still want passage?' the captain asked, tapping his fingers on the table.

'Possibly. I want to check out another possibility yet.'

'Good luck with that, lad. I think you'll be sorely disappointed. When you come back for passage, if I've closed up shop here, find me on the *Isabella*, at the third jetty. Name's Parmenio.'

'Thank you, captain. God willing, I'll be long gone before then, but if I am as stuck as you seem to think I am, then I shall seek you out.'

Captain Parmenio returned to his work, scouring the charts, only looking up once and shaking his head at the dispirited figure leaving his office.

Skiouros trod the boards back towards the door wearily, aware of the high likelihood that he would be forced to seek out the captain again. The problem there lay in the fact that, if the assassination of the sultan went ahead today as the conspirators planned, there was a very real chance that all foreigners in the city would be locked up or executed, especially if Hamza Bin Murad was the man in charge of the aftermath. Would there be a captain and a ship to visit by the time the storm passed?

No. His one hope lay on the far side of the peninsular city.

The streets of Balat were deserted, the winds battering at Skiouros' back as he scurried along towards the stone frontage of the house of Judah ben Isaac – an island of permanence and wealth in a poor wooden world. The door was shut and there was no sign of the hulking doorman, David. Such inaccessibility was anathema to the Jew's business, but with the storm the way it was it was hardly surprising that the door had been shut for now. The cold winds would have wreaked havoc inside and David might have frozen, or drowned.

Approaching the door, Skiouros reached up and grasped the cord attached to the bell clapper, shaking it back and forth with enough vigour to make the noise heard over the howling winds. For good measure, he then hammered on the door three times, then a pause, then three more times; the knock of a repeat and known customer.

There seemed to be no sign of stirring from within and Skiouros strained to hear above the howling of the dreadful wind, finally turning in a mix of disappointment and irritation, preparing to leave, when the door opened with a quiet click.

A gleaming black pupil glared out at chest height, framed by black curly hair.

'Shalom... lady?' he hazarded. 'Would it be possible to speak to Master Judah ben Isaac?'

The eye narrowed for a moment and the door slammed shut, leaving Skiouros standing confused and wind-blown in the street. After half a minute longer, the irritation began to outweigh the confusion in him, and Skiouros reached out once more to rap heavily on the door, just as it swung open again. Arresting his reaching hand and trying not to stagger, Skiouros righted himself and looked up into the eyes of David.

The big man who habitually stood at the door was, in a word, unkempt. His ringlets looked straggly and greasy – unwashed or brushed, and a field of dark stubble grew across the lower half of his face. His usually neat attire was stained and creased and, to cap it all, a long tear marred the right breast of his shirt, leaving ragged strands and dangling thread.

Skiouros realised that he was staring – a dangerous thing to do with men like David.

'I wonder if I...'

'Go away.'

Skiouros blinked. 'I'm sorry if this is an inconvenient time, and normally I would simply return later, but I'm trying to arrange transport from here and I really need my money.'

David's eyes turned baleful and Skiouros winced for a moment. A little more deference might have been politic.

'In!' snapped David, swinging the door open and standing aside.

'Not the office. Up the stairs; to the back.'

As Skiouros stepped inside and gingerly shuffled along the passage, the large man closed the door behind him and followed, urging him up a flight of half a dozen stairs and into a large room – a hall even. In all his years of visiting the house, Skiouros had only ever attended in the two office rooms, never penetrating into the heart of the building.

Something about the hall struck Skiouros as strangely familiar and it was only as he was being ushered past it into a side room that he realised what it was: the building had once been a chapel or small church. That was why it stood as a singular stone building among all the wood. Beneath his feet, the marble tiles in hexagonal shapes were a sight seen in so many Byzantine churches. The columns had been plastered over in white, but were clearly ancient. The walls, similarly, were plastered, with only small, high windows, but recessed shapes spoke of three tall windows now blocked up.

He was still frowning over this strange discovery when he was none-too-gently urged into a side room.

Within, a wizened man sat behind a desk covered in ledgers, stacks of tablets and scrolls and paper books along trestles at the other side of the room. The man was a Jew, as his appearance confirmed, and perhaps the right age to be more or less contemporary with Judah ben Isaac – an uncle, perhaps? Or maybe an older brother? His hair was long, as was his beard, both mostly dark grey and speckled with white, but like David he had clearly not bathed in a few days, and his drab, plain clothing showed a similar tear on the breast.

'What's happened?' Skiouros asked quietly, a cold certainty forming in the pit of his stomach that something unpleasant had befallen the Jewish businessman.

The old man looked up from his work, his eyes two hollowed, shadowy pits of grief. He peeled his gaze away to David and asked something in his own language. David's reply was short and sounded less than positive.

'You came for money, boy?'

Skiouros nodded. 'I came to collect the change from a currency exchange, after Master ben Isaac's transaction fee, of course.'

'Then, young man, you have chosen an inopportune time. My brother is with God now, helped there two nights since by a man with a heart black with murder.'

'I... I am sorry to hear that, sir. You have my condolences. Did he...'

Skiouros searched hurriedly for a way to confirm his suspicions about the perpetrator without causing offence. 'Was it a random attack?'

David appeared at his side, his eyes narrowing.

'Clearly not. And apparently not even because he was one of God's true children. It appears that he was questioned brutally before he was sent to God. If I find out that you caused his end, I will revisit his doom on you, Christian.'

'Calm, David,' the old man said, and his tone was weary and sad. 'Judah had stolen the fruit from many a man's pie in his time. We are sitting shiva: it is not a time for accusations and anger.'

'It is also not time for business, uncle, but here you sit with father's ledgers.' David shied away from the angry glance of the old man and stepped back once more. The brother of Judah ben Isaac beckoned, and Skiouros stepped forward to the table.

'I wish it could wait, Master ben Isaac, and I am truly sorry to interrupt your grieving, but I am unfortunately bound by my own troubles.'

'You are not of us. You do not understand shiva. Some would be insulted by the presence of an outsider, unless he is here to sit shiva with us, of course.' He looked up past Skiouros. 'Go to Ama and help her, David.'

The big man lumbered away, grumbling under his breath.

'Now,' the old man said, leaning back and steepling his fingers, 'you have business with my brother. He would wish it settled, if it could be. I am working through his accounts now, so tell me about your business.'

Skiouros felt the prospects brighten and nodded. 'Master Judah – may God bless his memory – was transacting a particularly complex exchange of Mamluk coins into akce for me, I think via Venetian ducats. The exchange should have been complete by now, but I realise that there may be something of a delay. The problem is that I am bound for Crete as soon as I can find a ship that will sail, and I have no more time.'

The old Jew's eyes narrowed.

'Mamluk coins?'

'Yes.'

'Then I fear you are set for disappointment, young man. My brother was returning from an exchange in the Venetian enclave when he was set upon. He was left in the street outside with a Mamluk coin on his tongue. I fear your money is gone – perhaps taken by the very thugs that sent Judah to God.'

Skiouros closed his eyes for a moment, trying not to panic. Without a small fund, he would find it almost impossible to find passage from this benighted city.

'I am working through his records,' the old man went on, gesturing to the ledgers. 'I have already been back a week and there is no mention of your transaction, I am afraid. He must have done it as a private commission and kept no record. I cannot see how I can be of further help.'

The young visitor pinched the bridge of his nose. The nightmare morning was worsening by the hour.

'Is there any way you can arrange passage from the city in its stead? I know that Master Judah had cargoes arriving and leaving the city every day. Perhaps I could find a place with one of those vessels?'

The old man shook his head.

'No ships are leaving. Even the small ferry boats to the Anatolian coast on the far side of the Bosporos have been grounded. Not even a fisherman sails today.'

'What of land caravans?' Skiouros asked, trying to keep the edge of desperation from his voice.

'Only to Anatolia – to the Asian shores. The Wali of Hadrianople controls all land routes to the north and west and his taxes are too restrictive for my brother's business. It is simple, young man: nothing comes in or goes out until the ports open.'

Skiouros sagged. Every way he turned this morning a door shut in his face. He was trying very hard not to feel as though his brother was trying to keep him 'on task' from beyond the veil. His mind began to wander as the old Jew started to rattle off the details of different routes and why they were closed, when they would be open and whether they would help with a journey to Crete.

It was odd that he'd spent the night talking to the ghost of his Muslim brother in a former Christian church, and now here he was trying to strike a deal with a Jew in another such building. Even the damn Romani witch he seemed fated to keep bumping into had started spouting religious rubbish at him.

He frowned.

'Quo vadis!' he grumbled. He'd heard the phrase before, quoted by priests.

'What was that, young man?'

Skiouros blinked, clearing his wandering thoughts and focusing on the old man. 'Oh, just something an old woman said to me. Must be her Romani language.'

'It is in Latin, boy, not the Romani tongue. "Where do you go", it means.'

'She called me Petros, I think. Or Theodoros. I didn't understand her tongue.'

The old Jew leaned back again and narrowed his eyes. 'Theodoros?'

'I think so.'

'Interesting. This was once the church of Saint Theodoros. My brother found it amusing to make his home here and conduct usury in the house of the Christian God.'

Skiouros bit his lip. It was beginning to feel as though something was going to great lengths to keep him here. Much as he claimed not to believe in fate, it was becoming abundantly clear that fate believed in him.

No hope of leaving the city until the storm had cleared, with only a matter of hours until the sultan's life would be torn from him by a Mamluk hand, plunging the city and the whole world into chaos. And Skiouros no longer had more than a few akce to his name; not even a room in the city any more.

'I am at the end, Master ben Isaac. Without that money, the last door just closed on me.'

'I do not understand, young man.'

'Everything's been taken from me. I have nothing, and something is about to happen that I cannot change or stop; something awful. I wanted nothing more than to be gone, but I cannot even do that. I am stuck here with my future, which is looking increasingly unpleasant.'

The old man shrugged.

'In the words of Ben Sira, "Do not worry about tomorrow, for thou knowest not what the day will bring forth."'

'Somehow that doesn't comfort me a great deal. Thank you for seeing me, anyway. My apologies for intruding on your grief.'

The old man nodded with a sad smile.

'Sometimes, my boy, even when there seems no way out, one is standing right above the trapdoor.'

Skiouros nodded, trying not to comment on how double-edged and disheartening this extra snippet was. Instead, he turned and strode towards the door, pausing just within, as the old man scraped back his stool and crossed the room behind him.

'Come. I will show you out. Blessings of God go with you, whatever this day holds.'

'Thank you,' Skiouros said with little enthusiasm as he was escorted back through the hall and down the stairs and passage to the front door.

As the heavy wooden portal closed behind him with a click, Skiouros stood in the street, shivering in the wind, and felt utterly lost. The first droplets of the next bout of rain spattered on his forehead and he sighed. Back to the church then? To sit with Lykaion's remains – perhaps to bury them while there was still a graveyard to do it in? Perhaps to take his life in his hands and flee through one of the city gates into the wilds full of wolves, bandits and Turkish soldiers and mercenaries?

No. It would not be long before the sultan came out of the Palace for his religious observances and the Empire would lose its head, both literally and figuratively. By then, Skiouros could be outside the great Aya Sofya with the crowds and might even see the assassin take his shot.

If he was stuck here while the world fell into hell, he was at least going to watch it start to burn.

Chapter 10 – Apocalypse

* Pazar (Sunday) morning *

The streets were already crowded as far back as the curve of the hippodrome. Skiouros grunted his sour mood at the gathered Turks as he pushed and jostled his way between complaining, shouting citizens, all gathered for the dual purpose of celebrating Ashura and trying to catch a glimpse of the great Bayezid the Second, Sultan and Master of Istanbul.

All they would see from back here amid the curving ruins of the seating stands, however, would be the distant ripple of waving arms among those at the front, acknowledging the lord's arrival. Skiouros tried not to think of them as sheep but failed as he elbowed a heavy-set man out of the way, pushing on between a young merchant-type fellow and two children before the big man could grab him and administer a clout round the ear.

Skiouros was, of course, lithe and small and an expert at moving swiftly through such crowds, evading capture or pursuit; today, though, he was not a thief – nor a fugitive – but one of those very sheep come to watch the great sultan arrive and to see the events of the holy day unfold.

He was, however, anticipating rather different events to those being awaited by the bustling crowd. They mourned the passing – centuries ago – of the great Hussein Ibn Ali, while he came instead to watch the passing of another renowned Muslim leader.

Pushing on, he passed the great ruined walls of the Kathisma – the Imperial box from which those men who had once ruled the Roman world had watched the Blues race the Greens; the Whites race the Reds. He remembered hearing the stories of those halcyon days from the ageing tale-spinners in the taverns of the Greek enclave; men who remembered the Byzantine realm and the last Emperor – Constantine Palaiologos, the eleventh man to bear that great name and the man who lost the city of his famous namesake to the Turk.

He remembered the story of the night the people rose up against their master in this very hippodrome. He couldn't remember the reasons in the long and involved tale, but the master storyteller had vividly described the explosion of violence in this great elongated arena, the fleeing of the emperor to his palace, the burning, looting and pillaging in which the people of Constantinople almost destroyed their own city, the siege of the palace and finally the arrival of the army under its generals. The soldiers of Byzantium had marched into this very hippodrome and executed every living thing that stood before them until the riots had ended in a sea of blood.

Did history repeat itself?

Skiouros could hardly claim to know the mindset of the Ottoman people, but he very much suspected that the reaction of the gathered multitude to the murder of their sultan before their very eyes would mirror the great riots that had shaken Constantinople those eons ago. If they were to discover that the death blow had come from a Mamluk no foreigner would be safe within reach of the city; but if they were to discover it was at the behest of a Janissary commander? Then the city would tear itself apart.

Whatever happened in the next few hours, the prospects for the survival of a poor Greek thief looked bleak.

Slowly he closed on the great Aya Sofya – the greatest mosque in the Ottoman world and once the greatest Church in the Christian one. It remained largely unchanged in form since the days it had housed crosses and images of the saints. A golden crescent had risen from its great dome upon the city's fall, and a few years ago a slender wooden minaret had risen from the corner closest to the palace, but that was the sum total of the visible changes to the building's exterior. The enormous, beautiful bulk of the Aya Sofya rose from the sea of excitable citizens like a giant tortoise.

Behind the great church where the mourning rites for the holy day would be held before the sultan and his viziers, Skiouros could just see the towers and walls of the Topkapi palace where the court resided.

The closer he made it to the gate in that wall, the more densely packed the crowd would become. Concentrating, Skiouros peered at the Aya Sofya. He had been to its doors more than once and had even slipped inside on a particular occasion a few years ago, though only very briefly. To be caught in the Ottomans' most sacred holy building would not go well for him.

He contemplated whether he could get inside today to watch the proceedings but, even before he remembered that the sultan was unlikely to even reach the building, he had decided against that course of action. Death would await a Greek Christian caught loitering in that place, but to be discovered within as a Greek Christian disguised as one of their own? Every conceivable torture would be visited upon his stained pale frame before he was allowed to die. No. It would not be worth the risk.

Anyway, nothing would happen inside.

It was between that forbidding door and the nearby palace gate that the murder would be carried out.

He found himself wondering how it would be done.

It could not be carried out with a hand weapon. Apart from the fact that escape for the assassin would be impossible and that the blame would then be irrevocably tied to the Mamluks, there was no guarantee that the Janissaries guarding the sultan would let him past. Even if they were of Bin Murad's own orta of guards, could the conspirators really plan all of this and allow for even the possibility that the guards might have a sudden flash of conscience and save the sultan?

No.

It would be done with some sort of missile. A dart would never reach him, surely? A gun would be the best for the distance, but they were not entirely reliable – certainly not enough for a professional assassin. Especially with the atmosphere as damp as it was. Several times the Ottoman musket brigades had been laid low by wet powder.

A bow, then. Even though wet weather played havoc with a bow string, it would survive better than the gunpowder required for a musket, and the bow could be sheathed until the last minute. Either a crossbow or a recurve sinew and horn affair; both would be perfectly suited to the shot. A poisoned arrow, too – just in case the initial blow was not a direct kill. And a poison that would most likely be traced to the Greek populace, too – laying the blame squarely away from both

Mamluk and Ottoman. Not something clearly Arabic in origin.

So how would a man be able to get a clear shot? On the few occasions that Bayezid had graced the streets of the Ottoman city with his presence, he had ridden proudly on his great white mare, every inch the conquering hero like his father. A shot would still be difficult from among the crowd.

He would have trouble, unless he could find a high place.

Skiouros' eyes were drawn up to the undulating roofline of the Aya Sofya, and then beyond that to the tall, narrow wooden minaret.

Would he really choose such a place? There would be no easy escape from a minaret if he was seen taking the shot, and that was a distinct possibility in such a high visibility location. The roof might be better, with more places to fire from and plenty of cover and escape routes.

But the minaret would give him the best clear shot.

Despite the knowledge that he was really powerless to do anything about the coming disaster, Skiouros found that he was moving forward with ever-increasing urgency, as though trying to reach the killer before the shot could be taken.

As he reached the walls of the great mosque, he moved along them, squeezing past hopeful watchers and avoiding the thrown detritus of half a dozen small children sitting high on the window sills. At the corner, he stepped onto an old Roman block that had had an iron ring driven into it for tethering beasts. Standing now a head above the crowd, he had a clearer view of the minaret.

Looking somewhat rickety, the narrow wooden tower with its balcony and roof at the top was only wide enough to contain one tight spiral stair that ran down to the upper floor of the great former church, where it met an opening in the wall. That doorway, Skiouros knew, led on to an interior staircase which gave access to the main church or the upper galleries. From there escape would be easy, blending into the crowd.

Yes, it was the best possible place for an assassin to shoot from, and once the man was down the minaret and into the bulk of the church, he would be free, but that journey from the high balcony to the interior would be risky. If he was seen too soon, he could find his escape route sealed and himself trapped in the tower.

The great Bab i Humayun – the massive and monumental gate in the walls that sealed in the grounds of the Topkapi palace and was little over a decade old, stood sealed tight, brooding at the great church perhaps a hundred and fifty feet from the minaret.

This was almost certainly where it was going to happen.

A deep, ear-splitting boom rang out across the crowd and, startled and shaken, Skiouros spun round in a panic, suddenly convinced that somehow the assassination had already happened. Could they really have used a cannon?

The reactions of the people packed around him were almost identical, the crowd surging in a panic at the sudden explosion. But there was no smoke; no damage.

Confusion reigned for a silent and eerie second.

And then the rain came.

The deafening crack had been the Anatolian storm finally opening up above the Bosporos and the sky was becoming noticeably darker with every heartbeat. There had been no cannon – no explosion. The storm that had wreaked havoc on the southern reaches of the Ottoman Empire had finally reached its heart.

Skiouros shuddered at the apparent symbolism of the timing.

Once, during a bad storm back in Hadrianople, Father Simonides had recounted a tale of the end of days when four riders would appear, bringing Armageddon in their wake. Skiouros had scoffed at the tale, even within earshot of the old priest – an impious move that had earned him three hours' work scrubbing the church's tiled floor – but Lykaion had sat transfixed by the story, drinking in every word with wide, terrified eyes.

And now, as the sky went from mid-grey through purple and finally to almost black, the rain pounding down so hard it hurt the head with every droplet and felt like a blow from a plank of wood, the chill air rent with deafening crashes, that unbelievable tale was suddenly all too credible. Skiouros found his eyes swinging up to the sky, looking for those four riders on the roiling crest of the storm.

He was alone in his panic. The sea of Muslim watchers around him heeded no such tale for their end of days. They were instead either looking around in confusion or ignoring the violence of the storm, concentrating on the gate through which Bayezid the Just would emerge to the acclaim of his people and the shot that would snatch away his life.

It was then, as Skiouros scoured the boiling black sky, that a movement caught his attention from the corner of his eye. His gaze was drawn to the top of the wooden minaret.

A figure!

The assassin – for it had to be him – moved in the shadow of the minaret's doorway, barely visible but for that single moment when he had leaned out of the shade to take in the view of the ground below with its seething masses. Skiouros' breath caught in his throat and his eyes returned to the level. It was almost impossible to see anything other than a writhing sea of heads and arms. Even the trees and the walls and ruins of various buildings were somewhat indistinct behind the crowd.

There were soldiers.

Some of them were Dervishes from the city's Bektashi monastery in their finery, bearing ornamental pole-arms. Others were low-level yaya infantry: unarmed, but resplendent in their uniforms nonetheless. Others still were Janissaries, both on- and off-duty. Even if any of them could do anything, they would be unlikely to listen to a word said by a peasant and might well simply arrest him, or even beat him. But there was little chance of reaching them through the crowds anyway, so that fact was moot.

What could he do?

Nothing.

The imam of the great Aya Sofya would have to climb that minaret, of course, to issue the call to prayer, but it would be too late by then. The sultan would be in position within the mosque before the call went out so that the crowd followed him to prayer, rather than vice-versa.

And he would be dead by then.

At this point, the imam would still be in his chambers in the mosque, while the killer stood on the minaret, waiting.

Watching.

The world was about to end. Skiouros' world, and that of the peaceable Ottoman Empire.

It surprised him, the extent to which he was able to view these events with a certain detachment. He had never been as invested as his brother in this affair anyway, but the death of Lykaion and his own inability to affect the outcome in any way – or even to flee the scene effectively – had lent him the final tool with which to sever his connection with the matter.

He was an observer of the End of Days and nothing more.

Another crash of thunder rang out and a brilliant white flash lit up the sky, creating a strange pattern in the clouds like the veins in dark marble. It looked for all the world as though a great slab of black stone was descending from the heavens to crush the city.

It might as well be.

Skiouros reached back for his hood to pull it over his head and take some of the pounding pressure of the rain, but paused and dropped his arms to his sides once again. Somehow the battering of the heavy droplets felt like a massage on his scalp, leaving him not enough space to think clearly, which was comforting and simple. His hood fell back again, sodden and unused.

A sense of calm acceptance had suffused him at last – a feeling that had been building all morning, and indeed ever since his weird night-time conversation with his brother's shade.

It was with this sense of peace, his face upturned – not so that he could see the assassin, but rather to savour the cool calming effect of the lashing rain – that he realised something was happening. Almost regretfully, he lowered his gaze to the crowd once more and opened his eyes, allowing conscious thought back in.

The great gate to the Topkapi palace had opened, the gap widening as the Janissaries heaved on the heavy doors. Figures had appeared on the battlemented walkway at the top of the gate.

From his position on the ancient block, some way back among the masses and at the corner of the great mosque, Skiouros had a good all-round view over the heads of the crowd. He could easily see the minaret and the gate, his eyes flicking back and forth between the faint, vague humanoid shadow in the tower and the figures atop the gate, his eyes straining in the gloom and the downpour.

But for all his clear vision, he could not quite tell what was happening; the seething crowd and the hammering rain and cracks of thunder drowned out all sound. Something was happening at the front. It was not the sultan's arrival, though.

When Bayezid emerged from the gate it would be on horseback, surrounded by mounted aides and guards, with Janissaries forcing back the sea of people and opening up a path ahead of him.

Clearly that was not happening as the crowd remained immobile, intent on the gate.

A red and white robed figure had appeared on the walkway among the Janissaries there. As Skiouros squinted into the gloom and the sheets of water pouring from the sky, he could see that the finely-robed man – not the sultan, surely – was addressing the crowd.

Whatever he was saying was totally lost in the distance, but it had apparently not gone down well with the masses. From ahead, near the gate and the minaret, angry and disappointed shouts and cries were rising. Interspersed among them were wails of anguish and sobbing. Suddenly the whole crowd seemed to be distressed.

It was not the mourning sound Skiouros expected on the Day of Ashura. He had witnessed the annual holy day before. A rhythmic beating of the chest was more expected; not this sudden distressed shouting.

His heart fell.

The shadowy figure at the minaret's top could be the imam after all, and not the assassin. Had the Mamluk already struck? Perhaps he'd found some method of ingress to the Topkapi palace, poisoning Bayezid in the same manner in which his colleague had dispatched the Janissary Agha?

It was over, then.

Not with a great, earth-shaking event, but with a speech. Even from his detached and impassive viewpoint, Skiouros could feel it as something of a disappointment. Such a calamitous happening with such far-reaching effects should be heralded with more than a downpour and a few words.

A well-dressed man in front of Skiouros muttered something about waste and turned, looking up at the sky angrily.

The thief frowned as their gazes met, his diminutive stature negated by the stone block on which he stood.

'What was that all about?' he asked dispassionately, his Turkish barely marred by an accent these days.

The man lowered his gaze to Skiouros, his nostrils flaring. 'The sultan!'

'Yes?'

'He is not coming out because of the rain!'

Skiouros stared at the man.

'Can you believe it?' The Turk snapped in angry disbelief. 'A man who has fought off the Mamluk Sultanate for a decade! A man who commands an army of thousands and rules the greatest empire the world has ever known, and he's not leaving his palace because of a storm!'

Skiouros continued to stare at the indignant nobleman for a long moment and then suddenly exploded in helpless laughter.

The nearest members of the crowd, seething angrily at the sultan, irritated by the rain and this betrayal of their enthusiasm, turned to regard this giggling imbecile with surprise.

For a long time, Skiouros laughed, unable to stop. He had not laughed so loud and free for years. In the past week, he and Lykaion had faced dangers galore. They had wracked their brains and put their lives on the line, sneaking around the city and spying, fighting off killers to prevent an assassination and they had failed in the end, only to discover that the weather had done their job for them!

Bayezid the Just was alive.

Alive because of the rain.

It was almost too beautiful to believe.

He was crying, of course, at the now-needless death of Lykaion, but the tears mingling with the endless streaming, life-saving rain, were as much of relief as frustration and grief.

The world would not end today, despite the storm.

God had sent the tempest not to cloak his four apocalyptic riders, but rather to shield the sultan against his enemies. What did that mean?

It meant that Skiouros could yet leave the city and go to Crete with captain Parmenio, so long as he could find finance for the passage.

Such a thing should be easy enough for a thief.

But as he thought of the picking of purses, he realised that the past days had changed something in him. In a moment of epiphany, he suddenly knew that he was not the conscience-free thief had had been these recent years. He had thieved to survive in the city and he had done that only in order to be there for Lykaion when he was needed. Lykaion no longer needed him, and now he could leave the city. And that meant that his days of cutting purse strings might well be over.

If he could only afford the journey.

Perhaps God, if he existed, was giving him a chance? Perhaps it was Lykaion. Whatever it was, the world had not ended, and he couldn't help but feel there was a reason for it.

A flash of lightning drew his eyes skywards again and he caught a momentary movement on the minaret: the swirl of a cloak.

It was no imam, after all.

The figure in the shadows high above was the assassin.

A thrill ran through Skiouros as he saw the figure disappear, descending the stairwell into the minaret tower and down to the Aya Sofya.

There was a reason for it all, then.

The danger to the sultan and therefore the whole of the city and

Empire was not over. It would never be over as long as the assassin remained at large. Bayezid had escaped today with his skin intact, but the Mamluk killer – the last of the three in the city – would try again and again until the lord of the Ottoman world lay dead.

Skiouros had been given a gift. He alone of the entire throng knew not only that a murderer was intent on the sultan's life, but that he was here, now. Thwarted, yes, but free and ever-able to make further attempts.

The assassin had to be stopped. That was why God had sent the storm. Even the flashes of lightning might have been to draw his attention to the Mamluk's presence.

What could he do?

The question was far from new but the inflection was different now. All morning he had asked that question but in a rhetorical, fated way, knowing that the answer was 'nothing'. Now it had become a genuine enquiry. Now there was an answer, if only he could find it.

He could hardly face the assassin down – he knew that.

The first of the three Mamluk killers he'd faced had been prevented from dispatching him only by Lykaion's timely intervention. The second had been part luck and part knowing the ground better than his enemy. This third time, there was nothing to help him. Skiouros knew this area – the heart of the Ottoman world – little better than the Mamluk would. He knew only the streets, not the buildings themselves. And the killer would be faster and stronger than him.

Skiouros smiled.

But now the Greek thief was no longer a Greek thief, at risk if noticed. To any casual observer, he was now an impoverished Ottoman youth, whereas the Mamluk, for all his cloak and anonymity, would be plainly discernible as one of the Empire's enemies if he could only be exposed.

Skiouros did not need to face the assassin in combat. All he had to do was draw him to the attention of the authorities this time, and they would do the rest.

His mind began to race. What next then? The assassin was already down the minaret and even as Skiouros peered at the upper floor of the Aya Sofya he could see the scurrying figure. The unmistakable shape of a bow protruded from the assassin's shoulder as the wind caught the cloak while he darted from the wooden minaret across the narrow walkway and through the door into the mosque.

There was only one feasible exit from the Aya Sofya. Oh, there were many doors, but today they would be under guard. With the sultan expected in the great mosque, each exit would be guarded by Janissaries.

So the Mamluk would have to leave by the main public entrance, trusting to his cloak to keep him hidden from discovery.

Even as his reasoning reached this conclusion, Skiouros was pulling and heaving his way through the crowd. Angry, irritable citizens shouted at him and he even caught a few warning blows as he pushed them aside.

He had to be there first.

He would be.

The rain was coming down so hard now that it was almost as difficult to push through as the crowd it was battering, the regular cracks and crashes of thunder and flashes in the sky only increasing in intensity with every passing moment. Skiouros skittered and slid on the paving as he rounded the now unused baptistery of the ancient church, barging his way through the mass of bodies, unheeding of the annoyance he was causing.

He would beat the killer to the exit.

He had been given an opportunity to stop all this; to uphold the vow he'd made in the ruined church of Saint Polyeuktos to see this through to the end. No simple crowd was going to stop him now.

The north-western façade of the great mosque rose from the sea of heads, impressive and ancient. The triple-arched porch that stood proud off the exonarthex was packed with people, all unmoving, trapped in this mass of humanity. Here and there a figure pushed and struggled in or out of the mosque, but most were content to stand in place and wait for the imam to issue the call.

In fact, as Skiouros closed on the central arch with its open doors, he could faintly hear the call to prayer now, in broken, distant fragments amid the pounding rain and the hum of the crowd.

Almost as though the enigmatic warbling had been a trigger, the assembled masses began to pound their chests with their hands – the traditional mourning for Ashura – at least as far as the press of people allowed.

Not wishing to stand out as anything other than a devoted native, Skiouros began to hammer his fist to his sternum even as he pushed and weaved through the crowd.

By the time he reached the entrance arch itself and leaned back against the ancient brickwork, beating the rhythm on his chest even as he heaved in weary, gasping breaths, the crowd had begun to push into the building. The guards within, informed that the sultan was not coming after all, had stepped aside and allowed the wide space kept clear for their master to be filled instead by members of the public. The sudden opening up of the inside relieved some of the pressure near the doors and Skiouros closed his eyes for a moment, feeling the change in the atmosphere around him as a small quantity of air circulated despite the blanket of rain, ripping away the smells of stale sweat and spices that had marked the citizens pressed to him.

A cleansing breath.

His eyes snapped open and focused seemingly automatically on the cloaked figure that moved improbably against the flow of people. As the Ottoman population surged in through the door to the place they would remove their footwear for their devotions, one single figure was moving against the tide.

Almost like a gift from God, the assassin was moving towards Skiouros as he navigated the surge of bodies. The thief could quite clearly make out the slight lump at the cloak's shoulder that betrayed the bow carried beneath it and the hump at the hip where the quiver of arrows jutted. No one else had noticed, but then such tell-tale shapes were hardly clear and obvious signs to those who were not already looking for them.

Skiouros took a deep breath.

The next few moments would likely be among the most dangerous in his life, and yet he felt somehow calm, and even eager. The assassin closed on him, eyes glinting in the deep shadow of the hood as he scanned the crowd, apparently not even noticing the young man leaning against the wall. The Mamluk was beating his hand against his chest in a half-hearted manner, enough to be in keeping with everyone, while not concentrating on the task or rhythm.

Skiouros allowed his gaze to drop to his own chest as his hand slammed into his sternum again and again.

The cloak moved past, within touching range.

With a sudden flourish, Skiouros' hand stopped beating, reaching out instead to grasp the murderer's cloak by the shoulder.

Skiouros' eyes came up, focusing for one moment on the three Janissaries standing in a huddle nearby before drawing back to the man and the knot of grey cloak in his grip. With every ounce of strength he could muster, Skiouros hauled back on the cloak.

The assassin – caught completely off guard – staggered, almost falling backwards with the tug. Then, in a God-given moment, the brooch holding the cloak closed bent and came apart. Skiouros almost fell as the garment in his hand came free.

'Assassin!' he bellowed as he lurched against the wall, raising his free hand to point at the man suddenly exposed in the midst of the crowd.

'Mamluk!' he added at the top of his voice, in order to draw extra attention to the man's clearly Arabic, southern features.

There was a strange, almost deafening silence as if the world held its breath, and then an almost instantaneous crack of thunder and flash of lightning, lighting up the man as the crowd pulled back around him, opening up as much panicked space as they could.

'Mamluk assassin!' Skiouros cried again, throwing the cloak at the man.

Maddeningly, somehow the Janissaries had been lost to sight as the crowd moved, a roar of angry disbelief rising from the massed throats. Skiouros found that he was standing in a rapidly widening circle with the killer as the crowd pulled back.

If the authorities ever needed a clear indication of the man's guilt, the recurve bow over his shoulder and the quiver at his waist would do the trick.

But the authorities had been obscured by the heaving crowd.

For a desperate moment, Skiouros wondered if the assassin might afford himself the time to deliver a blow to his accuser. It would be easy enough.

But then the man was gone from the widening circle. Pushing his way into the frightened, angry crowd, the assassin disappeared directly across from the mosque's door.

Skiouros felt the sudden lurch of his hasty plan going awry. He'd assumed that the authorities would leap to his aid, especially when the killer's identity had been clearly revealed. He'd even thought the angry citizens would lend their aid. What he had not banked on was the crowd not only rearing back from the Mamluk in panic, but also accidentally preventing the Janissaries from getting near.

Before he even realised the danger he was putting himself in, he was pushing through the press after the fleeing Mamluk, still yelling his accusations so that the guards could tell where the killer was, despite their vision being obscured by the crowd.

Gradually, as he pushed across the wide square outside the Aya Sofya with its press of worshippers, the mob began to thin out. Here and there as he heaved and scrambled, ducked and weaved, he caught a glimpse of his quarry, moving with equal difficulty.

And then suddenly, Skiouros burst from the last press of people into open space, only to discover that the killer had vanished.

The pursuing thief came to a halt, panting, far enough from the crowd that he had a reasonable view of his surroundings. Behind him the people were still pushing into the Aya Sofya and half a dozen Janissaries were visible, ploughing through the mass towards him, their high, flowing white cap decorations marking them out above the massed heads.

Desperately, aware that if he lost the assassin now he would likely never find him again, Skiouros scanned the area, his eyes narrowed, squinting into the gloom and the deluge, trying to spot something of use.

A faint bumping noise drew his attention directly ahead.

A battered, rickety wooden door bounced twice against the frame before coming to rest, betraying recent passage.

Where did the door go? The simple whitewashed wall in which it was set was unadorned and windowless. It was clearly no house or business. With a nervous swallow and a quick upcast prayer that he was right, Skiouros bellowed 'This way!' and ran to the door, flinging it open.

He barely had time to register the darkness and the musty damp algae smell before the arrow grazed his cheek, sinking into the wooden door frame.

The first thought that struck him as he ducked back was that the stairway he'd almost fallen down within must lead to one of the innumerable ancient cisterns of the city.

The second was that the assassin's arrows were almost certainly poisoned.

Panic gripped Skiouros as he wondered what to do. To rush on down the stairs into the darkness with an assassin lurking somewhere inside would be a potentially suicidal act. His head spun round and his gaze played across the retreating backs of the crowd. In their push to get into the great mosque and out of the horrendous weather, the mass of people had swamped the pursuing Janissaries who, while they were probably still in pursuit, were currently nowhere to be seen, buried in the heaving throng. If he simply waited for the soldiers to catch him up and sent them in, the Mamluk killer could be anywhere. It all depended on whether he wanted to catch him badly enough to risk his life further.

That particular thought brought back the issue of poison. While Skiouros had nothing to do with such killings himself, and even tended to steer clear of the sort of groups who would perpetrate them, his profession had brought him into contact with paid killers or their masters from time to time. One thing he did know was that any Turk or Mamluk (or even Christian for that matter) who valued their pay would utilise poisons on their blades or missiles. There was always a chance that the shot would not be a killing blow, and so it must be accompanied by a guaranteed backup.

The poison would be deadly. Should he abandon all of this and get to a healer?

He suddenly began to shake and spasm as if freezing ice-water had infused his veins from head to toe, and panic wracked him. He was going to die.

It occurred to him in the objective, sensible part of his mind that it was almost certainly a reaction of his body to the mere thought, especially since he was standing in cold, battering rain. If a poison had worked its way into his blood in the space of a few heartbeats and was having such an effect he would be dead before he reached the bottom of the stairs – and there would be nothing anyone could do about it.

Trying to focus on the positive, he forced his fear down and was not surprised to find the deadly chill in his veins subside with it.

All in my head. It's all in my head.

That was not a comforting thought either.

By the time he was coming to a conclusion about what he should do, he was already inside the door, ducking to one side in case his silhouette gave the assassin another easy shot. No arrow came. His back against the cold, slimy wall, Skiouros paused for a long moment to let his eyes accustom themselves to the environment and his ears stop pounding enough to hear anything useful.

Despite having felt like several minutes of life-or-death decision-making, it had in effect been a matter of seconds between being struck by the missile and now returning to the dark. Certainly less than half a minute.

As his eyes began to take in the cistern in its cavernous gloom, his eyes were already supplying further details.

199

There were no footsteps of a man moving downstairs – the killer must already be at the bottom. The sound of a vast quantity of water in an enclosed space came up from below, lapping low waves hitting stone, all echoing eerily around the huge cathedral-like space. But there was more to the water sound than that. As his ears scanned the constant echoes of lapping, he recognised rhythmic splashes.

The splashes of oars.

A boat.

The thin beam of light that issued from the door above was gloomy in itself, dulled by the deep grey of the storm, but it picked out the uniform grey trunks of a forest of columns soaring up through the darkness to terminate in arches at the top, holding up a solid roof that would have been the floor of something above, no longer standing. There were fragmentary ruins of some ancient basilica there, as he knew from previous visits to the area, now interspersed with the small mansions or large townhouses of the wealthier Turks.

Across the darkness, towards the far end of the cistern, he could see the light picking out the undulating surface of the stored water, white flecks and shifting shapes on a sea of ebony.

But there was another shaft of light, too.

It was hard to make out until the eyes adjusted, especially with the outside light being so dim, but a square opening in the roof some distance away in the gloom cast down a beam that picked out an ever-shifting rectangle on the water below.

His eyes narrowed as they took in something else – something that their first three passes of this other light source had missed. It was all but invisible, but it was there.

A rope hung down from the hole in the ceiling towards the water's surface.

Skiouros was skittering lightly down the slippery, ancient steps long before he realised that perhaps this was not the best thing to do. Could he not have simply gone back outside and found a way into the lots behind this entrance, to locate the opening?

Ah well; his course was not truly set as he descended a little too far and too fast and felt his foot slip into cold water. He had already reached the bottom. His mind reeled. There was no walkway. No platform or wooden jetty. What had made him presume there would be in a damn cistern?

A snapping sound alerted him to the danger even before the

thrumming sound of the approaching arrow reached his ears, and he dropped to a crouch, his legs and backside sinking into the icy water in blackness. The arrow clattered off the wall just above his head, roughly where his chest would have been.

Now that his eyes were accustomed to the darkness, he could pick out the shape in the gloom. A small coracle-like boat was approaching the descending shaft of light and the dangling means of escape. He could now see the shape of the killer, reaching out with one arm to retrieve his bow from the boat's bottom even as he pushed against the water with the oar in the other.

Skiouros could almost have laughed, had he not been in such mortal danger. Even as the assassin reached to grasp the rope it suddenly disappeared upwards with the 'zizz'-ing sound of rope being drawn hurriedly across an edge. The assassin's fingers closed on empty air.

A curse in Arabic rang out across the water, quickly followed by a tumult of calls in both Arabic and Turkish. The square of light above was suddenly blotted out by the arrival of figures and then the entire cistern resounded with a deafening crack. Even as Skiouros' ears rang and the sound echoed a thousand times in such quick succession it was almost a vibration, the meaning of the sound sank in.

A gun shot.

That meant the Janissaries. No one else in the city would be carrying a gun. Apparently they must have known about the other roof-exit and, having been alerted to the assassin's escape route by Skiouros' shout, had rushed across to seal it off.

His elation at the sudden reprieve was shattered a moment later as he realised that the killer had not been harmed and had, in response, turned his boat and was now rowing with all his might back towards the stairs.

Skiouros' heart leapt. Should he run?

The question became moot a moment later as the door above clattered and more Turkish voices echoed from the top of the stairs, challenging the Mamluk assassin to surrender. That was it. The man was trapped.

The thought of what might happen when a deadly killer found himself trapped only occurred to Skiouros as the first arrow splashed into the water close enough that it pinned his cloak to the mortared wall just below the waterline.

His wide eyes sought out the shape of the assassin drifting along the water's surface towards him, using the momentum he had previously built up, as he neared his original point of entry. The figure was standing in the boat now, heedless of the danger of capsizing. His bow was held taut in one hand and the other was busy nocking the next shot while several more arrows projected from his fingers, held at the ready.

Skiouros, even in deadly danger, had to be impressed as he saw the man's arrow leave the bow, only to be replaced by the next, dropping from his finger-holds and into position just in time for the string to be drawn back and the bow fired again.

The first arrow grazed his shoulder as he disappeared beneath the water's surface, but the man's curious technique allowed for the most astounding rate of fire. Even as Skiouros opened his eyes under the water, peering through a blossoming red cloud from his wounds, he saw the staccato shots bounce from the wall two heartbeats apart. Then, three shots later, there was a gap. Skiouros wondered for a moment whether the man had run out of missiles, but then the water exploded as one of the Janissaries at the stair top hit the surface, an arrow through his neck.

Skiouros waited. He waited with the patience of a man aware that drowning might not be the worst result of this dive. Finally, as his chest burned and his lungs screamed and his mind began to shake, producing black spots in his vision, he pushed up and broke the surface next to the bobbing corpse of the Turkish soldier. The water tasted faintly metallic from the blood diffusing in it.

There was no sound of arrows. He turned, pedalling in the water, and almost suffered an involuntary loosening of the bowels as he saw the boat perhaps three feet from his head and closing. Desperately, he pushed himself out of the way, holding up an arm to stop the boat striking him on the head, and peered up nervously.

Rivulets of blood were running from the boat's side into the water and his gaze focused on the slumped form of the assassin, a second mouth opened beneath his chin and grinning evilly with a crimson smile. The blade that had inflicted the neat, professional wound was still in the man's hand.

Of course he had killed himself.

What else could a professional killer do with no way out and his supply of ammunition drained?

Another wave of panic broke over him – the feeling was becoming so familiar it almost felt like the norm now. He struggled desperately as arms hooked under his shoulders and hauled him from the water. He was aware that he was punching and kicking with little actual success, until a hard, ringing slap across the face made him stop.

The Janissary officer who had delivered the blow and who was one of the two men holding him up, grinned, revealing a wicked face with two missing teeth.

'Calm, boy,' he commanded in a deep voice, his Turkish stained with the provincial twang of a Balkan upbringing.

'Sorry sir,' he replied in his best Turkish, trying not to look the man in the eye.

'You were the one who alerted us?' Despite the upward inflection, it was clearly a statement rather than a question, though Skiouros nodded regardless.

'Well done, boy. Many's the man who'd have run in panic or turned his face from such a thing.'

Skiouros became slowly aware that two more Janissaries standing knee-deep in the water were hauling the dead assassin's corpse from the boat. The officer turned to them.

'Is he…?'

'Yessir. Dead by his own hand, equipped like a professional assassin and as Mamluk as they come.' The man plucked an arrow from the mortar of the wall and held it up in the feeble light. 'This bastard was meant for the sultan, I reckon, sir.'

'Indeed. There will have to be an investigation.'

Skiouros swallowed nervously. Any investigation could well unearth things that would damn him to a very painful and public death. Fortunately, such a nervous reaction would have been entirely in-character for a poor Ottoman waif, and the officer gave him a sympathetic smile, marred by those ugly gaps left by his missing teeth.

'But not for you, lad. Go on. Get out of here and go with the blessing of Allah and his prophet.'

'Salaam alaykum,' Skiouros replied with great relief, not feeling the slightest unease at invoking such heathen greetings. After all, peace was peace, whoever's God sent it.

As he shuffled past the man and contemplated the staircase up to the dim light, through which he could hear the rain pounding down on the world, the officer said 'Wait.'

Turning, Skiouros' blood ran cold. What had the man suddenly realised? His fearful eyes fell upon the officer running his hands across the body of the killer, checking for anything useful. The Janissary turned back to Skiouros with something in his hand and tossed it across to him.

Instinctively, the thief's hands shot out and grabbed it before it fell. For a moment he was worried that such speed and agility had betrayed him as more than a mere peasant, but the man was still smiling. Skiouros peered down at the parcel in his hands. A heavy purse. His eyes widened as he looked back up at the officer, a question in his gaze.

'For your trouble. I wouldn't handle this filth's change, anyway.'

The officer had already turned back to his task and all four soldiers were paying him no further heed. With the sudden pulse-pounding elation of a man who has gone from nothing to everything in half a heartbeat, Skiouros climbed the stairs back to the real world.

Chapter 11 – The source of all evil

* Pazar (Sunday) evening *

S kiouros hovered in the shallow arched recess that had once been an access gate through the Bucoleon palace walls, watching the dreadful evening flash, boom and pour down with a mix of distaste, fear, and cold, diamond-hard resolution.

The storm had, against all expectations, continued to worsen all afternoon. Though it had seemed like midnight even at the height of the day, beneath the dark purple sky and the constant crashing and flashing, what had appeared to be the most dreadful storm of Skiouros' young life had, in fact, proved to be merely the prelude to the main show.

Now, torrents of water like rivers ran down every street carrying muck, slurry and debris with them in unpleasant waves. Miraculously, given the undulating terrain of the city, every road was a watercourse now, even at the crest of the hills. Some time just before what could laughably be termed 'nightfall', Skiouros had even seen a dead man, bloated and grey, float past, attached by torn clothing to half a fallen tree. The shattered remains of street-hawkers' carts washed past alongside the corpses of wild dogs and cats. Tiles smashed in every street, torn from the roofs of the ancient buildings by the sheer force of the eddying, whipping, roaring winds, and even heavy tiles and loosened bricks were being carried away by the swift currents of the street-rivers. The rain seemed to change direction every ten minutes, sometimes pounding down vertically and bouncing three feet back up from the cobbles, and at others driven by the awful gales to an almost horizontal gradient that felt like a sideways waterfall if you happened to be out in the street.

No one was out in the streets now.

People who had been had died; hit by flying debris, washed away into alleys where they were drowned, unable to fight the current and constant rush of water long enough to suck down a lungful of air. The sky that had looked like a sheet of black marble hovering over the city had expanded to reach each horizon, making it practically impossible to estimate the time of day.

The thunder and lightning in a normal storm would approach and then pass, the sound and light coming ever closer together until they struck at once, and then gradually parting as the tempest moved on. Not so today. The thunder and lightning that had ravaged Anatolia seemed to be circling the great city, never moving more than a mile from the walls before returning. It was almost as though God had singled out Constantinople for punishment.

Skiouros could imagine what was being shouted by the priests back in the Greek enclave, where they would be whipping themselves into a flagellative frenzy to abate the almighty's displeasure. Likely the Turkish imams were up to similar insanity – Skiouros couldn't remember whether the faithful of Allah whipped themselves, but they likely had their own version if not. Everyone with a deep-seated fear of their God would be currently looking at the sky and praying so hard they almost soiled themselves.

It was a horrendous storm.

But… it was a storm, plain and simple, for all its destructive powers. Skiouros had made the conscious decision to ignore it as far as possible.

He had bigger issues to confront.

He hadn't realised that initially, but then, following the death of the assassin in the cistern, he had been more concerned with his own apparently miraculous survival and the possibility that he might yet not be clear.

Having left the cistern, the young Greek had clambered up into the 'light' of the city, scurried across the square and into the shelter of the crumbling tetrapylon that had once been the great Milion monument at the heart of the Roman city. Within the refuge of the Milion, he had slumped against a pillar, his eyes roving around the square, his mind racing. Few stragglers of the crowd that had thronged it earlier had remained to brave the storm and witness the excitement of Janissaries pursuing a villain; most had ignored all the fuss and scurried in out of the weather, into the Aya Sofya or one of the other new mosques nearby where they could grieve appropriately for the day of Ashura – though with one wary eye still on the almost Biblical storm.

The first worry that had gripped Skiouros had been the likelihood of poison. There was no doubt in his mind that the assassin had poisoned his weapons, but both wounds he had taken – to shoulder and cheek – had been grazes, the shoulder a little deeper but still a flesh wound caused in passing. He had felt no ill effects so far but, regardless, had just decided that it might be an idea to visit one of the Turkish physicians when the second consequence of his subterranean encounter had made itself clear to him.

As he had reached up to brush away the torrents of water from his brow, he had realised how pale and pasty his hands and wrists appeared. A quick check had confirmed that, although his cinnamon stain had survived the periodic exposure to rain, several minutes of ducking underwater had removed most of it, the latest pelting rain finishing the job. He was almost a pale Greek again now. Moreover, the rain running down his face had a filthy brown tint, confirming that the khave dye in his hair was fast clearing out too.

He would not be welcome at a Turkish physician now, and Skiouros had long since lost any respect for their Greek counterparts who seemed to believe that freely-flowing blood solved everything from a headache to a venereal disease. In the end, with his options narrowed, he had muttered a short prayer and trusted to his luck that any poison had not had enough contact to take hold in his system.

The lack of weakness or other symptoms arising over the past four hours seemed to have borne out that theory.

And so he'd stood for a moment, wondering what to do next, until he remembered the purse clutched in his soaked hand. With some trepidation, given the money's source, he'd unfastened it and examined the contents. A few silver akce rattled around amid golden coins of Mamluk denominations and even a few Ottoman sultani and Venetian ducats. The assassin had seemingly been prepared for payment in any currency. Skiouros had found it difficult to estimate the value of the purse, given its wide variety of coins, but it would be not far off the value of the hoard he had lost in the company of Judah ben Isaac.

It would certainly be enough for a cabin in the first ship that sailed.

That had settled his mind: as soon as the storm passed, he would be on the first foreign ship out of Istanbul. Possibly even Captain Parmenio's vessel, though it would be troublesome explaining away the shift in his ethnic background since their last meeting.

Still, there would be no point in even trying to book passage until this great tempest had moved on and left the battered city to pick itself back up.

And in the meantime, that left one great task that Skiouros felt compelled to undertake.

Over the past few days all three assassins had met their end. It would be nice to think that the sultan was now safe, with his would-be killers gone, but such a thought was naïve indeed. The resources of the Mamluk Empire were reputedly close to bottomless and their ranks of assassins would run to numbers far in excess of three. Within a few weeks of word of their failure reaching Cairo, three more could easily be on a ship bound for Istanbul. The great Sultan Bayezid the Second would not be safe yet; not as long as the Mamluks felt inclined to keep sending their hired killers.

Which meant stamping out that inclination. Two men in the city had both the power and the will to repeat the attempt: Hamza Bin Murad of the sultan's Janissaries, and Qaashiq, ambassador from the Mamluks. Other than they and their master Prince Cem, away in the Roman Pope's custody, Skiouros knew of no one involved.

It had not taken a great deal of consideration to come up with a suitable and feasible way to deal with the spy and the traitor without having to involve the authorities.

That afternoon had been spent preparing his plan and then beginning to put it into action. He had to find a way to draw out the two men, and it would have to happen simultaneously. If some accident befell one of them, the other would seal himself up tight and unreachable. So they had to fall together, else they might not fall at all.

That part had been relatively easy to plan, assuming the aid of the urchins that inhabited the dangerous structure beside the Bucoleon and other parts of the city.

Then the two men would have to die.

It would have been nice if Skiouros could somehow let them know why it was they were dying or who it was that snuffed out their life, but he was under no illusion that both men were stronger, faster and better trained than him, and to reveal his presence to them was to risk failure and death. They would have to go to their paradise blinking in wonder and never knowing why. The fact that they would die would have to be enough.

The afternoon had passed in preparation and, though Skiouros was now chilled to the bone and soaked to the skin, back to his original pale Greek look, he was as satisfied as he could be that everything was in place and ready.

What happened next was in the hands of God.

Taking a deep breath, Skiouros ducked out of the ruined arch and scurried down the street towards the dangerously unstable former palace where the homeless waifs hid from the elements.

The street outside the Bucoleon, with the garden of statue bases and the pharos tower, was one of the few in the city that was almost entirely level, and had consequently filled to ankle depth with filthy water that had run down from the hills, forming a sluggish, slow-moving lake that froze the feet and lapped the shins. Things that did not bear close investigation floated in the flood, some of them still thrashing in their rodential death throes. A lost shoe of surprisingly high quality floated past and Skiouros was relieved to note that it was empty. A sudden gust of wind threatened to hurl him from his feet and dump him back in the water and he had to lean forward into the gale, his arms wrapped around him, hood whipped back from his head as the rain battered his face.

A glow of warm light emanated from a number of windows in the Bucoleon palace as he passed, but no one would be studying the streets through them in these conditions, and many had shutters across them or drapes drawn inside the glass. One of the interminable cracks of thunder split the sky as he passed, making his ears hurt, and he had the impression off to one side of a white flash as a jagged javelin of divine fire lunged down from the black sky and struck somewhere on the hilltop near the Aya Sofya.

Skiouros turned his attention back to his destination.

The sagging building beyond the currently-occupied palace had once been a glorious and decorative affair and Skiouros approached the open doorway noting the plinths upon which had once sat the same statues of lions as still graced its neighbour. Nervously glancing up at the dangerously bowing ceiling inside the door, Skiouros stepped in out of the rain, almost overbalancing as the constant pressure of the wind in his face disappeared.

He cleared his throat. Should he shout? Would he be heard over the storm outside if he did?

'What d'you want, Greek?' snapped a young, unbroken voice in thick Turkish with an Anatolian accent.

Skiouros spun around to see a boy of perhaps seven summers leaning against the frame of a side door, his arms folded in a pose of thorough confidence. The thief took a deep breath and squared his shoulders.

'I've a job for you,' he replied in perfect Turkish with a local twang.

'Fuck off.'

Silently, Skiouros reached into his new purse and selected three silver akce, holding them up between his fingers for the boy to see.

'Be worth your while.'

'You looked outside, Greek? Ain't no one goin' out in that for a few coins.'

Skiouros smiled. The boy might ooze confidence and bravado, but Skiouros was a student of avarice and of the 'tells' of the human body, and he'd seen the flash of hunger in the boy's eyes as the coins appeared, however brief it might have been.

'I think you will. Given the bad weather, I'll double it,' he added, drawing out an extra three coins.

'Ten.'

'No. Six. It's enough to eat for a week if you're careful.'

The boy put his fingers in his mouth and gave a shrill whistle. Skiouros felt eyes on him, the hair on his neck standing up in preternatural nervousness. In the next three heartbeats a dozen figures appeared in doorways and corridors around this main hall. The thief mentally kicked himself for his miscalculation. The urchins would be used to the Janissaries next door giving them commissions, and those men would be big and dangerous and well-armed. That the ragged inhabitants of this place might not react the same way to a young, reedy foreigner had not occurred to him.

'I think we might just take that purse from you anyway,' the boy said quietly. 'Evhad and Bekir have acquired a taste for white flesh, but if you're lucky we might put you out of your misery first.'

Skiouros felt his pulse quicken and noted glinting knives appearing in a number of hands. His thoughts raced and he found himself wondering what the boy meant by a 'taste' for white flesh. Neither option that leapt to mind was encouraging or pleasant.

They outnumbered him and he stood little chance against them for all his speed and age advantages.

'Really?' he asked with a heavy drip of sarcasm. 'Allah sends a storm of vengeance across the city to sweep away the faithless, and you would risk his wrath by betraying the Qur'an and committing murder?'

The boy frowned.

'What do you know of God, Greek?'

'Not all those of a fair complexion are ignorant in the ways of Allah and his prophets.'

As Skiouros stood, trying to keep his nerves well hidden beneath a veneer of Ottoman confidence, he watched several of the older waifs converging on the speaker. There was a brief muttered conversation, from which Skiouros caught a few words only, but one of them happened to be 'Janissary'. They suspected him of being one, very likely. After all, very few foreigners knew the ways of Islam unless they had been brought to the Empire in the Devsirme intake and converted by the city's soldiers, just as had happened to Lykaion those years ago. Good. Let them think he was a Janissary if it got the right results.

Finally, the small huddle seemed to reach a consensus and the five of them stepped forward. Skiouros noted with some relief that the other watchers melted away into the corridors and doorways as though given some unheard command.

'Eight akce and all up front. You're unknown to us.'

Skiouros stood and deliberated. Really it was a paltry amount from such a rich purse, but he did not wish to appear too easily swayed. A real Janissary might be tempted to argue them down or simply walk away and find another waif. After a while he gave an arrogant shrug.

The apparent leader stepped forward to meet him, the others melting back into the shadows. This really was a lot more troublesome than Skiouros had expected.

'You know where to go?'

'The barracks up in the old forum on the Third Hill.'

Skiouros felt relief flood him. He'd had a feeling that these boys had run such errands time and again for the Mamluk ambassador, and the answer seemed to confirm it.

'Yes. To the orta commander Hamza Bin Murad. He is to meet my

211

master in the usual place as soon as he is able.'

The boy simply nodded.

'Why're you out of uniform?'

Skiouros glared at him. 'Such curiosity can be dangerous.'

The boy shrugged and reached out for the coins. Skiouros dropped them into the outstretched hand and then fished five more from the purse and added them to the pile.

'Be quick, and avoid the hill by the hippodrome. It's a fast-flowing river now.'

Without a word, the boy wrapped his fingers around the coins and loped off out of the front door. Skiouros turned to regard his surroundings and was relieved to note that there was no sign of any observer now. With a release of pent-up breath he turned and followed the messenger out into the storm.

Now for the other message.

It was not hard to find another urchin, lurking in a side street a few blocks away. It was a risk – he knew that the Mamluk sent his messages with urchins from the gang in the abandoned palace and while there was always the possibility that Bin Murad had a similar arrangement, he had no evidence and would have to trust to luck that the Mamluk would not be suspicious of a messenger he'd never seen before.

The young lad, shivering and soaked, was huddled in the lee of a tall house, his emaciated body providing very little protection against this horrendous weather. Where the streetwise urchins of the Bucoleon were tough and prepared, this young fellow almost fell over himself to grasp the three coins protruding from Skiouros' fingers.

'There may be more chances in future to earn a few coins if you do this properly.'

The boy nodded, staring greedily down at the coins in his palm.

'You know where the Bucoleon palace is?'

The boy frowned for a moment and then nodded, his face lighting up with understanding. 'Near the pharos, by the sea.'

'That's right. You need to knock on the main door. Don't get frightened by the Janissaries inside. If you tell them you're there to speak to the Mamluk ambassador they'll let you be. When the man comes out, you need to give him this message.'

He paused, wondering whether the boy would have the memory for it, but he had to trust in the lad's need to perform the task well in the hope of future lucrative work.

'Tell him that the Corbasi wants to meet him in the usual place immediately.'

The boy frowned. 'Which Corbasi?'

Skiouros paused as a crack of thunder rent the sky, the air thick and electric. Once the deafening noise died away and he could be heard again, he addressed the boy by the flash of white light that bathed the street.

'That's none of your concern, and he will know. Have you got that?'

'The Mamluk ambassador. Corbasi wants to meet him immediately in the usual place.'

Skiouros nodded. 'Then go.'

As the boy scurried out into the rain, Skiouros watched him nervously. All the pieces of the game were now in place, but something was making him nervous. He wondered for a moment whether it would be prudent to follow the boy and make sure that he delivered the message correctly, but quickly decided against it. Now, it was more important to be in place and ready.

Hurrying back through the streets, he closed on the Nea Ekklasia confidently, sloshing through the ankle-deep water, detritus bouncing from his feet and eddying away. There were no casual observers to hide from today, and not enough time had yet passed for either of the villains at the heart of this matter to beat him to the church.

The ruined wooden door to the peristyle garden that sat to the church's rear was in a worse state than even a few hours ago, the billowing winds and blown waste bouncing from the broken rotted planks and weakening them ever further. He'd taken the precaution of jamming it shut, just in case, but a hefty kick sent it flying inwards once more – a kick that almost saw him overbalance and tip into the water as the current and winds tugged at his other leg.

As he moved into the colonnaded garden, pushing the gate closed behind him, he was suddenly struck by how much it now resembled a public bathing pool. Where the currents had allowed a small amount of drainage from the complex and had kept the water level down, the central garden area had been contained within a low wall which had turned it into a wide pool.

For a moment, as he realised that the water level within the complex appeared to have risen a little even despite the drainage, he feared for the execution of his plan. Would it be washed away with the endless downpour? No. It was still safe to rely upon, and should be so for an hour or two yet unless the weather changed dramatically.

Quickly, he followed the cable around the inside of the peristyle, safely sheltered beneath the colonnade, finally coming to the church's rear door and noting with satisfaction and relief the fact that it still stood unbarred. With the flick of a thumb he lifted the latch and swung it open, stepping in out of the rain.

A small puddle had formed just inside where the ill weather had leaked in beneath the wood, and Skiouros stood for a moment after he'd quietly shut the door and dropped the latch, adding a thousand new drips to the growing lagoon. At least footprints wouldn't matter. There would be no trackers and no pursuit today.

With the nervous swallow of a man who had wagered every last penny on a long shot, Skiouros turned and nipped through the kegs of powder, along the narrow aisles and to the vantage point from which he and Lykaion had fallen deep into this mire of murder and treachery in the first place.

Barely had he dropped into position when the main door at the front of the church slammed open and booted footsteps clattered across the marble floor, unseen.

'Come out!' called an authoritative voice in a local Turkish accent.

Bin Murad!

Skiouros' blood ran suddenly cold. Come out? It had to be a bluff. He crouched slightly lower, only one eye visible through the narrow channel between kegs, his knees threatening to tremble, his breathing suddenly troublesome.

'It's no use hiding. There's no way out. My men are already hemming you in.'

Skiouros closed his eyes for a moment, his heart pounding as a cold knot of fear bound his gut tight. Now, as he concentrated, he realised he could hear not only the echoes of Bin Murad's footsteps repeating back and forth around the walls, but also those of several other men.

Quietly, he turned on his heel and started to creep back towards the rear door.

'When we find you, I will have your skin peeled from your frame and pinned to the wall. You will be salted like a side of meat and then, finally, when you do not believe there can be any deeper agony, I will have you slowly slid, arse-first, onto a sharpened stake above the Gun Gate, where you will die slowly over two or three days for the delight of the ships passing along the Bosporus once the storm is gone. What do you think of that, son of Nikos?'

Skiouros almost tripped. Bin Murad somehow knew his identity!

Desperate now to reach that private exit from this place, he rounded the corner at the end of a line of kegs and a fist with the dimensions and force of a battering ram smashed into the side of his head, driving his senses from him and spinning him momentarily into a terrifying, confusing blackness.

He must have been stunned, rather than knocked truly unconscious. Skiouros could picture the blurred passage between the rows of kegs as he was dragged unceremoniously by one foot to the church's centre.

His head bumped down to the marble again with a painful crack and he lay still. Would it go better or worse for him if he continued to feign unconsciousness? Certainly, he would prefer to be out cold, given the throbbing pains in his jaw and the back of his head. Yes. Silent and immobile was the way to play it until he had a better idea of what he could do...

'Fool,' Bin Murad snapped, crossing to lean over and look down at him.

Despite his initial intentions, Skiouros found he had opened his eyes and was looking around with panicked, jerky motions. Bin Murad had a twisted and very unpleasant smile wrapped across his mean, piggy face.

Three other Janissaries stood around, the one who had hit him very close. He had been dumped just inside the central open space, close to the first circle of kegs and radiating passages.

'What happened to your brother? I had assumed it was Hussein Bin Nikos I was going to have at my feet when the little sewer rat brought me a message without the correct codes and told me it was from a Greek Janissary out of uniform. Not that I'm unsatisfied with the result, you understand. I've had the desire to bring you to justice for a number of years – ever since I found out about your flight from the Devsirme a decade ago – but it is irksome that I still have to hunt down your brother now.'

Skiouros spat – a futile gesture in the circumstances.

'He's beyond your reach, traitor.'

Bin Murad's smile turned even more malicious, his eyes acquiring a dark twinkle that promised pain.

'I think you'd be surprised at the length of my reach, boy; and a man who removes an unfit ruler to replace him with the rightful sultan is hardly a traitor. In the new Istanbul I shall be a hero. Once new assassins have been brought in – though I might even do it myself now.'

'You think selling the power of the throne to Egypt is a laudable thing, commander? You can skin and execute me, but you'll find yourself heading down the same path once the Mamluks have a foothold here.'

'We can handle the Mamluks, boy. They're useful at the moment, but their time will pass,' Bin Murad said, dismissively.

'Is that so?' snapped another voice. Painfully, Skiouros turned his head to see Qaashiq, the Mamluk Ambassador, striding into the church centre. For the first time, he did not appear to be accompanied by Janissaries, but had four men at his shoulders dressed in fine mail shirts and with distinctively Egyptian features.

Before Bin Murad could even reply, two of the approaching Mamluk soldiers jerked their fingers on their short, lightweight crossbows, sending bolts slamming into the chests of the two most outlying Janissaries, the pair sprawling back against the kegs of black powder, gasping with agony and surprise. The remaining Janissary soldier, standing only a few feet from the commander, instantly unslung his musket and began the loading procedure, but one of the Mamluks had ratcheted back the cord on his crossbow by hand and placed a bolt in the groove before the Turk could even unstop his powder cartridge – ironic, given his situation.

The Janissary dropped his gun and raised his hands as his eyes fell on the missile pointing at his face, becoming all too aware that he stood no chance of firing first.

The other Mamluk archer had lowered his crossbow; the three of them drew their curved scimitars while Qaashiq simply folded his arms and regarded Bin Murad with cold, dead eyes.

'I fear you are mistaken about who is expendable, commander. You have been convenient thus far. You are no longer so.'

As he finished speaking, the man beside him snapped the trigger of his reloaded crossbow, sending a foot-long ash quarrel with a heavy iron point straight through the remaining Janissary guard's left eye and into his brain until it struck the rear of his cranium and came to rest, an inch of flight protruding from the ruptured iris.

Wearing a frozen expression of stunned disbelief, the soldier simply sagged and collapsed back, falling to the floor like a sack of grain. One of the other fallen men was gasping and clutching at the flights of the bolt jutting from his chest, every breath bringing bubbling pink foam to his lips. The other – the man who had recently delivered a ringing blow to Skiouros' head – was splayed out on the floor, apparently expired, though Skiouros could see the man's eyes swivelling towards the sword hilt at his belt. The crossbow shot had struck his shoulder, merely wounding him.

To Skiouros' astonishment, the Janissary widened his eyes and made a shushing face at him. Laughable. As though Skiouros was likely to help.

But then what else could he do? The Mamluk was unlikely to help him.

'Turn around, Qaashiq,' Bin Murad said with an angry snarl. 'Walk out of here and I will make nothing of your dishonourable actions. Else I shall be forced to deal with you.'

The Mamluk let out a belly laugh, still standing unconcerned, his arms folded.

Skiouros saw the nearby fallen Janissary's hand inching down his leg and realised that he was not going for the long sword in its scabbard, but for the short, finely-crafted Indian throwing knife that was sheathed next to it. He would never manage to stand and reach the enemy with his sword, but a good throw from the floor would remove at least one of them, even if he died for his efforts.

At that particular moment, as Hamza Bin Murad and Qaashiq stood locked in a battle of wills, glaring at one another, the Mamluk soldiers each concentrating on the Turkish officer, no one was paying the slightest attention to the fallen wounded Janissary or the scruffy – apparently unconscious – Greek next to him. They probably hadn't noticed him at all yet.

But the moment this lunatic threw his knife, every Mamluk in the room would be peppering them with crossbow bolts.

Skiouros heaved in a deep breath as quietly as he could, bracing the sole of his boot in a wide crack in the marble flooring caused by the constant shifting of heavy ordnance over a number of years. Waiting for little more than a heartbeat, he watched the Janissary's eyes drop to the knife for which he reached.

For a split second, and that time only, not a single eye in the room was on him.

Heaving with his wedged foot, he pushed himself back into the avenue between the crates, out of the direct aim of the Mamluks.

Before the first shout went up he had rolled over three times, taking him far enough into the passage between keg stacks to disappear from the sight of anyone but the fallen, wounded soldier. As Skiouros scrambled to his feet, he glanced back in time to see a bolt strike the fallen man in the neck, appearing through his vertebrae in a spray of blood. The Janissary hadn't even managed to wrench free his throwing knife before Skiouros' sudden burst of activity had drawn unsought attention to the area and brought about his death.

As the man slumped back to the floor, gurgling and pumping crimson, his eyes starting to glaze, withered Skiouros with their accusatory steel.

The young thief fled.

With no thought for subtlety or silence, he pounded back along the alleys between kegs, not even pausing to risk a backwards glance. Whatever was happening there would hardly draw him back. Nothing now would stop him running.

As he rounded the last corner and laid eyes on the small door that led to the colonnaded garden, he could hear Bin Murad back in the central circle of the church, snapping out orders to hunt him down – orders that were apparently being contested by Qaashiq, there being no Turks left upright to follow their commander.

Good. Let them argue, so long as they stayed where they were.

Even as Skiouros' hand reached for the latch to open the door, his eyes slid sideways to the cord that he'd followed into the building when he arrived.

It had taken a great deal of care this afternoon to anchor that precious cord in position. The slow match was not kept in the same stores as the explosive powder for obvious reasons, and he had been forced to pay well above the odds to procure it from a contact of dubious legality in the Forum of the Ox.

He had lavished attention on its setup, the near end finishing in a carefully-spilled pile of black powder right next to an opened keg. The entire length had been coated with a fine layer of pig grease, which would not hinder its burning but would stop the water from rendering it useless should the rain become too close. The cord had run unbroken around the inside edge of the doorframe, by the hinge, leading out to the garden, where it ran the entire length of the peristyle garden, pinned to the wall at a height of four feet, safely out of the weather.

Let them argue! It would be the last damn argument either of the sons of bitches would ever have.

Allowing the door to close partially behind him, he nudged in place the brick he'd left out specially, which kept the portal slightly ajar and would allow the fuse to pass around the frame unhindered.

It was a masterful work of planning and he knew it. It was sure and weatherproof. The fuse start was at a good distance from its end, and even though he knew little of explosives, given the number of kegs stored in that place it was very unlikely that anything would live through the blast.

Barely slowing, he smiled grimly to himself as he neared the far end of the garden and reached for the flint and steel he'd left on a small ledge for this very moment. Turning, he glanced back at the brooding bulk of the Nea Ekklasia, grey against the purple black of the night sky, as he began to flick the flint and steel above the small packed pile of tinder that formed the start of the long fuse.

'Sorry, Lord.'

It was a shame, even with the church long out of use, to resort to its destruction just to remove a spy and a traitor, but Skiouros was no warrior. When fighting was not an option, you used your wits and whatever God put in your hands. Today, the Lord seemed to have put the entire New Church of the Byzantine Emperor Basil I square into his hands.

The tinder caught and there was a fraction of a second only for Skiouros to panic that he'd been sold defective match cord before it began to flare white with a smoky, cloying vapour. Skiouros stepped back a few more paces to stand next to the broken door that led out to the street, sheltered from the constant battering rain by the colonnaded portico.

With vicious, grim satisfaction, he watched the white blaze move down the covered side wall of the garden, eating up yard after yard of fuse as it approached the centuries-old church and its enormous stock of black powder.

His heart almost leapt from his chest as the figure of one of the Mamluk soldiers stepped into the doorway from inside the church. The man held his crossbow primed but instead of trying to target Skiouros, he simply threw it, unheeded, to the floor.

Skiouros stared in astonishment for a moment until he realised what had happened. The soldier had not spotted the Greek lurking in the shadows at the far end of the garden. Perhaps the dark of the night had hidden him; perhaps it had been the sheets of rain lashing down. One thing was clear: the man had cast aside his crossbow because he had spotted the white flare and suddenly needed his hands.

The thief watched with sinking spirits and near panic as the darker-skinned Egyptian swiftly unhooked a curved knife from his belt and snicked a section out of the fuse over a foot long. The approaching white flare fizzled and winked out as it reached the gap. The plan had failed! Only moments from completion, Skiouros had been foiled by a foreign thug's almost coincidental arrival on the scene. Had he been half a minute longer in discovering the door...

Nothing remained now but to flee and hope he made it away from the city before his details were spread through every harbour.

Secure in the knowledge that the man would not have time to reach for and ready his crossbow before the target was out of sight, Skiouros stepped to one side, pulling open the garden's ruined exterior gate just as a deep, low, threatening rumble of thunder rolled across the city, seemingly directly above him.

'Yes. Thanks a bundle, Lord,' he snapped, his eyes rising to the black, veined marble sky before he stepped out of the garden.

It was only the fact that he cast his eyes heavenwards that allowed him to view the flash that followed the rumble only a fraction of a second later.

The white lance of lightning, jagged and forked, stabbed down out of the ebony sky, searing Skiouros' retinas with its brilliance. Before he blinked in the green-purple blot that was all that he could process, he heard the crash of glass and stone join the bang of the thunder.

His eyesight returned as the flash vanished again into blackness, leaving a jagged streak burned across his vision. He realised even before he heard the noise where that line of white had terminated.

The Nea Ekklasia.

The first bang was surprisingly subdued – more of a deep, vibrating 'whooomp', as though it had occurred in some subterranean chamber.

The Mamluk guard in the doorway had frozen in position and was turning to the church's interior when the first external sign of the detonation occurred, molten black furnace flames blooming from every aperture in the building.

Fragments of the foreign soldier showered the garden along with rubble from the church, passing Skiouros and clattering against the wall – pieces of bone and chunks of armour and weapons. All that remained of the doorway was a billowing deep red fireball, trimmed with black. Glass was flying from windows and pieces of brick hurtled across the garden.

Skiouros stared, stunned. Something throbbed in his arm, and he looked down to find a piece of bone jutting from his flesh. Not his own, but part of the Mamluk who had been standing in the doorway and which had struck him with as much power as any crossbow bolt.

Even as he watched, Skiouros frowned to see the fireball suddenly retreat, sucked inwards like a blazing tide, back into the doorway, leaving an eerie darkness.

He had witnessed enough fires in this mostly wooden city in the past eight years to spot the danger well in advance. A retreating blaze was merely a lull between the first, smaller explosion and the second, much greater one.

Panic suddenly washed through him.

Within moments he was through the broken door, heedless of the wound in his arm, running up the slippery street, the water washing around his ankles, things bouncing from his feet, rain hammering at him like a thousand workmen with tiny hammers, the whole city bathed in an eerie dark glow.

He slipped and fell twice.

The first time was swift and he was instantly back up and running. The second coincided with the main detonation. He didn't pause to look back; he didn't need to. There was no need to confirm the death of the men inside. He had perhaps underestimated the explosive power of so much black powder – but then he wasn't a soldier; he'd never had call to use firearms. The total obliteration of the building and its occupants was elegantly announced by the debris that rained down over the streets of almost a quarter of the city.

He might not know cannon and gunpowder, but he did know the architecture of the churches he'd been climbing these past years. The pieces that were falling from the sky were not just roof tiles and pieces of window. They were half-columns and whole floor slabs, ancient foundation blocks and sections of wall, the detached bricks still held together with mortar.

Some of the falling rubble was the size of Skiouros. Some was larger – frighteningly larger. As he ran, praying fervently and desperately to a God of whom he was suddenly finding it very hard to deny the existence, pieces of the Nea Ekklasia's foundations and superstructure came down among the houses at the sides of the street, smashing through the roofs and passing through two or three floors, demolishing entire buildings.

The whole event, though he saw none of it directly, was lit weirdly by the sooty orange glow from behind him.

It was the brightest light the city had seen since before the storm began and bloomed at its darkest point.

Skiouros did not stop running until he reached the highest point of the road. Ahead, it descended a gentle slope towards the walls of the sultan's great Topkapi palace. Off to the left, on a higher terrace, stood the great Aya Sofya and the ruins of what was once a Roman palace. To the right was the channel of the Bosporus, seething as the rain pelted its surface, with Asia ravaged beyond.

And behind...

Skiouros finally turned and looked back down towards the Nea Ekklasia.

The rubble had stopped falling and the glow had died away to a gloomy red.

The Nea Ekklasia had gone.

Not only, in fact, had the Nea Ekklasia gone, but many of the surrounding buildings had come down due to the explosion or possibly to the heavy masonry debris thrown at them by the blast. A wide swathe of black destruction stood near the Bucoleon palace, marking the 'resting place' – if you could call it such – of a Mamluk spy and a Janissary traitor.

A slow smile broke out across Skiouros' face even as the population began to take to the streets, braving the torrential rain and the appalling winds to peer in astonishment down at the wide crater with its shattered piles of stone, twisted, writhing columns of rising smoke and small, dotted fires gradually burning out in the downpour.

Apparently God had not disapproved of Skiouros' plan.

Perhaps God was even a little too annoyed at the recent purpose to which his grand house had been turned.

Laughing lightly to himself in a slightly manic fashion, Skiouros sank to his knees in the rushing water and then sat back on his ankles, watching the last glows of orange fires blacking out in the rain.

It was over.

Despite everything, it was actually over.

'We did it, brother.'

Five miles south, a band of lighter sky heralded the end of the storm approaching across Anatolia, twinkling stars beyond bathing the Empire with a myriad of possibilities for the future.

Epilogos

* Istanbul - Capital of the Ottoman Empire.
Year of Our Lord Fourteen Hundred and Ninety.
Autumn.
Sali (Tuesday) *

It was hard to even imagine this was even the same world, let alone the same city as the one through which Skiouros had fled in dark and rain, amid the death and destruction that had heralded not the end of the world, but the preservation of it.

The sun shone cold, but far still from freezing, in a sky marred only by a few white horses' tails of cloud. The streets were still coated with debris – some of the worst sort imaginable – but most of the water had gone, drained away from the hills of the city into the Golden Horn, the Propontis or the Bosporos that surrounded the headland on three sides. Barely a house remained fully intact, with shutters torn off, roofs completely stripped away, walls collapsed and worse in some cases. Those older wooden houses that suffered weak foundations had collapsed altogether. Somehow, despite the constant torrential downpour, a conflagration had managed to start in the area of the Monastery of Saint John of Studios, demolishing several neighbourhoods before the rain and public effort combined had succeeded in stopping it.

Nothing, of course, came close to the destruction wreaked by the freakish lightning strike that had detonated the powder store of the Nea

Ekklasia and destroyed a wide swathe of some of the more ancient and impressive structures in the city. The more dilapidated building of the former palace of the Bucoleon, recently inhabited by some rather unfortunate waifs and strays, had been one of the more important structures to collapse in the blast, and the pharos tower had taken enough of a knocking that it might soon go the same way.

From a doorway in the Greek enclave a sprightly figure stepped, his whole bearing announcing his pleasure, relief and satisfaction to the world. It would take a careful watcher to spot the haunted look in the eyes that spoke of loss and pain, but even that already had a light veil of acceptance over it that would thicken with time.

Skiouros adjusted the cloak, pulling it close against the chill, and then paused. With a smile, he unfastened the clasp and swept the garment from his shoulders, tossing it to one of the homeless beggars lining the street, who grabbed it and hurriedly tucked it into his bag, eyeing his peers at the roadside suspiciously.

The former thief paused in the cold, clear air, the glorious sunshine glinting from glass and small puddles that remained in the deeper ruts. He'd not appreciated how glorious the cold bright weather had been until the great storm had swept across it. Skiouros stretched and threw his arms wide, turning slowly.

This was his city.

He had been baptised into the church in Hadrianople, but he had been 'baptised' in Istanbul more than once. For that was something he realised now in a way that he'd never been able to before: it mattered not how long the Greeks grumbled and moaned in their enclave, or how long the Jews clung to the old ways here; this was no longer Constantinople. It was not the city of Constantine and never would be again. It was Istanbul – the capital of the Ottoman world and the seat of the Sultan Bayezid the Just.

And that was fine. It was right. It felt right.

After all, he – a Christian and a Greek – had been instrumental above any other force in keeping this culture in control here in the past week.

Funny, really. For the first time, he had seen it as a Turkish city with Greek inhabitants and not as a Greek city living under a conqueror, and yet in that same moment, for the first time in his life he had felt truly at home here. It was his city. The city that had claimed his family and where a part of Lykaion's spirit would forever remain, whatever happened to his head. It was the city that had taken a young farm boy and forged him first into a thief and then into a tool for vengeance and justice.

And as much as his view of the city had changed, so had his view of himself. Skiouros was no longer the young thief who had stolen apples in the market or cut purses to survive. Somehow, subtly, he had changed in that single week.

And now he would leave, despite being finally at peace with this great city.

The ports had opened by order of the vizier; the first ships would sail today and Skiouros would be on board one of them. He was no longer running away – there was nothing here to run away from any more. He had no ties and no debts. He had a purse of monies in several currencies and was a virtual unknown. The world was a blank parchment on which he could map out his future.

As he finished his slow circle and peered down the street towards the Lycus valley and the harbour of Theodosius, he smiled. Somehow he doubted this was the last time his booted feet would tread the stones of Istanbul. The place had become home.

But before he could ever settle into it, there were things he must do. One cloud still hung over the horizon, forever threatening and very much out of reach: Cem Sultan. The brother of Sultan Bayezid, who had conspired to capture the throne and had been part of all this from the plan's conception, remained alive, if in captivity, to plot anew. Somehow – though Skiouros could not navigate the possibilities in the eddies of his thoughts – one day he would see Prince Cem face justice for what he had done.

But that was for the future, and Skiouros was still a young man with many summers ahead. Lykaion had wanted him to quit the thieving, and so he would, but that left a hole in his life that needed to be filled with something. He would find out soon enough what that was, but one of the first plans that had struck him in the night was that he needed to learn his letters, whether that be in Greek, Turkish, Latin or even Saxon. Crete would be his melting pot and his starting block. From there he would just have to see what transpired.

With a business-like squaring of the shoulders, Skiouros began to stride down the street. There would be more than one vessel in the port that he could try for. He would like to throw in his lot with Captain Parmenio. Something about the slightly dishevelled trader had struck a chord with him and he felt a strange pull towards the man – a kindred spirit? – but that might not be practical. The good Captain would be expecting a Turkish boy, not a pale Greek. Would he be able to approach the merchant as a different passenger entirely and book a cabin? Somehow he suspected that despite the change in colouring, Parmenio would recognise him instantly. The questions that might arise then would be uncomfortable at the very least.

Anyway, now that he and Lykaion were no longer the focus of the Janissaries – who were currently engaged in trying to put the city back together and hold back the riots and looting that threatened to break out all over the place in the wake of the storm – now that he was no longer their focus, he could safely approach any captain for passage.

'The storm has passed.'

Skiouros turned and slowed as he passed the Romani woman, his face registering not an ounce of surprise. Strangely, he felt almost glad to see her.

'Perceptive as always, old witch.'

The woman narrowed one eye and cocked her head, giving her the disconcerting appearance of a raven as the corvid bones clicked in her hair.

'Farewell to you, thief, priest and assassin. We shall not meet again.'

For a moment, as he came to a complete stop, Skiouros considered enquiring as to her meaning but, knowing it would be futile and lead only to further enigmas, he shrugged. 'I will return, but not soon, and you are old. Go to your rest well, old woman.'

The witch cackled and rubbed her hands together.

'Remember that wherever you voyage, what you are is only what you are. It is not who you are.'

'Sound advice, I expect,' he laughed.

'Have you not forgotten anything?'

Skiouros frowned and then raised an eyebrow. 'Lykaion, you mean? I will come back for him, eventually – when the time is right.'

'Brothers should travel together. With the sons of Anatolia ruling the city, the head of a fallen Christian will not be treated with respect. Remember my words: Tu Petros, sa-phal Theodoros – you Petros, your brother Theodoros.'

'I swear that the longer I stand listening to you, the less sure I am of anything,' Skiouros laughed, though his eyes had clouded slightly. 'Fare you well old witch.'

'Travel well and to good ends, young thief.'

Turning his back on her, Skiouros strode on down the street. As his feet skipped lightly across the paving, the young man found himself picturing that plain, unadorned wooden box that contained the head of a noble soldier being broken and abused by Ottoman construction workers. His step slowed more with every flash of the image and by the time he had reached the next major junction, he had already decided on a new course of action, no longer with the heart to curse the witch for her advice and her prophecies.

The slope up towards the walls and the former church of Saint Saviour was gentle and he had hardly broken a sweat by the time he arrived at its entrance. His pulse quickened as he realised that the door was open.

Hurrying and starting to fret, he ducked in through the door, wondering whether to announce his presence. Three hairy, dirty men were lugging sacks and shouldering hods, making their way to the centre of the church. Work was beginning again. In mere months this might be a mosque.

Grateful for his light step – the men had not noticed his arrival as they scraped and crashed around with their loads – he ducked off to the left and ran into the north chapel, where he hurriedly retrieved the box he sought from the altar.

It was so unexpectedly light that he'd whipped it open to make sure the head was inside before he realised what a bad idea that might be. Just a few days had passed, but already the change was nightmarish, transforming the head of Lykaion into this worm-eaten, rotting thing. Somehow the wooden reliquary had been designed tightly enough that it seemed to contain the smell and the unpleasantness until – like Pandora's box – it was opened to unleash its evil.

Skiouros stood and dry-heaved, spitting onto the rubble pile for a few moments after sealing the box shut once more. He would remember not to do that again.

But in a way it had been cathartic.

What was in there now was just a thing. It was no longer his brother. It represented him, certainly, but it was nothing more than a representation now. He wondered for a time whether it mattered if the thing was dealt with by the workers? Lykaion's memory and spirit would live strong regardless. But the answer was still yes. He had to take the only surviving part of the older son of Nikos the farmer with him until finally he found somewhere appropriate and safe for him to rest.

Pausing at the doorway to make sure the workmen were busy with their labours, Skiouros scurried across the narthex and out through the door into the cold, refreshing air, where the first few chilly lungfuls removed the last hints of decaying taint from his senses. Dipping into the pile of workmens' gear outside, he grasped a small, torn hemp sack from the rubble and stuffed the box inside as he walked on.

Gradually, the panorama of the city opened up as he moved down the hill, turning corners until he could finally view the great sea of the Propontis splayed out to the distant horizon. Somewhere beyond that lay Crete and the west. His eyes dropped to the shore, where he could see the great port of Theodosius, its harbour walls resembling two arms reaching out to embrace the sea. Ships were already plying their way through the water.

Somehow, despite the fact that he had no plan and no real idea how he was going to go about leaving, he had the feeling that everything would sort itself out. Perhaps it was the unusually positive statements of the Romani witch and her uncanny insights, but he was feeling optimistic and perhaps even lucky.

Not a head turned as he passed through the Forum of the Ox, a small trade market being set up at one end. Briefly he was tempted to swipe a pomegranate from a stall as he passed, but he stopped himself in time, even as his arm extended.

This was not him; not his path any more.

With a strange smile, he passed on through the streets, down beneath the great crenelated tower of the Gate of the Jews and out to the harbour.

The place was so different from his last visit. Ships and boats were everywhere, some stationary, others moving. The sound of carpenters and shipbuilders rang out all around, mixing with the calls and shouts of traders and their teamsters, all beneath the cacophony of the gulls that whirled and swooped.

The feeling of positivity rising, Skiouros made for the Merchants' Hall but came to a sudden stop as he reached the dockside itself. His eyes strayed up to the great dark wood of the solid, beautiful ship that sat by this jetty, its figurehead a once proud and beautiful blonde girl, now weather-cracked and almost colourless.

'Isabella.'

It had to be a sign. He'd never been a man to believe in signs or omens, or even the direct interference of God, but hadn't he seen it first-hand in the form of a fiery lance that had destroyed the Nea Ekklasia? God did intervene, but it was said that he helped those who helped themselves (a phrase he'd always rather liked in his thieving days).

He stood for only a few heartbeats, his face turning this way and that, his gaze switching back and forth between the Merchants' Hall where so many possibilities of travel lay and the bow of the *Isabella*, slowly rising and falling by the jetty.

'Alright, God. You win.'

With a smile, he turned and strode up the jetty. The long, wooden walkway was manic, with stacks of cargo waiting to be loaded and crewmen and port-workers of every age and nationality up and down the space going about the business of preparing for the voyage.

Skiouros ducked in and out of the stacks of crates and heaps of sacks, pausing here and there as workmen sweated past with loads on their backs. As he rounded what appeared to be a huge stack of fabric bales, Skiouros almost stumbled into the line of figures. In surprise, he stared at the queue of half a dozen men in long black robes, their small black cylindrical hats forming a tell-tale shape beneath the cowls of their cloaks.

Monks!

'Good afternoon,' he said amiably to the rearmost one.

The monk at the back of the queue, a short and slight figure compared to the rest, turned to Skiouros and the thief could just make out the pale, young face of a handsome boy within the hood before his eyes registered with suspicion the rectangular parcel the young monk was carrying beneath his arm.

His eyes slid down to the box beneath his own armpit. It was almost like looking in a strange monastic mirror. Skiouros fought the urge to laugh.

'You've a familiar looking parcel there.'

The young monk simply looked at him, his face immobile, and Skiouros frowned.

'Have I offended you, brother?'

At the head of the line, a tall, narrow figure in the same black cloak turned and Skiouros saw a bushy white beard in the shadow of the cowl.

'He will not answer you. Our novices are expected to remain silent in contemplation of their path.' His voice took on an irritated, haughty tone and Skiouros could picture the nostrils flaring in the hood. 'And show some respect, as a good Greek should. This is no 'parcel', but a relic of unsurpassed value.'

Something inside Skiouros clicked into place and he bowed his head with a slight, almost hidden smile.

'Of course, father. My apologies. May I ask after the nature of this most holy item?'

There was the faint suggestion of a huff of irritation within the cowl.

'We bear the head of Saint Theodoros to safety at the church of Saint Titos in Heraklion, where it will sit in grace next to the skull of that church's great namesake. This heathen hell-hole is no longer a fitting place for a saint's bones. The Patriarch is trying to ship out all relics to good Christian lands.'

Skiouros had to fight to stop himself laughing out loud. God certainly did move in ways most mysterious, as priests said. The old father had turned away again, clearly annoyed at these interruptions by the ignorant. As Skiouros stood at the rear of the line, wondering what to do, a man with long, greasy black hair and a pointy beard arrived at the front, tying his locks into a pony-tail and folding his arms before addressing the father.

'There are too many of you, father. Your passage was only booked for four, and three of those are in hammocks.'

'The hierarch assured me that he had arranged passage for us all. We are expected to join the community at the monastery in Heraklion. This is simply not good enough.'

A polite discussion – bordering on argument – ensued between the ship's purser and the head priest. Skiouros looked around. Not a single pair of eyes was on him.

Damn it. It was just too easy.

Some helpful workers had dumped a large pile of used crates next to the one of cloth bales towering next to him.

'Oh come on, God!'

But he'd only promised himself no thieving, and there were a multitude of sins that escaped that appellation. God would surely forgive him? Had the Lord not engineered all this just for him? It was hard to deny it.

The black-clad novice with the box under his arm issued barely a hiss of breath, let alone a squawk as he was suddenly jerked backwards off his feet into the privacy afforded by the two piles of goods.

The four brothers from the Pammakaristos monastery faced the ship, their attention locked on the negotiations between purser and father, the heated debate masking the strange noises from among the piles of goods at their rear. Within half a minute, the novice was back at the end of the line, decorative holy reliquary beneath his arm, clutched tight as though his life depended upon it. One or two flies hovered hopefully near the box.

An agreement was reached between the two men and it was announced that extra hammocks would be provided at no extra charge on the understanding that the church would look favourably on the activities of Captain Parmenio in the future. Skiouros counted three heartbeats before the line of monks started forward towards the boarding plank. He lowered his head so that his face disappeared within the gloom of the cowl. A novice would be expected to keep himself so attired at all times, very helpfully. The only thing that might give him away was the fine quality leather of his boots but, with the shuffling gait set by the old priests, his feet were safely hidden in the voluminous robe.

As a stack of cloth bales was strong-armed past them towards the mobile platform and its winch, Skiouros smiled. Behind him, the empty crates were shoved onto a cart to return to the warehouses, heedless of the rough-sandalled foot that protruded from one of the larger boxes. The novice would wake with a headache, and for that Skiouros couldn't help but feel sorry, but there it was: God helped those who helped themselves. By the time word of the lad's failure to board reached Crete, Skiouros would be long gone.

His nostrils were still stinging with the pungent stink of rotten meat, despite the fact that the sea air had blown the smell away almost instantly, and he flapped the flies away from the box as he approached the boarding plank.

The journey to Crete would take almost two weeks, unless Captain Parmenio felt the need to push things. It could be difficult to keep the persona of the novice with the box for all that time, but Skiouros had a feeling that the young man was hardly expected to do anything more than hold the box and shut up, so perhaps it would not be as tough as all that. He'd given up thieving… not lying. Maybe that would be next when they reached Crete.

Off to the right, between the third jetty where he had boarded and the Syrian merchantman that sat at the second, an old, unadorned wooden box continued to bob in the harbour's water for a few moments before disappearing beneath the surface, taking the fabled head of Saint Theodorus with it.

* Heraklion, Crete: Year of Our Lord Fourteen Hundred and Ninety *

It had not been an easy crossing of the Cretan Sea since the last stop at Santorini, with the winter gales now truly here and the howling winds whipping the oft glass-like surface into white peaks and green-grey troughs that threatened to smash and swallow the Venetian caravel. Skiouros had never sailed before, other than short crossings of the Bosporos in ferry boats, but had quickly discovered that it felt natural and freeing. In fact, he would have loved the voyage had he not discovered, through judicious eavesdropping that first afternoon on the ship before they sailed, that Brother Ianni, the novice whose place he had taken, was a martyr to sea-sickness. Consequently, he had been forced to overeat the worst, fattiest and most rotten foods on board in order to appear ill at all times and dutifully throw up repeatedly, spending much of the passage at the ship's rail, day and night.

But now, even as his pale green-grey face, hidden in the robe's voluminous hood, puckered for another session triggered by the piece of old fish he'd found beneath his hammock and stuffed into his mouth this morning, he eyed the approaching land and sighed with relief as he leaned across the rail and emptied his gut.

Heraklion was accorded all the honour of a capital, and it certainly was sizeable and well defended, but to one who had come from Istanbul – the most powerful city in the world – it still seemed a little provincial.

The enormous, solid shape of the harbour fortress bobbed towards them, occasionally obscured by the crash of a salty wave against the ship's side, soaking Skiouros' already sodden robe.

Beyond the huge, heavy bulk of that square castle the harbour walls enclosed a port that looked calm and quiet compared with the sea beyond. Behind that the city opened up, huge strong walls stretching out to each side to protect the island's main city.

It would be good to set foot on land. He had loved the journey and

233

the chance to see so many ancient and fantastical places en-route, but the constant sickness required by his guise had drained him and made his sight-seeing as much a chore as a joy.

In a way, although the illness deception had left Skiouros exhausted and frail, thin and colourless, it had really been a godsend. Despite the requirement to maintain his garments and keep his peace, it would have been exceeding difficult to maintain the guise of the novice constantly throughout the journey, particularly at meal times. The fact that he could not eat with the other passengers, as he only nibbled when desperate and even then often vomited shortly after, made his seclusion easier. His seemingly constant illness and foul smell kept everyone at bay, crew and travellers alike, and that was the true saving grace to his disguise. In fact he had hardly had even a moment of human contact since the journey had begun, barring the one strange incident, of course.

Four nights ago, the *Isabella* had put into port at Agios Kirykos on the isle of Ikaria, a small merchant port on a beleaguered island under the protection of the Knights of Rhodes and regularly beset by Ottoman pirates. Captain Parmenio had felt that, despite his carrying trade authorisations from the vizier in Istanbul, it was better to seek the protection of such a place for the slight detour than to run directly through enemy-infested waters without restocking and seeking the latest reports of pirate activity.

The men of the ship's crew had variously stayed aboard to go about their tasks or headed for the nearest drinking and whoring establishments in town, and the other five monks had made for the church to pay their respects and devotions. Skiouros had found that, once again, he was ignored and left to his own sickly devices.

He had waited until everyone else had gone ashore or busied themselves with various tasks, and had then finally disembarked and sought the one place he knew none of the sailors would go: a quiet local tavern. After days confined aboard ship, the men of Parmenio's vessel sought companionship and raucous entertainment, not a quiet repast. Let them have it. After days of eating rotten fish and soggy biscuits and even half a rat at one point, Skiouros had sought real, honest food and a cup of plain, even watered, wine. It stood to reason that, though the town would have probably more than one bawdy house for visiting sailors, many of the locals would prefer to frequent a quiet, sensible inn.

He was right.

It took very little time or effort to locate the Poseidon's Table and confirm that its clientele consisted almost entirely of old island men, fishermen and farmers, every one an indigenous soul. Outside the door he had removed the monk's robe, hat and hood, returning to the plain if filthy clothes beneath, before entering. He had gratefully ordered a plain meal of lamb, bread, olives and vegetables, paid for it and a cup of wine and sunk into a seat by a table near the roaring log fire. It was the most comfortable he'd been in weeks.

Perhaps the desire for that was what had made him drop his guard so much. Stupid, really. Four days from the end of the voyage and he'd put his guise in danger for the sake of a warm fire and a good meal.

He had almost shrivelled into his seat when the two men walked in. Captain Parmenio had looked around the inn with satisfaction, his eyes lingering for just a moment too long on Skiouros before returning to the bar. Nicolo, the Venetian purser with the pony tail and pointy beard, had transacted with the innkeeper and the two men had then undergone what looked to Skiouros like a completely fictitious deliberation about where to sit before crossing to Skiouros' table and asking in polite Greek whether they could take the empty seats.

The two officers had spent the following hour discussing the ship and its cargo, possible destinations for their next voyage, trouble they were having with two Spaniards on the crew and other such mundanities, occasionally conversing genially with Skiouros, politely enquiring as to the situation on the island and the piracy in the local waters.

Skiouros had fluffed his way through local gossip with standard replies that would fit almost any island town. When it came to piracy he avowed no knowledge, being a simple shepherd, and suggested they ask one of the knights at the watch house by the other end of the bay. Parmenio had smiled and agreed, turning back to his conversation with Nicolo.

As soon as Skiouros had finished his meal and downed his wine, he had made as polite an excuse as he could and hurried from the bar, unravelling the monastic cloak and slightly crushed hat he had been using as a cushion and shrugging into it as he descended the dark, winding street back to the small dock where the *Isabella* sat gently bobbing in the dark waters.

For some time that night and the next day, Skiouros had

judiciously avoided both the officers in his choice of vomiting positions, but the pair had paid no particular attention to him anyway, and his panic had soon eased. It was a coincidence. After all, neither man had ever seen Skiouros' face before without its darkened, Turkish pigmentation or concealing shadowed hood, so there was no real reason they should have thought him anything other than an islander.

Still, when two days later, the caravel had stopped at Santorini due to the sighting of potentially enemy vessels, Skiouros had opted to stay on board and play the sick novice once more.

Since then things had run as smoothly as a writhing, bucking, dipping and swaying ship could allow, and now Skiouros felt his spirits lift as they neared the harbour.

The box containing Lykaion's head had been taken from him on the first night by one of the senior priests, who seemed not to trust the abilities of the sea-sick young novice to keep it safe. They appeared to think that he would accidentally drop it over the side in his constant retching. Truth be told, he was glad of their decision. After all, he would be relinquishing the box into their hands when they arrived, so they might as well carry it whilst aboard.

The great fortress at Heraklion's harbour entrance slipped past, heavy cannon bristling from every embrasure to cover the nautical approaches to this city, Venice's eastern jewel. The change in the ship's motion as it slipped from the choppy waters of the sea into the calm harbour was instantly noticeable and Skiouros peered into the spray, aware that the clouds above the island were threatening drizzle, and watching the huge warehouses, arsenals and mercantile buildings of the port sliding towards them, the jetties reaching out in welcome.

He almost jumped as a figure settled at the rail to his left, and then others to the right. The monks had gathered to watch their destination approach. After decades of living under the Ottoman regime they had returned to a Christian world, and their joy and relief was almost palpable.

Skiouros lowered his face so that the hood covered his features more thoroughly and watched the water pass for several more minutes until the ship slowed, shouts echoing back and forth among the crew. Sails were furled and slowly, the caravel approached the wooden jetty.

The young 'novice' leaned on the rail, his eyes roving across the city that would likely be his home for the foreseeable future as the crew went about their tasks, throwing and hauling ropes and cables and performing the many arcane little jobs that seemed to be required even to manoeuvre a ship through a tiny arc. Suddenly the hull bumped against the jetty, making the monks jerk back, gripping the rail to stay upright.

With another two bounces and a long grinding of timber against timber – a sound that brought a reproving glare for the crew from their captain – the *Isabella* arrived in Crete.

Skiouros smiled within his hood. Whatever happened now, he was finally here. He could start to carve out whatever future he wished, but at least it had begun. Lykaion would be taken to rest safely in honour in the church at the heart of this strong citadel, where he could remain until the day Skiouros could take him home in safety and not place him in danger of abuse and destruction. That he rested in a Christian church was perhaps a little inappropriate, given his beliefs, but Skiouros didn't think that God – or Allah for that matter – would mind; he was certain that Lykaion wouldn't.

Then there was the matter of his letters. Here – a Greek land under Venetian rule – he was likely to find someone to teach him any number of languages. He had enough money in his purse to see him out a number of months and by then, he would have settled on his course.

Unfinished business...

He knew what the end result of his new life would need to be, but how he would navigate the twisting channels of fate to reach that end was still an unknown. One day he would see Prince Cem, the usurper Sultan, pay for his part in events that had shaken the world and killed Lykaion, son of Nikos the farmer.

One day... but not today.

A boarding plank was run out from the deck down to the jetty, wooden ridge-strips nailed to its surface to aid the grip of the passengers' booted feet. Skiouros remained at the rail for a while, watching as the various paying passengers with whom he had had no contact disembarked. Finally, the monks began to move along the rail and descend.

At the jetty, the purser was giving them directions to the church – somewhat unnecessarily, given that the top of the great dome and its ornate bell-tower were visible above the warehouses and other buildings that lay between. As Nicolo finished his explanation, the priests thanked him and began to stride along the jetty towards the port. Skiouros, still at the bottom of the boarding ramp, to the rear of the group and lagging behind, paused and raised a hand.

'Rest well, Lykaion. I'll come back for you.'

As the monks disappeared with their 'holy' relic, Skiouros hesitated. He didn't want to be too close to the brothers so that they noticed him and made sure he joined them at the church, but he also couldn't afford to separate until he was safely away from the jetty where he could lose the black robe and melt into the crowd. Nicolo began to mark the passengers off his list as the crew started unloading the goods with a winch and rope further back along the jetty.

After what Skiouros deemed an appropriate pause, he stepped down the last two feet of plank, turning as though to hurry and catch up with the rapidly disappearing black shapes of the other monks.

Nicolo stepped in front of him, folding his arms.

Skiouros frowned and made to duck past him, but the purser merely sidestepped and gestured up the plank with a pointed finger. Skiouros felt his spirits sink. Turning, he saw Captain Parmenio at the top of the ramp, beckoning.

Acknowledging defeat, Skiouros stomped disconsolately back up the plank, Nicolo right behind him, almost breathing down his neck.

'Get up here,' Parmenio sighed.

Skiouros stepped onto the deck and shuffled in front of the captain, a dozen different stories and excuses fighting their way between brain and mouth, none of them quite reaching the level of credibility that he would need.

'Tell this young man what we do with stowaways, Nicolo.'

The Venetian purser, his Greek slightly accented yet fluent, cracked his knuckles.

'We throw 'em overboard, captain. Or if we're on land still, we hand 'em over to the authorities.'

Parmenio raised an eyebrow and waited. With a sigh, Skiouros peeled off the cowl and removed the small cylindrical hat.

'Technically, captain, I don't think I count as a stowaway. The purser here will no doubt corroborate the fact that precisely the right number of passengers disembarked.'

'Don't get clever,' snapped Nicolo, delivering a stinging smack across the back of Skiouros' head from a hand adorned with at least three gold rings.

Parmenio narrowed his eyes.

'Some poor sod of a novice has had to go back to the Patriarch in Istanbul and tell the head of his church that he was mugged! At least I hope he did. You don't have the look of a murderer...'

Skiouros' heart skipped a beat. 'He's unharmed,' he said quickly. 'A lump on his head, maybe, but that's all.'

'You've put me in an awkward position, young stowaway. See, the Patriarchate in Istanbul is going to want to know what happened to the man who mugged their novice. He's going to make enquiries and find out that I transported the right number of monks. And I still have to visit Istanbul from time to time. See the difficulties you've put upon me?'

Another slap from behind snapped Skiouros' head forward.

'You didn't know,' he replied shrewdly. 'If you hadn't stopped me now, you could have pleaded innocence.'

'I still can. But I want to know two things before I even contemplate agreeing to that.'

Skiouros nodded hurriedly like a drowning man who sees a rope tossed from the shore.

'Firstly,' Parmenio said calmly, 'I want to know what it is you're running from. See, I'm not daft. You may not be made up like a Turk any more, but you've been desperate to get away from the city, and that makes me twitchy. I don't like the idea of trouble following you to my door.'

Skiouros sighed and sagged a little. Well, he'd given up the thieving and he'd said he'd give up the lying too when he arrived.

'In truth?'

'In truth.'

'In truth, I was wanted in the city, but for something I hadn't done. The danger's passed now, as the bastards who were after me died in the storm. To be absolutely honest, I'm not really sure what I'm planning to do next, but in the long-term I'm not running away. I'm running towards.'

Parmenio's eyes rose to meet the purser's behind him and some strange look passed between them. Finally, the captain nodded.

'And the other thing is: why, if you have nothing to hide now, did you sneak aboard as a monk when you have enough money to buy passage? You told me you had plenty when we first met, and the monks may not have noticed your rattling, bulging purse on the journey, but it caught the attention of more than one of my crew.'

Skiouros drew himself up straight.

'That, I'm afraid, is something a little personal and close to my heart, and of which I would rather not speak. Were I to pay you for the passage now, would your curiosity perhaps wane a little, captain?'

Parmenio's face hardened for just a moment and then cracked into a smile.

'Give me the fare and get going, lad. I've business to attend to. But no matter who you speak to, you were never aboard the *Isabella*. And I've never seen or heard of you.'

Skiouros nodded wearily and withdrew his purse, rummaging in it until he'd produced enough ducats to pay for the crossing. Finally, he fastened it again and dropped it back inside his robe, handing over the small pile of coins.

'Thank you, captain. May God smile upon your ship and your voyages.'

'And may he look the other way where you're concerned,' Parmenio countered with a sly smile. Nicolo gave him a quick, light slap across the back of the head and stepped away.

With a last, nervous smile at the two sailors, Skiouros turned and hurried down the plank to the jetty.

Crete, at last. Now where would an ex-thief with a monk's robe and a bag of miscellaneous coinage find a bite to eat?

As the young man passed the port warehouses, shrugging out of the black robe, he whistled an old Greek tune – a favourite of Nikos the farmer and his elder son, Lykaion. Turning the corner to the city proper, he smiled with relief as he cast the robe, cowl and hat aside into the shadows at the lee of a large building.

The old Romani beggar reached up and grasped the crumpled garment that had landed in his lap, turning it over and examining it. A priest's robe.

Fascinating!

Running his wizened brown hands through his wild, long, black hair and causing the bones to click and rattle, he rose and limped off towards the city in the wake of the young man.

END

Author's Historical Note

*T*he Thief's Tale was born of three factors. Firstly, the 'beloved rut' in which I find myself. I love the Roman era and am more than happy writing novels set within it until the *vacca* come home, but occasionally I feel the need to write something different, even just as a palate-cleanser. If this book had not been what it is, it would have been some other non-Roman work. Yet the novel is still in semi-familiar worlds. The Constantinople (or Istanbul) of 1490 is still echoing the world of the Byzantine Empire, which in itself is the last great flowering of Rome. And so, while very different from my standard milieu, it is also close enough to hold that same fascination.

Secondly, my love of the city. A few years ago, before our kids arrived, my wife and I went to Istanbul for a week. Most tourists, it appears, visit some 5-10 great, world heritage sites and are sated. Not us. We walked the backstreets in search of the fragmentary remains of churches centuries-gone. We walked the circuit of the walls – in my wife's case with feverish sunstroke! We visited everything we could find of historical Istanbul. I now know of many other sites which will help fill my next visit, but I feel as familiar with any inch of that city as I do with other cities in which I have spent more time. We turned it inside out in a week, and it was the city we discovered beneath the skin of tourism that I have tried to put across.

Thirdly: I found a single event. The final events in this (mostly fictitious novel) might seem somewhat farfetched, and yet they are the most true. The lightning strike in that great storm that detonated the Nea Ekklasia powder house that year is not well recorded. You will not hear it spoken of or see it in any general history, but if you delve into the world of early Ottoman Istanbul, you will find it referenced. That simple explosion – which is noted historically as having dropped blocks of masonry even on the far side of the Bosphorus! – is the linchpin around which I built my plot.

Skiouros and Lykaion are fictitious. So are Ben Isaac, Bin Murad, Qaashiq and the Cretans. The story is a tale of a fictional assassination attempt by fictional conspirators foiled by fictional heroes. It is, after all, historical fiction. But the civil war between the brothers Bayezid II and Cem Sultan is real enough, as is the war with the Mamluks. Bayezid paid the Pope a small fortune on an annual basis to keep Cem in custody. I would elaborate further but for fear of ruining sequels. The events revolve around real people as well as fictional, and real circumstances. It is a view of what might have happened.

As a quick note on architecture and dress, this is – for me at least – one of the most complicated times and places to research and write. The world of this tale is still very much a Byzantine one, and the Ottomans, while now flooding the city, had only been there a few decades. There were surprisingly few mosques and a lot of churches. Istanbul at this point is the ultimate melting pot, bringing the architecture and culture, dress and religion of Asia and the east into a meshing contact with the medieval/late-Roman culture of the west. As such, Turkish jackets and trousers are in as much evidence as Italian doublets and braes. Istanbul is treated as having mostly wooden housing, which it would have done during both the late Byzantine and early Ottoman eras, and fires have always been the plague of the city.

I have similarly used a variety of naming conventions, often trying to tailor it to the point of view of the narrative. The Greek inhabitants almost certainly still called the city Constantinople long after its fall to Mehmet the Conqueror, while to many it was already Istanbul. Hadrianopolis became Adrianople, which then became Edirne. I have homogenised the first two to make it Hadrianople for the reader's ease, denoting its solid Latin and Greek roots. I have used Bosporos for Bosphorus, and yet the Turkish Aya Sofya for the great church of Justinian. Essentially, I went with what seemed appropriate at the juncture. I hope it read well for you.

The story was never intended to have a sequel but, as often happens to me, I was almost constantly battered with inspiration as I wrote and the arc for a second and third book fell into place before I was even halfway through this one.

I hope Skiouros has entertained you. Feel free to drop me a line and discuss the book or anything about the late Byzantine or early Ottoman world if you so wish. Details are on my website.

For now, thank you for reading and Skiouros will return in *The Priest's Tale*.

Simon Turney. January 2013

If you liked this book, why not try other titles by S.J.A. Turney

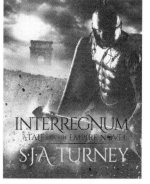

Interregnum (Tales of the Empire 1)

(2009) *

For twenty years civil war has torn the empire apart; the imperial line extinguished as the mad Emperor Quintus burned in his palace, betrayed by his greatest general. Against a background of war, decay, poverty and violence, men who once served in the proud imperial army now fight as mercenaries, hiring themselves to the greediest lords. On a hopeless battlefield that same general, now a mercenary captain tortured by the events of his past, stumbles across hope in the form of a young man begging for help. Kiva is forced to face more than his dark past as he struggles to put his life and the very empire back together. The last scion of the imperial line will change Kiva forever.

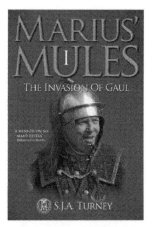

Marius' Mules I: The Invasion of Gaul

(2009) *

It is 58 BC and the mighty Tenth Legion, camped in Northern Italy, prepares for the arrival of the most notorious general in Roman history: Julius Caesar. Marcus Falerius Fronto, commander of the Tenth is a career soldier and long-time companion of Caesar's. Despite his desire for the simplicity of the military life, he cannot help but be drawn into intrigue and politics as Caesar engineers a motive to invade the lands of Gaul. Fronto is about to discover that politics can be as dangerous as battle, that old enemies can be trusted more than new friends, and that standing close to such a shining figure as Caesar, the most ethical of men risk being burned.

* Sequels in both series also available now.

Other recommended works set in the Byzantine & Medieval worlds:

Strategos - Born in the Borderlands

by Gordon Doherty (2011)

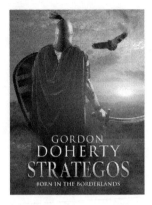

When the falcon has flown, the mountain lion will charge from the east, and all Byzantium will quake. Only one man can save the empire . . . the Haga! 1046 AD. The Byzantine Empire teeters on full-blown war with the Seljuk Sultanate. In the borderlands of Eastern Anatolia, a land riven with bloodshed and doubt, young Apion's life is shattered in one swift and brutal Seljuk night raid. Only the benevolence of Mansur, a Seljuk farmer, offers him a second chance of happiness. Yet a hunger for revenge burns in Apion's soul, and he is drawn down a dark path that leads him right into the heart of a conflict that will echo through the ages.

Tom Swan and the Head of St George

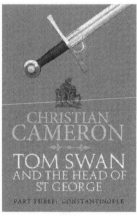

eBook series by Christian Cameron (2012)

1450s France. A young Englishman, Tom Swan, is kneeling in the dirt, waiting to be killed by the French who've taken him captive.

He's not a professional soldier. He's really a merchant and a scholar looking for remnants of Ancient Greece and Rome - temples, graves, pottery, fabulous animals, unicorn horns. But he also has a real talent for ending up in the midst of violence when he didn't mean to. Having used his wits to escape execution, he begins a series of adventures that take him to street duels in Italy, meetings with remarkable men - from Leonardo Da Vinci to Vlad Dracula - and from the intrigues of the War of the Roses to the fall of Constantinople.

Made in the USA
Monee, IL
08 December 2023

48530717R10150